"WELL DONE . . . PURE ENTERTAINMENT."
—*St. Louis Post-Dispatch*

"ANOTHER FAST-PACED TRIP BACK IN TIME. . . . Readers should enjoy this ingenious tale."
—*Booklist*

TWICE UPON A TIME
Allen Appel

"A HIGH-SPEED, DEFTLY HANDLED SEQUEL TO AP-PEL'S SUCCESSFUL TIME-TRAVEL FANTASY *TIME AFTER TIME* . . . HISTORICAL FICTION THAT WORKS!"
—*Kirkus Reviews*

"RIVETING . . . A UNIQUE BLEND OF HISTORY AND SCIENCE FICTION."
—*Library Journal*

"ENTERTAINING, WORTHWHILE READING THAT PACKS A PUNCH."
—*Voice of Youth Advocates*

"HARD TO PUT DOWN."
—*The Midwest Book Review*

"A COMPELLING ADVENTURE . . . BUILDS TO A GRIPPING CLIMAX AT LITTLE BIGHORN . . . AMUS-ING AND EXCITING."
—*The Coast Book Review*

ALSO BY Allen Appel

PUBLISHED BY Dell

Time After Time

Twice
Upon a Time

A NOVEL BY

Allen Appel

A DELL BOOK

Published by
Dell Publishing
a division of Bantam Doubleday Dell
Publishing Group, Inc.
666 Fifth Avenue
New York, New York 10103

ISBN: 0-440-20576-X

Reprinted by arrangement with Carroll & Graf Publishers, Inc.
Printed in the United States of America
Published simultaneously in Canada

March 1990

10 9 8 7 6 5 4 3 2 1

OPM

Dedication

To Colonel Leo J. Conway, U. S. A. (Ret.)
A brave and generous man.

Acknowledgments

Thanks to my wife Sherry, as always; to Bill Garrison, as usual; to Catherine Bell for her valuable advice; and to Karin Johanson for squaring me with the Librarian of Congress. To Bhob Stewart for going far above and beyond simple friendship; and Kent, on whose shoulders it all comes to rest.

I have chosen freedom, and I have paid the price.

Stephen Callahan, *Adrift*

Then

It was the last hour before true dawn.

Alex Balfour stood at the top of a hill.

The world was white with snow.

Down in the small valley the land was smooth and round beneath the heavy drifts. On the crests of the hill that surrounded the valley, the soldiers of the Seventh Cavalry stood with their horses. Custer's order had been whispered through the ranks: remove overcoats and remain perfectly still, no swinging of arms, no stamping of feet.

Alex did not feel the cold.

Nearby, wet snow slid from a branch with a muffled thump, and the branch, now free, rose, knocking snow from other branches. All eyes turned toward the tree and men waited with held breath to see if they had been discovered. A small brown deer looked out from beneath the tree, stared for a moment, and turned silently and disappeared. Down below a dog began to bark.

To Alex it was as peaceful as a Christmas card. There were tamarack and lodgepole pines on the hillsides, and sheltering cottonwoods on the valley floor. A narrow iced-over stream, the Washita, meandered between the rows of cottonwoods. He could see a cluster of tepees on the banks of the stream. As the sky began to slowly gray, the cluster became a village. The dog continued to bark.

At a signal the men mounted their horses. There was a faint rustle and stir of equipage; the tiny clink of bits and stirrups, the creak of cold leather, the shifting of horses as they moved beneath the weight of their riders.

Below, the flap of a tepee pushed back and an Indian wrapped in a blanket came out into the cold mist to beat the barking dog into silence. There was no danger; sane men did not make war in the dead of winter.

For a moment it seemed as if the world were trapped inside a glass ball. Time hesitated on the keen edge of the moment. For a single heartbeat the Indian stared up the hill at the riders surrounding the village on three sides. And then the glass shattered as the man turned and howled a warning, and from the far hill the regimental band broke into Custer's theme song, the Scottish air "Gary Owen," and the riders spurred their mounts and the attack began.

He watched, his interest quickening. The deep snow sprayed from the horses' hooves and showered from the limbs of the burdened pines. The branches sprang up as if in salute as the men rode through them, and the first rifle shots slapped and echoed in the winter dawn. The soldiers cheered as they poured down the hill.

Indians ran from the tents, insects boiling from a hive, women and children heading for the creek, men shouting as they leapt onto their own horses or knelt to fire at the flow of soldiers that coursed toward them, an avalanche of blue uniforms and charging horses and cascading snow.

Lines and points of muzzle flare winked and flashed from both sides, from the hillsides and from the valley floor. The three streams of men that flowed down the hillsides met and merged on the flat in the Indian camp, and there was a twisting, swirling madness as the charging horses trampled screaming women and children and ran down fighting warriors. The pale morning sun broke over the hills. The air was blue with smoke from the rifles. The white snow was spattered with blood, bright and steaming.

He watched in horror and felt his soul and his mind fill with pain. It was all too clear; perfect. He seemed to see and hear each shot, each blow of the saber, each scream, each cheer. He seemed to feel them all separately and in unison until it was he who was screaming, but he had no voice. He struggled to run, to hide, but he could not move, could not turn away, could not shrink from the dreadful moment.

And then he was free. The wind seemed to blow through him, to scatter him. Now he felt the bitter cold, but only for an instant, and then he was away, home.

His mind quickly sealed it all away, walled it up, insulating him against the pain. It was too soon, too much for now. Later, he would remember.

Now

Chapter 1

"What do you know about Indians?" Molly asked.

Alex Balfour cradled the telephone between cheek and shoulder as he struggled to pull on his running shoe. "Indians," he said, loosening the laces. "Let's see. They're short with brown skin and large doelike eyes."

"Not those kind of Indians."

The shoe slid on. He moved the receiver to the other ear and bent over to tie the laces. "That's about the extent of my knowledge. Sorry."

"Alex."

He stood up and tied the drawstrings of his shorts. He looked around on his dresser among the clothes piled there for his T-shirt, the one with the holes in it. Molly was always throwing it away.

"Alex, wake up, this is Molly Glenn calling from the news room of the *New York Times*. We have no time to be fooling around. *American* Indians, Alex, not *Indian* Indians."

"Just a second," he said, putting the receiver down on the bed table and slipping on the T-shirt. It gave him a perverse pleasure to think that he was, in his own small way, slowing the progress of the *Times*. He pictured a vast printing press, blurred belts of newspapers racing along in unending streams, and he, Alex, poised over the giant machine with an enormous monkey wrench, about to plunge it into the very bowels of the monster. . . .

He picked up the telephone. "Alex," Molly said, beginning to sound exasperated, "we are talking Native Americans here. As in Geronimo and Apache. In this case, as in Crazy Horse."

Yes, there was a definite edge in her voice. No need to push too far. "Well, why didn't you say so?"

A sigh from the other end. "All right. Are you ready now? What are you doing anyway? Did I wake you up?"

"I'm getting ready to go run. I've been up for hours. The bed was still warm on your side when I got up."

"Hah." She knew him too well to believe that one. Molly was the only journalist that Alex had ever known who, of her own free will, got up and went to work early. Very early. She got out of bed between five and six in the morning, and she was at her desk before seven o'clock. She said it gave her time to accomplish something before the day's distractions began. Alex, on the other hand, liked to stay up at night. This caused a certain amount of confusion in their lives, but it also meant that Molly was home a lot earlier than the other *Times* staffers who went to work at a fashionable 11 A.M.

"All right, so I didn't get up at the crack of dawn. Now, what was the question?"

"The category is Indians, Alex. Gee, for a guy who can remember everything, you've got a lousy memory."

"I don't remember everything, I just read a lot. I'm a historian, or at least I used to be. Remembering things is a part of my job."

Alex edged down to the end of the bed and looked at himself in his dresser mirror. He needed a shave. He had dishwater-blond hair and a very light beard, but today he definitely needed a shave. On him the Don Johnson look came off as a dirty face. "There are a lot of Indians," he went on, "or at least there were. Just exactly who or what are you interested in?"

"Crazy Horse." She stopped for a minute, and he could hear the rustle of papers. "Yep, that's the one. Crazy Horse."

He didn't even need to think very hard on that one. Indians, especially renowned war chiefs, had been a passion of his as a boy. For a moment he remembered sitting on his bed, leafing through the pictures in one of his father's research books. "He was a Sioux," Alex said. "Architect, or rather strategist, of the Battle of the Little Bighorn. Actually he was a very strange Indian, very mystical. Why are you interested in him?"

"Well, you know how I get these weird assignments. I think it happens because I come to work so early; the guys on the night shift get in something strange so they look around the office and there I am, sitting at my desk all bright and cheery, so I get stuck with it."

Alex had an image of Molly at her desk. Bright and cheery was a good description, though she was using it facetiously. Molly had the reddest hair he had ever seen. Heads always turned when she walked into a room; an Irish beauty with pale creamy skin, blue eyes, and a wonderful smile. She was a favorite on the staff. Not only because she was pretty, but because she was a good reporter.

"An Indian out in South Dakota has gone on some sort of a rampage," she said. "He claims that he's the spiritual and physical heir to Crazy Horse. He shot two white men who were doing a land study on the reservation."

"As far as I know," Alex said, trying to remember, "Crazy Horse didn't have any children. At least none that lived. He was married at least twice, once to two women at the same time, but it isn't thought that any of his children survived. Actually, I don't think he was much interested in women. He liked to sleep on the ground in the rain, sometimes in caves. Women aren't much interested in sleeping on the ground."

"You can hardly blame them, can you?" He could hear her tapping on her desk with a pencil while she thought. "Can you research him for me sometime today? I'll work on it from this end, but I'll be doing background on the guy that's gone berserk. Christ, I hope he's not a Vietnam vet," she said to herself more than Alex. "You know how good you are at this sort of thing, Alex. It would be a big help."

"That's it, flatter me. I'll do it—it's not as if I've got anything else to work on."

"Well, you come up with something for me, and I'll take you to lunch on the *Times.* You go run and get your historian-researcher brain working. I'll see you at home this evening."

"Right," he said, standing. He stretched, said good-bye, and hung up the telephone. He peered into the mirror over the dresser, rubbed his face, and thought about growing a beard. He looked tired; was he getting old? Maybe a beard would make him look younger. He searched for some overt sign of disease, some wasting illness, a jaundice in the eyeballs. Nothing there, just the erosions of everyday life. The face of an ordinary thirty-six-year-old guy who stayed up late watching old movies on his VCR. He sighed, rummaged around on the pile of clothes on his dresser until he found his Walkman, left the room, and went downstairs.

He stopped for a moment in the hall and looked at his two original Monets. They were oil still lifes, one a bowl of fruit, the other a vase of flowers. The flower picture was crooked so he straightened it. The paintings were unknown to the art world, any member of which would have fainted at the thought they were up on the wall in a private home. They had been left to him by an old friend who had died. He looked at them every day and remembered his friend. At first he had worried about thieves, but then he realized that your standard New York dope addict was too stupid to know what they were. They'd take his TV, his stereo, and his VCR, but they'd leave the only thing that was worth serious money. He unlocked the door and stepped out on the porch.

The day was cool, early spring. The sort of rare day when New York seems clean and hopeful. Alex put his foot up on the wrought-iron railing and did a few stretching exercises, warming the muscles in his legs. He squatted and heard his knees crack. I'm getting old, he thought, thirty-six. Growing a beard won't help. I stay up too late and I don't have a regular job, and it's been a year now.

• •

One year.

He had gone, then, far away, and done things that now he

could scarcely believe. Except for the pictures in the hall, and the scar on his arm, there was little to remind him of that time. He touched it absently, the scar, rubbing the raised weal of flesh the way you rub a lucky charm, worry beads, a rabbit's foot, something to give you hope for the future, allay the troubles of the present, bring back the past.

He had gone into the past. There were no other words for it. There he had come alive. And afterward there was a time of healing, and then a time of waiting, and now there was only time as the past faded away and became simply memory, and that was not enough.

On the surface it was a pleasant life. There was Molly, who knew what had happened, who believed in him; money, inherited from a despised father, enough money to do whatever he liked. But what did he do? What did he want? He read books, watched old movies and ran to keep his body in shape. He kept a sailboat that he and Molly spent their vacation on every year. He cooked their meals and cleaned the house and didn't mind either chore. He liked walking the streets of New York looking at the old buildings, the ones that had character and charm and reminded him what life had been like in the past. And he searched for something else, even though he knew he wouldn't find it down an alley or around a corner, no, it was somewhere else, somewhere you couldn't walk to, somewhere that you couldn't find just because you were looking.

• •

As he stood on the stoop he could hear New York muttering to itself in the near distance, the way crazy people sat on street corners and muttered, a constant undertone. His house was a pleasant old brownstone on a side street of pleasant old brownstones in Greenwich Village. He put on the earphones of his Walkman. The murmur of New York disappeared beneath the beat of fifties rock-and-roll. He jumped down the three steps to the sidewalk and began to run.

After he had healed, and after he had waited, he had seen and felt the effects of his present creeping back in, insulating him in a symbolic layer of fat, and in a pleasant but mind-numbing bubble of everyday life. He fought it. The fat he could conquer—he could run and work his body—but his mind was something else. Had it not been for Molly and had there not been that hope that it would happen again if he just waited, and a certain rueful sense of humor about what he was and what he had been, he would have immersed himself in his books and his movies and his comfortable house until one day there might as well be no more Alex Balfour, just a dusty pile of old books, probably an empty whiskey bottle, and a television set tuned to nothing, flickering away in the permanent twilight of his heavily curtained living room.

And so he ran. He used the Sony to drown out the world around him. At first he had listened to classical music, and then he had taken to listening to recorded books, and then he had switched to rock-and-roll because running was boring and he needed that extra energy that fast hard music gave him. Not new rock, which he didn't like or understand, but old rock, from the past. He alternated days between Jerry Lee Lewis's early Sun recordings, Chuck Berry's *The Great Twenty-Eight,* and a best-hits album by little Richard. When he got tired of the tape, he listened to the radio, an oldies station with a minimum of commercials and the occasional news and weather. Every once in a while he would catch himself singing along; he could tell when he was doing it by the pained looks on the faces of the passersby.

He'd gone through a succession of tape players. The sweat from his hands got into them, and the constant bouncing seemed to take a quick toll on the lighter types. He'd finally arrived at a heavier-than-fashionable model and had an electrician weld the earphone jack to the body of the player so it wouldn't pull out while he ran. The whole rig had considerable heft, but at least it wouldn't fall apart.

He was listening to the radio as he ran. The news came on just after "Duke of Earl" by the Chandlers. The lead news item was a cheerful reading of hopeful economic indicators. He was getting ready to switch over to his tape when the next item caught his attention. He ran under the white marble arch into Washington Square, dodged a drug transaction between a dreadlocked Rastafarian and a suit-and-tie businessman, and turned up the volume.

"Late last evening near Rapid City, South Dakota, two representatives of the All West Power Corporation were shot and seriously wounded as they were collecting soil samples on the remote Pine Ridge Indian Reservation. Shortly after the shooting, a caller to the *Rapid City Post* identified himself as John Raven, an Oglala Sioux, and claimed responsibility for the incident. The *Post* reports that Raven stated that he was the legitimate heir to the great chief Crazy Horse and was announcing his leadership of an uprising that would return the tribe to the old ways of living. Authorities have refused to speculate on the motive for the shooting or the identity of the man, saying only that both Indian police and the FBI were on the scene and would soon begin a massive search into the rugged terrain of the nearby foothills. The two men who were shot are presently listed in critical condition."

Alex turned off the radio.

So far, there seemed to be little known, or at least little that was being released to the media. He wondered if Molly was going to have to go away on the story. He hated it when she went away. He tried to picture the reservation landscape, remembering a summer trip out West the year after he started college. An image of long stretches of brown prairie with broken hills and high backdrop mountains came to mind. A dead brown land with a constant wind. Patches of sagebrush and low spiny cactus. He turned a corner and headed toward the Strand bookstore.

Indians. All right, he would see what his man Hal at the Strand had hidden away on his shelves.

He could feel it then, in his mind. It shifted, just a little, as if it were beginning to come awake. That special thing that was his, that ability that could take him away from all of this, the present, and into the past. He felt it move and his heart moved with it. In anticipation and fear. It was as though he were a child, lying awake in the night, staring at the ceiling. A small boy who hears, from the empty room above, the lurch and slide of something large and clumsy as it comes awake and begins to move.

Chapter 2

"Tell me about Crazy Horse," Molly asked. "Did you find anything?" She was sitting on a high stool beside the butcher-block kitchen counter. She had changed into her faded old blue jeans and a soft white sweatshirt with a picture of a duck on the front. The red of her hair seemed to focus the color in the room, the faint peach of the walls and the natural wood of the tables and chairs. Every kitchen should have a Molly, Alex sometimes thought as he watched her sitting on her stool. Conran's should list them in their glossy catalogues: beautiful, functional, intelligent, never breaks down, comes in one color only, stunning red with peaches-and-cream base. Priceless.

Alex was at his large gray commercial gas stove, surrounded by his tools: Cuisinart, blender, mixer, pots, cutlery, and cookbooks. This was their usual arrangement, Molly on her stool, Alex at the stove.

Alex cut four slices of bacon off a large chunk and threw them into a heavy, black iron frying pan. The bacon hissed and popped on the hot metal.

Molly liked to watch him cook. He was very good at it, much better than she was, and he enjoyed it. He had been cooking ever since his parents had died when he was seventeen years old. He and Molly had lived happily together in college and he had been the cook even then. Several years after graduation they had separated over a difference of opinion on the question of marriage; she for, he against. Then she had come back after a ten-year hiatus that included, on her part, a failed marriage and an attempt at living the good life in sunny California. She had been back for one year and they had gratefully fallen back into their old patterns.

He took a chicken out of the refrigerator and began cutting it into pieces.

"Indians?" she asked again as he put her favorite teacup and saucer in front of her and filled the cup from a Chinese teapot.

"Chicken," he said. "Chicken with fennel. A very old recipe, from the Italian Renaissance." He picked up a small jar and dumped a few seeds into the palm of his hand. He put several of them onto her saucer. "A neglected herb." He bit into one of the seeds. "People in the olden days used to put them into keyholes to keep out the evil spirits." Molly put a seed into her mouth and crunched it between her teeth. He watched her grimace as her mouth filled with the sharp bite of anise.

"The Puritans took the seeds to church to munch on during long sermons. They were called 'meetin' seeds.' Supposed to keep you from getting hungry." He turned back to the stove and moved the bacon to the side of the pan. He put in the chicken and arranged the pieces carefully. He turned back to her. "Indians. Yes, I found some things," he said, wiping his hands on a dish towel. "Stay put; I'll be right back."

He went into the living room and came back with an armful of books. He stacked them on the kitchen table. "Here you go." He picked up the top book. *The Great Sioux Nation* by Fred M. Hans, Mari Sandoz's *Crazy Horse,* considered the definitive work on Crazy Horse. Wissler's *Indians of the United States,* Cyrus T. Brady, *Indian Fights and Fighters,* and Royal B. Hassrick's *The Sioux: Life and Customs of a Warrior Society.* And assorted others. You've got enough here to keep you busy for a while."

Molly looked at the pile doubtfully. "Do you think I need to read all of them?" she asked.

He laughed at the look on her face. He went to the stove and moved the chicken pieces around. "And there lies the difference between the historian and the journalist," he said.

"Well, it's certainly one of the differences." She shook her head. "I don't have time to do that much research. I'm in the middle of a breaking story—I can't stop everything and take three days off and read all of those books." She looked back at the pile. "Three days, God, it would take me a week. They'll have caught the guy, jailed him, and he'll be out on parole before I get through the background work. This is why we interview people. We find someone who's already read all the books and ask him what we want to know."

"I know, I know. Somehow it seems to me like cheating, though. So they haven't caught him yet?"

"Not as of six o'clock. The last we heard he had disappeared into the hills."

"Have you found out anything useful?" He licked his hand where a drop of flying grease had landed and burned.

She shook her head. "Not much. His name is John Raven, and he's an Oglala Sioux. Lives on the Pine Ridge Reservation in South Dakota. Something of a militant, a member of the American Indian Movement. He was probably at the takeover at Wounded Knee back in 1973. That's about it. There's a fair amount of confusion over his motive. Most of the reports about his staging an Indian uprising seem to be overreactions and exaggeration. As near as I can tell, he merely called the local newspaper and said he'd done it because the surveyors or whatever they are were trespassing on Indian land."

Alex turned the chicken one more time, sprinkled on a tablespoon of flour and a small handful of fennel seeds, stirred for a minute, and then poured in a cup of white wine. The wine splashed into the pan, releasing a cloud of fragrant steam that made his eyes water. He turned down the fire and dropped in a handful of almonds and covered the pan. He checked the time on his old Bulova pocket watch and put water in a pot for the rice. "Let's go into the living room. I'll put the rice in and the salad's made so there isn't anything to do in here for twenty minutes. And take the books—if you won't read them, the least you can do is carry them."

• •

Alex picked up one of the books and ran his hand over the spine. "It's hard to believe, but I bought all of these for less than fifty bucks. They're all used, but they're in great shape."

Molly looked around the living room with amusement. The walls were covered from floor to ceiling with shelves of books. They were an addiction to Alex. He would no more pass up a used-book store than an alcoholic would a drink. Many of them had been inherited from his father, who had been a historian and a writer. Alex's father was a subject that they did not generally discuss. He occupied a special niche that defied light conversation. Alex hated his father for emotional neglect and active abuse, for dragging him and his mother around the world through jungles, deserts, and forests in search of locations he then turned into wildly successful historical novels. Alex and his mother would sit in their tent, surrounded by various dangers, waiting for his father to come back from his expeditions. It was only a year ago that Alex had learned that his father was not in those same jungles and forests, but years away in the past, doing his research *in situ*. To the world, Alex's father was dead; to Alex he was alive somewhere in the past, as dangerous and deadly as a rabid rat loose in a child's nursery.

"Your man John Raven has picked a spectacular role model in his choice of Crazy Horse," Alex said. "I looked through these this afternoon, and they're all in agreement on one thing: Crazy Horse was probably the finest, and one of the last examples, of a truly free Plains Indian."

"Why was he so special? I don't know anything at all about him." She shifted around on the couch so she was facing him.

"The reason that you don't know anything about him is because twentieth-century white America isn't much interested in the history of the Indian. If I were to name a white American who was well known at the time you wouldn't have the same problem. Try George Armstrong Custer."

"Everybody knows Custer. Custer's Last Stand."

"Very good. Then you should also know that Crazy Horse was the Indian who defeated Custer at the Little Bighorn."

Molly frowned. "I always thought it was numbers that defeated Custer. That he was short of manpower, and long on ego, and was eventually overrun by a superior force."

"That's the generally accepted opinion, and there's a lot of truth to it. But it discounts any intelligence on the part of the Indian, which is a typical white man's way of looking at things. It's easy to say, in hindsight, that it's obvious that Custer and his six hundred men had absolutely no chance against Crazy Horse and his three thousand warriors, but that doesn't take into account any factors other than troop strength." He pulled a book from the shelf and opened it. "Napoleon concluded from his Egyptian campaign that a European soldier against an Asiatic or an Oriental enemy, one on one, didn't have a chance. No matter what the differences in weaponry. The native was always too clever. Three to five Europeans *might* have a chance against the same number of natives—if they were properly dug in or well led on an offensive. But from there on up, the odds change dramatically. Twenty or more Europeans, armed with the best weapons, could take on fifty or even a hundred natives. Europeans and, in our case, American troopers of the Seventh Cavalry, had discipline, training, and fire control. And Custer knew this. He'd gone to West Point and studied his Napoleon. Sure, he underestimated the number of Indians he was up against, but even if he had known their true strength he still would have gone ahead."

"It sounds like insane odds to me, six hundred to three thousand," Molly said.

"It's not so crazy when you know more about Custer. He was one of the greatest military heroes of his time, just behind Grant and Sherman in the eyes of the American public. An incredibly brave cavalry officer who had one chief tactic that he used in any military situation: charge. Mount up your men, draw your sabers, dig in the spurs, and charge. And usually it worked. At least until he rode down into the Bighorn valley."

He put the book back on the shelf and sat back down. From the kitchen came the ding of a timer.

"Dinner," they both said together.

• •

Alex opened a bottle of deep red California Zinfandel and poured it into their glasses. He put a trivet on the table and served the chicken from the same black iron skillet that it had been cooked in. Molly made appreciative noises while she ate the first few bites. "I wouldn't have thought that you could tame fennel seeds. You seem to have subdued them quite nicely. And the almonds are great."

"Fourteenth-century Italians were great almond cookers," Alex said. "Now we smoke them with chemicals and serve them up on airplane flights."

They ate for a few minutes. "So, anyway, Crazy Horse," Alex said, taking another piece of chicken and a second mound of rice. He spooned some of the pan juices over the rice.

"Crazy Horse was born in 1839. It's said that he was odd even as a little boy. Very introspective, very quiet. He had light skin and light curly hair." Alex drank some of his wine. "As a boy he was called Curly. Generally Indians don't take their serious name until they have a vision or do some brave deed. Sometimes he was called Light-Skinned Boy."

"Very literal," Molly said. "I guess I would be Red-Haired Woman."

"Probably. I, of course, would be known as Cooks-with-Fennel. So, Curly grew up like most normal male Plains Indians of the time, inculcated with the manly virtues of great bravery, supreme fighting skills, endurance, brute force, and the ability to withstand major amounts of pain." He pushed back his plate and served the salad. "The way the Indians fought is interesting. Actually killing someone was all right, but it was a much higher honor to count coup. To count coup, one would ride his pony up to the enemy and simply touch one of them with a stick or his hand. Then he would make a mad dash back to his own lines. This tended to keep down the loss of life, which was important as male Indians were needed to hunt and sit around bragging and telling stories and such. But when they decided to fight the white man, this sort of warfare wasn't very productive. An Indian would dash in to count coup, and your average Bluecoat would simply blast him out of the saddle. Very unsportsmanlike.

"Are you finished?" Alex asked, pointing at her plate. "If you are, I could get you some dessert. There's ice cream."

She waved a hand. "I've had quite enough. I'll get fat if I'm not careful. You go ahead."

He carried the dirty plates and the leftover chicken into the kitchen. He got the ice cream out of the freezer and brought it to the table. He ate it straight out of the cold plastic container.

"So, did he ever have any children?" Molly asked. "That's the crux of the matter, isn't it? At least as far as I'm concerned. This guy, John Raven, says he is the direct descendant of Crazy Horse. If he really is, that makes it a little different than if he just made it up."

"I think there's more to it than that. Even if he's simply chosen Crazy Horse as his make-believe ancestor, he's done it for a reason. He's going to also accept Crazy Horse's attributes and his philosophy—otherwise why bother to choose a particular person?"

"How can you eat all that ice cream and never get fat?" she asked.

"I run my ass off every morning." He spooned out the last of the ice cream, put the top on the empty container and set it on the table.

"So here you've got your guy, John Raven, who sees someone as his enemy. In this case it's a big corporation or the minions of the corporation, those guys who were digging holes on reservation land. Incidentally, did they die?"

"Not yet, but it's a distinct possibility."

Alex nodded. "Anyway, John Raven decides that he must smite his enemy. Rushing in and hitting him with a little stick isn't going to seem like much in these modern times, so he shoots him. Or in this case, them. Under the circumstances, Crazy Horse probably would have done the same thing. His point was to stop these men from doing whatever they were doing and set an example. Very effective. Consider that point number one. Point number two is his vision quest."

Molly looked at him with her head tilted to one side. "And that is . . . ?"

"Perhaps the key to your Indian's motive. For the Sioux male, the vision quest was a central part of his existence. It gave meaning, order, and direction to his life. Visions were induced in a number of ways. There was the really tough way, like the Sun Dance ceremony, and then there was the slightly easier method of going to some remote place and going without food or sleep for an extended period. That usually brought it on.

"Curly, he wasn't known as Crazy Horse yet, had his vision when he was fifteen years old. He saw a great warrior riding a horse, floating in the air. The warrior gave him a series of instructions: he should never take anything for himself; before going into battle he should throw some dust over his pony and over his own head; he should wear a small stone behind his ear and a single eagle feather in his hair. There was a whole list of things.

"Curly's father, old Crazy Horse, said if Curly did what the dream warrior indicated, then he would never be killed or hit by a bullet. He said that Curly must be like the warrior, that he must lead the people and never take anything for himself. And then he said that from then on Curly's name would be Crazy Horse, and he himself would be known as Worm."

"Worm?" Molly asked.

"Yep. And don't ask me why. I don't have the slightest idea."

"So what's the point of all of this?"

"The point is this. I said there were two primary considerations: That John Raven would take his identity, in a tribal sense, directly from Crazy Horse. And that he would, if he were truly following the old ways, have had his own vision quest, which would have given him some indication of how he was to live his own life." He paused. "Or maybe he's searching for his vision now, and all of this is part of his quest. Anyway, if it were me, trying to find John Raven, I would want to know how serious he was about his own Indianness, this business of following the old ways, and not just as a militant, but personally. If you know that, you have a chance of finding your man. His personal direction would dictate his physical direction."

Molly finished her tea and set it on the floor. "All right, I see your point. But visions and magic aside, did Crazy Horse have any descendants? And could John Raven be one?"

"Possibly. Probably not." Alex shrugged. "No one knows."

Chapter 3

"Kill the pony herd. Kill them all."

He was in the village. He seemed to be standing among the blue-coated soldiers. It all came back to him, as if he had never left, the sweeping charge of the soldiers, the bitter cold he did not feel, the snow, the killing.

"General, there's eight hundred goddamn horses in that herd, surely . . ."

"My orders are to kill the pony herd, Captain Benteen. Carry out those orders."

It was Custer. Just like in all the photographs; the handsome face, the famous long blond hair, the pale blue eyes. He was dressed in a suit of fringed buckskin. An aide stood at his side.

"Yes sir." The gray-haired, stout, older soldier turned and walked stiffly away. Custer looked around, as if taking inventory.

The ground around him was strewn with the bullet-ridden bodies of Indians; men, women, and children, animals, horses and dogs. Like the playroom floor of some giant, malevolent child. The sun was up now, and the snow was bright with splashes of blood that had begun to melt into pink slush beneath the boots of the living and the bodies of the dead.

Custer walked toward the center of the village, or what once had been the village. The soldiers were pulling down the te-pees, piling them together and burning them. The air was thick with smoke and the smell of burning buffalo robes. A soldier stood guard on a crowd of captive Indians, mostly women with children, and a few old men. All of them were wrapped in blankets. Many of the women had slashed their cheeks in mourning. One of Custer's scouts stood with the guard. The scout was dressed in greasy buckskins and a large Mexican sombrero. He was chewing a wad of tobacco and cradling a very long, large-bore rifle.

"Have you interrogated the prisoners, Sam?" Custer asked the scout.

"Well, General, I guess I have, though I ain't got much out of them under the circumstances. As you might expect, they're still a bit perturbed over what we've done to their husbands and fathers." He leaned to the side and spit into the snow. "This bunch seems to be a mixed band, mostly Cheyennes with some Sioux and a few Kiowas. I believe they're part of a larger group that's scattered all along the river downstream. Which is something we ought to keep in mind. Most of these belongs to Black Kettle, or used to. He's dead, as of a short while ago."

The scout stopped talking and everyone looked toward the far side of the meadow as shots suddenly erupted, paused, and continued, accompanied by the screams of dying horses.

"If you're going to take this bunch with you, you'd better save out enough horses from that herd for them to ride," the scout said. "And a few of the tepees."

Custer's eyes narrowed for a moment; then he nodded at his aide. The aide trotted off toward the sound of shooting.

"I do have an interesting proposition for you, General," the scout said with a lopsided grin. He nodded at the Indians and a fat squaw moved forward, pushing a young girl in front of her. "This fat one started in on me as soon as we had them rounded up. Says she's got a present for Long Hair." He nod-ded at the woman. "This here's Me-o-tzi. That translates as something like 'Little Grass That Shoots in the Spring.' As you can see, she's a fine-looking woman, for an Indian. The fat one says she's to be your bride." He tilted his large hat back and leered at Custer.

Custer studied the woman. She was around twenty years old, slim, with beautiful straight jet-black hair that fell to her waist. Somehow, amidst all the horror, she looked as if she'd just bathed and combed her hair. She was wearing a pale gray, beaded elkskin dress. "As you say, Sam, she is indeed a fine-looking woman. For Indian or white. You may thank the old one for the offer, but explain to her that I already have a sits-beside-the-fire wife." He waved his hand to indicate that the women were to return to the others. The fat woman began to rail at them, but the scout cut her off with a command. He lifted his rifle, and the woman fell silent and stepped back.

"Anything else?" Custer asked.

"Only thing might be one of the old men. They stayed behind to rear guard while the others waded down the river and got away. One of them's a chief, or at least he used to be. Name's High Cloud. He's a Sioux. Smarter than most of them usually are, speaks a little American."

Custer nodded. "I'll speak with him later, after we're out of here." He looked at the throng of captives. "I'm letting the officers have their pick of the squaws. But keep them away from that one." He gestured at the woman, who was still standing apart from the others. "Me-o-tzi, didn't you say? And give her a tepee of her own." The scout spit again, switched his chew from one cheek to the other, and smiled. Custer turned and walked away, toward the sound of shooting. Alex seemed to draw back to the edge of the village where he could watch, though he did not want to.

He watched the soldiers drag the dead to a long shallow trench and dump them in. He watched the final tepees go into the bonfires. He watched the last of the ponies fall and lie heaving on the pile of horses that covered what would be, in the spring, after the snow had gone and the grass had greened, a lush meadow of flowers and tall prairie grass. He watched because he could not turn away, could not close his eyes. He watched because he was not here, but far away, asleep. And then it began to fade, and he awoke.

• •

He stood in his second-floor bathrobe, dressed in his green terrycloth robe and his fuzzy slippers, trying to open a bottle of aspirin. He had awakened with a terrible headache and a faint memory of pain and grief and the remembered smell of burning leather and the coppery odor of blood. The light in the bathroom was too bright. It hurt his eyes and his head. His hands shook.

He finally got the arrow and the notch lined up and thumbed the lid off with a small pop. He looked toward the bathroom door, which was open an inch or so, listening to see if the sound had awakened Molly. He took off the lid and laid it on the sink. He began picking at the edges of the tamper-resistant foil that covered the mouth of the little jar. His head beat in time with his heart.

It was happening again; he did not doubt it. He wasn't sure what he had dreamed, but he knew it would come to him. In time.

He gave up and punched a hole in the foil with his eye-tooth. He peeled away the covering. He tried to pinch the ball of cotton and pull it out. It slipped away and ended up down inside the bottle. Little lights began to twinkle in the corners of his eyes, and nausea grew with the pain. He stopped to rest, leaning on the sink, and looked up, not at the mirror where he expected to see his face, but instead found he was looking at . . .

an enormous building. Involuntarily, he drew in a deep breath and began to hyperventilate. He felt his heart skip a beat. The room around him was gone, his house was gone, New York was gone, and here he was on a bright moonlit night dressed in his bathrobe and fuzzy slippers in front of an opera-house type of building, a palace, or a temple, or something, grand and ornate. He made a conscious effort to slow his breathing. He knew what had happened because it had happened to him before, but still it shocked him as it would any sane man, this leap into the cold sea of time. It occurred to him that at least the weather was decent. Nice night for a trip, a disembodied voice in his brain pronounced, followed by a peal of maniacal laughter.

The quickest, most accessible hiding place was right in front of him, behind the columns on the huge porch of the building. He shuffled up the steps and moved behind a column. It was dark there. The marble was cool to his touch. He found that he was still clutching the small pill bottle. He put it into his pocket and inventoried his possessions: one partially opened bottle of pills, one ragged tissue left from a bout of flu contracted the preceding winter. Not much to work with.

He carefully peered around the column. Where the hell was everybody? It was like a giant set of some classical architecture, a Roman city closed for repairs, a ghost town. On either side of the plaza in front of the building were huge statues of headless winged horses. He looked up and down the mall. More strange buildings. No people.

He went back behind the column and sat down and leaned against its base. He looked at his feet. Those damn fuzzy slippers. Molly had bought them for his birthday as a joke. Some joke. He tried to assign a date or place to his surroundings, but came up with nothing. Architecture had always been one of his weak points. But from what he could see from his present vantage point, none of the buildings seemed to be in the style of any of the other buildings. It was as if he were suddenly thrust into a great opera set built by one of Wagner's mad gods. The drama of it was unmistakable, but the sense of it escaped him. What would happen when day came? Would it remain empty? It seemed unlikely. And what would he do? Stroll around in his bathrobe like an escapee from a mental ward? He didn't even know what century he was in, much less what country.

All right, where am I, when am I, and where is everybody else? He focused his senses. Accept the fact that it looks strange; forget that for a moment.

Listen. Nothing. Quiet, and he hesitated to complete the thought, as the grave.

Smell. The odor of new asphalt clung to the night air, redolent hot tar now cooled. Beneath it hung the smell of recently dug earth traced with touches of sawdust and fresh-cut timber. He understood.

This place, wherever, whenever, and whatever it was, was new. Freshly built. The smells were smells of construction. There were no people because no one lived here, first of all because it didn't look like a place where people would live, but also because it wasn't finished. The statues of the winged horses had no heads because they were incomplete. Maybe it really *was* a giant stage set. Maybe he was in Hollywood. He had a momentary image of a director, a man with a beret pulled backward on his head and a large megaphone, "All right, who's the guy in the pajamas on the set?"

A faint sound caught his attention. Small squeaks like an ungreased wheel. A metal wheel, rolling on pavement. Muted voices. Alex got to his knees and pressed himself against the column. Fear pumped adrenaline into his bloodstream. Fucking bathrobe, fucking stupid slippers. What if he had to run? He was naked beneath the robe.

The squeaking grew louder. Mingling with what sounded like the scrabbling of claws on metal. The voices had resolved themselves into curses. Alex took a deep breath and peered around the column.

His eyes provided the information, but his brain was unable to process it. He had once read about a man, blind from birth, who had regained his sight and was shown a streetcar. The man had been unable to identify the streetcar until he went up and ran his hands over it. Alex recognized the dilemma: even though one sees, one does not necessarily understand.

Two men, about fifty yards away. The one who was riding was white, the one walking was black. The vehicle looked like an immense child's tricycle. A small seat was positioned between two large wheels that were fully five feet high, and a foot-and-a-half thick. There was a handlebar attached to a little guide wheel in front. The man who steered was doing the cursing. Alex moved back behind the column while he tried to sort it out. What the hell was it?

"Goddamn you, you black bastard, keep that yellow dog

moving. They got to run together or this thing ain't going to work at all," the white man shouted.

"He running now," the black man said.

The trike picked up speed until the man on the ground was trotting.

The man riding almost sang with excitement. "All right, you bitches, let's go, let's go, the Captain going to want this thing worked out right now. You want to eat, you got to run. I'll whip your mangy asses. I'll beat you miserable curs. God-damn, boy, poke that right-side dog with that stick. Make her move!"

As the light of the moon fell on the strange group, Alex could see that the high, wide wheels contained two dogs, one in each wheel, and they were running in a basketwork cage, much as gerbils run in tiny exercise wheels. The man on foot poked a stick through the basketwork and prodded the dog nearest him. The dog stopped running and smashed his head against the wire, barking and snarling his rage. Alex could see the white of the teeth in the moonlight as they gnashed at the wire.

The right-hand dog was stopped, but the other one was still trying to run. This halted the forward progress of the machine and began moving it in a circle. The rider turned the stick hard to the left, which didn't stop the turn but did begin to tilt the vehicle. The far dog began scrambling harder to keep up-right, and only when the black man leapt up and hung onto the rising wheel did the tricycle right itself and stop moving.

"I'm going to kill that bitch," the rider said as he climbed down. "Gimme that goddamn stick. I'll beat her until she can't run nor walk nor crawl."

"No suh," the other man said, backing away. "We hurt these dogs and we might's well start looking for some other line of work. That is if we able. You know what Brannon do to men who don't do what he bids. He say get the damn dogs ready, and that's what we best do."

"Hell, we'd just as well put *you* in the cage, which is what I suggested in the first place. A set of matched niggers would work better than these bitches." The man kicked the wheel and set off a new round of barking and teeth gnashing. "God-damn it. All right. Let's get 'em moving." He climbed back up in the seat and the black man talked soothingly to the dogs for a minute. The strange group wobbled off again, slowly, away from Alex, down the roadway, into the dark. He sat back down behind the column and rested his head in his hands until the world began to fade around him.

• •

"It happened, didn't it?" she asked. She was sitting up in bed with the sheet wrapped around her. He was standing by the bed. They both knew what she meant.

"Yes," he said. He had come back, into the bathroom, just where he had left. He'd even put the bottle of pills back into the medicine cabinet.

"How long have I been gone?"

She shrugged. The light was still on in the bathroom, spill-ing through the partially open door.

"I don't know, when did it start? I woke up an hour ago." She turned and looked at the clock radio on her bed table. "It's three A.M. now."

He sat down on the bed and took off his slippers. Even in the dim light he could see black smears of fresh asphalt on the soles. "I had a nightmare." What was it? Horses? Something about horses. "I had a headache. I got up to take some aspirin, I guess it was around midnight. That means it's been almost three hours." He moved up the bed and leaned against the headboard beside her. She reached for his hand.

"Where," she began, faltered, then went on, "where were you? Where did you go?"

He shook his head. "I don't know. It was very strange. Hard to explain." He thought about the tricycle.

She leaned against him. He put his arm around her so her head lay against his chest. Her body was tense. "So," she said, "here we go again. Tell me what happened."

He pulled her tighter and put his cheek against her head. He told her. She lay so still at times he thought she had fallen asleep, but when he hesitated she would tell him to go on. By the time he had finished, dawn was beginning to seep in around the edges of the curtained windows.

"But why?" she asked. "Why then, whenever it is, why that place?"

"Why any of it?" he said. "We've never understood why it happens." He frowned. "I can't stop it, you know that. It's part of me. My father could do it, hell, maybe *his* father could do it. It has to be genetic, as much a part of my DNA as the color of my hair, The point is not so much why or how it happens, but what the *purpose* of it is. What is it I'm supposed to do? And does anything I do make a difference?"

"Circles. It always comes back around on itself. I wish it would all just go away."

He remembered the cool clean night air and the excitement. The singular *strangeness* of it all, and still the excitement. The danger. He did not want it to go away.

"There must be a reason for it." He turned toward her. It was light enough in the room to see her face as she watched him. "What do I have in my life now? What am I doing in *this* place?" He gestured to the room around them. "All I have is you. I don't do much of anything else, nothing that makes any difference." He paused, trying to put it into words. "After the last time, after I had been in Russia . . ."

"And almost died," Molly interjected.

"Yes." He nodded. "And almost died—I came back to my old life and I could see how empty it was. I used to feel as if I lived my life in Plato's cave, watching the shadows on the wall. Then I realized that that wasn't right, this *was* real, my life here, and that was the problem. What do we do? I study what men did in the past, and you write about what other men do in the present. That's about it. The only danger comes from speeding taxi cabs and drug addicts bent on stealing our stereo." He stopped and shook his head.

"Yes, I almost died back there, but . . ." he looked at her and she could see it in him, the power, and knew there was no stopping it. "I didn't die." Now he looked away and remembered another place, another time. "Christ, Molly, back there, back there I was alive."

Chapter 4

Molly sat in the kitchen at the counter in a patch of bright early morning sun. Her freshly washed hair gleamed crimson, but her eyes were tired and dark. She drank tea from a lemon-yellow Fiestaware cup that she placed on a dark blue saucer. She watched Alex make himself a cup of coffee.

The splash of sunlight, the cup and saucer, the sun-warmed wood, and the shiny appliances seemed to her somehow out of sync, cheery evidence of a normal world where people did not visit faraway times in the middle of the night. For a moment, as she watched the liquid tremble in her teacup, she wished her life to be safe. She smiled at the thought. She wished that she was standing by the stove, dressed in blue jeans and sweatshirt and an apron, making breakfast for, what the hell, why not go all the way, her husband and their two adorable children. In her mind she shooed them out the door, the children to school and Alex to some regular job. She was tired of crazy Indians, a boyfriend who had some frightening ability to go places that the laws of physics did not allow him to go, of always wondering what was going to happen next.

"Do you want some breakfast?" Alex asked.

"No," Molly said, shaking her head.

"You look like you want something."

Molly smiled. "Well, whatever it is it isn't in the refriger-ator." She shook her head again. "I was just sitting here feeling sorry for myself. Wishing for things I wouldn't want if I had them." She looked at her watch. "Seven o'clock. I haven't been this late in a year."

"We were sort of busy last night. You're allowed to sleep in."

"*You* were sort of busy. I was sitting in bed wondering where you were. You have any more ideas on that subject?"

Alex poured himself another cup of coffee. "Not really. It could have been anywhere. I'd guess, just from the clothes and the feel of things, that it was later than 1865, after the Civil War anyway, and before 1890. It won't be that hard to work out—I've got a lot to go on."

"And I have to go to work. You'll call me if you find out anything?"

He nodded and kissed her on the forehead. It was worse for her than it was for him. He at least got the excitement. It was like a drug, or the taste of some exotic fruit or fish that if incorrectly prepared could poison you. When he went back there was a rush of exhilaration, a feeling of absolute freedom; fear, yes, but there was so much more of life in it than he normally had. He was glad that it had finally happened, but he tried not to show it because it was something he did alone, without Molly, something that she could only participate in through his recounting. And Molly was not the sort of woman to sit on the sidelines and watch.

"I'm off to my Indian," Molly said, climbing down from the high stool. "I'll see you tonight." It was half a question. Would he be here?

"I'll be here."

• •

He debated skipping his morning run so he could start his research, but he didn't. He'd been running every day for so long it had become a firmly entrenched habit. When he didn't run he felt mildly guilty and mildly sluggish all day long. So he ran.

After his bath he walked the length of his bookshelves pulling out possibilities. The collection of books covered all four walls of the living room and was representative of his family's history for the last sixty years. Alex, his father, and his grandfather were all historians. Much of his grandfather's library went to Yale, where the old man had taught, but some of it was here, as were his father's books as well as Alex's. One whole section of shelves was devoted to videotapes, mostly of old movies and television shows. Alex's interest in the past, he resisted using the word *obsession,* was concentrated more on the immediate past than the further reaches. But from what he had seen last night, the time period he was looking for had to do with his grandfather's immediate past rather than his own.

He pulled Dixon's *History of American Architecture,* Peale's *History of Transportation,* and the original edition of *American Clothing and Costume.* Basic stuff, used by researchers everywhere. Alex's library was particularly strong in this type of book, as his father had used them extensively in his own career.

Alex sat in his deep, old soft plush easy chair, and he put the books on the floor beside him. He pulled up a low coffee table and opened the oversize history of architecture. He started with the 1800s and leafed through every page until he found what he was looking for. It wasn't difficult, any buildings as odd and as big as those he had seen last night, even seen in darkness, would have to be remarked upon somewhere.

And here they were. The Philadelphia Exposition of 1876. The building he had hidden in was the Memorial Hall, and the huge railroad station was the Main Exhibition Building. The expo rated a section all to itself. He found nothing in the transportation book about dog-powered vehicles, but then he had not held much hope for that. The book of clothing simply showed what was normal for the period.

The next step would be a trip to the public library to soak up general information. In a way he felt as if he were arming himself for a mission. An intellectual Rambo. Only he was not going into the jungles or the woods and he wouldn't be taking any firearms. Information would be the ammunition, and he intended to get as much of it as he could before he made the next trip. The phone rang.

"They're sending me out there," Molly said "Our fleeing Indian is still missing."

"I suppose you have to go," Alex said, regretting having said it the moment the words were out of his mouth. She didn't complain about where he went, so how could he complain about her doing her job?

"I have to go. You know that."

"I know. What I really meant was I'll miss you. I'll worry about you."

Molly laughed ruefully. "That'll be a switch, won't it? I know that's what you mean. I'll miss you, too. And I'll also be worrying about where you'll be. Look, I don't leave until tomorrow, so we can talk about it tonight."

Alex hung up the phone. There was something else that bothered him, but he didn't have the nerve to mention it to Molly. Something his father had told him the last time he'd gone back. If he was going to return from the past, he needed someone here as an anchor. Molly was his lifeline from then to now. He had to have someone who cared that he came back, someone who would keep him alive in the present. Molly. So, yes, he would miss her, yes, he would worry that she might get hurt, and God help him, yes, he would worry that if Molly wasn't here he might be trapped back there. Tie it all up and what have you got? A heavy load of guilt, love, and fear, one that he would just have to carry no matter what happened.

• •

The first thing to do was to see his friend Dave at the library. Alex had an odd assortment of friends. Most of them were tradespeople he had dealt with over the years until they'd achieved the status of friend. There was Hal down at the bookstore, Armando at the liquor store—they discussed various wines and beers for hours on end—Matty at the corner grocer's who would save out the best and most interesting vegetables for Alex, Rolf the butcher, and Dave at the library. Every once in a while one of them would come by the house, but generally they simply met after work at a bar to have a few beers.

"You teaching a new class?" Dave asked, handing over several reels of microfilm. The librarian had been in one of Alex's classes at the New School.

"They canned me, Dave. I thought you knew that."

The bearded librarian shook his head. "Nope. You haven't been in for a long time. Not since you were teaching that Russian history class. How come they fired you?"

"Well, I couldn't really blame them. I missed about a month of classes."

"You been sick, man? You do look sort of skinny."

Alex laughed. "No, nothing like that. I just got unavoidably called away. How much have we got on these reels?"

"You got six months of the *New York Times* there, starting January one, 1876. You looking for anything in particular?"

"No, just looking. Just some general research, nothing serious."

The librarian nodded. "Let me know if you need anything else."

Alex wound the film onto the pickup reel and felt a moment of déjà vu as the first pages flickered onto the screen. As a history major in college and as a teacher afterward, he had spent great periods of his life in front of microfilm machines, reading the papers of the past. If you added up the amount of reading time, research time, and student and teaching time, and then threw in eating and sleeping, he wondered how much actual living he had done.

He sat in front of the machine for five hours, getting up only to ask for new reels and to go to the restroom. He stuck with the newspapers, New York and Philadelphia. When his eyes refused to accept more newsprint, he switched to magazines, *Harper's, Atlantic,* and *Scribner's.* He found the layout not much different from the newspapers. At five o'clock he nodded off over an article on the Philadelphia Exposition by William Dean Howells, and he decided to call it a day. He was stuffed with information, glutted with mounds of words that needed to settle before he could utilize the mass of information. This had always been his method; pour it in, fill it up, and let it percolate until it was a useful part of him, ready to be called up when needed.

• •

Potatoes. Quennebecs, Matty had said, holding up a small potato. Last of the season, fresh from the ground, saved them out just for you, Alex. Matty was a fanatic when it came to freshness. You want your fish fresh, right? Your bread? Who wants to eat stale bread? So why not vegetables? Alex agreed.

Alex washed the potatoes, skins on, cut them up and put them into the pot. Water. Onto the stove, medium heat.

"You ever go to a World's Fair?" he asked Molly. She was on her stool, he was at the stove.

"Just one, the last one. Knoxville. I had to cover it for the paper I was working on. All I remember is long lines, mediocre food, and films of what the world would be like in the year 2000."

Alex nodded. "I was there. I also went to Montreal when I was a teenager. Same thing. The hit of the fair was a circular building where you stood in a crowd and watched a three-hundred-and-sixty-degree film of people riding a roller coaster. 'Sensaround,' I think the effect was called. 'The Way People Will Watch Films in the Year 2000.' Jesus." He turned to Molly and leaned against the refrigerator. "You know, the year 2000 is not that far away. I'll be fifty years old." He had a mental image of the two of them, just as they were now, here in the kitchen, with gray hair and wrinkles, like children in oldster makeup. He tried to visualize how either of them would really look, but he couldn't do it. Is our own aging process impossible to visualize? Would it all really be the same, Alex and Molly? He shook off the image. His mind was unable to cope with the future, unwilling to forecast, powerless and anemic when forced in that direction.

"The Philadelphia Exposition was different," he said, taking two small strip steaks out of the refrigerator. He glanced at Molly, wondering if she was listening or going over her travel itinerary. It didn't matter much. What he needed was an audience in front of which he could formulate his thoughts. It was the teacher in him, rising to the fore. "Expos today are always dealing with what life will be like in the future. We're geared to technology and what it will mean to us as individuals. Back then, this is 1876, people were interested in their past, where they'd been, rather than where they were going."

"I'll be back in a minute," Molly said, "I've got to check my reservations."

Jeez, Alex thought, I'm holding her spellbound. But he understood. She'd been running around all evening packing her bag and getting ready. She was supposed to fly out early in the morning and be in South Dakota by noon. One hell of a cultural leap. She was nervous and distracted, and so was he. As usual, he fell back on his pedantic nature; he'd give them both a lecture to calm their nerves.

He put his cast-iron skillet on the front burner, salted the bottom of the pan, and turned the fire high. He felt vaguely guilty about the salt. High blood pressure, the silent killer, sitting there in the frying pan waiting to leap into his arteries. What was left? Modern science was taking away all his pleasures. He quit smoking years ago, recently cut back on his drinking, ran every day, and now he was worrying about salt? He thought over the miles of hundred-year-old newsprint he had read during the day and couldn't come up with a single warning about how the reader would drop dead if he didn't stop doing something that wasn't good for him. The salt was turning brown. He threw in the two steaks and stepped back as they seared onto the hot pan. He took a piece of frozen gingerroot out of the freezer and peeled it. He checked the potatoes, turned the fire down, flipped the steaks over, and shaved the ginger onto the meat.

"All right, I'm confirmed for the morning. Now what were you saying."

Somehow the lecture mood had left him. He already missed her, and she hadn't even left. "Just babbling about what I read at the library. Nothing important. Do you know how long you'll be gone?"

"That's the third time you've asked me that this evening. I'll be gone until they catch John Raven, I guess. Or until the story gets too old or too stale or they call me back to do something else. There's no way of knowing."

He nodded and checked the potatoes. Done. He dumped them into the colander and turned off the fire under the steaks. Molly put the potatoes into a bowl as he put the steaks on a platter. He put a couple of tablespoons of hot mustard, a pat of butter, and a splash of white wine into the pan, turned the fire back on and stirred it around. He poured the mustard-ginger sauce over the steaks.

Molly sighed as she got the salad out of the refrigerator. "This is probably the last decent meal I'll have until I get back. What do Indians eat, anyway? Do they have restaurants on reservations?"

"I don't know what they eat these days. They used to eat wild animals, primarily buffalo. Pemmican, squash, corn, turnips, and all manner of nuts and berries. These days they probably eat junk food. As for restaurants, I never saw one on a reservation. You ever been to a reservation?"

"Nope." They sat down at the table and began eating.

"Well, they're pretty sad places. Brown and empty. At least the few I've driven through. I don't know, maybe they look better if you're an Indian. I don't see how, though. I don't envy you."

"I don't mind as long as I get a good story out of it. There's not enough vinegar in the salad dressing." She smiled at him.

"Next time, my dear," he teased, "make it yourself. After a week of beef jerky you'll remember that salad dressing with great fondness."

"And you, too. I'll remember you with great fondness."

"Yes."

Chapter 5

She was already asleep when he went to bed. She had gone up while he was still washing the dishes. He stood in the doorway and looked at her in the dim reflected light from the hall. She was so quiet when she slept that he sometimes had to stop himself from waking her up to see if she was still alive. Her hair fanned out around her on the pillow. He could see the outline of her body beneath the sheet. Maybe it wouldn't happen again. Maybe he wouldn't go away, maybe he'd just stay here and wait for her to come back and everything would be normal. Maybe.

He turned off the hall light and walked softly into the dark room. He took off his clothes and piled them on the floor and got into bed. Molly mumbled something and turned to him. He could feel her soft breath on his cheek.

• •

He opened his eyes.

It was the smell that had awakened him. He was lying flat on his back. There was no sound. He lay still and attempted to sort it out. It was thick, all around him, the smell of hides, leather, animals, sweat, smoke, dirt, bodies, all commingled into something new, a smell like a color never seen. A shifting sort of thing that eluded his attempt to classify it, not bad or good, those terms didn't fit, it was different, overpowering yet somehow satisfying, like the smell of fresh bread and frying meat and onions.

He turned his head slowly to the side. He was lying on an animal skin with long thick fur. The individual hairs tickled his nose. The air was warm, and he was naked.

There was a faint light. Above him, where the roof was, he could see a hole, and through it the darkness of a night sky with a few stars. Where the hell was he?

It had happened while he had been asleep. No headaches, no whirling lights in the corners of his eyes, nothing like it had been before. This time he had gone to sleep, and now he was somewhere else. He suppressed a wild urge to get up and run, knowing that he was not asleep, that Molly would not wake him up and say, Alex, it was just a dream.

He listened. Closed his eyes and slowed his breathing and listened, sorting out the sounds. Outside, wherever he was: crickets; there, a snort from an animal, a large animal. Horse? Cow? Pig? What the hell, bear? Far away, an owl. Nothing else. Outdoor sounds. There didn't seem to be much in the way of walls, just that little round window high up on the ceiling.

Now, inside. Breathing, the long soft sound of sleep. Not his breathing, but someone else's. His body instinctively tensed, his fear fastening on the sound. He willed his muscles to relax. He made himself count to one hundred, slowly, while he stared at his feet and relaxed all the muscles in his body.

He sat up very quietly. If he had to flee he at least ought to know which direction to flee in. There was a faint diagonal line in the wall in front of him. He eased onto his hands and knees and crawled toward it. He was acutely aware of his nakedness. He put out a hand and felt the line, found that wall was not a wall, but a covering, an animal skin, and that the line of pale light was a flap in the covering. He pushed it back and leaned out.

There was a moon, almost full, bright against the land-scape. They were on a rolling plain. In the distance there were mountains showing as a line of jagged dark against slightly lighter sky. It was cooler outside than it was in the tent. He looked up at the sloping walls and corrected himself. Not tent; tepee. Holy Jesus, he seemed to be in an Indian tepee, and that was so strange that for a minute it didn't even frighten him. Around them were two other tepees, and farther away what seemed to be a large grouping of military-style tents. He pulled the flap back down and sat back inside.

It took a moment for his eyes to adjust, but he could plainly hear that the breathing was now different; faster, shallower, and he knew whoever it was there in the tepee with him was now awake. He could see the pale form, sitting up. He pulled one of the skins over his lower body.

A voice. "Tu-we. Ta-ku?"

What? "It's all right," he whispered. The words were repeated. He had no idea what they meant. He was very good with languages, knew a lot of them, but this was not one he recognized.

"It's all right," he said again, unable to think of anything that would work any better. He could see her now, see that it was a woman. She, too, was naked. He couldn't make out her features, but long black hair framed her face, falling to high round breasts.

She leaned forward toward him. She reached out a hand and touched his shoulder. He leaned forward and touched her on the shoulder as she had done.

All right, time for a moment's analytical thought. It looked like he was in an Indian tepee, or what he thought an Indian tepee should look like, and this woman was speaking a language that might very well be American Indian. At least she hadn't screamed or run away, so maybe he wasn't headed for instant death. She moved toward him. He could see her face now; round eyes that were wide open, high flat cheekbones that were almost Oriental. She seemed somehow familiar. Faint memory stirred, fragments of a distant dream. She peered into his face, put out her hand again to his shoulder, touched him, squeezed his arm.

It seemed as if she was checking to see if he was real. He could almost hear her thinking: Is this real or am I dreaming? Quite normal under the circumstances, Indian or no Indian.

The amazing part was that she didn't panic. She showed less fear than he was feeling.

"It's not a dream," he said quietly. He put his hand on her shoulder and squeezed just as she had done. Long ago he had seen his father use the same imitation technique while making contact with primitive tribesmen. The idea was that the repetition was an indication of friendliness, or at least that you weren't about to commit some act of mayhem.

She moved even closer and peered at his face, tilting her head to try to see better. She felt around at his legs and touched them beneath the animal skin. She seemed to be waiting for him to do something.

She rose up on her knees and brought her face quite near his. He could see her clearly now.

"Nape-yu-za." Her voice was calm. He got up on his knees facing her. She was only slightly shorter than he. They were so close he could feel her breath on his face. He could smell her, part of the smell in the air, warm. For the first time in his life he understood what the odor of musk was. She leaned against him.

Her breasts rested against his chest. He might have pulled away. There was a moment when he could have, but he didn't, and she leaned into him. Her cheek was against his, not moving, just there.

Quite suddenly the fear shifted, metamorphosed into a wave of desire that had as its focal point that place on their two bodies where they were touching, her breasts, the nipples clearly felt against his chest. And then there was obvious indication that he was indeed a man, flesh and blood, no ethereal spirit.

She touched him, squeezed him, roughly. And laughed. He almost pulled away, but then she was on him, like a cat, quick. She laughed a low sound and pushed him onto the animal skins. She stretched herself on top of him. He felt her supple back, ran a hand down her smooth flank. Her skin seemed to be covered with a light fragrant oil. And then it was all swift movement as she impaled herself on him like some eager Christian throwing herself onto the stake, and there was no more thought, only their two entwined bodies on the pile of thick fur, and he was unbound, endlessly, unquestionably, alive.

• •

And then he woke. He looked at the clock beside the bed. One hour; he'd been gone for one hour, and in that hour he'd . . . what? He could smell it on him. The smell of hides, and the smell of her body. He looked at Molly. She'd hardly moved since he came to bed. He suppressed a wave of panicky laughter. *He* had, oh, yes, indeed, he'd moved around quite a bit. He quietly swung his legs over the edge of the bed and went into the bathroom.

He closed the door. He turned the brass taps of the bathtub so the water ran quietly. He leaned against the sink and watched the old claw-footed tub fill with steaming hot water. He cupped his hands over his face and smelled the essence of the woman, remembered her supple quickness and wondered how he had gotten himself into this, and what it all meant.

He lowered himself into the bath. He eased back and watched the water rise to the drain, just below the faucets. He sat back up and carefully washed himself.

He had almost fallen asleep in the tub when Molly opened the door. "Alex? What are you doing? It's three o'clock in the morning." She rubbed her eyes.

"Taking a bath," he said, stupidly.

"I can see that," she said, coming into the room. She was naked. "The question was, why are you taking a bath at this time of night."

"I just came up," he lied. "I was watching a movie on TV. One of the original Frankenstein movies. I fell asleep." Christ, he'd almost said he was watching an old Western. The guilt began to rise up in him like a pile of earth being pushed up by a bulldozer. He feared he would smother in it.

"You're getting all wrinkled. How long have you been in there?"

"Not long." It didn't seem he could utter a complete sentence that wasn't a lie. How had he sunk so low in so short a time? he wondered. He didn't want to lie to her, had never really done so in the past, but what could he say? *Molly, I've just been somewhere back in the past screwing an Indian woman? And it was fantastic? I'm sorry?*

She turned to the linen closet and pulled out a large green towel. He had a moment to reflect on what a great backside Molly had. A very good front side as well.

"Get on out, and I'll dry you off. I'm sorry I fell asleep before you came up—I was just so tired from not sleeping last night."

She's sorry, he thought, getting out of the tub. Jesus Christ, she's sorry. No, Molly, it's me who's supposed to be sorry, I'm the one who's the rat, it's me, Alex, world's biggest heel. She began to dry him. He watched her breasts sway as she rubbed him.

"You're dry," she said, running a hand down his belly. "I think it's time we went back to bed." She leaned against him and kissed him.

• •

In the morning she was gone.

Chapter 6

For three days and nights he waited. The house was empty and he was lonely, and when he went out he was even more lonely because there were so many people on the streets, and he had nothing to do with any of them. That was one of the problems with having only one close friend. When that friend was gone, you were alone.

Armando tried to tempt him with a case of Gartenbrau from Madison, Wisconsin. "Special for you, Alex, a great beer, something new, try it, you're going to love it." Matty at the grocery store saved him some tiny green beans flown in from France. He bought it all and ate and drank and the beer was wonderful and the beans great, but it didn't help.

He sat in his chair and read books. Information poured into him and filled up some of the space that Molly left behind. She called to tell him where she was staying, a small motel in Rapid City, but when he called her back the next night there was a message saying she would be out for several days and that she would call him when she returned.

Every morning he ran, pushing himself, covering real distance, then back home to the bathtub and another book. He read everything he had on the Civil War; he did slavery and Reconstruction and then the death of Reconstruction. He studied the Plains Indians and the military men whose job it was to crush those Indians. He read about the politics of the 1870s, and the art and literature of the time. He studied old maps of the Philadelphia Centennial Exposition.

When it happened, he was sitting in his chair drinking a beer, but he was at least fully dressed, and as the little lights in the corners of his eyes began to flash and his head began to ache he felt the fear again, and wanted to stop it, but knew he couldn't, wouldn't if he could. He stood up and picked up his blue jacket and put it on; I'm just going for a little trip, he thought crazily, and he sat back down and gripped the arms of the chair, breathed in deeply, let loose his breath and found himself sitting on the ground in the strong sun of a spring afternoon looking up at a tall, large black man. "Where in the name of Jesus did you come from?" the man said. "And why you sitting in the dirt?"

• •

Molly leaned back in the hard green plastic motel chair and looked at the screen of her Toshiba computer. The modem was hooked to the telephone and she was ready to send, but at the last second she hit the print button instead. Even though she had been writing her stories on computer for years now she still liked to see a hard copy when she used one of the new portables. The small, dot-matrix printer buzzed that high, whiny, zipper sound as it spit out the news story she had spent the last hour writing. It was the first since arriving the day before, mostly background since not much had happened. The editors back in New York would probably cut it to shreds, but it was done and soon would be off and she could get down to some real work. The printer fell silent, surprising her as it always did by its speed. She tore off the roll of paper and read the story over quickly.

RAPID CITY, S.D., May 16—After four days of intense man-hunt, law enforcement officials here have found no trace of the Indian who shot and critically wounded two employees of the All West Power Corporation. At the time of the shooting the two men were involved in taking soil samples on the nearby Pine Ridge Indian Reservation. The All West

Power Corporation and the Oglala Sioux Indians have been involved in a land dispute that dates back to an 1868 treaty between the U.S. Government and the Sioux nation. The man wanted in connection with the shooting, John Raven, an Oglala Sioux, allegedly shot the technicians without warning and then fled into the nearby wilderness of the Badlands. Combined efforts of local and reservation police and the nearby Rapid City, South Dakota, FBI office have turned up no leads on where Raven may be hiding.

Spring has just recently come to this beautiful but desolate landscape. The grass has turned from a dry winter brown to an intense green, spotted with clumps of colorful wildflowers. Overhead an immense sky stretches unbroken from one horizon to the other across the wide prairies, virtually unchanged from the time of the great Indian battles.

"It's a rough territory," says local rancher Everett Stoddard. "These Indians know this area very well. If they're going to get him, they're going to have to pack in there and prepare to spend some time at it." Mr. Stoddard, whose family has ranched here for 50 years, works as a guide for hunters and is working with law enforcement officials on the manhunt. A full-scale operation is presently being outfitted, and searchers hope to be on the trail by the end of the week.

While Mr. Raven's motives are as yet unclear, the shooting seems to have stemmed from a long-standing dispute over the rights of the Sioux Indians and the large corporations who want to utilize the prospective deposits of valuable resources that are thought to exist in large quantities in this area. John Raven, known as an Indian activist involved in other altercations over many of the same issues, has worked for the Indian rights movement in the past, and was one of the defenders during the 1973 Wounded Knee takeover. While acknowledged as a militant on the rights issues, Mr. Raven was not thought to be violent by local officials. Generally considered to be a hard worker, and an intelligent and persuasive speaker, Raven had long espoused a return to the more traditional ways of the Indians. "He knows this land," a reservation policeman declared. "If he's in the Badlands, and there's no reason to think that he isn't, then we're going to have one hell of a time working him out. With his ability and know-how he could stay lost for a very long time."

And so with a three-day lead into this rugged territory, Indian activist John Raven promises to be a difficult quarry for these searchers. Questions of motive and intent, as well as the basic issues of Indian rights, continue to cloud the investigation the way the early morning mists hang over the prairie. Questions of legal issues that go back more than a hundred years are involved, and long-standing enmities between Indians and whites hinder the investigation. Amongst all of this, one thing is abundantly clear; if John Raven continues to hide, he will be very difficult to find.

Molly put the roll of paper into the desk drawer. The desk was green to match the walls with a top of brown plastic that was supposed to resemble wood. She typed in the proper code and pushed the send button. The telephone modem silently dialed the correct number, connecting her computer to the *Times* office in New York. The machine sent the story while she sat and wondered what Alex was doing, reminding herself to leave a message for him in case he called this evening. She was being picked up by one of the Indians who had worked with John Raven. He was going to take her to meet one of the American Indian Movement leaders. She looked out the window at the overcast sky and the flat land stretching into the distance. Very difficult to find. Yes, she had no doubt that John Raven would be difficult to find. But the personal representative of the long arm of the *New York Times,* Molly Glenn, was quite willing to follow him down the rabbit hole and ferret him out. You can run, John Raven, but you cannot hide. At least not forever.

• •

The black man's voice was low and rough like the bass-pedal chords of an old church organ. From Alex's vantage point on the hard ground, the man seemed to grow out of the earth like an old oak. He was dressed in a starched white shirt, rough, black high-water pants, and worn ankle-high black shoes. The shirt stretched taut over heavily muscled arms. The man's neck was as thick as a chunk of firewood, and his upper body was a V-shaped slab. He looked like a Negro Mr. Clean. His skin was a deep smooth brown, the color of bayou water, his face broad and round with a flaring nose. His hair was cropped close to the contours of his massive head. Alex stood up and brushed off his jeans. The man loomed at least four inches over Alex's six feet.

"You always go about that way? Appearing on the ground like that?" Alex couldn't think of any reasonable answer. The truth was out of the question, and he couldn't come up with a quick lie to cover the circumstances.

"Do you talk? Can you understand my words?"

"Yes," Alex said, feeling stupid. He had dreaded this moment, caught in the act, had thought about it many times, and now it was here and there was no way out of it. "I was just . . . well . . ."

Another black man joined them. This one was as tall as the first, but reed thin with yellow skin, foxlike eyes, and a curved blade of a nose. "What you got, Abraham?" He looked Alex up and down.

"Man just turned up sitting on the ground. I'm standing here looking for some business and the man appeared at my feet like a gray dog on a foggy day. I don't know whether or not he can even speak much."

"Where you from?" the second man asked. "You from this country? Speak American?" He turned back to the larger man. "He's probably from some far country. They're all over this place."

"Yeah, but see, he just came out there on the ground. I was watching in his direction, and he didn't come from nowhere I could see."

"I can speak English," Alex said. "I'm from New York." Hell, there were a lot of strange things from New York. These guys didn't exactly look like world travelers.

The big man nodded. The thin man stared at Alex then

looked away, saying, "What you bothering with him for anyway, Abraham? You're supposed to be shining shoes, not talking to some New York man. You move on and get some business, leave this man be. 'Less he wants his shoes shined." All of them looked at Alex's running shoes. The second man snorted and walked away. "You get to work, Abraham," he said, glancing back at them. "I don't want no shiftless men on my name."

The man called Abraham stood and watched the other man walk away.

"I guess you'd better do what he says," Alex said.

The big man shrugged. "He ain't really my boss, he just thinks he is. He thinks he's got light skin enough to tell others what to do. I don't pay him any attention. You seen those men from Ja-pan?" Alex shook his head. "You came from New York, I never been there, but I've heard of it and met men from there. These other people from Ja-pan, little yellow people, they're from a further place even than Africa. They're building them a house down that way," Abraham nodded in the direction the other man had gone, "Built it without any hammers and nails. They used little saws that they held with their feet. Strangest thing you ever did see. Didn't make hardly no noise. People laugh at them, but they build their house just as fast as any of the others."

"I haven't seen them," Alex said. He looked around. They were standing in front of a low building with a broad veranda with chairs and tables. There was a striped awning on the roof. People, mostly men, were walking around, but no one paid them any attention.

"You seen that envelope machine?" the black man asked.

"No," Alex said.

"Now that's something. They finally got that thing working, and it turns out all these little envelopes for writing paper just as fast as quick-as-you-can. Folds them up and puts on the glue." He reached in his pocket and took out a piece of paper and handed it to Alex. Alex unfolded it. It was an envelope, slightly larger than your ordinary business size. He looked at the large black man, unsure of the correct response. "They give it to me for nothing," the man said, shaking his head again. "You never saw anything like it."

Alex handed the envelope back. All right, he thought to himself, it seemed as if no one was going to call the police on him. Actually they couldn't call the police if they wanted. If this is the Philadelphia Exposition, and it certainly looks like it, he thought, that means it's 1876 and the telephone has barely been invented.

"Do you know what day it is?" Alex asked. "The date."

"The day is a Saturday. We got off tomorrow. I don't know the day of the month exactly though I know it's April. Don't you all know what the days are up in New York?"

"Well, I've been on the road. Lost track of the time. What's that building?" Alex pointed to the building behind them.

"That is the Public Comfort Building. When this Exposition gets open people will come in those gates behind the building and put their hats and coats in there. Get a meal or a cream out on the veranda. Get their shoes shined or their hair cut. Or do their necessaries. That's where I work, only I'm supposed to walk around and ask folks if they need their shoes shined or help them find their way around. It ain't open yet, but there's lots of folks coming out here from town and all over. New York, too."

For the first time Alex suspected that the man had not really bought his nonexplanation. There was a glimmer of something, amusement maybe, in the man's deep brown eyes that said he'd go along, but that he wasn't fooled.

"You must know the park pretty well," Alex said.

"Yes, sir, I know it right well. I been here for three months every day, and they took us all around and showed us all the exhibits that they got so far, and I keep up with it, checking it each day so I know what's new. We open up next month and I'll be helping folks, so I got to know it. They pay me pretty good, besides what I get for the shoes." He lifted a wooden box up by the leather strap and shouldered it. "I got to go now, Mr. New York." This time the smile was not only in his eyes. His mouth was wide, the teeth white and even.

"My name's Alex Balfour," Alex said, extending his hand.

The man took it, looking a little surprised. "Well now, it's a pleasure, Mr. Balfour. My name is Abraham Freeman, and if I can help you with anything you just come and get me. I spend my mornings here at the Comfort, and my afternoons out on the grounds." Alex's hand felt like a child's in the black man's grip.

They shook and Abraham flashed his smile again and headed off down the concourse.

Alex watched the broad back for a moment, breathed deeply, and looked around. He walked down a freshly asphalted path and sat on the ledge of a partially completed fountain. A quartet of semiclothed, very buxom female statues held up an ornate tray that would someday flow with water.

He did a top-to-bottom inventory. He was wearing his lightweight blue jacket and a long-sleeve white dress shirt with the sleeves rolled up. Blue jeans and running shoes. So far his clothing had not been a problem. He had his Swiss Army knife and his father's pocket watch. He took the watch out and checked the time. One fifteen. He had seventy-five cents in change: two quarters, two dimes, and a nickel. In his wallet he had a bunch of useless business cards that he couldn't remember why he was saving, several credit cards, and twenty-five dollars. Two tens and five ones. He wished he'd made a stop at his local money machine before he'd left, but he didn't even know what the currency of the time looked like. The great researcher. He could tell you in absolute detail the coming events of the Hays/Tilden presidential race, but he didn't even know if his own money would get him thrown in jail. He put his hand in his jacket pocket and found his tape player. He hadn't noticed that it was in his pocket when he put the jacket on. He felt the row of buttons along the top without removing it and wondered what tape was in it. For a moment he fantasized setting up an exhibit and selling franchises to make tape recorders, and then realized he'd have to invent the battery industry, plastics, transistors, and magnetic tape, just to name a few of the components. It was definitely a machine-from-the-future, but he didn't think it was going to do him much good.

One thing he did know was the layout of the exposition. He had found a map of it in his book on architecture, and he had studied it long and hard. The fountain he was sitting on was the Bartholdi fountain. Bartholdi was the man who was sculpting the Statue of Liberty and Alex knew that somewhere on the grounds was the upraised arm of that statue, with a plea for donations to complete the project. Behind him was the Public Comfort Station, and behind that the main gates and the railroad tracks to Philadelphia. On either side of him were the two largest buildings, Machinery Hall and the Main Exhibition Building. In front of him the rest of the expo spread out over more than two hundred acres of gardens and state buildings and restaurants and exhibits from all over the civilized world. Now that he had oriented himself, he had a sinking feeling as he realized that that was about as far as research would take him: now he was on his own. That was the thing about maps. Most people, including Alex, had a way of confusing the map with the territory. Now it was time to find his way in this world.

Chapter 7

As Alex had told Molly, he had been to a World's Fair in Montreal as a child, and to the latest one in Knoxville. There had been other fairs, but the unfortunate experience of the first had been borne out by the last: long lines, bad food, suffocating crowds, and the constant harangue that he was witnessing the World of the Future.

The Philadelphia Exposition was not the World of the Future, but of the past, and as Alex wandered the grounds he realized that he was living a historian's dream. This fair celebrated America's one hundred years of freedom, looking to the past for its inspiration. It was also a compendium of the present, full of the requisite advances in the worlds of art, industry, and agriculture, but it drew its strength from the Revolution, and the life of the people who lived one hundred years before. What Alex was getting was a double dose of history, a microcosm of two distinct periods.

He wandered around for hours, unable to look at anything for very long until some new and exciting exhibit drew him on. Finally, the delayed shock of the time shift, like a massive case of jet lag, seemed to physically drag him down until he went back to the Bartholdi fountain to sit down to rest.

Abraham found him just where he had left him. By that time Alex was hungry and thirsty as well as tired. And perfectly willing to let the big man take him in hand. Abraham took him to the Catholic Total Abstinence Fountain and got him a free drink of water that the Catholics cooled by forcing it over a huge chunk of ice, replenished daily, the water being nature's True Bliss and Healer according to a tract he received along with his ice water. A marble Moses sixteen feet tall gazed down at them from atop a group of sculpted Europeans famous for aiding the patriot cause of 1776. Lafayette and Pulaski watched as Alex drank his cool, clean water and found it truly finer than any alcoholic beverage ever to pass his lips except maybe a few special beers and George Dickel whiskey.

Abraham sat him down in a chair kindly supplied by the Catholics, even though a few of the sisters seemed to take offense at the giant black man and his disheveled friend. Abraham smiled at them all.

Alex showed Abraham his money and asked if it was spendable. "You got some funny notions of money in New York," Abraham commented. The dollars were too small and while the two dimes might pass, the nickel and the quarter were no good.

"It looks like you broke, Alex, and that is the truth. You're not gonna last long on two funny dimes—you got to have some jack. You got any people you can have help you out? Anybody here in Philadelphia?"

"No. Not a one."

Abraham shook his head. "I don't believe I'll ever understand white people. A colored man could always find someone from his homeplace or some kin to help him out. Even if the kin is just his black skin."

Alex thought about it and realized that he would have had a great-grandfather alive in these times. But he was probably in Boston. Besides, what was he going to do, knock on the man's door and announce himself as his future grandson? An interesting, but dangerous, idea. He felt the lump of his pocket watch in his jeans. "I don't suppose there are any pawnbrokers around here?"

Abraham pointed in the vicinity of the main gate. "If you

got something you want to get rid of I know a place right outside that fence. You got to go out the front and down around the side where some men have got up a whole 'nother town out there. They call it Centennialville, those that are trying to be nice about it. Most people call it Shantytown or Dinkyville. It's just beer gardens and circus games and some other things that a colored man ain't going to have any part in. Gambling and some say women. They got men there to buy just about anything. People come up here to see the fair and get caught up out there and lose what money they got. There's always a man around to try and cheat you." He shrugged. "It was me I'd seen about a job or something before I'd try that course."

Alex thought about it. It might be better to save the watch until he was really in trouble. Was he really in trouble yet? That depended on your definition of trouble, he guessed, but at the moment he seemed to have a friend and was in no drastic danger that he could perceive. What the hell, why not take an honest job for a change?

"What kind of work do you think I could get?"

"What kind of work can you do? That'd be where I'd start figuring."

Alex laughed. "I'm a historian. Got any use for one of those?"

Abraham looked at him with new interest. "This whole fair here has to do with history. Might be as they'd be able to use you. What kind of history do you know?"

"All kinds. What kind do you want?"

Abraham looked at Alex then away. "I don't suppose you know any history about colored people."

"Sure. I've had a couple of classes of black history. Do you think they'd be interested in that?"

Abraham leaned forward over the small wrought-iron table. For a moment Alex was afraid the table would fold under the man's weight. "You went to a school that taught about the colored man? Where was that school?"

"In New York."

"New York. I got to see this place. The truth is I don't think these people 'round here going to be interested in what you know about the Negro race, but I am. See, I can read and write some, but I need to know things that I can't find no one to teach me. Maybe you can. We got kind of a school where we live—Elias teach us to read and write, how to talk better. But we ain't got much in the way of history." One of the Catholic Abstinence workers came over and picked up their water glasses. Abraham glanced up in annoyance.

"If you two are done here there's others that would like some water," the worker said. She was a thin, spinsterish-looking woman with a mean little mouth.

"Yes, ma'am," Abraham said. "We just about finished here. Dat was mighty fine water, ma'am. You all are doing a fine thing here. 'Bout de best water I ever did hab." He stared at her with a foolish expression. She hesitated and then moved away. "Look," Abraham said, turning back to Alex. The foolish expression had disappeared with the woman. "You don't have no money, no place to sleep, nothing to eat. I do. If you can be around colored folks you can come back to where we stay, just outside here. They got special rooms, little houses, built for people who work here, colored people. I'll keep you and feed you if you'll tell me some of your history about my people. I need to know that."

"You asked if I could be around colored people. What did you mean by that?"

"Just what I say." Abraham's eyes never left Alex's. "I don't know any white man who could sleep in a room with colored men. But you're different. Something about you. White people have all got a look to them, even the ones that help us. That look says that we're different, no matter what happens. Some look with hate, some pity, all kinds of looks in between. You're different. You look at me like I'm just me. I've never seen that before in a white man."

"I can live with blacks," Alex said. "Doesn't make any difference to me. And yes, I'll teach you your history."

• •

Alex waited for Abraham by the main gate. The crowd leaving the exhibition grounds had the same feel as any crowd of people leaving work. A stray piece of music from a beer commercial floated through his head, "It's Miller Time," guys slapping each other on the back, heading for the nearest bar to wash down the day's dust. He had a moment's nostalgia for his own time.

He drew some curious glances, but no one stopped to comment on his unusual clothing; blue-jean pants that had only recently been invented, white Nike running shoes with a red swoosh. At least the jeans are 501's, he thought: button fly.

He was again struck by the curious mix of what he knew, as learned from books, and what he was seeing. The people were just people, dressed in clothing that was not all that unusual, but at the same time they were different, primarily in the details. As the details added up, the workers streaming out of the gate began to look foreign to him even though there was no overall fact or look he could point to.

Their clothing was mostly wool, dark and heavy, and not particularly clean. Most of the men wore hats, bowlers and caps, mustaches and beards in the fashion of Ulysses S. Grant, their president. Most of the faces that were not bearded needed a shave, and many were pockmarked and scarred. The men were solid looking rather than fat. And there seemed to be no Hispanics, something vastly different from your average crowd of New Yorkers.

There were fewer women than men. They wore complicated, uncomfortable-looking dresses and hats. The men stayed mostly with the men, the young women linked arms and walked together. He could see Abraham coming, a head taller than almost anyone else in the crowd.

"You stand around with your mouth open like that something going to fly in it." He put his hand gently on Alex's back and steered him through the gate. "Let's go home and get us something to eat. That Catholic water is sweet, but it don't do much to fill a man up. Uncle'll be there and he be cooking up something."

Alex allowed himself to be moved along by Abraham and the crowd. Outside the grounds they turned left down a wide street that ran along the fence around the exposition. Many of the workers stopped at a set of tracks and began to climb onto horse-pulled trolley cars. The smell of horses and dung was heavy in the still evening air.

"Where are we going?" Alex asked. He felt like a child beside Abraham.

"Home. It ain't much, but then none of us got much to speak of. People generally leave us alone so that's all right. A place to sleep and to eat and I slept in a lot worse. Ate a lot worse, too." He glanced down at Alex. "I told you before it's all colored men. If you want to go somewhere else you better get going."

Alex laughed. Somewhere else? Where? Back home, West Tenth Street? "Abraham, I told you before, I don't care about that. I don't have anywhere else to go. I appreciate you helping me. I don't care that you're black and I'm white."

Abraham gave him a long look and nodded. "You may not care but everyone else does. I can't figure it—I guess I'm going to have to study you some more. Down here," he said, pointing down an alleyway flanked by rows of rough low individual wooden buildings separated by five feet of dirt yard. A few chickens scratched in small pens behind the shacks.

The alley felt claustrophobic after the expanse of the exhibition grounds, close and mean and poor after the grandeur of massive buildings and ersatz temples.

Abraham led him up a short dirt walkway to one of the shacks. He opened the door and motioned him into the dim room. It was still early evening, only dusk outside, but a kerosene lamp burned. The one window in the room was covered by a piece of burlap. The air was heavy and hot. It smelled of burning coal and bodies and wood and old food. Alex stopped just inside the door, waiting for his eyes to adjust.

"I don't know what you looking for, mister, but I think you got the wrong place. Ain't no whites here. What you looking for be down at the other end of the row." The voice was old and rough. The flame on a kerosene lamp danced, throwing a stooped shadow onto the rough plank wall. An old gray-haired black man stood holding the lamp. He lifted it higher and the flame reflected from his rimless spectacles. "Nothin' here but niggers."

"It's me, Uncle," Abraham said, pushing past Alex. "He with me."

The old man's head turned toward Abraham. "Abraham, what you brought home with you now? You know you can't be bringing no white man in here." The head swiveled back to Alex.

"It's all right, Uncle," Abraham said, taking the lamp from the old man and putting it on a high shelf. "Alex, this old man is Jim, but most everybody calls him Uncle. Uncle, this is Alex Balfour. He's going to be staying with us." The look on the old man's face was clear even in the dim light. "He's different," Abraham went on. "Give him time."

The old man looked back and forth between Alex and Abraham and sighed. "If you're coming in, you might's well come all the way in." The old man turned back to a wooden table where he was working.

Alex closed the door and looked around the room. Heat rose from a pot-bellied stove that was vented through the roof. There were three straight-backed kitchen chairs and two wooden crates to sit on. The table where the old man worked and a row of shelves made up the rest of the furnishings. The old man muttered to himself as he chopped greens with a heavy knife.

Alex turned and found Abraham watching him. "Change your mind?" Abraham asked.

Alex shook his head. A flicker of movement caught his eye. For the first time he noticed a curtained doorway. Alex could see a man there, partially hidden by the dark of the room and the black cloth of the curtain. "Well, now," the man said, "what has the cat brought home this time? A mouse, yes? A white mouse."

"Watch your tongue, Elias," the old man said softly. "Don't take no education to see the man's white. Don't take no education to keep quiet, neither."

The man stepped into the room. Alex felt the gaze on his white skin like the light, flickering touch of a blind man's fingers. For a moment the two of them stared until at last the man turned away. "Of course, you're right again, Uncle. Old habits die hard." He turned back to Alex and held out his hand. "Elias Wheatly," he said.

Alex stepped forward, said his name, and shook hands. The hand was hard and callused, contrasting with the intellectual look of the man. Rimless glasses like Uncle's, except here they gave an impression of intelligence rather than age. He was Alex's height, but thinner. He had a triangular face with a wispy goatee. His skin color was lighter than either Uncle's or Abraham's, more cinnamon. He looked at Alex with an amused, cynical expression. He wore a white shirt and black pants like Abraham's, with the addition of an unbuttoned vest. "Forgive my manners." He flicked a hand to indicate his earlier reaction. "Seeing a white man in one's home is seldom a good sign."

"I brought him," Abraham said. Alex had almost forgotten Abraham. For all his size he was overshadowed by Elias. The light in the room seemed to center on Elias, as if he were the acknowledged focus of everyone's attention, the ringmaster in this small show.

Elias motioned to one of the chairs. "Sit down, please," he said, pulling up one of the other chairs for himself. They all sat except the old man, who lifted the lid on a pot of boiling water and put in handfuls of chopped greens.

"Now tell me," Elias said, "why Abraham has brought you, besides his propensity for bringing home strays. He'd bring home those Indians of his if they'd let him."

"I found him sitting on the ground," Abraham said. "Came right out of nowhere, far as I could tell. We got to talking and later on I found him again, except this time he was wandering around about to die of thirst. Seemed so lost I had to help him. He's from New York."

Elias nodded at the information. The smell of salt pork and greens began to fill the room. Alex felt his stomach contract and growl.

"It seems he's also hungry," Elias said. "All right, we'll feed him. And do you need a place to sleep?" Alex nodded. "Bed and board. Abraham obviously has some plan for you. It should be interesting at any rate. Do you know I've never slept in the same room with a white man? I expect none of us has. Yes, interesting."

Elias smiled a small smile and Abraham smiled a wide, white smile and in the shadowy room Alex thought of Cheshire cats and cats in general and Elias's earlier remark; and mice. White mice.

Chapter 8

Molly pulled herself up into the high seat of the old Chevrolet pickup truck. She put her pack on the floor next to the gearshift and flipped her long ponytail over her shoulder. "Molly Glenn," she said, holding out her hand. "You're Mr. Two Horses, right?" The tall Indian took her hand.

"You can call me William or Will. 'Mr. Two Horses' sounds a little stupid, doesn't it? You're younger and prettier than I thought you'd be."

"So are you," Molly said, almost without thinking. The "younger and prettier" remark was not new; every time some man said it to her it grated on her nerves. It meant that any reporters from the *New York Times* should be men, or if women, old and ugly. "I'm older than I look," she said.

"So am I," William Two Horses said, putting the truck in gear, looking as if he were sorry he'd let her into it.

He had a round face with high cheekbones and a strong nose. His skin was smooth and dark, the color of the dry copper-colored bluffs that lay in the distance. His hair was long and glossy black, tied into two braids. She tried to put an age to his face. He looked young, maybe in his early thirties, and his skin was so smooth and clear it was almost like a woman's. He wasn't pretty, but he was so good-looking he came close to it. The strength in the cheekbones and the hooked nose and the broad brow saved him. Gravel crunched and scattered under the tires as they pulled out of the motel parking lot. A beer can rolled around among other assorted trash on the floor of the pickup.

"Where are we going?" Molly asked.

"Henry Sands said to bring you back to the reservation. Said the *New York Times* was on its way, and I was to make sure you got through." He shrugged. "Here I am."

She'd put the call through to Sands that morning. Before leaving New York she'd made the rounds, and she'd pulled together all the names and leads she could get from some of the national-staff reporters. She'd read clips from the last ten years and found Henry Sands's name coming up over and over from the Wounded Knee days. Sands was the AIM, American Indian Movement, man on the Sioux Pine Ridge Reservation. She'd get in touch with the more official Indians in the Bureau of Indian Affairs later. It was her experience that if you started with the government types you were fighting obfuscation from the moment you walked in the door. Better to find the unofficial, the unauthorized version first, and work backward. That way you know some of the right questions to ask when you get to the people who are supposed to have the answers.

"Tell me about Henry Sands."

The Indian looked out the side window at a tall tablelike bluff of streaked red-and-gray rock, as if deciding what line to take with her. She'd seen the reaction before; it meant that the decision was being made whether to speak to her like she was a reporter, or a person. People who were being interviewed usually told reporters what they thought the reporters wanted to hear. They told other people the truth. Sometimes Molly got the truth right away, and sometimes she didn't. It was part of her skill to convince people that while she was indeed a reporter, she was also a person. Just like it was part of her skill to separate the fact from the fiction.

"Henry is old. Eighty-two years this spring. He's the leader of the Indian community on the reservation. People will tell you that Johnny Teller is the leader, that he's the chief, but he isn't really. Teller is the BIA man, the Bureau of Indian Affairs. He and the rest of the reservation council are voted in by the Indians who bother to vote, which aren't many. We've tried it that way and it didn't work. When we won an election legally they just cheated us out of it. Henry is the real leader. He was one of the first old-time Sioux to join the AIM, back in the early days."

She could tell that Will Two Horses had yet to decide if she was anything more than just a reporter. He was giving her the unofficial official version. Or the official unofficial version.

She watched the road. They were coming into the Badlands, some of the most spectacular scenery in the world. She had been through the area once before, in a station wagon with her parents and her two brothers. All she remembered was fighting over how much of the back seat belonged to each child. *Mom, Mom, Davey has his leg on my property.* There was a vague memory of giant cliffs, huge towers of rock looming outside the station-wagon windows, her father shouting at them to look at the scenery. But she had been a little girl, and the towers were scary, so she had concentrated on protecting her portion of the car seat.

"Is Sands an Indian name?" she asked.

"Henry's parents joined the Episcopal Church before he was born. Back when the churches got to pick various reservations to run. They gave him the name Sands. Henry has lots of names." The Chevy shuddered in the wind. Airborne grit sprayed the cab with a hissing sound, audible above the roaring engine. It was an old truck, painted an aquamarine color not seen much after 1959. The dashboard bore the evidence of various past abuse; missing knobs, a large hole where a radio had once been.

Molly watched the towers of rock seem to grow as they passed among them. There was no other traffic. No other life that she could see. She was a child again and in her imagination the rocks came alive with a great slow presence, a race of stone beings from another world, set down here to watch the tiny truck as it wound its way between them. She pushed the image away and turned toward the Indian. "And after we talk to Henry Sands?"

"That depends on Henry. If everything seems all right then I'll take you out to where John shot the company men. Do you want to see it?"

"I want to see everything that has anything to do with the story." She could see his grip tighten on the steering wheel and knew she had made a mistake.

"The story?" he said.

"Yes, the story. I know that to you it's a lot more than that but to me it's a story. That's what it has to be."

"Sure. We wouldn't want to get involved, would we?"

"Not at the expense of the work. I have to maintain a certain objectivity or I can't do my job. The reason I'm here is I'm writing a story for my newspaper about John Raven and why he shot those two men."

"No," he said, gritting his teeth, "the reason you're here is that we've got to put up with you people nosing around because you are the *New York Goddamn Times* and we need all the publicity we can get because there's more here at stake than just our poor friend John Raven. We have to go along with every white reporter who comes in looking for an Indian story with a decent amount of blood to titillate the readers of the morning news. Shit!" He hit the steering wheel. "Why do I let you people do this to me?"

She sat staring out the window. She'd heard it before. It was better to just let it work itself out; there was no use in arguing about it. They rode in silence, listening to the wind muscle the truck around on the two-lane blacktop.

"I understand what you're saying," she said mildly. He looked at her with the sort of look that she expected, a don't-give-me-that-bullshit look.

"Believe me, it's not the first time it's come up," she said. "I'm interested in every aspect, all sides of this thing. I want to hear everything you can tell me about why it happened. I want all the background I can get. I could have started with the FBI and the BIA people—in fact they're going to be very unhappy that I didn't. But it's still a story to me, and nothing that happens is going to change that. Just like you're an Indian and I'm white, and nothing that happens is going to change the color of our skins. You need me because I'm the free advertising for your cause. That's all right with me, I'll trade that for information."

"How about the truth? Are you interested in that?"

She gave him a modified version of the look she'd just received. "Don't insult me."

More silence. He watched the road. The poorly muffled roar of the engine seemed to fill the whole world. "All right. Sorry. This business is getting on everyone's nerves. We've got FBI men stomping around the reservation in their big black city shoes, and Johnny Teller's goon squad roughing up anyone involved with AIM, and the BIA threatening us with U.S. marshals and SWAT teams, and all because one Indian went crazy and shot a couple of white men who had no right to be where they were, doing something they had been told not to do. Everyone wants John Raven's ass, and they think the way to get it is to beat up enough of our people until someone breaks."

"Is it? Will someone break?"

"No. John Raven is up in the hills, or down in some gulch, and I don't know where he is and neither does any other Indian. Whoever wants him is going to have to go after him on their own. They know that, of course—this isn't the first time this sort of thing has happened—but they'll still go through the same motions; beating people up, threats, arrests. That's just the way our authorities go about their job. Which is the main reason you're here, at least as far as we're concerned. Not the publicity for the cause—we get enough publicity for that. What we need is protection. Those two white men aren't the only ones who'll be shot before this is through. I can guarantee you there'll be dead Indians before it's over. I want you right there out in front, ready and able to tell your Eastern readers just exactly what's happening. The goons will be less likely to kill people if they think the world is watching over their shoulder. You want a story? All right, Ms. Glenn, you're going to get it."

The silent monuments receded behind them. They had made it through the land of the giants. Now they were into the land of the Indian.

Chapter 9

They sat at the wooden tables and ate the greens from thick, chipped, white bowls. There were small quarters of spring turnips and dark pieces of smoked pork neck bones. Alex noticed that the spoons were embossed with the name The American Restaurant. Uncle tore a loaf of wheat bread into chunks and passed it between them. They ate without speaking. Alex ate his portion carefully, willing himself to eat slowly. The bitter greens were laced with shreds of smoky pork, strengthened by the pale green broth. The combination of elements: hunger, excitement, and simple excellence, made it an extraordinary bowl of soup. He soaked up the last of the liquid with the bread and finished it with a small sigh.

"More in the pot," Uncle said, without looking up from his own bowl. Alex sensed that if he took another bowl, which he wanted to do, he would be eating their breakfast. He shook his head no. "Thank you. It was very good."

Uncle nodded. "Spring greens come up on the train to the restaurant. They throw away the little ones and the tops. Fools. They throwing away the best parts." He paused and then went on as if he'd made up his mind about something. "You looking for work?"

"Alex looking," Abraham said. He picked up his bowl and drained the last drops. "He's a history man. Like a teacher."

Elias laughed. "I'm afraid there isn't much call for historians You might be able to get on at the Public Comfort, like Abraham. Or at the restaurant with Uncle. Shining shoes or cleaning up. Most of the work here is in the service area. Good jobs for people who've spent their lives pulling cotton and being slaves, but not much there for a teacher."

"Anything will be fine," Alex said. "I need money, not a career. Where do you work?"

"I'm a mechanic. I work on the looms for the Philadelphia Weaving Company."

"Elias been to school," Abraham said, as if exhibiting a prize. "He lived here up North his whole life."

Elias nodded. "I've even been to New York a few times. I believe that's where Abraham said you were from?"

The door pushed open. The tall, light-skinned man who had spoken to Abraham earlier in the day stood in the doorway. The man looked at the four of them at the table.

"What the hell is he doing here?" There was no need for any of them to ask who was being referred to.

"I brought him," Abraham said. "Ain't no business of yours, Cato."

The man eyed Alex and stepped into the room. "If he's bringing trouble, it's my business. I got a responsibility around here. You bring someone in here like this I want to know it. What if something happen to him, what'll we do then? Everybody be in trouble then."

"You don't need to worry about me," Alex said, his voice sounding too loud in the small room. He looked around the table at the others. "I'm all right and I intend to stay that way." He looked at Elias, who looked back at him with no particular expression, as if telling him that he was on his own. The tableau held for a moment, and then Cato looked at Abraham. "Maybe," Cato said, slowly. "What you doing anyway?" he asked Abraham. "You going out there this night or staying here? Said you were going out this afternoon."

Abraham looked at Alex. "I'll be fine," Alex said. Abraham stood up.

"I guess I'll go for a while. Said I would, so I will. I'll be back, but he can sleep on my bed if he wants."

"We'll work it out," Elias said. "You go on ahead."

Abraham nodded and moved around the table. "Why you always want to be going for the big nigger?" he said to Cato as they went out the door.

The room seemed larger after Abraham left, or maybe just emptier. Uncle cleared the bowls and put them in a bucket. He rummaged around on a shelf and came back with three wineglasses, putting them on the table. Another trip to the shelf produced a gray stoneware jug with a cork in the top. The elegant wineglasses seemed to float above the rough plank table, elevated by sheer grace. Alex touched the rim of one of the glasses, his finger finding a minute chip. "Going for water," Uncle said, picking up another bucket and leaving.

Elias pulled the cork and filled the three glasses with amber liquid. "Dandelion wine," he said. "Uncle makes it. When we got here last year the fairgrounds were covered with dandelions. Now it's asphaltum." He picked up his glass and raised it to Alex. "To Uncle, our storyteller and our winemaker." He took a sip and put the glass on the table in front of them.

"Uncle works in the American Restaurant. He's the dishwasher, no matter that he's a better cook than any of the white chefs there. He was a slave, worked in a kitchen on a plantation in Georgia. That's where they gave him the name Uncle. Most slaves changed their names after emancipation but he kept his. All the little kids come to him for stories." He shook his head and went on. "After emancipation he walked here. He's worked as a dishwasher ever since. He brings home what they throw away, the greens, the bowls, these," he touched his wineglass, "the damaged goods." He drained the glass and poured himself another. Alex tasted the wine. It was tart, green and grassy. "He makes it with the flowers, the heads of the dandelions. Sometimes we eat the leaves, in the spring, but the wine is made from the yellow flowers." They drank in silence.

Alex felt the wine begin to warm him. The burlap covering over the window occasionally fluttered in a current of cool evening air. He could feel Elias watching him, weighing him, sifting the evidence. He felt no threat, but rather an intelligence that probed lightly, cautiously.

"Abraham said you'd gone to school in the North," Alex said.

Elias nodded. "Yes. I've had an education. Better than most, white or colored. I have a trade, though I had intended to be a lawyer. That has not proven to be possible," he added dryly.

"Where are you from?"

Elias smiled. "Right here. Or very near here. To Abraham, who is originally from South Carolina, Philadelphia is North. You probably think of New England as North, or New York State. To a slave, North has a connotation that is not attached to a compass." He nodded at Alex's now empty glass. "By all means, have some more."

Alex reached for the wine, filled his glass, then looked at Elias. Elias nodded so Alex poured him another glass as well, hoping that the wine would lower the barrier that lay between them. Elias seemed to sense his purpose. "Let's make a deal, as they say, Mr. Balfour. I'll tell you something about us and you tell me something about yourself. Something a bit more substantial and realistic than your magical appearance. From New York. All right?" Alex nodded. Elias stood and turned up the wick on the oil lamp. It flared and smoked briefly then steadied, pushing the shadows a little farther toward the corners of the room. The door opened and Uncle came in. He put the bucket of dirty dishes on a low bench and poured in the water. He began washing the bowls with a rag. Elias rose and put a glass of the wine on the bench beside the old man.

"I was born," Elias began, "in a small community twenty miles from here, the Ephrata Society. You've heard of it?" Alex shook his head. "No? Many have. It's famous in its own way. A religious community, formed in 1731. My parents were the only colored people who lived there. I was never quite sure whether we were the only ones because of fear of having too many Negroes on the part of the white leaders or simply a basic enmity toward such a strict religion on the part of colored people. Also one of the rules was a belief in celibacy as being most pleasing to God, which kept the population down in general. My parents, and others in these later years, did not believe in celibacy, and while they lived apart from the stricter members, they were tolerated and accepted to a degree. Which was a great deal more than the rest of our country was able to accord my poor race.

"It's quite an interesting place. It's still there if you'd like to visit sometime. The old days of vigor are gone, but the members carry on. They use no metal, everything is built from wood, the utensils are all made of wood." His voice assumed a measured solemn tone. " 'So that there was neither hammer, nor ax, nor any tool of iron heard in the house while it was building.' You know your scriptures?"

Alex smiled. "No, I'm afraid where I come from we've given them up."

"New York, then, is a godless land?" Elias asked mockingly. "At any rate," he went on, "what has been most important to me was the excellent school I attended. The best in the area—pupils came all the way from Baltimore. This was the primary reason my parents stayed in the community, the opportunities for a colored child to receive an education anywhere else being virtually nil."

"But surely in the North it was possible for blacks to attend school."

Elias was quiet for a moment. "Alex, I'm not sure where you're really from, but it isn't the New York that I know. A man's business is his own so I won't press you on your past, but·if you intend to stay with us there are things you should know. First of all, it would be wise to stop referring to us as 'blacks.' 'Black' is a race term, on par with the ubiquitous 'nigger.' We prefer to be 'Negroes' or 'colored.' And to answer your question, no, it was not necessarily possible for Negroes to attend school, even in the North. Your grasp of race relations seems to be as weak as Abraham's. He believes that the South is pro forma bad, and the North, just as pro forma, good. Before emancipation there was virtually nowhere in this country a colored man could receive much of an education. That is why my parents' choice of staying at Ephrata was such a wise and important one. At least for me, though there were benefits for them as well. I can read and write, and a good bit more. Most Negroes can do little of either, though now you'll find them in schools everywhere, or at least you could. Things seem to be changing again. . . ." He hesitated.

"In what way?"

Elias thought for a moment. "I'm not sure. There are stories from Georgia, South Carolina, the southern states primarily. A group calling itself the Ku Klux Klan has been threatening and beating Negroes who have attempted to better themselves. You don't see it in the newspapers, but we hear the stories. Even here in the North, in the cities, there seems to be a shifting of attitudes. As I say, I'm not sure."

"You talking about trouble and it's plain to see that it's coming," Uncle said, sitting down at the table. "I knew all this other was too good to last, knew it all along. This white man here may be different, but the rest of them is going to take everything back again. Just like there weren't no war, just like Lincoln never was. What we got to do is the same thing we always done, pull in our heads like turtle, and look out for our own."

Alex found himself no longer a part of the conversation. It was as if he would occasionally simply fade away, or as if his existence were so far above or beneath notice that he would be forgotten or dismissed, turned up or down, like the smoky kerosene lamp.

"You want me to go find Abraham?" Uncle asked. "You know that Cato likely to get him in trouble."

Elias looked toward the door as if he could see through it to wherever Abraham was. "No, not yet. He'll be all right for a while." He looked back at Alex and said, angrily, "You don't understand any of this, do you? Where in hell do you come from? What are you doing here?"

"I'm a man just like either of you." Elias's words drew an answering anger from him. He struggled with it for a moment, then went on. "You're right, in your way. I'm not from the New York you know. But you said a man's past is his own business. Let that part of me go for now. I think I can help you, or at least help Abraham, give him some of the information he wants." He stopped. It was wrong for him to be angry. To him the past, this time, was known, at least intellectually. Compared to him, these people lived in darkness. Their frustration and caution, under the circumstances, was a reasonable reaction. "Do you want me to find Abraham?"

Elias stared at Alex. His face was hard. "Yes, maybe you should." Alex started to stand but stopped when Elias raised his hand.

"Let me tell you about Abraham before you go." The anger was still there. Alex sat back down. "I'm not sure how you see him. You look at things in ways I don't yet understand, but I know what others think. You can see it when they look at him. He's big, not that there aren't other men just as large, but his spirit is big. Abraham was a slave but he was never beaten down by slavery. Most of us were, even those of us who wore no chains. He has a great curiosity about things, about his fellow man, white and colored. Has he told you of his interest in history?" Alex nodded. "I haven't been able to help him with it. It's curious, but I know ten times as much white history as I do of my own race. It was never taught in school, of course, not even the excellent school at Ephrata.

"Whites think that Abraham is dumb. Big and dumb. He smiles too much, he never dissembles. He does what's asked of him. When people cheat him, and they do so quite often, both white and colored, he simply laughs if off as part of life. But we are afraid, Uncle and I, that his curiosity will one day get him into serious trouble. It is not possible for a colored man to live with so little guile. He's out there now, down at the other end of the row where the amusements are offered, with that damn Cato who takes him along as a sort of bodyguard, and he's looking and he's trying to learn and it's like a large curious child just waiting to make a mistake." Elias shook his head. "People envy big men. I pity them. People wait for them to fall, look for ways to push them. At least some people do. Little people. A big colored man, especially one who trusts others, is vulnerable. Maybe you can help us. Maybe you can teach Abraham what he wants to know. But I have one other piece of advice." He stared at Alex grimly. The room felt hot and airless, as if all the oxygen had been breathed up or burned.

"You don't seem to understand this basic fact," Elias went on. "Colored people don't like white people. This is true, and yet most whites never understand it. It is a white world, it is your world, and there is very little in it for us. You have taken it all and given us nothing but those things you value too lightly to keep for yourselves. Your politics are not ours, your police, your precious rights, your economy, your amusements, none of these things can be ours, and yet you expect us to like you. Just as Old Massa expected his darkies to stick by him. No, it is not so." He shook his head. He was speaking quietly, almost to himself. "The darkies deserted Massa just as fast as their feet could carry them. We care nothing for you." He looked up at Alex, stared at him. The chair creaked as he leaned back, unclenched his hands. He nodded. "Yes, go find Abraham."

• •

It was a long walk, or at least it seemed so. The only light came from the windows of the shacks along the dirt track that threaded toward the sounds of crowds and a distant calliope. The alley, the doorways, the stoops, were empty. The long row of shacks ended, and he crossed a field, knee-high with weeds that swished against his legs as he walked. The moon was bright and the weeds seemed a strange silvery color.

• •

The midway was not very wide, and it was crowded. It was lined on either side with open-faced huts and tents that offered games, prizes, money, food, drink, and fleshly pleasures left mostly guessed at. The scene was lit by a row of wooden torches jammed into the ground at regular intervals, wound with rags that burned with thick yellow flames and oily smoke. Men pushed along laughing and drinking, being hailed by the barkers that stood in front of each establishment, advertising the wonders inside.

"Cards, gentlemen, card games for everyone! Double your money and more!"

"Cold beer. Cold beer. Blood's Triple-X Dublin Stout. Pale ales and beer!"

"Get your meat pies, meat pies!"

"See the Wild Man of Borneo! See the Wild Children from Far-off Australia! See the Fat Woman, the Two-Legged Horse, the Five-Legged Cow!"

"See the Egyptian Dancer and her famous dance of the Seven Veils!"

"The lovely Madam Serena tells your fortune! She tells all! She knows all! And she is beautiful!"

And that is where he found Abraham. Cato was talking to two other Negroes, who eyed Alex and walked away as he approached.

"If you looking for Abraham he's in the shadow over there, looking at the picture of that damn Madam Serena. Next to the Egyptian Dancer. He wants to go in and get his fortune told. I told him that it don't signify nothing, told him that she shows you more than the future, but you got to pay to see it. They ain't going to never let no colored man in to see no white woman anyhow. Abraham thinks she can say what will happen. He believes. I told him to stay over there and watch if he had to, but to stay out of the way. You take him back before he gets into trouble. He comes down here every night and stands around, someone going to notice him pretty soon. He's too big and dumb not to be noticed."

• •

"Abraham."

"Go away, Alex."

"Let's go back, Abraham."

"No. She knows, Alex. Says so on those signs."

"No, Abraham, it's just a show. Walk back with me."

Abraham stared at the painted pictures of Madam Serena, a fat white woman with coal-black hair and a veil. "I got to know what's going to happen, Alex. I want to see."

"It's not for you to see. It's not for anyone to know. Walk back with me. I'm afraid to go alone."

Alex pulled him away. Around them in the night, shadows danced and the flames curled and smoked and colored the crowds of whirling, laughing, braying men, colored them with the shades and shifting incandescence of the eternal fires.

Chapter 10

Alex tipped back the box he was sitting on and leaned against the wall of the house, feeling the rough-cut lumber scratch against his back. He watched men, and occasionally women, working the pump that supplied the water for this end of the row of houses. When he sat forward he was in the bright morning sun; when he leaned back the shadow of the house fell across all but his shoes. He alternated between the two. The box, made of thin crating, threatened to fall apart beneath him, exposing him for the fool most of these people thought him to be.

If you were to have asked him back in his own time what his position was on race, he would have presented his credentials with modesty, but pride. He was a liberal and had always tried to act upon his beliefs. He felt, as much as was possible, that he was without prejudice; a clean slate in matters of race, religion, and gender. But here, as he painfully learned, none of that mattered.

Sometimes he felt like climbing up on his box and shouting at them—*Stop looking at me that way, I marched on Washington, I worked the Poor People's Campaign. I've been gassed. I've given more money than any of you will see in a lifetime. I've paid my goddamn dues.* But he was still white. Standing on a box and shouting wouldn't change the color of his skin.

He had learned these harsh facts: his past did not count for anything here, these people did not like him, did not trust him, did not want any advice from him. They wanted him to go away. He stayed because Abraham wanted him to, and because some stubborn part of him down deep inside said no, damn it, I will not be moved.

He could have found somewhere else to live. He had two weeks worth of wages that he shared with Abraham, Elias, and Uncle. He had landed a job pushing a sedan chair around the grounds, although as yet there were no paying customers to be pushed. There were two types of pushers: those, mostly educated young white males, who acted as guides, and a larger contingent of all races whose job was to push the fairgoers wherever they wanted to be pushed. The guides were the elite troops, the others simply muscle.

In the mornings he roamed the grounds with his empty chair, learning all he could about the exhibits. He had been issued a heavy, bound catalogue of all the fair's proposed exhibits. He was supposed to study the catalogue on his off hours. In the afternoon he did odd jobs, from basic construction to delivering messages.

He occupied a strange social position, seemingly above any of the Negroes by virtue of his color, but lower than any white because it was known that he not only consorted with said Negroes, but actually lived in a house with them. One day he pushed Abraham around in the chair briefly, for a joke, and was told that if the nigger sat in the chair again both of them would be fired on the spot.

There were those lower than Alex, though, lower than the lowliest Negro, or Chinaman, and these were the two Indians. Alex always thought of them the way Elias and Uncle referred to them, as Abraham's Indians. One old man and a young woman, prisoners of the War Department, symbolically staked out as a living exhibition supposedly for the edification of the masses, an educational display whose garbled purpose was lost somewhere between their capture by George Armstrong Custer at his battle on the Washita and their day-to-day existence in a buffalo-skin tepee that afforded them only marginal privacy from the leering, prying eyes of those who stopped to watch and jeer. Abraham's sense of decency and curiosity had lead him to "collect" them the way he had collected Alex. He helped the Indians by giving them food and bringing whatever small amenities he could scrounge that might make their existence more endurable. Abraham could not bear to see anything hurt. He brought home injured birds, baby mice, and all manner of wounded animals. Alex, and the Indians, were simply larger versions of these crippled creatures.

He had taken Alex to the Indians the day after Alex started work. Alex had stood dumbfounded before the old man and the woman. It had flooded in on him, the memory, standing on the hill and watching the battle, and after, seeing Custer with the prisoners. The old man had been with the prisoners. The woman was the one singled out for Custer. The memory was whole, complete with all the dread and pain he felt at the time. And there was more. The woman was the one, oh, yes, that he had been with in the tepee; now he knew that. It had been dark, he had been confused, overwhelmed, but it was she. It all fit together, the dreams and events coming together and sorting themselves out until the memory was complete. These were not just Abraham's Indians; they were his as well.

The old man nodded at Alex. The woman looked at him and he could see that she, too, remembered, and then she turned and looked away.

"Alex here is a history man," Abraham told the Indians. "He's going to teach us about the Negro race. Maybe he can teach you about your people."

The old man looked from Abraham to Alex. The two Indians were sitting on a striped blanket. There was a low fence that gave them a circular yard extending ten yards around the tepee. The Indians were inside the yard, Alex and Abraham outside. The old Indian stood and walked to where the fence separated them.

"What is there to learn?" the old Indian said.

"He could talk some when they brought them in," Abraham explained to Alex, "but I been teaching them some more words. I bring them food when we got it. The army don't give them much. His name's High Cloud and hers is Little Spring, but she don't hardly talk."

"Why?" High Cloud said to Alex.

"Why what?" Alex said. The old man was thin and had skin the color of tanned hides, a wrinkled face that resembled the Indian on the front of the nickel, or that used to be on the front of the nickel. He was wearing a buckskin shirt and trousers and moccasins. The woman had on a cotton blouse and a soft leather skirt that reached to her ankles. She sat cross-legged on the ground, not looking at any of them.

"What is history? What is to learn?" High Cloud asked. He had clear intelligent eyes that looked steadily at Alex.

"Well," Alex said. "History is knowing about the past. You learn it because it helps you understand the present." He gestured around them. "It helps you understand this." He felt vaguely foolish.

The Indian followed Alex's gesture and looked around. There was a blue-coated soldier who leaned on his rifle and watched them from a small guardhouse nearby. There was a row of cannons on display, ranging from the size of a bicycle on up to a huge monster that looked capable of lofting barrels at the enemy. On the other side of the guardhouse was an old Conestoga wagon with a canvas top and high wooden sides. The rest of the fair spread out around them.

"Why do you need to understand . . . this?" the old Indian asked. On the word "you," he had touched Alex's chest.

Alex looked around, embarrassed, as if he'd been telling a stupid story. "So you'll understand what it really is. So you'll know what to do in the future. So you can plan . . . not you exactly, but people . . ." He trailed off. The Indian looked at him, waiting. When Alex didn't go on he turned and walked back to where the girl sat. He looked back at them.

"I will teach you something," he said to Alex. "As a favor to my good friend Abraham." He waited a moment while they all watched him. "This," he raised his hand to indicate the exhibition, the cannons, the people, the whole world, "is a dream." He stared at them for a moment longer, then sat back down on the blanket.

As they walked away Abraham told Alex that sometimes the Indians were like that, they had to get used to a man before they were easy with him. Then a huge steam foghorn near the front of the War Department Building had bellowed a demonstration warning and Alex had jumped and spun around as if stung or slapped, and he had seen the old Indian, High Cloud, watching him and smiling.

• •

Elias had brought in an advertisement he had picked up somewhere. He tacked it up on the wall of the house. For several nights Elias read the advertisement to the others after dinner, explaining each of the unfamiliar words in great detail, leading discussions into the mysteries of the white man's world. And that was the crux of the joke, that this was a product for white man's use, to treat a white man's ills. The point being that somehow whites brought such plagues upon themselves.

There was a picture of an erudite gentleman with a thick bushy mustache and heavy imposing eyebrows. The caption identified the man as Professor Percival H. Ingles, author of the book here offered, and director of the Peabody Medical Institute. The ad copy announced that more than a million copies of the book, *The Science of Life: or, Self Preservation,* had been sold. It then listed a summary of its compendious contents.

It treats upon MANHOOD, how lost, how regained and how perpetuated; cause and cure of exhausted vitality, Impotency, Premature Decline in men, Spermatorrhoea, or Seminal Losses (nocturnal and diurnal), Nervous and Physical Debility, Hypochondria, Gloomy Foreboding, Mental Depression, Loss of Energy, Haggard Countenance, Confusion of Mind and Loss of Memory, Impure State of the Blood, and all diseases arising from Errors of Youth or the indiscretions or excesses of mature years.

Elias particularly liked to dwell on the errors of youth and the excesses of mature years, asking Alex if he would amplify just what errors of youth a white man was prey to. Abraham, who, like Uncle, had to have most of the magniloquent terms explained, soon had the broadside memorized and liked to intone the litany in his profundo bass, dwelling on his favorites: Seminal Losses (nocturnal and diurnal), and in particular that finest of all words, broken into at least five solemn syllables: Spermatorrhoea.

Alex grew so sick of hearing the ad that he instituted his evening history lesson. His audience was usually Elias, Uncle, and Abraham, and occasionally Cato, who professed indifference but stayed to argue and question as much as the others.

"Two hundred and fifty years ago the first black settlers came to America aboard a Dutch ship that had robbed a Spanish vessel of its cargo of African slaves bound for the West Indies. These twenty Africans were traded for food and supplies."

"They the first slaves, the foreparents?" Abraham asked. Alex sat on a stool that Abraham had appropriated from the Public Comfort Station. Elias, Uncle, and Abraham sat at the table. Uncle peeled small withered apples from a bag on the floor.

"They weren't slaves then," Alex said. "They were indentured servants. They sold their services to settlers for a specified amount of time, usually from two to five years. At the end of that time they were freed. They had the same economic opportunities that a freed white servant did; they voted and participated in public life. This pattern continued for at least forty years, almost to the end of the seventeenth century."

"When was that seventeenth century?" Abraham asked.

"Two hundred years ago," Elias said.

"I don't understand," Abraham said. "If we was free so many years ago, how come we slaved after that? How come we slaved for so many years? How come it took so long and we got to live through slavery days just so to get back where you say we started out to be?"

"Don't seem fair, somehow," Uncle said. "Not that fair have much to do with colored folk anyhow."

"The decisions of slavery were based on economic considerations," Alex said. The language of academia was a balm to most teachers, but here in this bare room the words were small comfort. "The people who ran America, the Englishmen, decided that there was a great need for labor in the country. There just weren't enough people to do all the work. They chose Africans to do that labor. They had tried to make slaves out of Indians, but that didn't work. Indians could escape and hide with their brothers who were usually just over the hill or across the river. Besides, Indians seemed to sicken and die under slave conditions. Then they tried it on poor white people: criminals, debtors, petty thieves, and prostitutes. But whites were under the protection of recognized governments, and they could escape and easily blend in with the crowd. This left Africans. They were strong, they were inexpensive, they were visible, and the supply seemed inexhaustible. Why not?"

"Why not?" Elias said, slapping the table. "Because it was wrong, it was evil! How can you even ask that question?"

"I'm sorry," Alex said, "it was rhetorical." Abraham looked at him for an explanation of the term but Alex just shook his head. He wondered if it would not be best just to quit, though he didn't think they would let him now that he had started. They hungered for information, but it was so difficult to give it without treading on sensibilities. There was no scholarly distance or anesthetic of time. But maybe words always hurt, he thought, even in his present. Maybe the distance he felt was an attribute of his privileged position; teacher, high above the lowly students.

"Of course it was wrong," he went on, "even back then they knew it. They had to do two things so it would work. First, they had to establish an ideology of racism that justified what they did." He stopped Abraham's question with a raised hand. "They had to think up reasons that made it seem all right. And secondly, they had to break up the bond that existed between white and black servants. In the beginning people didn't see differences because of color; they grouped people in other ways. The most important way was class, ruling class and serving class, and then whether or not you were a

Christian. It's difficult for us to realize, but in the early days people didn't see themselves as black and white, they saw themselves as who was up and who was down. And all the downs stuck together no matter what their color."

"I find that difficult to believe," Elias said. "Skin color is a rather obvious difference."

"I said it was difficult to believe, but that doesn't make it false. In those early days there was a large class of servants, both black, excuse me, colored, and white, and they lived together, intermarried, ran away together, played together, until there was a large population of mixed-race people. There were prejudiced people, but racism, as we know it today, was unknown. That didn't come until the community adopted prejudice as a method of ruling and controlling a particular group of people. By instituting racism as the prevailing philosophy, the aristocrats and the planters and the people who ran the colonies were able to separate white from black, isolate the blacks so they could be exploited."

Abraham looked to Elias for a translation. "He's saying the white people made up lies about colored people so the poor white people would hate us. That they had to have someone to do all their work for them because they were too weak to do it themselves."

"I already knew that part," Abraham said. "About them being too weak to work."

"Now that is the truth," Uncle said. He cored the apples and put them in a pot and put it on the stove.

Alex sighed. "This is very hard for me."

"Damn. Hard for you? You don't know what hard is," Elias said. "Hard is having it done to you, not having to talk about it."

"You want me to stop?" Alex flared. "You asked me for it. I don't like it either, but there it is. It happened, but I didn't do it, don't forget that."

"We forget nothing," Elias snapped. "Yes, we asked you to tell it, and you will. No it's not easy, and there's not a goddamn thing any of us can do about that. But you'll tell it because we need to know."

"Alex," Abraham said, "I asked you. I know it's hard, but Elias is right, we need to know. I'm asking you again to stay and tell it."

Uncle stirred the apples and said into the steam that drifted up in the still air from the pot, "It's a story. Some stories harder to hear than others, but they still need to be told. The tongue is steel, and that's for sure, but every one of us is a hard-grown man. We can stand for it, all of us, without any of this fighting. It's natural enough, but it won't do us any good. You stay, Alex; I'll feed you some fine applesauce, and tell you some of our stories. Applesauce take away some of the hurt."

Alex looked at the hard gaze from Elias, and the need in Abraham's eyes, and nodded. He would stay.

Chapter 11

Molly remembered Alex's description of the Indian reservations he had seen: brown and poor. As the truck wound down the dirt track through the crumbling arroyos, past weather-beaten houses and broken-down trailers with skewed television antennas, she found his description succinct, but apt. The monuments of the Badlands were behind them, in the past, and this was the unrelenting dull face of the sad present. The land seemed abandoned, the houses and trailers man-made artifacts left behind like cheap furniture to be thrown out and hauled away.

Will Two Horses looked at her and read her mind. "Not exactly Central Park, is it?"

She raised her eyebrows and smiled at him. "You know Central Park?"

"I went to law school at Columbia." Her eyebrows went up another notch. "I'm not only John Raven's friend, I'm his lawyer. I'm also a lot of other people's lawyer."

"Appearances are deceiving," Molly said.

"Now there's an understatement of the first water. That's been our problem since you set foot in this truck. One of our problems, anyway." He rolled down his window and the cool air rushed in, blowing away the accumulated engine fumes.

"You're looking at this land through white eyes." He went

on quickly to forestall argument. "You said it yourself. It's a matter of skin color, something neither of us can change. We are all culturally bound. You look around and see rocks and dirt and scrub pines. I look and see the places where the animals hide. Rocks and hills that the spirits inhabit. I see the history of the land. It's my history, not yours. There's no reason for you to know it." He thought about it while he turned the wheel sharply, guiding them around a deep pothole. "Think of it this way. Maybe I would come into your house in New York City and see a plate on a table, a broken old plate that had been glued together. To you, it's the last plate left from your great grandmother's table setting, a sentimental heirloom, broken by accident and then clumsily glued together by your repentant child. To me, it's an old broken plate. To me," he nodded at the land that stretched around them, "this is my home. There was more of it at one time, the plate was once whole, once part of a larger set, but now it's all we have left. Would you throw away your plate?" He glanced at her for a moment. "Of course not."

"No, I wouldn't. But I also wouldn't shoot someone who was fooling around with it."

"If it were your house, would you shoot him? What if you found two men drilling a hole in the side of your house?"

"I would call the police."

His laugh was short and harsh. "The police, yes. Here on our land if two men were doing such a thing the police would come and help hold the drill. Maybe supply a little dynamite to blow down one of the walls. Indians do not call the white man's police. When you are talking to Henry Sands, notice the holes in the walls of his home. They are bullet holes. Put there by the police."

Will swung the truck abruptly into a dusty yard in front of a two-story wood house with a sagging screen door and a dog asleep on the porch. There were several rough-hewn outbuildings, and a corral behind the house. In the corral, two bay horses lifted their heads from the sparse grass and looked at them as they drove by. The dirty yellow dog pricked his ears as the truck rolled to a stop. In the ensuing, almost overwhelming quiet, Molly could hear the click of the cooling engine and the constant moan of the wind as it swept through the bare yard and around the house, and over the brown hills as it had done, always. The wind relented from the moan to a sigh, a lonely, unloved, whispering sound. Molly wondered how anyone could ever live in such a land.

A child peered through the torn screening on the door and disappeared back inside. They waited in silence until an old man stepped out onto the porch. Will Two Horses climbed out of the Chevy. Molly waited while the two Indians spoke briefly. Both of them looked toward her so she got out of the truck, shouldered her day pack, and walked to the porch.

"This is Henry Sands," Will said. "Molly Glenn. From the *New York Times*."

Molly shook the offered hand. It had the dry rough feel of old corn husks. "Come inside out of the wind," Henry Sands said. His voice had a high singsong quality, the voice of a young man.

Henry Sands was dressed in heavy twill work pants and a red-checked flannel shirt buttoned to the neck. They went through a front room with two aging couches and a plastic La-z-boy recliner. The floors of all the rooms were covered with a black-and-white checkerboard linoleum. Two heavyset women with long black hair and round faces stood by the stove in the kitchen. They smiled shyly and left through a curtained doorway into another room. Molly could hear the mutter of a television set through the curtains, and upstairs, the thump and laughter of children.

"We will have coffee with our talk," Henry Sands said. Will and Molly sat on tubular steel kitchen chairs with plastic seats at the worn white metal table. Henry poured coffee from a flecked blue coffeepot into bright red metal cups of the type fashionable with college students of her time. The handles of the cups were always too hot to hold, but they were cheap and colorful.

"I have never read the *New York Times*," Henry Sands said, passing the coffee cups. If the hot metal bothered him, he did not show it. "I understand that it is a very powerful organization. During Wounded Knee there were several reporters who came into the town when we took it over. They stayed with us for some time and seemed to be careful men."

"I read the stories they wrote," Molly said.

"Yes," Henry said. "We have not seen much of these reporters since then. There have been many stories, many of our boys have been killed since then, but the *New York Times* has not come to find these things out. Why is that?"

Molly felt herself flush. It was one thing to be challenged by someone like Will Two Horses. She was used to that, but this ingenuous question from this grandfatherly old man embarrassed her. She could think of no good answers. Perhaps there were none.

"I don't know," she finally said, honestly. "Perhaps those who decide such things didn't feel that these stories were important enough to our readers."

The old man nodded. "Yes, not important to your readers. But now that John Raven has shot two white men, it has become important." Molly nodded. "He is not a bad man, John Raven," Henry Sands went on. "Since he has joined the AIM he has become very eager, as have many of our young men. This is good."

"He shot two men," Molly said.

"He did not kill them. Had he wanted to kill them he would have. He is a very good shot, I have seen this myself. I understand your point, though. You think this is perhaps too drastic a step? Yes, well, it has caught the attention of the *New York Times,* do you understand?"

"Yes, I understand," Molly said, "but if he is captured he will be put on trial for attempted murder, and he will surely go to jail for a long time. If the men die, which is possible, they may sentence John Raven to death."

The old man drank his coffee although Molly could still hardly touch her cup. Will Two Horses was taking tentative sips at his.

"It is not important if John Raven goes to jail. Many of our boys are in jail for things that they did not even do. Yes, it is better to go to jail for something you actually did. And he is also prepared to face death. He would not have acted were he not prepared for this. I understand that this is difficult for you, that you do not see things the way we do, but John Raven has chosen a path that to us is an honorable one. That he may meet death on the path is of little consequence."

Molly remembered Alex's description of an Indian fight, the warriors rushing forward to touch his enemy with a stick, the odd brave notion that it was the *idea* of the wound, the sudden possibility of death, the symbolism that was important. "But what is the point of it all? What is the purpose?"

Henry Sands smiled. "He has done it to save the land. The spirits have told him to do this thing. It is they who have decided that we can no longer stand by while the white men drill holes into our land and search for the uranium and build their mines and plants and poison us with their wastes." He laughed. "What else could he do?"

"Was it the spirit of Crazy Horse who told him to do this?"

"Possibly," the old man said. "He seems to think so. Does it make a difference?"

"It makes a better story for the newspaper," Will Two Horses said dryly. "She has her readers to consider."

Molly went on as if she hadn't heard him. "I would think it would make a difference in deciding what John Raven will do next." She remembered the night Alex told her about Crazy Horse and the vision quest. He had said then that this might be the key to John Raven. Or at least to finding him.

"That is for John Raven to decide. The spirits are speaking to him, not to us. Sometimes a warrior must fight alone."

"But what about those who are trying to catch him and bring him in?"

"What about them? They will try to catch him. John Raven knows that."

Molly felt as if she were pushing a very heavy rock up a very long hill. "Don't you want to help him escape? He's an Indian, you're an Indian. He did this for the benefit of your tribe. He was trying to save your land. Don't you care about that?"

Henry Sands looked at Molly through very old eyes, and she felt small and young, as if she were being looked at by a patient father who knows that there are too many years between them to bridge, but who is kind enough to keep on trying. "Your questions have no answers; they are too simple. John Raven is a son to me, but it is his life that he is living, not mine. I cannot speak for him. I cannot save him. I do not wish to take away from him that honor that he is searching for. He will find it or he will not. It is the search that is important. If during his search John Raven helps his people, helps the land, then that is good. I would not have him be caught by our enemies, nor would I have him die. But it is not up to me."

"Then who is it up to? Who is responsible?"

It was very still in the house. Henry Sands looked at her kindly as he said, gently, "It is up to John Raven. He is responsible. It is his life."

• •

She stayed for dinner. The two silent women she had seen earlier were two of Henry's daughters. They came back to the kitchen and turned into two normally chatty women who went about the task of preparing a meal for at least twelve people. Molly estimated the number to be twelve, but she never really came up with an accurate count of the playing, laughing children. The women worked with a minimum of fuss and an air of good humor and resignation. Good humor because they seemed naturally inclined toward it, and because Henry Sands sat at the table drinking unending cups of black coffee and telling stories and jokes. She could tell that the jokes had been told before but that they were still appreciated, the way one comes to appreciate the scratches and hiss on an old and much-loved record.

"What were General Custer's last words?" Henry asked. Molly shook her head.

"Take no prisoners."

The husbands of the two women were brothers. They ate with the rest of them, but said little at the table. They were both short and stocky with barrel chests and long unbraided black hair. Their round faces had high cheekbones and black eyes that looked steadily at whoever was speaking. The children were numerous and active and sat still only long enough to eat their mashed potatoes and chunks of stewed venison.

After dinner, the women washed the dishes and the men retired back to wherever the TV set was located, and she and Henry and Will had sat at the table and still Henry talked, now about his early life and finally about the takeover at Wounded Knee where he had taken the final steps of allying himself with the American Indian Movement.

They loaned her a flannel-lined Montgomery Ward sleeping bag and gave her the couch in the front room to sleep on. Will had declined the offer of the other couch, saying he would sleep in the truck. Molly fell asleep only minutes after she heard the truck start and quietly roll out of the dirt yard.

• •

The door slammed open, and a bright beam of light struck her full in the face. She sat up with her arm in front of her eyes, trying to see into the glare. A heavy male voice with a western accent said, "Shit. Look at that hair and those tits. That ain't no Indian."

She pulled the sleeping bag up to cover herself. "Turn out that light," she demanded in as firm a voice as she could manage. "What's going on? Who are you?"

There was the sound of boots walking toward her. The light remained fixed and unrelenting. She was aware of two figures, indistinct behind the glare.

"I believe that is our question, not yours," a milder voice said. "Who are you, and where are the others?"

Molly could hear someone coming down the steps from the second floor of the house. For a second the light seemed to waver, but then it stayed on her.

"Leave her alone, What do you want with us?"

The light moved to Henry, standing in the doorway, wearing a sleeveless undershirt, work pants, and no shoes. His hair was mussed. Molly picked up her shirt, put it on, and pulled her jeans on in the sleeping bag.

"Don't be moving too quick there, lady," the first voice drawled. "Pity you had to go and put on that shirt."

"Who's in the house, Henry?" the mild-voiced man asked. "How many Indians in the tepee?"

Henry reached to the wall and flipped on the lights. The two men were both big and wore hunting jackets, cowboy boots, and Stetsons. The man with the drawl had a thick belly that hung over his hammered-silver belt buckle. The man carrying the light switched it off. "Get them down here, Henry—I want everyone here in this room where I can see them and count them. Just holler up the steps. I want you here where I can see you. Tell them anyone tries anything funny has got big trouble." He pulled the jacket back over the grip of a long, holstered pistol.

"Now just for the record, miss," he said, turning to Molly, "Who are you, and what are you doing here?"

"I don't need to answer any of your questions," Molly said.

The man nodded and turned back to Henry. "Get 'em down here, Henry, we don't have all night. Might as well get the women and kids down here, too. I want to see all the Indians in this house down here where I can count them and look at them."

"Well, mister," Henry said, smiling and smoothing down his ruffled gray hair. "Turn around real slow because there's most of them right behind you."

The two men turned around to face Will Two Horses and the two silent brothers. Will was fully dressed and carrying a rifle that was pointed dead center at the heavy man's gut. The other two Indians were shirtless and shoeless, but held rifles across their chests.

There was a long silence.

"Fuck you, Chief," the fat man finally said. "Three little Indian pricks with cheap rifles don't add up to one pissed-off white man. And I can tell you I'm beginning to get kind of pissed off here."

"Shut up, Harvey," the smarter-looking man said.

Harvey looked at the other man with open disgust. "Shit, Mr. Owen, these chicken shits ain't going to shoot anybody."

"I said, be quiet." Owen looked at the fat man until the

other looked away. "Can we do something with these rifles?" Owen asked. His voice was controlled, careful.

"Not quite yet," Will Two Horses said. "We wouldn't want Harvey there to get too relaxed." Harvey looked around as if he were going to spit on the floor, but then thought better of it.

"I want you out of my house," Henry Sands said. "Outside. Then we will talk."

The two Indians in the doorway backed out onto the porch and stood at either side of the door. Will backed carefully out and stood by the steps. The two white men stepped onto the porch and down into the hard-packed dirt yard. Henry and Molly followed onto the porch. Will walked to a Jeep wagon sitting in the yard, reached in through the open window and flicked on the lights. The two white men were caught in the beams, lit like two deer being spotlit by poachers. The Indians and Molly moved to the side, out of the light.

"You going to run down my battery," Harvey said. No one paid any attention to him.

"Names," Will said.

After a moment's hesitation Owen responded. "Frank Owen, Federal Bureau of Investigation, and this is Harvey Blanchard from the local sheriff's office. We're here on official business."

"You come on business while we sleep?" Henry Sands asked. "You smash in my door on your business? What is this business?"

"We're looking for an Indian, John Raven. He's wanted for attempted murder. Any felony committed on federal trust land is an FBI matter. We had reason to believe he would be here. If we'd called ahead we knew he wouldn't be here when we arrived."

"He isn't here anyway," Will said. "Don't you listen to the radio or read the newspapers? He's somewhere out there." The barrel of the rifle moved a half an inch in the direction of the night then back again to Harvey's stomach.

"Shit," Harvey said.

Bugs, some of them large, began to swim in the cones of the headlights. A huge moth fluttered out of the darkness and lit on the bumper of the wagon. Only Molly seemed to notice. The moth's wings were green and brown, patterned like two huge eyes.

"I do not know you, Mr. Owen, you must be new here. You could do better than to follow the advice of the local police," Henry Sands said. "Their first response is to come onto the reservation and shoot a few holes in my walls. It has never done them much good. It is also illegal."

"Do you know where John Raven is?" Owen asked. "Or where he might be?"

Henry shook his head. "He is where Will Two Horses has said he is. If you want him you will have to look for him out there."

"Takes an Indian to find an Indian," Harvey said. "You could find him if you wanted to."

"You have many tame Indians to help you. The reservation police. I am surprised you have not brought them along this night."

"I didn't want them," Owen said, "I thought the two of us could handle it. Make less of a fuss."

"Yes. Two white men against the Indians. Surely that should have been enough. But it wasn't." Henry turned and walked back to the door of the house. "If you have business with me, Mr. Owen, come and see me during the daytime. Do not kick in the door, knock on it." He reached to the side and knocked twice on the wooden frame. "Put them in their cars, boys, and come inside. It is too cold to stand in the yard."

The two white men hesitated and then walked to the car. The barrels of the rifles followed them across the yard. They opened the doors and climbed inside. The engine ground then caught.

"Wait a minute," Owen said from the passenger seat. "For the last time, who are you?" he asked Molly.

"Molly Glenn. I'm a reporter for the *New York Times,* I made an appointment with your secretary this morning. I'm to interview you at two o'clock this afternoon. It's been very interesting, Mr. Owen, seeing the FBI in action. You can be sure it will be in my story."

Owen just looked at her. "Let's go," he said to Harvey. The wagon backed out of the yard and swung out onto the dirt road.

They all walked into the house. "Get the women and kids from out back," Henry said. "They're in the usual place." One of the silent Indians nodded and left. "They were out of the house before the white men arrived," Henry said to Molly. "Will heard them coming and got them out. The boys were outside with Will when they drove up. I am the decoy, the sleepy old Indian. If they would learn to leave their cars and trucks farther away and walk in, they might surprise us, but they never do. They never have. They do not seem to learn from the past."

Chapter 12

Alex rolled his sedan chair down the wooden floor of the Main Building. He was taking a shortcut to Machinery Hall to look for Elias. Main was one-third of a mile in length, but the trip down the wide center aisle was considerably shorter than the meandering paths outside.

Carpenters were completing the last of the finish work on the massive Electric Echo organ in the English Tower of the building, clearing up their tools and the leftover sticks of trim wood, making room for the pipe tuners who were already swarming over the keys and pedals and stops. Great groans from the bass pipes echoed through the building, punctuated by shrieks from the soprano end of the keyboard. There were three different organs in three corners of the building in various stages of completion. Alex wondered if the building, the largest in the world, would be large enough to contain all the music the organs could produce if it was decided to play all three at the same time. Alex checked his catalogue of the exhibition. As heavy and complex as an old-time family Bible, he kept it on the empty seat of his chair so he could look up any details he was unsure of. It informed him that the other two organs were a Hillborne L. Roosevelt, slated for the north transept, and a Hook and Hastings at the east end of the building. These were the sort of facts he was supposed to know, and an inability to call them up on demand could result in his dismissal. Pop quizzes were part of a chair-pusher's life, attended to personally by Alex's boss, Albert P. Riddle, Esq., sole owner and proprietor of Atlantic Amusements. Albert liked to refer to his little tests as Riddle's riddles.

Riddle, known to many behind his back as Albert "Pisshead" Riddle, was a rat-faced little man who had successfully tied up the chair concession with a series of well-placed bribes to lesser members of the Centennial Commission. Besides the chairs, which were rented by the hour, he sold stationery, postage stamps, and opera glasses. He also rented canes and umbrellas and had a side business in cheap souvenirs. Albert, who saw himself as a sort of merchant prince, was destined to make a bundle from the exhibition. "Detail," Albert would squeak, "that's what's important in this business." He would line the pushers up behind their chairs for inspection each morning. "You there," he would point at one of them, "what's the combined weight of all the goods in the art department?" A nervous throat cleared. "Two million one hundred thousand and nine hundred pounds, Mr. Riddle."

For Alex it was easy. With his trained memory he retained almost everything of what he read. So while Alex was not the most diligent pusher, often parking his chair in some out-of-the-way spot while he wandered among the exhibits, he was known for his grasp of the facts. The other guide-pushers were divided in their assessment of Alex; some hated him for his ability, others were glad he was there to take the heat off them. So when he was called upon by Riddle, half of them scowled while the other half heaved sighs of relief.

"You there, Balfour. How many men in the Centennial Fire Department?" Alex clicked his heels together and pulled himself to attention. "One hundred seventy-five men, two stations, fifteen call boxes, and seven steamers housed in Machinery Hall on call with a full head of steam at all times, sir!" Albert couldn't decide if Balfour was in some way making fun of him, but his command of detail was undeniable.

Alex rolled his chair along, watching the workmen assembling the exhibits that lined the wide aisle. The pounding of hammers, the babble of foreign voices, and the moans from the organ filled the huge room, bouncing around inside to create a pandemonium of sounds that became one sound that was almost a solid presence. The only really quiet spot under construction was the Japanese House, which was still being meticulously handcrafted by the solemn Japanese workers.

The chair rolled easily, two large wheels in back, two small wheels in front. After a few days Alex had overcome the feeling that he was actually a male nurse, endlessly rolling some invisible invalid down the pathways of all 236 acres of the exposition. He had just passed the French exhibition when Albert P. Riddle popped out from behind a huge cloisonné vase.

"Halt!" Albert commanded, holding up one hand. "Attention, Chair Guide Balfour, it's time for Riddle's riddles." Albert picked up Alex's copy of the exhibit catalogue and seated himself in the chair. "Proceed," he said, waving them forward.

Alex had the same problem that Albert did. If Riddle was unable to decide if Alex was constantly putting him on, so Alex wondered if Albert's strange manner was some sort of permanent inside joke, amusing only to Albert's internal audience of one, himself, an adoring fan more than willing to supply Albert the Witty Player with an unbroken murmur of praise and adulation.

"Here! Here!" Albert flapped his arms in Alex's face and pointed off to the right to the British Exhibition. "In here." He grabbed the arms of the chair as Alex swung them rapidly under the red flag with black lettering marking the entrance.

The amount of material on display in any section of the exhibition was overwhelming. In later expositions, photography would take over much of the display space, but here, where photography was a fairly new phenomenon and primarily restricted to its own pavilion, actual *things* were exhibited in such profusion as to deluge the onlooker with a myriad of objects artfully displayed in a forest of beautifully crafted dark wooden glass-fronted cases.

Fortunately Alex had studied the British Exhibit at great length. There was a young Irish woman working in the millinery section who so reminded him of Molly that he had spent hours wheeling his chair between the display cases studying the contents and sneaking looks at the red-haired young lady as she worked. He was still excited about the exposition and all its fascinating historical aspects, and during the day he was always occupied. But the nights, lying on his thin pallet, brought Molly back to him. He missed her. And always there was the knowledge that it was she, their connection, that tied him to the present. Without her he would stay here, in the past, forever.

He pushed Albert solemnly past a fifteen-foot-tall skeleton of some extinct lizard, forelegs propped up on a chunk of petrified wood. Alex paused to intone the creature's scientific name, which was clearly written on a label, and then he rolled by a series of giant tapestries hung from the ceiling, past cases of fanned laces, books, brass and silver musical instruments, guns and cutlery, cloth, furs, silk dresses, and entire furnished bedrooms.

Alex turned a corner and stopped in front of a large case containing a seated wax figure. He still wasn't used to the profusion of these wax figures that were everywhere, lifelike, frozen in noble attitudes. He studied this one, recognizing the face from a college textbook picture.

"Thomas Carlyle," he said, "Scottish philosopher." He moved the chair closer to the case. Carlyle sat in an easy chair, his face almost covered with a shaggy beard and mustache, his cheeks sunken and his eyes grim. Alex realized that somewhere in this world there was a real live Carlyle, writing books and railing at civilization in tones and words and ideas that few would remember or respond to a hundred years in the future. But in this time he was so revered that he had been immortalized in wax and given an easy chair to relax in. He tried to remember what philosophers had been represented in any of the modern world's fairs he had attended.

"What about these?" Albert asked. He pointed at a row of suits of armor.

"Armor, from the fifteenth and sixteenth centuries," Alex said.

Albert got out of the chair and walked up to the metal suits. "Little guys, like me." He smiled as if he'd just discovered a wealthy ancestor.

"Not really," Alex said. He lifted a plate on the chest and showed Albert a leather hinge inside. "People are always saying that our ancestors were smaller than we are, but it's not true. Armor was hinged all over; when you put it on it stretched out. When you stand it up like this it all scrunches together and looks small."

Albert frowned. "How about those beds we passed back there. Those old-time beds were a lot shorter than ours are."

"People slept sitting up—the beds didn't need to be as long. People are pretty much the same height they always were." He shrugged, as if to say, Don't blame me if people slept sitting up.

Riddle's frown deepened, looking somehow cheated. "I never know when you're kidding me, Balfour. If you weren't so good at this job I'd fire you. Where the hell did you say you were from, anyway?"

"New York."

Riddle shook his head once and walked away. He stopped and turned to Alex. "There's something funny about you, but I can't put my finger on it. You live with niggers, and you know too much. Jeez, you know more than I do about this stuff. You want a better job? You want to manage this end of the operation, sit in the chairs and ask the questions?"

Alex considered this surprising turn of events, but couldn't really see himself rocketing around tossing out questions to pissed-off pushers. Besides, he wasn't here to have a career, he was here because . . . well, he didn't know yet, but it wasn't to rise through the ranks of Atlantic Amusements. "No thanks," he said.

Riddle raised a finger and pointed it at Alex as if he were pulling a trigger. "Right. It's up to you. Stop leaving the chair around when you're supposed to be working. Somebody steals it and I'm taking it out of your pay. Got it?" Alex nodded and Albert walked away in search of another malingering chair-pusher he could terrorize with a few riddles.

• •

Alex pushed the chair out of the British Exhibit and back down the long aisle past the exhibits from the British Colonies, Sweden, Norway, and Italy. He paused by the doorway of the building to watch a crowd of workmen and visitors around two large mirrors, one concave and one convex. There were always large crowds here, laughing and marveling at this strange phenomena, which he'd heard compared to Dickens's Fat Boy and someone named Daniel Lambart, whoever he was.

He went on out the door of the building and crossed the intervening courtway, along the asphalt paths that starred out from between the two great buildings onto the main roadway of the exhibition.

He wheeled his chair through the open doorway into Machinery Hall, a vast building only slightly smaller but even noisier than Memorial Hall. He pushed his chair along what seemed to be thousands of different types and manufacturers of sewing machines to the weaving section, where Elias worked keeping the machines of the Philadelphia Weaving Company functioning smoothly. A woman whom Elias had introduced him to, a plump pleasant girl named Sally, sat at a Jacquard loom turning out bookmarks bearing a remarkable likeness of George Washington with the flowing script "Father of Our Country" emblazoned in white letters against red and blue.

"You seen Elias, Sally?" Alex asked, yelling over the roar of machinery.

She reached up, turned off her loom, and swiveled on her stool to face him. "That tall yellow colored man just ran in here to get him," she said worriedly. "He said there was trouble with someone over at the Indians'. They both took off out of here like the devil was after them."

"Watch the chair," Alex said as he turned and ran, down the long aisle, past the clanking, purring, growling, banging machines that promised a bright new future and praised the glories of the past.

Chapter 13

Alex burst through the doors of Machinery Hall and turned onto Fountain Avenue at a dead run. He skirted the tables and chairs of the Catholic Total Abstinence Society and headed down the broad mall that ended at the Sons of Temperance Fountain.

Ahead of him was the Government Building and behind that was the Indian encampment and Elias and probably Abraham and whatever trouble awaited him. He ran easily and was surprised that even after several weeks of not running he still seemed to be in pretty good shape. He sprinted by the Turkish Café and skirted an ornate popcorn stand where a small crowd watched curiously as he passed.

He jumped the narrow-gauge railroad tracks and for a moment was paced by one of the small trains carrying workmen to the California Building. There were cheers and jeers as the workmen pointed and shouted at him. After the train drew away the only sounds were his own breathing as he sucked air into his lungs and his Nikes hitting the gravel path as he made the final turn around the front of the Government Building. The perimeter of this quintessentially Victorian structure was ringed with displayed cannon, obstacles that Alex had to dodge as he came around the back side. (Rodman gun, he thought, swerving around a twenty-foot cannon; weight, one hundred fifteen thousand one hundred pounds, throws a shot of one-half ton and requires two hundred pounds of powder.) He circled the back end of the old Conestoga wagon that had been used by General Sherman on his long march to the sea. He stopped and stood panting, trying to catch his breath.

A small crowd of men were facing the Indian encampment. In the center, inside the small fenced-in yard around the te-pee, was Abraham holding a struggling smaller man. He held the man by his shirtfront and was looking into the crowd for help, like a small boy who had caught some loathsome thing and now didn't know what to do with it. Alex pushed through the crowd.

"He was sneaking into the tent, Alex," Abraham said, catching sight of him. "I took him away from Little Spring—she had him, she would have killed him."

"I told him to turn him loose," Elias said, appearing at Alex's side. "He won't listen to me."

"If I turn him loose he going to run!" Abraham said.

A drop of red blood dripped onto Abraham's arm. Alex stepped closer and looked at the man held by Abraham. The man's face was slashed and bleeding on one side. "Tell him to let me go," the man whined. "I wasn't doin' nothin'."

"Tell the nigger to turn him loose," someone in the crowd said. "It ain't right."

"Hold on to him for a minute," Alex said. The man's face was bleeding in four parallel lines from ear to chin. The blood twisted down his neck and disappeared under his shirt collar. The man touched his cheek, smearing the perfect lines. He looked at his hand, rubbing the bloody fingers together.

"Damn. That squaw tried to kill me." He looked up at Abraham. "This nigger was going to finish me off."

Alex looked at Abraham for more information. "Little Spring caught him sneaking in under the tent. He was going to steal something. I was coming to give them food when I heard him let out a holler."

"The nigger grabbed him and started beatin' him," a man in the crowd said. "I seen it all."

"What the hell is going on here?" a soldier said, pushing

through the crowd. "I go off station for two minutes to take a piss and you damn fool Indians and niggers got to get into some kind of trouble. I never should have let you come around here with that food anyway."

The guard was young, probably twenty, with a boyish face that was flushed and frightened. Alex knew that he was supposed to stay and watch the Indians, and he would be in trouble for leaving his post. "All day long I got to stand over there and watch the old chief and the squaw just sittin'. Nobody comes around but the nigger and people trying to cause trouble. I just had to go, nobody could blame me for that."

"This bitch tried to kill me," the bleeding man said, jerking his head toward Little Spring.

The two Indians had been standing by the front of the tepee. The old man stood watching the crowd with no discernible expression on his face. The woman, Little Spring, watched the group of men with disgust, her eyes dark with anger. She spoke to High Cloud in a low voice. He nodded and approached Alex.

"This one," he said, nodding at the bleeding man, "tried to climb in through the back of the tepee. He came to steal. Little Spring caught him. Give him to us and we will kill him for you." He nodded to the woman. "She will."

"Just wanted a goddamn souvenir," the man said. "All they got's trash anyway. Just two goddamn Indians, not even niggers." He pointed at Abraham. "This black bastard butted in. What the hell's he think he's doing grabbing at a white man?"

"Catching a thief," Elias said, angrily. "A white thief."

"Now the other nigger's gonna start with his sass," the man said. "We gonna take this?" he shouted at the crowd. "First it's the goddamn Indians, now it's the goddamn niggers. Where's a white man stand around here anyway? We got to listen to this?"

The crowd, which had grown, seemed to move within itself, muttering. "Hell, no," someone called. "Not from niggers."

"Or red niggers either," someone else hollered. A few men laughed.

Alex noticed the soldier backing away through the crowd to

his guard box. There wouldn't be much help from that direction.

He stepped into the Indians' yard and pulled Elias along with him. He told Abraham to turn the thief loose. The crowd began to split and move along the fence, unsure of its next move. The bleeding man hopped over the knee-high fence and swiftly blended into the crowd. "Goddamn niggers," Alex heard the man shout as he slipped away. "Goddamn nigger lovers."

"You fools," Elias said, his high voice cutting into the crowd. "Where do you think you are? This is not the South, we are not slaves. You can't get away with this anymore. We're free!" he shouted. "Can't you get that through your thick heads? We are free men!"

A rock the size of a fist caught Elias full on the mouth. "Free to eat rocks, nigger," someone shouted and laughed. All of them inside the yard began backing toward the tepee.

Elias bent over, spitting blood. A rock cracked into Alex's temple with a snap of quick pain. Blood coursed into his eye. Abraham moved in front of all of them, spreading his arms to protect them. A large rock thudded off his chest. He seemed to expand, the way a sponge expands as it picks up water; only Abraham was soaking up evil and growing to shield them against rocks and threats until he seemed a great presence that the small and the weak could hide behind, a tree whose trunk and limbs would shelter them.

The crowd hesitated.

Then Alex heard it. A strange squeaking and the scrabbling of claws on metal and muffled curses and barking and growling and the grind of the metal wheels on gravel and around the old Conestoga wagon came that high strange nightmare of a tricycle with the two slobbering panting dogs caged within the great wheels, and seated up on the little tricycle seat was a man with silver hair and a clean blue uniform and a gun in a saddle scabbard strapped to the handlebars. By his side ran the black man Alex recognized from his night on the porch, which now seemed so long ago, the man with the stick, the black outrider who banged on the wheels and shouted at the dogs, "Whoa now, dogs! Back now, dogs! That is enough now, dogs."

And the crowd turned toward this apparition and fell quiet. Stones dropped to the ground.

"Holy Mary, Mother of God," someone said.

The tricycle stopped, and the man on the high seat swung easily to the ground and walked toward them. "Well, now," the man said. "And what have we here?" He was tall and broad and looked about fifty years old, well preserved and strong. The crowd split as he walked through. "Well, my boys, having a little fun with the Indians? Having a little entertainment? Is there not enough work to be done without this diversion?" He looked sharply at the faces of the men, as if memorizing each of them for later use. He came to the low fence and stopped, looking in at Alex and the others. "Very interesting," he said, nodding.

He turned back to the crowd of men and stared at them. "Would you care to throw some rocks at me, then?" he said lightly. The crowd began to fall away. "No? And why not? Because you've no brains in your head? Because you're a bunch of chicken-livered sons of bitches who are too cowardly to act like men? That's it, crawl away, go back to your jobs or wherever you've come from. I've seen you—you can depend on that. I've seen you and I'll remember you." He turned his back on the crowd, dismissing them from his consideration.

"Are any of you badly hurt?" he asked.

Alex looked at Elias, who had a piece of cloth pressed to his mouth. He shook his head and looked away. Alex lowered his arm and found his cut brow had stopped bleeding. "I think we're all right," he said.

The man nodded. He had ruddy skin and light blue eyes. His carefully combed silver hair was thick and swept straight back. He studied Abraham then fixed his gaze on Alex. He seemed mildly puzzled by Alex's inclusion with the blacks and the Indians. "Ah, yes," he said, "you're the white man who lives with the coloreds. I've heard of you. I presume you have an explanation for all of this. Balfour, isn't it?"

Alex nodded. "I can tell you what happened. It's not the

fault of any of these people. A man tried to steal something and then the crowd . . ." The silver-haired man held up his hand.

"I'm the chief of police of the exposition. My name is Brannon. I'll expect you in my office first thing tomorrow morning. You can," he stopped while he studied Alex, then went on, slowly, "explain it to me then." He glanced around and spotted the guard sitting in his small hut. He seemed about to go speak to him, then changed his mind. He walked back to his dog-cycle and swung up onto the seat. He nodded to the black man with the stick.

"Go, dogs!" the man said, banging the near wheel. The dogs sprang to their feet and began to run up the insides of the wheels. The cycle began to move, the chief of police steering them in a perfect, even circle. "Go, you dogs," the black man shouted, dropping into a slow trot. They moved off, around the wagon and between the cannons, toward the front of the building.

Little Spring bent and went into the tepee. Abraham turned and took Elias by the arm. "I'm going to take him to the Comfort," Abraham said. "We got to clean this up. Clean you up too, Alex."

Alex shook his head. "I'm all right. I'll be along." What he wanted to do was be alone for a few minutes. His legs were beginning to tremble with delayed shock. He felt as if he'd just escaped from a head-on car crash. He nodded to the two black men. "You go ahead." Elias and Abraham walked away.

The old Indian sat down on his striped blanket and looked away into the distance to somewhere that did not include Alex or any other man in this place. Alex walked to the fence and stepped over. He turned at the sound of a throat being cleared.

A small man stood watching him. The man had bright eyes and a thick shock of red hair with a matching bushy mustache. He looked like an extremely intelligent hawk. He looked very familiar.

"Yes, well, that was something," the man said. "Yes." He took a long puff on a large cigar, looking up at Alex as if waiting for his explanation.

"Hold it there, mister," another voice said. Alex and the small man both turned to face the guard who was behind them, carrying his rifle across his chest. "No smoking on the grounds. You'll have to put that cigar out."

The small hawklike man fixed the guard with a threatening look. The guard stepped back. "That's the rules, mister. No smoking of any type on the grounds." The red-haired man glanced at Alex, then back at the guard. He shook his head in disgust. He took the cigar out of his mouth, dropped it, and ground it under his heel. He turned to Alex.

"Isn't that the goddamnedest thing you ever heard? Here I've just witnessed a scene of near murder, several men left torn and bleeding, stones thrown and a lynching narrowly averted, and this chucklehead comes up and tells me there's no goddamn smoking allowed." He turned back to the guard. "Just what the hell *is* allowed? Maybe I'll just go and blow up the Government Building. That'd probably be all right, wouldn't it?" The guard just stared at him, afraid to say anything more.

The small man sighed and turned to Alex. "I think that son of a bitch just took the record." He sighed again. "Clemens," he said, holding out his hand. "Sam Clemens. Don't tell anyone, I'm not supposed to be here."

Alex automatically shook his hand, unable to think of what to say. Here he was shaking hands with Mark Twain, arguably America's greatest writer, and he couldn't think of a thing to say. He ran a series of dates through his mind and the title *Adventures of Tom Sawyer* clicked into place, like three cherries snapping into place on a slot machine. Early 1876, he was sure of it.

"I've read your *Tom Sawyer,* Mr. Twain," Alex said. "It's a wonderful book."

"Really now," Twain said, rocking forward on his toes and staring up into Alex's eyes. There was a hint of a smile under the mustache, the smile of a man who is about to win a large poker hand. "That's interesting, seeing as how it won't be published until next month."

Chapter 14

"Where are we going?" Molly shouted over the roar of the accelerating engine as they pulled out onto the highway. "I thought Rapid City was back that way." She pointed her thumb toward the bed of the truck.

"You'll be back in plenty of time to meet with the FBI," Will Two Horses said. He shifted into high and settled back in his seat.

"I didn't ask when I'd be back," Molly said. "I asked where we were going."

"Before I tell you where we're going, you tell me what you thought about last night. He glanced at her. Molly watched as a large tumbleweed bounced across the highway in front of them.

They had gotten up at daybreak and eaten breakfast. The women and children filled the kitchen with laughter and noise. No one seemed upset about what had happened during the night. They referred to it as the ambush and laughed it off when she tried to bring it up while they were eating.

"I'm not sure what to think," Molly said to Will. "Of course, it was outrageous and illegal, but I get the feeling that it isn't exactly the first time it's happened."

"That's for sure," Will said. He was wearing his long hair

loose today, under a beat-up cowboy hat. It reminded her of the sixties when all her friends had long hair, men and women. It was a style that, when she looked back on it now, seemed silly. But on Will Two Horses, and the two silent Indian brothers, it looked right.

"Henry's the point man for AIM here on the reservation. When the shit hits, Henry's the man who usually has to take the brunt of it. The local police hate him because he's the real leader, the spiritual leader of the tribe. And they can't buy him off. So they shoot up his house and they roust him out of bed and they harass his children. They killed his wife."

It seemed as though the sound of the engine had suddenly ceased, though she knew it hadn't. She watched the hills roll by.

"How do you know?"

"After Wounded Knee in 1973 there were sixty killings on this reservation in just three years. That's sixty *unsolved* killings. Henry's wife, Little Hawk, was one of them. She was driving back from a women's meeting late one night; someone pulled up beside her and shot her with a twelve-gauge shotgun. There was never any serious attempt to find out who did it."

She turned on the seat to face him. "What the hell is it that makes everyone here hate each other so?" she said angrily.

"It all started," he said, "when the white man decided it was America's manifest destiny to conquer and rule every inch of this country. It started when the Indian decided that he would fight to keep his land." He jammed the truck into a lower gear and swung them off the highway onto a blacktop road. The truck leaned to the right. She saw a sign along the side: WOUNDED KNEE 5 MILES.

"I want to show you where I came into this," he said. "Where Henry made his first stand, he and a lot of other Indians. I know that much of this sounds like bullshit, cowboys and Indians, manifest destiny, stuff out of a book. But it's real, and it just doesn't go away. People still die for it. It's not a story, Molly, this is life."

• •

They stood on a low hill looking down on a small town. He had loaned her his wool-lined buckskin coat, and she was wrapped in it. The sky was clouded over and gray. A small, bright red church stood out defiantly against the monochromatic dirt color of the few other buildings and the land around them.

"I was fifteen," Will said. "This is where I crawled into the encampment." He pointed to a gulch that ran off to their right, toward the town. "It was at night and the army had their perimeter set up all along these hills where we're standing. I came down the gully with a little pack on my back and my heart pounding to where I thought it was about to burst. I'd taken a Magic Marker and colored my sneakers black so they wouldn't stand out in the night."

• •

Will Two Horses, fifteen years old and afraid, lay in the bottom of the gully listening to a group of soldiers talking and drinking coffee about twenty yards up over the lip of the gulch to his left. He was close enough to smell the coffee and hear them laugh. He'd been crawling down the gully for three hours and now he was afraid to move for fear of being heard, afraid that when they did hear him they'd put a few thousand rounds of M-16 fire into the ditch and come over and investigate after the smoke had cleared. *Well hell, Fred, looks like we got a good Indian down here.* Suddenly someone started up a jeep, so he wriggled off the way he'd been taught by his father, creeping along like the black-widow spiders and the poisonous snakes and all the other wildlife he was sure were down here in the dirt with him. Scorpions, whip tails upraised, just waiting for a skinny kid in blue jeans and a black turtleneck and painted-up sneakers.

It was a four-hundred-yard crawl and while his mind got a little easier about the soldiers behind him, he began to worry about the Indians out there in front. He knew there was a bunker up ahead that marked the Indians' perimeter, and that there'd be a guard and he'd be surely armed and probably pretty nervous what with a sizable portion of the Eighty-Second Airborne and a good piece of the Sixth Army of the United States sitting up on the hill, waiting for anyone down below to show his head so they could put a bullet in it. But he'd come too far to quit now and besides, the alternative was to crawl back the way he'd come, and he wasn't ready to try that. He'd take his chances with the Indians.

• •

"I hitchhiked over from Miles City, Montana. My dad had a job working in a sawmill there. We all knew what was going on down here. It was on the TV every night and in the papers. My parents, who were pretty conservative, pretended like they weren't much interested, but every Indian in the United States was watching Wounded Knee and waiting to see if there'd be another massacre." They started down the hill along the lip of the gully. Will was looking down into the cut in the earth, talking almost to himself.

• •

His breathing was too loud, but he couldn't quiet it. His elbows were scraped and sore from dragging his body over the rocky ground. He decided he must be within the Indian lines. He moved into a crouch and slowly lifted his head up over the edge of the gulch and almost screamed when the barrel of a rifle touched him lightly on the forehead. "I've got one bullet," a soft voice said. "It's only a twenty-two shot, but it'll put a nice hole in your head. You want to tell me real quick who you are?"

"Will Two Horses, Oglala, from Miles City. I want to help."

The rifle tapped him lightly two more times. "Come on up out of there real careful, Will Two Horses. There's a bunker right behind where I'm lying. Let's go."

Will crawled out of the gulch and toward the low blocky bunker silhouetted against the starry night sky.

It was made of cinderblock, and as he lowered himself down into it he saw, by the light of a candle, two Indians dressed in black, each holding a hunting rifle, silently watching him. On the front wall of the bunker was a surveyor's transit behind a black cloth over an opening.

The Indian who had found him picked up a small radio. "Security, this is Eagle Nine, we've got another walk-in out here. Actually he's a crawl-in. Can you send someone out to take him off our hands. No movement from the military as far as we can see. Over." He put the radio down on a small ledge. Suddenly the night exploded as shells slammed into the cinderblocks, knocking chunks of gray gravel down onto them and filling the air with fine grit. The candle was blown out and the breath was knocked out of him as one of the Indians fell on him, pressing him to the dirt floor. The bunker shook as the shells raked the ground around them. The firing stopped. In the sudden silence their breathing was a loud rasping sound. A small noise came up out of him before he could stop it, the sound of a rabbit in a wire snare. He cut it off as soon as it came out. No one mentioned it. They lay there, the man heavy on his back, for another several minutes. Finally, the man on top sighed and rolled off and sat up. "Welcome to Wounded Knee, kid," he said.

• •

Will picked up a small round rock and threw it at a clump of grass near a pile of broken cinderblocks. The quiet town was still several hundred yards away. Molly thought that was where they had been heading but now Will stood and just looked, as if this was as far as he wanted to go.

"There were around four hundred of us in there. Indians from all over the country. A lot of them came in at night the way I did. The army had outposts set up, roadblocks, guards walking the perimeter, but we got through anyway. We brought in ammunition, food, medical supplies, everything we needed. Henry Sands was in there from the beginning, handling the logistics of keeping people housed and fed. We had a clinic manned by our medicine men, a field kitchen, a sweatlodge, housing, a radio room, a security setup that was better than the army's. Frank Fools Crow and some of the other chiefs and headmen were handling the negotiations with the United States."

She watched him pick up another stone. This time, instead of throwing it, he cleaned it in his hands and handed it to her.

It wasn't a stone, it was a piece of lead. "Slug from a thirty-caliber machine gun," he said. "Probably from one of the APCs. I did a Freedom of Information inquiry a few years ago, got some documents from the Pentagon for a case I was working on. The figures are emblazoned on my brain. Being shot at has a tendency to fix your interests.

"Al Haig was the commander that authorized and planned the action against us. The list of materiel that the army expended here is pretty impressive. Seventeen armored patrol carriers, one hundred thirty thousand rounds of M-16 ammunition, forty-one thousand rounds of M-1 ammunition, twenty-four thousand flares, twelve M-79 grenade launchers, six hundred cases of C-S gas, one hundred rounds of M-40 explosives. Helicopters and Phantom jets flew overflights every day." He shook his head. "And those damn thirty-calibers. One day we took four thousand rounds from one of them before lunch. We heard them bragging about it on the radio."

"Were many people hurt?"

He looked at her as he thought back. His eyes were somehow older than they had been, a gray that matched the color of the sky.

"Three men had been hit when I got here. M-16s in the leg, hand, and stomach. The medicine man took out the bullets. They all recovered.

"We were a little underarmed compared to the army. We had hunting rifles, shotguns; one guy had an AK-47 he'd brought back from Vietnam. No helicopters or jets. We had to use a little ingenuity to keep them scared enough that they wouldn't just drive right in and take over. First thing we did was stay up all one night painting coffee can lids black and hooking wires to them. The next day we made a big show of walking the perimeter and burying the lids. We heard them on the radio warning all units that we were mining the fields and roads." He laughed. "Shit. Then we painted a long pipe black and hung a beaded Indian belt over it and set it up where they could see it. They decided that it was a fifty-caliber machine gun."

Molly held the slug in her hand. It was warm, flat on one

side where it had hit a rock. It was heavier than it looked like it should be. It was an ugly thing, and she wanted to throw it on the ground, but she felt that Will Two Horses wanted her to keep it, that he'd given it to her as more than just a curiosity. She put it into her jeans pocket and stuffed her hands into his coat. She pulled the collar up around her ears, thankful that he had loaned it to her. She felt mildly guilty, that he must be cold. The wind blew fitfully, spraying them occasionally with fine sand that stung her eyes.

"You said there were negotiations. What did your side want?"

"Not much, just that the government obey the law. We wanted a presidential treaty commission to review our Dakota treaty of 1868. Not a *new* treaty, understand, we simply wanted the president to go over and implement the old, legal treaty. We also wanted the government to prosecute our crooked tribal officials and their goon squads for criminal actions and harassments against us. In other words, we were asking the United States government to implement and obey their own laws."

"And?"

"And they turned us down, of course. Just like they always have."

Will looked back at the little town, at the Catholic church on the north side, and remembered.

That's when they had the first killing. He had been alerted that three Cessna airplanes were going to fly over and parachute in some badly needed supplies. He had been assigned to the detail that would collect the supplies because he was one of the fastest runners in the camp. He was known variously as Black Sneaker, Deer Boy, Night Hawk, and a few other names that he had collected in honor of his speed.

• •

They waited in the Hawk Eye bunker, he and two other kids, one a girl with long black hair that floated out behind her as she ran, and a boy who was new but who would become his friend. The bunker had a bird's eye painted on top so the planes knew where to make the drop. They waited and listened and soon enough they heard the far-off buzz of the approaching airplane. They crawled out and squatted behind the bunker and watched as five parachutes bloomed high in the sky, the supply canisters hanging beneath them. The wind pushed the parachutes slightly off course, and Will heard the other boy curse as they watched them crumple to the ground fifty yards in front of the bunker.

"Get them at night?" the other boy asked.

"We need them now," the girl said. "One of them's got medicine that they need at the clinic."

Will leaned out and looked at the canisters lying in the dirt. There was no real cover between the bunker and the army outposts in the hill beyond. But if the wind picked up it could catch the parachutes and drag the canisters even farther away. "Let's do it," he said. "We can get in at least three of them before they start anything." The others agreed so he stuck his head into the bunker and told the two Indians inside what they were going to do.

As he ran he imagined that his sneakers were not high-top Keds, but two eagles, young ones, eagles that would fly him to the canisters. There he would become a deer, a buck with a wide rack of horns and powerful legs to lift and run. If he fought he would become a bear, a grizzly. He stopped and dropped to the ground, unstrapping the canister from the parachute, working quickly but carefully. He saw the girl, who was quicker than he, loosen the straps on her canister and pick it up and begin her run back. He would pass her on the way, he was Deer Man, he was the fastest. The first shot kicked up the dirt ten yards away, the second halved the distance. He shouted at the other boy, who was still struggling to unstrap the parachute, to forget it and head for the bunker. He shouldered his own canister and started to run. The girl still led, the unencumbered boy was next, and Will was last.

The bullets whined by his head. He could see the puffs of blasted cinderblock as the bullets began to pound the already scarred gray surface. "The church," he shouted, "the church!" The girl in front swerved to the left and headed for the Catholic church that sat another fifty yards beyond the bunker.

They made it inside, throwing open the door and diving for the floor as the first bullets began chewing into the wooden walls. The canisters hit the floor and rolled crazily, spinning in circles as several sleepers who had been resting on bunks shouted and fell to the floor.

Frank Sun Boy Early River slept soundly on one of the bunks. Frank was an Apache who had hitchhiked cross-country from North Carolina to be with his brothers at Wounded Knee. His specialty was crossing the army lines at night to bring in people and supplies. He had been out all the night before, practicing his trade, and he was very tired. The sound of firing, kids, canisters hitting the floor, and shouting woke him up. He sat up in his bunk. Will watched him sit up just as a thirty-caliber bullet came through the wall and smashed through Frank's head. Blood sprayed the room, exploding in a red mist that hung suspended in the air as Frank's body flipped off the bunk onto the floor. The warning in Will's throat came out as a howl of horror, no thought, no word, just a long howl of pain and shock as Frank Sun Boy Early River kicked once and lay still in the widening pool of blood that Will could smell and taste. Could *still* smell and taste.

• •

"Will?" She shook his arm. He spun toward her and for a moment she saw something in his eyes, a sort of madness that frightened her, a look of unfocused horror. She stumbled back, away from him, tripped over a rock and went down. And then he was over her, the look now changed, picking her up off the ground, and for just a moment she was weightless in his arms. The look in his eyes frightened her in another way because she felt an answer in herself, felt it rise unbidden and somehow confirm a thing that had been there between them all day and now bubbled to the surface where they could both see it, feel it. *No,* she thought, *I will not.*

Chapter 15

Alex dressed quickly in the dim light of the room where they slept. He could see Abraham, lying on his pallet, watching him. He pulled on his blue jacket, the zipper making a slight, alien sound that had never been heard in this time or world. Alex felt the weight of his Walkman in the pocket of the jacket. He pulled it out, carefully wrapping the cord from the headset around the body of the machine. He placed it under his small pile of spare clothing on the shelf near his thin mattress. He had not played it in this time, afraid that he might run down the batteries, not knowing how long they might last or even if there was any reason to hoard their precious power. He knew Abraham was watching, and he knew that no one would touch his things. They were four men sleeping in the same room and their privacy was as absolute as honesty and courtesy could afford. Uncle was already gone to his work at the restaurant, and after Alex left, Abraham would rise, and after him Elias.

He crossed the long mall area in front of Machinery Hall on his way to the administration section of the Public Comfort Station. He was on his way to Chief of Police Brannon's office, as the chief had ordered, and he had the distinct impression that if he was late things would not go well. First thing in the morning, Brannon had said. Alex had a quick mental image of himself wearing a sign (I WAS LATE) inside one of the large wheels of the dogcycle, being prodded by the black man with the stick as the chief stood aside and watched with a smile.

Alex was sitting in a small anteroom when the chief strode in, glanced at him, and pushed through a low wooden railing that separated the room into two sections. He was dressed in the same tight high-buttoned uniform he had worn the day before. The chief took off his hat, hung it on a coatrack, and went into his office. There was no secretary.

Alex wondered, as he sat waiting to be called, if secretaries had been invented yet. He mentally catalogued the missing items from the office: no telephones, switchboards, receptionists, typewriters, or computers. No noise. There were two wooden file cabinets and a set of shelves with pigeonholes for mail. Next he would be counting the boards in the walls. He felt as if he were waiting to see the principal.

"Balfour," the chief said from the other room. Alex walked into the inner office. Brannon sat behind a wide old-fashioned desk that was littered with various forms and papers. His rosy complexion denoted either health or an early-morning drinking habit. He studied Alex carefully.

"Mr. Balfour," Brannon began mildly, his voice a pleasant tenor, "why do you live with niggers?"

Alex felt himself flush. "Is there a law against it? Living with colored people?" he asked, trying to keep his tone vaguely respectful.

Brannon glanced at the papers on his desk as if there might, indeed, be a law, and it might be somewhere handy in the pile. He shook his head. "No. At least there isn't a written law. Not yet anyway. But it's still highly unusual." He looked back up at Alex. His gaze was steady, giving no clue to thought or purpose or even mood.

Alex shrugged, unsure of what response would be best under the circumstances. He had learned, or was in the constant process of learning, that measuring the attitudes of this time with a modern yardstick usually led him into complicated territory where each mistake led to another until he had built himself an elaborate trap. One that he usually promptly and neatly fell into.

"I needed a place to stay when I arrived and Abraham and his friends were kind enough to provide one."

Brannon nodded. "But you continue to reside with these men."

"We have," Alex said, searching for the correct words, "become friends." He thought about it and wondered if it was true, if the web of intersecting needs that made up his relationship with Abraham and Elias and Uncle constituted a form of friendship. He thought it did, for his own part, but the longer he stayed with the others the less he seemed to know about what they felt about him.

"Let me tell you something, Mr. Balfour. I don't know where you come from . . ."

"New York," Alex interrupted.

Brannon waved his hand. "All right, New York. But here in Philadelphia we have a set of standards that generally precludes the mixing of the races. It certainly precludes a white man living in some shantytown shack with a bunch of coloreds. It breaks a rule, you see, and when rules get broken the next thing that happens is that laws get broken, and when that happens it upsets me. We've a wonderful fair here, but it's a very delicate operation." He leaned back in his chair and clasped his hands over his stomach. "In a way it's much like one of those machines they've got on display. Complicated. But as long as all of the pieces, the gears, rods, belts, and pulleys, all remain in their proper places doing their proper work then everything runs along smoothly. But as soon as one of the parts gets out of alignment, well, then the whole thing is liable to seize up and go straight to hell.

"Now," he paused while he shuffled through some of the papers in front of him, "that little incident you were involved in yesterday. That sort of thing happens because people aren't behaving the way they're supposed to. We've that nigger Abraham mixing in with the two Indians. And we have you mixing in with the niggers. And we have that fool who wanted to get into the tepee and steal something or mess with the woman or whatever he wanted to do. At any rate, it was the combination of these factors that made a small incident, a minor breakdown of the machine, suddenly threaten the entire mechanism."

"It was hardly our fault that . . ." Alex interrupted, his hand going unconsciously to the scab over his eye where he'd been hit with the rock.

"I'll thank you to wait until I've finished, Mr. Balfour," Brannon said, raising his voice. "You see, you're still making the same mistake. It *was* your fault because you were involved in a situation that you had no business to be in. You and that Abraham. We've been watching him. If we weren't going to get rid of the Indians, I'd have stopped him some time ago." He paused.

"What I want you to do, Mr. Balfour, is several things. Soon General Custer will be with us to take care of his Indians. It was a pretty idea to have them on display, but I've finally convinced the Centennial Committee that it's too dangerous to continue. That little fracas yesterday put the capstone on my arguments. General Custer is going to come and make arrangements for P. T. Barnum to take the chief and the woman off our hands. That damn Barnum's been hounding me about it from the day we brought them in here." He held his hands out palms up and smiled, as if Barnum had been badgering him night and day. "What I want you to do is make sure that your friend Abraham understands that this is white man's business, and that he's to stay away from the Indians until this affair is completed. Do you understand? He's to have nothing to do with the Indians. If he persists, he will surely lose his job, and perhaps more."

Alex stood and looked at the man while he tried to put it into perspective. The names alone were enough to give him pause: Custer? Coming here? P. T. Barnum? And how was Abraham going to act when told that his Indians were about to be sold to the circus like a couple of trick ponies?

"Negotiations will take several days, perhaps longer," Brannon went on. "But I want them out of here before we open. I want you to do what I've said, and then report back to me on

Thursday about this matter. I want to know if we're going to have any problems." He stopped and examined Alex carefully.

"You look perplexed, Mr. Balfour, but there's nothing for you to question. It's very simple. You're part of the machine. If you do what's expected, everything will continue to run smoothly. You take care of the nigger, and we'll take care of the Indians. Report back here on Thursday." He stood.

"Wait a minute," Alex said. He glanced around the room, aware for the first time that there wasn't even a window to relieve the feeling of claustrophobia that had begun to settle around him. "You can't just sell people like cattle. You just had a war that settled that point."

"No, Mr. Balfour. Lincoln said that you can't sell a black man. He didn't mention anything about Indians. Indians are our enemies. They are killing honest white settlers, and there are no restrictions on our behavior toward them. You say they can't be sold? They could be *killed*. Don't you find that a more exacting punishment? General Custer killed the sons and husbands and friends of these particular redskins, but he graciously saved their lives. They should be grateful. Besides, these things are not for you to question."

"But . . ."

"Be quiet." He walked around the desk and stood beside Alex. He was slightly taller and broader and the uniform gave him an added presence. Let me tell you something." He leaned close. Alex could smell him now, old sweat in the wool uniform, the coffee and breakfast on his breath. "If you get in my way you'll rue the day you ever showed up in my bailiwick. I'm a tolerant man, Mr. Balfour. Except when it comes to niggers. And Indians. I'll protect them as long as they're part of the exposition, that being part of my job. But don't push me. I've got my limits when it comes to niggers and Indians."

• •

Alex climbed into the horse-drawn carriage and paid his seven-cent fare, found a seat along the open side, and sat down on the hard wooden bench. He saw only a few other passengers. The Centennial was the last stop on the line out of Philadelphia before the vehicle turned around to take passengers back to the city. The carriage jerked forward and he tried to shake off the encounter with Brannon, tried to make sense of it and decide what he should do.

The carriage rode on a set of tracks and was pulled by two weary-looking horses with sway backs and blinkers. This was his first trip into Philadelphia in 1876. He would have rather spent the time just looking, but Brannon kept getting in the way of the scenery.

As he understood it, he was supposed to keep Abraham away from the Indians until P. T. Parnum came and bought them from Gen. George Armstrong Custer. It echoed like some strange joke. But it was no joke, he was certain of that. As he looked from the long bridge over the Schuylkill River he could see several fishing boats and a small ornate steamboat. A line of passengers stood at the rail of the white steamboat. One of them waved and Alex waved back.

As the carriage moved through the crowded city streets, he felt a cold squeeze of apprehension, not just because of the Indians, but because the changing scene outside the carriage showed that he was entering a new and dangerous world. A world that smelled of burning coal, horse manure, wet garbage, and odors that hinted at worse. Here crowds of men and women walked or rode along the muddy, sometimes paved, sometimes unpaved, quagmirelike streets. Here rows of shops displayed a forest of gaudy signs advertising hundreds of unfamiliar products. Around it all was a whirl of shouting men, the din of construction, and the sounds of horse-drawn traffic, all compounded by sheer weight, size, and numbers into a solid sense of corporeality that seemed impenetrable. He thought about all the dangers of this world that he had tried to ignore up to now: cholera, yellow fever, all manner of contagious diseases, rotten meat, adulterated food, criminals, lunatics, thought about them and realized that he was as prey to them as anyone else. Even if he had an advanced knowledge of these dangers, in the end, there was little he could do to protect himself.

It was too much. For once his curiosity and enthusiasm were overwhelmed. The motion of the carriage over the rough cobblestones made him sick to his stomach. He closed his eyes and leaned forward, covering his ears with his hands.

"Excuse me, but are you all right?" a man said, sitting down on the bench next to him.

Alex sat up and took a deep breath. He looked at the concern on the man's face. "Yes," he said, and as he said it he realized that he probably was. These moments of paranoia might be justified, this world *was* a dangerous place, but so was New York City in his own time. And here was a stranger who was concerned, someone who was offering help. He remembered his first day at the exposition when Abraham came to his rescue. There was danger, but there was also kindness.

"It's a beautiful day," the man said, sitting back in the seat. "Spring is here, that's for certain."

The bus lurched as it rode over a switch on the rails. Alex held on to the side of the seat, but the man beside him, obviously more experienced, swayed with the movement and remained firmly upright. He was a big man with a large, impressive head and a rough beard. His face seemed comforting, and, at the same time, familiar. He was wearing a linen shirt with a scarf thrown over the shoulder and rough workman's pants stuffed into boots. Alex assumed he was a conductor or driver's assistant.

"Can you tell me," he asked the man, "Where I can find the LaFayette Hotel?"

"Certainly," the man said, nodding. "You're on Broad Street at the moment. This line rides the length of it. You'll want to stay on until you get to Sansom Avenue, which you'll find by the sign for the Adams Express Company that runs the length of the second floor of the corner building. The LaFayette is the third building down. There's a striped awning out front if I remember rightly. Quite a good hotel, one of the best in the city." He looked closely at Alex. "If you're all right I'll be getting back up front." Alex nodded. The man smiled and walked the length of the car. He had a pronounced limp, but he easily leaned out the open door and swung himself up on the high seat beside the driver. He put his hand on the driver's leg and they both laughed.

The horses pulled the bus down the narrow street and into increasingly heavy traffic. The driver shouted at the drivers of mule-drawn carts and horse-drawn carriages of all sorts. The bus slowed but never actually stopped. Vehicles seemed to vaguely obey the rule of keeping to the right, but other than that there were no rules that Alex could discern. What continually struck him was the sheer number of horses. He knew that horses were the primary means of transportation, but the knowledge of this did not prepare him for the endless equestrian parade. He tried to picture Broadway in New York during rush hour, and then replaced the cars in his mind with horses and mules, complete with the omnipresent odor of manure. Undoubtedly a mess, but would it be that much worse than modern exhaust-spewing, gridlocked traffic?

Alex saw his street coming up on the left. He stood and leaned out the side of the bus the way he had seen others do and dropped to the ground, jogging forward to keep his balance. He looked around, feeling that there should be some applause, but there was only the busy street swirling around him.

The LaFayette did indeed have a series of striped awnings that ran from the front out over the sidewalk. It was a tall, narrow building, five stories high, painted a light cream color with a small awning over each of the windows. It had an air of European opulence, built on solid American values. Fancy but democratic. The desk inside was manned by a thin clerk in a severe black suit who looked him over carefully. The small lobby smelled of cigars, sweat, perfume, and coal.

"Mr. Langhorne," Alex said. "He's expecting me."

The clerk waited a moment, as if deciding whether or not Alex should be admitted, then gave a slight nod. "Yes," he said, with a faintly English accent. "Room 412. Mr. Langhorne," he gave the name a special emphasis, "is in."

Chapter 16

The climb up four flights of stairs reminded Alex that the day of the elevator had not yet arrived. The dawn of that day, though, was soon to come. He'd seen several prototypes of elevators at the exhibition, where they were referred to as perpendicular railways. One notable example was developed by a man named Otis who drew a large crowd of onlookers when his machine was raised several stories while he calmly perched atop the passenger car. At the top of the lift he pulled out a large knife and dramatically cut the rope that held the car and himself high in the air. The car dropped about a foot before his newly patented Otis Lift Brake kept it from plunging Mr. Otis to certain death. The crowd gasped and Otis smiled and took a deep bow, acknowledging the applause.

By the time Alex reached the top floor he was breathing heavily. He knocked on the door and a voice within told him to enter, which he did, into a haze of gray-blue cigar smoke that hung in a low still cloud.

"Ah, the mysterious stranger. You lived through the climb, I see," Twain said, looking at him from the bed. He was dressed in trousers and a white shirt with a dark green dressing gown over-top. He was lying propped up on the bed with a notebook and a pen in hand. "I had them put me up here to discourage visitors," he said. His voice was high pitched and slightly rough, as if the cigars had exacted a price. "So far the only person who's been discouraged is myself." He pointed to a wing chair near the foot of the bed. "Sit, I won't be a moment."

Alex sat in the chair and watched him write in the notebook. Twain had told him the day before that he would like him to call the next morning at the hotel. He was to ask for him under the name of Mr. Langhorne. Twain said he was interested in a man who had read a book of his before it had been published.

The only explanation Alex had been able to fabricate was that he worked for the printer of the book and had read it there, but he saw nothing but trouble and more lies down that road. An alternative would have simply been not to come, but the chance to meet and talk with Mark Twain was too good to pass up.

Twain tore the page from the notebook and laid it on the small table by the bed. "A letter to my wife," he explained. "I've been relating my experiences of yesterday. I have mercifully left out the part where that ass told me I may not smoke; I fear it would be too much for her. I spent much of last night lying in this bed choosing that particular circle of purgatory to which I would consign him." Twain blew out a puff of smoke while he looked up at the ceiling.

"And?"

"Number seven, I believe. Usually reserved for the sexually incontinent. 'Here the rocky precipice hurls forth redundant flames.' The sufferers are forced to record illustrious instances of chastity, over and over, until they are cleansed."

"You are cruel."

"Well, he was a chuckleheaded ass. At least I put him in purgatory, where he has the opportunity to better himself. Which is more than he did for me." Twain swung his legs over the side of the bed and sat up. "It's true that I smoke fifteen cigars a day," he took the one he was currently smoking out of his mouth and put it carefully on the endtable, "but I only smoke them one at a time." He took off the dressing jacket and hung it in a closet. He took out a rumpled coat that

matched his pants and put it on. Alex noticed that Twain
didn't have the usual dirty neck and blackrimmed fingernails
common to the males of this time. He also didn't smell of
sweat or the standard eau de cologne used to cover it up.

Twain picked up the cigar and puffed it back to life. "It's
almost noon. Shall we have breakfast?"

• •

Twain walked with a peculiar rolling gait, a bit like a sailor
or a slightly bowlegged cowboy. He ambled along, head back,
peering out from under his bushy eyebrows, hands in his
pants pockets. He was a nonstop talker, pausing occasionally
to look in a shop window. People on the crowded walkway
would sometimes recognize him and call to him, and he
would give them a grave nod.

"I have given your premature compliment on my book *Tom
Sawyer* some thought," he said. They were walking by a store
advertised as C. G. Henderson's Cheap Book Store. Twain
stopped and looked through the front window at the books for
a moment. Of the piles of books displayed, Alex could make
out *Reading Without Tears,* and a number of old-world ro-
mances, precursors of the bodice-rippers of his own day.
Twain snorted at the selection and walked on. "I have utilized
Pinkerton's principles and come up with the following." He
stopped and pointed at Alex's chest with his cigar hand. "You,
sir, are newly arrived from what has been a very long journey." He paused for effect, looking pleased at Alex's obvious
surprise. "You have come here from England. I'd bet my last
penny on it." He stuck the cigar into his mouth and grasped
both his coat lapels. "I've struck the mark, haven't I? I can see
it in your eyes."

"Why do you say that?" Alex asked, almost laughing with
relief after what he had thought Twain had been about to say.
The foot traffic on the sidewalk broke around them like water
around a rock.

"Child's play, Mr. Balfour. You said you enjoyed my book,
Tom Sawyer. This book, as yet in the process of being printed,
is not available in this country. Because of copyright questions, though, may God damn all questions of copyright. It has

been published in England for some several months. Ergo, you must have read the book in England, recently, and as you are standing here before me you have obviously arrived here from there. There you are; Pinkerton would be proud."

Here was his out, handed to him on a silver platter. He wished he'd thought of it himself. Having recently arrived from England would have been a better story than his "I'm from New York" excuse, but it was too late to change it. "I'm sorry, but you're wrong," Alex said, unable to resist giving it his own twist. "Or at least partially wrong." Twain frowned, looking down at the ground, and began walking again. Alex fell in beside him.

"Actually, my sister, who lives in England with her husband, sent me a copy of your book. So, as I said, you were partially right."

Twain brightened up. "Hah. Well, yes." They walked along slowly. Even though it was the middle of the day the light was dim beneath the almost continual row of awnings that projected out from every storefront. "It reminds me of a story," Twain said. "A little boy, son of a farmer, comes running up to his father. 'Father, Father,' the boy cries. 'Come quick, the hired man's up in the hayloft with the maid. He's got his pants pulled down, and she's got her dress up. We've got to stop them! They're getting set to pee all over our hay!' "

Alex laughed.

"It's like the father told the boy. 'Son,' he says, 'you've got the facts right, but you've drawn the wrong conclusion.' As I have." He gave Alex a small smile and led them through a heavy etched-glass and wooden doorway into the cool gloom of a restaurant.

The room was large and dim, lit by gas lamps that hissed faintly. The air was thick with the odors of burning gas, fried food, onions, and cigars. Most of the heavy, round wooden tables in the room were occupied by well-dressed men and a few women. They ordered from handwritten menus that offered a lengthy list of dishes, weighted toward meat, light on the vegetables. The prices seemed ridiculously low. Still, he wondered, fingering the small wad of bills in his pocket, who was paying?

Alex listened in amazement as Twain requested a bowl of oatmeal, two lamb chops, hot biscuits with marmalade, an omelet with a side order of ham, a cup of coffee, and a glass of whiskey. Alex ordered a beer and a roast beef sandwich with boiled potatoes and pickles. Twain recommended the sandwich, noting that they were a new rage among the upper classes.

"Now tell me what the hell was going on out at the exhibition yesterday," Twain asked, after their food arrived. He speared a piece of ham with his fork.

"Before I tell you about yesterday's trouble, will you tell me what you are doing at the exhibition?" Alex asked. "And why no one is supposed to know that you are here? Which, I assume, was the point of telling me to ask for Mr. Langhorne at the hotel."

Twain nodded as he chewed. "My friend William Dean Howells is writing up the exhibition for the *Atlantic*. He's coming down in several weeks, after the official opening. I decided to slip down before he arrived just to see it for myself. I was fortunate to see the Crystal Palace at the 1853 World's Fair. I was seventeen years old and thought it the most beautiful thing I had ever seen." He stopped eating for a moment as he remembered. "A real fairy palace," he said quietly. He shook off the memory and went on in a louder voice. "It fell down in a fire five years later. No structural integrity to iron once you apply a little heat to it. There's a lesson about life and beauty in there somewhere, but I'll need another whiskey to find it." He took a bite of his omelet.

"I don't want anyone to know I'm here because I'll have to have an opinion if it gets out. I'd just as soon Howells did the criticism. I'm expected by the public to have an opinion—and it has got to be a humorous opinion—about everything I lay my eyes on. You watch, before I finish eating, someone will come by and ask me for an opinion."

"But everyone seems to know who you are anyway. The

clerk at the hotel makes it clear that your name isn't really Langhorne. People on the street seem to know you."

Twain nodded. He started to speak but was interrupted by the waiter.

"Is everything satisfactory, sir?" the waiter asked.

Twain looked pointedly at Alex. "Yes," Twain said, "quite satisfactory." The waiter moved away. "See, what did I tell you? At least I didn't have to lie or tell a joke. Anyway, I don't mind that ordinary people know I'm here—I just don't want any editors to know. If I'm here privately that's one thing, but if I'm here publicly that's another. There've been instances when a man's public opinion and his private one have been the same, or at least there have been thought to have been instances. But I don't like to take a chance on it, not in print. I do too much of that sort of thing already.

"Now," he pushed back his plate and signaled the waiter for another whiskey, "about those colored people and those Indians. That head policeman that showed up at the end of the fracas, he said you lived with the coloreds. Is that true?"

"Yes," Alex said.

"I live with them myself. We've a colored cook and a driver. But the way he said it I don't believe we're talking about the same thing. I believe he meant you actually live with them."

"That's right," Alex said, feeling a small flame of anger kick on at this persistent denigration of his living arrangement. "We sleep in the same room. We take our meals together, use the same utensils, drink from the same glasses, sit in the same chairs, and breathe the same air." He finished up with more heat than he had intended. "And I'm getting tired of having to explain it as if it were a crime." He looked down at the table and drew a deep breath. They were quiet for a moment.

Twain cleared his throat. "In some places it would be. A crime, that is, Or at least it would have been not too long ago. It's still a thing that's going to cause comment, if not worse. This obviously gravels you, but I'm afraid you will have to accept it. It will be the customary reaction."

Alex shook his head. "Once again I'm forced to mention

the recent war. Why did you fight it if not for this sort of freedom?"

Twain snorted. "Excuse me, Mr. Balfour, but the War Between the States was not fought so that you might live in the same room with Negroes nor eat from their dishes. The thought of which rather turns my stomach. Lincoln himself would have looked askance at it. And I did not fight in that war; I retreated from it, all the way across the continent to the Nevada Territory." He waved a hand. "Be that as it may, might we return to yesterday? You have chosen a unique group to ally yourself with. When I came upon you you were drawn up in a defensive formation for the protection of two Indians. Your giant nigger was deflecting the blows. . . ." He stopped at Alex's pained look. "Good God, man, what's the matter with you now?"

"Must you use the word *nigger*?"

Twain looked to the ceiling in supplication. "It's what they're called—have you stepped from the surface of the moon? You are the most thin-skinned man I have ever come across. It is common usage among all classes." He held up both of his hands. "All right, all right, I can see in your eyes that we're never to get on at this rate." He sighed. "Does the word *colored* offend your delicate sensibilities?" Alex shook his head. "Good. Now, about the Indians. Your conduct of yesterday implies that you are also an Indian lover." He lighted a fresh cigar and sipped his whiskey, not noticing Alex's reaction to the term *Indian lover*. "I'm surprised you hadn't found a Chinaman to drag in and protect while you were at it. And maybe an abused dog. Is it your profession, or are you just naturally inclined toward it? The Good Samaritan had nothing on you."

Alex peered through the cloud of cigar smoke trying to see if he was being put on. Twain's eyes were almost shut and his face was impassive, but this seemed to be his normal expression. He decided that he was being kidded, or if he wasn't, he was tired of taking offense. At any rate, he got the point.

"I'm afraid I wasn't doing much protecting," Alex said, touching the dried scab over his eye.

"Yes, you really were. As a white man you carried a certain amount of weight; you exerted a shielding influence, I am sure of that. The savages were fortunate to have you there."

"I thought the savages were on the other side of the fence throwing rocks. The people on the inside had done nothing to warrant the attack. It's not the first time they've been badgered. It just went further this time. The fault lay with the white men, not the Indians, not the colored men. There's no question of that. There were brutes there, there were savages, and they were all white."

Twain's eyes now seemed completely closed. His arms were crossed over his chest and he was slumped back in his chair. He seemed to either be thinking or on the point of sleep. There was an air about him of a man who was using only a small portion of his powers at any one time, of a great engine simply idling.

"Ah," Twain said softly, "bless your heart, Mr. Balfour, now you're going to weigh in against the nature of man."

"Is there any other way to characterize those men? I don't believe I've ever been in a situation where I've felt such base, evil intent as I did from that mob. You were there, you saw it, can you deny it?"

Twain opened his eyes a fraction of an inch, just enough for Alex to see them catch the light from one of the hissing gas lamps. "Deny it? Yes, I certainly do deny it. Those men were simply acting out their individual natures, to call them evil is to give them credit for something that is beyond them. In fact it is beyond all men. It would be as likely to call a steam engine evil. Or even good, for that matter."

"And so man is a machine, nothing more. Is that what you're leading up to?"

"Yes."

"I don't believe it. I can't believe it. It's an old analogy that doesn't hold up."

"Old is it?" Twain nodded to himself. "All right, since my proposition seems to have whiskers, at least as far as you are concerned, perhaps you'd like to show me my error. Firstly, what are the materials of which a steam engine is made?"

"I'm no engineer. Iron, steel, brass, various metals."

"All right. Where are these found?"

"In rocks. Look, are we about to enter into some sophistic argument over the nature of man?"

Twain appeared surprised. "Mr. Balfour, you're the one who brought it up, not I. You sit there throwing out notions of good and evil and at the first touch of argument you cry sophistry. Do you believe what you say because it's correct, or just because it's simple, easy to believe? Why are you so afraid of argument? Are you afraid that I might change your notions?"

"No, it's not that." He stopped and tried to work it out. Just what was it? He could come up with nothing more than the fact that he just was not used to it. To thinking this way. He hardly ever argued with anyone. He and Molly shared pretty much the same value system. When he taught he was the teacher, and he'd never had a student who really challenged him. He tried to think of a time, outside of a freshman dorm room, when he'd heard anyone discussing ideas of evil or good. Had he come to his own morality through discovery, or simply by default?

"All right," Alex said, surrendering. "Metal is found in rocks. Not in a pure state, in ores." It would at least be interesting to see how Twain made his point.

"Could you make a machine out of the metal found in this state?"

Alex shrugged. "I guess so. It would be very weak, though."

"How would you make it stronger?"

"You'd have to mine the metals, treat them. Smelt the iron then turn it into steel. Combine whatever metals make up brass. This would make them stronger. Then you could build your machine."

"And this would be a better machine, you'd be able to do more with it."

Twain's face betrayed nothing. He smoked his cigar and asked the questions without signaling his intent. Alex could see where he was being led but was unable to stop the process.

"So on one hand," Twain said, "we have a machine built of

stone without much merit. On the other we have a fine metal one, capable of doing much work. Would you say that the one had more merit than the other?"

"Yes. Obviously."

"More personal merit?"

"What does that mean?"

"Would the machine be personally entitled to the credit of its own performance?"

"No, we're talking about machines. Machines simply do what they are built for. The one is neither good nor is the other bad, there's nothing personal about it. It has no choice in the matter. And I assume that your argument is that man is a machine so there is no personal merit in his performance either."

"Yes. What's the difference between the stone engine and the metal one? Shall we call it training, education? Shall we call the stone engine a savage, and the metal one civilized? The original rock contained the stuff of which the steel one was built, but along with a lot of sulfur and stone and other inborn heredities, brought down from the old geologic ages. Prejudices, let us call them. Prejudices which nothing within the rock itself had either the power or the desire to remove. These impurities, prejudices, had to be removed by outside influences, or not at all."

The waiter was standing by the table with the bill. Twain took it, to Alex's relief, and paid it. He picked up his glass and drank the last of his whiskey.

"Let us continue this discussion on the way to the exhibition. I want to go back and find something. I made a few inquiries before I left yesterday. All right?"

They both stood. Alex found that the two beers he'd had with lunch had left him a bit light-headed. It was the first alcohol, besides Uncle's dandelion wine, that he'd had since he'd come. One more beer and he'd be ready to discuss the nature of man as long as Twain wanted. Well, maybe two more beers.

Chapter 17

On the way back to the hotel, they passed an organ grinder with a monkey. The monkey was dressed in a tiny red suit and a fez and was begging with a tin cup. The only people who seemed to notice the organ grinder were the swarms of scruffy children who raced along the sidewalks, dodging the pedestrians and stopping only to yell at the monkey.

Alex knew that the cities of this time were overrun with these children, most of them orphans or the abandoned offspring of immigrants and prostitutes. They lived in boxes and barrels and cellar doorways, and they stayed alive by begging, stealing, and collecting and selling old rags and bones. Twain didn't seem to notice the children, as if they were so much a part of normal life they were not to be remarked upon. In fact, he wasn't remarking on much of anything but seemed to be mulling something over in his mind.

"You know, Mr. Balfour, you're a curious man," he said, without looking at Alex. "I referred to you as the mysterious stranger earlier today. I meant it." He stopped to light up a new cigar.

"There's nothing very mysterious about me," Alex said. He would just as soon dispense with this particular topic.

"No," Twain waved his hand, "you can't deny it. First, there's your speech. It's what convinced me that you'd just returned from abroad. I thought you'd picked up some mongrel accent over there, but that's not it. I can see that myself now."

"It's a New York accent," Alex said.

"No, no," Twain said, waving the cigar around. "I know New York. I'm quite familiar with New Yorkers. Your speech is shorter, clipped, as if the wool's been sheared off it. I can't quite put my finger on it." They reached the corner and Twain stopped. "We'll wait for the coach here." They were still in the shade of an awning. Twain rubbed his hands together and said, "It's a cool day, isn't it?" He buttoned the top button of his coat.

Alex agreed and zipped up his jacket.

"Hah!" Twain crowed, leaning close to Alex. "And what the hell is that?" he said, bending over and peering at Alex's zipper. "I noticed that damn thing when you came in this morning. The man's coat has no buttons, I said to myself. Just a curious strip of perforated metal up either side of the front. Brass, isn't it?"

"Uh, yes, I guess," Alex said. He suddenly had a vision of the changed future: Mark Twain, Inventor of the Zipper. No *Huckleberry Finn.* No wellspring from which Hemingway would claim the roots and greatness of the modern American novel.

"Look . . ." Alex began. Twain pointed at the zipper pull and raised his eyebrows. "Sure," Alex said, "but listen . . ." Twain tugged the zipper down a few inches then back up. A beatific look came over his face.

"Now, wait a minute," Alex said, stepping back. "All right, it's a new invention. But I don't have a patent on it yet. I didn't want anyone to see it."

"I can understand that," Twain said. "I'm an inventor myself. Mark Twain's Self-Pasting Scrapbook. Ever heard of it?" Alex shook his head. "No? Well, it brings in money every year. But this," he reached out and tapped the zipper, "this could be the boss. What do you call it?"

"A zipper."

"Zipper? Zipper. Not bad. You don't need an investor, do you?"

"No. Look, could you just forget about it? Isn't that the bus coming?"

Twain looked down the street. The horse-drawn coach was half a block away. "Oh, Christ," Twain said. He turned around and pulled up his coat collar.

"What's the matter?" Alex asked.

"It's that ass Whitman," Twain said. "Up there with the driver."

Alex looked at the man beside the driver as the coach stopped in front of them. It was the same burly, bearded man who had helped him on his trip over from the exhibition. Alex stepped up into the coach as several passengers jumped off the side onto the street. "No!" Twain whispered urgently.

Alex handed up his fare.

"Well, my friend, I see you're looking fit now," the bearded man said, taking the coins.

"Yes," Alex said. "Thanks again." He walked back into the car and sat down. Twain, now up on the bottom platform, glared back at Alex. He was all hunched over to the side like a cripple, his face turned away. He held his fare up in the air without looking and shuffled down the aisle. He dragged by Alex and went to the last seat in the coach. He beckoned as he slumped down.

Alex went back and sat down. "What's the matter with you?" he asked.

"I told you," Twain said in a low voice. "It's Walt Whitman. The pornographer. Don't you know who he is?"

Alex leaned out of the seat and looked at the backs of the men up front. Now that it was pointed out to him he could see it. His image of Whitman had always been from the famous Eakins photographs, taken when Whitman was very old. Large domed head with the halo of wispy hair, the sad eyes and the flowing white beard. This Whitman appeared to be in his mid-fifties and, aside from the limp Alex had noticed on his trip into town, hale and hearty.

Alex sat back up in the seat. "*Leaves of Grass,* right?" For a second he wondered if he'd just brought up another book that had yet to be published.

"*Leaves of Smut,*" Twain said. "I had to throw the book in the furnace. I was afraid my wife or, God forbid, one of my daughters might find it. Filthy stuff. Certainly not poetry." He laughed humorlessly. "The man's made a career out of one book. He adds more poems and prints up new editions. He actually writes his own reviews and submits them to magazines under false names. Everybody knows it. He's shameless." He shook his head.

"But you've got to admit there's a strength to his work."

"Oh, yes," Twain laughed again, "it's strong all right. No question of that. He sent a copy of the first edition to Emerson, who wrote—and God knows what was in his addled head when he did it—that it was full of wonderful wit and wisdom. So our friend Whitman immediately printed up another edition with the letter reproduced in full. You can imagine how that went over up in Boston. I did get a laugh out of that."

"But why are you hiding from him?"

"I didn't want him to recognize me. He collars anyone of any importance and puffs his book. It's vile work. I don't want anything to do with it."

Alex briefly considered going up and asking for an autograph. "I was pretty much under the impression that he was generally unknown."

Twain looked at him with pain. "That's what he'd like you to believe. I tell you, the man gets more press than anyone except that drunkard Poe. Both of them are forever being touted as the unknown American Genius. At least Poe had the decency to drink himself to death."

"He seemed nice enough to me," Alex said lamely. "Whitman, I mean. I never met Poe."

Twain glowered at him and slumped even lower into the seat. He put his hand to his forehead, shielding his eyes. "I'm going to just sit here until we get to the other end. If he gets down and heads in our direction let me know and I'll throw myself off into the street. Or into the river, I wouldn't care which."

"You don't want to discuss the nature of man anymore?"

"Not now," Twain hissed.

"Gee," Alex said, "that's too bad."

• •

They spent the three-mile coach ride in silence as Twain stayed slouched in the seat. His glower would deepen as snatches of song and laughter from Whitman and the driver occasionally floated to the rear of the coach. Alex showed his employee card at the gate and Twain the press pass he'd been issued by the Centennial Commission.

"I did some checking after I left you yesterday, Mr. Balfour," Twain said, as they pushed through the gate. "Over at the press office. What we want now is the French Department in the Main Building."

"This way," Alex said, pointing to the large building to their left. "Which brings up a point. Why don't you call me Alex and I'll call you . . . what should I call you?"

"There are a host of names I'd prefer you didn't use, but I assume you are speaking of familiar names. Most people refer to me as Twain. Some friends find it difficult to use my pen name, thinking it less natural, but after twenty-some years of use it has become as familiar to me as either Sam or Clemens. Perhaps more so. Call me Mark. Even though I'm traveling, as they say, incognito, it's a common enough name." He paused for a moment and looked up at the fountain with the barebreasted women holding up trays of cascading water. I stole the name from an old river pilot who wrote, or thought he could write. After he died it seemed of little use to him so I appropriated it."

It was warmer in the Main Building. Twain unbuttoned his coat and watched with interest as Alex unzipped his jacket. Alex pointed down the broad main aisle to the scarlet banner that announced the French Department.

Workmen were still hammering away in some of the exhibits, but one of the organs seemed to be in good working order. It pumped out a popular tune that Alex had heard people humming over the last few days. Catchy songs seemed to sweep through the population. He would hear them being hummed and sung by everyone, and then they would disappear, to be replaced as quickly as they had come. In this age without radio, records, or television, people sang to themselves and to each other with no self-consciousness as far as Alex could see.

The walls of the French Department were covered with huge elaborate tapestries in brilliant colors. The display cases held examples of Pallisey ware, bronze statuary, and a myriad of clocks. Next to a player piano, billed as the world's first, was a large piece of plate glass twelve by twenty-five feet. This exhibit puzzled Alex since it was the sheet of glass that was the exhibit. But it stopped Twain in midsentence.

"It's so clear," Twain said in a tone of wonder.

"It's glass," Alex said. "It's supposed to be clear."

"But it's so big," Twain said.

"It's not *that* big," Alex said.

"You've seen bigger?"

Yes, I certainly have, Alex thought. On many department store windows. But by now it had sunk in that for this time, this was a very large piece of glass, maybe the largest piece of glass in the world. To him it was perfectly ordinary, to these people it was a wonder of the age.

"All right," he said, "it's a huge piece of glass. I've never seen a bigger one."

Twain nodded with satisfaction. "Too bad it was the goddamn French who manufactured it."

They moved on to the carriage exhibit and there they found it, in a case all to itself, the Cynophere.

It was identical to the one that the chief of police rode. The wide five-foot-high wheels, the little steering rod attached to the small front wheel. The only missing accouterments were the dogs, and the black man with the stick shouting, *go, dogs, go, you dogs.*

" 'Cynophere,' " Twain read from a label on the front of the glass case. " 'Invented by M. Huret of Paris and exhibited by M. Norbert Belvalette, the celebrated Parisian carriage-maker. The finest vehicular achievement of the age.' Modest, aren't they?" he said to Alex and then continued to read. " 'The carriage is made of iron and steel and is both light and strong. The inside of each wheel is a treadway of perforated sheet iron. The vehicle is capable of speeds of ten to twelve miles per hour and is eminently suitable for short-distance commuting. A stock company is being organized in the United States and is interested in reaching interested investors.' " Twain took out a cigar and stuck it in his mouth. "Hmmm," he mused.

"What do you think?" he asked Alex.

"What do you mean?"

"As an investment," Twain said. "I think it has possibilities. If a person got in early with this it could be the Big Bonanza. How much does a dog eat, anyway? Less than a horse, right? You don't even have to buy them. They wander around all over the place. Dogs are free. Think about it."

Alex's first impulse was to tell him he was crazy. But then he thought about the giant sheet of glass. Twain couldn't know that the automobile was just around the corner, that steam power was about to give way to the petroleum age. He made a concerted effort to see it through nineteenth-century eyes. He waited while he tried to conjure up this vision. No, it was still a stupid idea.

"It's crazy!" Alex said. "Look at it, it's too heavy. You'd have to have two monster dogs like Brannon uses. To say nothing of the guy who runs along with the stick."

"You're right, the guy with the stick has got to eat, too. Besides, what if a cat ran across the road? It's all right here where you haven't got much of a cat population, but in the real world you'd be asking for trouble." He chewed on the end of his cigar. "There probably aren't any cats in France," he said, almost to himself. "They probably ate them all." He turned to Alex. "As a matter of fact, I'm surprised they even have any dogs left." He turned back to the machine. "Oh, well. It seemed like a good idea."

Alex led them back through the exhibit to the main hallway. They sat on one of the benches that ran down the center of the aisle.

"If they don't stop playing that goddamn tune I'm going to

shoot the organ player," Twain said. The organ was playing the same melody it had been playing when they came in.

"I don't know," Alex said. "It's kind of catchy."

"That's the problem. It gets caught in your brain until you can't get rid of it. Our cook was singing it the day I left Hartford." He sang along with the organ, " 'It certainly is most absurd / The fact can never be / My great grandaddy never was / Monkey up a tree.' There, now it'll be stuck in your head—maybe I'll be free of it. By the way, I'm leaving town tonight."

Alex had a sinking feeling. He'd come to think of Twain as a friend even though he'd only known him for one day.

"I've got to go to New York on business. Besides, they let you smoke in New York." He took the unlit cigar out of his mouth and looked at it. "I've got an idea for an article. I'll be back in a few days."

Alex felt his spirits rise again. He nodded.

"Get me a room at one of the hotels here on the grounds. Tell them I'm aware that they're not officially open, but that I'll put up with any inconveniences. Make it in the name of Sam Langhorne."

They stood up and Twain held out his hand. Alex shook it.

"It's been interesting, Alex. I still haven't figured out what it is about you, but I'll get it yet. Meanwhile, I hope that little song won't drive you crazy."

The organ had stopped but Alex realized that he was still singing the refrain in his head.

"It's called 'Too Thin, or Darwin's Little Joke,' " Twain said.

"Some joke," Alex said.

Chapter 18

John Raven lay on his back looking up into the sky. He was trying to see the exact moment when the stars disappear, the true moment of dawn, the beginning of day. Might as well try to catch the ghost of a bird, he thought. Or the wind. He watched the stars as they dimmed, and then there were no stars. As if he had fallen asleep. As if he were caught in some subtle shift that shunted men past that point without awareness, without thought. If he could find that moment, could exist within it, experience it, he thought, he could leave the night and become the day. Perhaps touch the sun.

His sleeping bag was warm. Nearby he could hear his horse pulling at the dry grass. It was a familiar sound, a tearing, and then the wet click of the horse's teeth. He drifted toward sleep. He was in a pocket canyon on the low slope of the Black Hills, the horse hobbled deeper in the trees. He had not gone north, into the Badlands as they would expect. A man could get lost in there, they would say, a man could get lost in there forever. Yes. But who would wish to be lost forever?

He'd gone south, then west. He would go around the Great Turtle, the Black Hills, skirt the edges, head north until he reached his next stand. Then he would fight, and they would know that it was not over, not forgotten, that there were those who would fight in the old ways until others would join them, and then still others, until there were enough. Or they would die.

He traveled at night and slept in the day. The land was spare and lonely and no one had seen him. No one would expect him. He had food, a little, and coffee to brew on the tiny fires he allowed himself. For a moment he remembered his father in the days when they all lived together, before the bad drinking, before his father left. He remembered how they would camp in the hills, just the two of them, away from the old silver trailer where they lived, and the trash heap of broken utensils and old cans, away from his mother and her whiskey. His father would tell him the stories of the old ways. He would teach him to make the small traps to catch rabbits and squirrels, how to build a smokeless fire in a pit, how to live off a land that many saw as barren, but others, like his father, saw as full of life, and giving of life.

He rolled over and listened to his horse chew. It was a sound that would bring sleep. The sound of not-chewing would bring him out of sleep, and out of the warm bag, but for now there was no danger. Perhaps he would dream tonight. Perhaps he would dream of Crazy Horse, his father.

Chapter 19

He couldn't bring himself to tell Abraham they were going to sell the Indians. Not until he'd considered all the alternatives. The look of confusion and bewilderment that would come as the man tried to understand, and worse, understand and be *reasonable,* kept Alex from it. He would not deliver that blow. It was as if he'd been asked to club a tame deer.

"I can't help the Indians? Can't take them no more food?"

Alex shook his head, unable to look the man in the eye.

"The chief say that? That policeman say I can't help them no more?"

Alex nodded. "That's what he told me."

"But why? What could be the reason for it?"

Alex sighed. "He said that it just leads to trouble. That if you keep hanging around the Indians, people are going to get mad, and there'll be trouble like yesterday. More and more people are coming in here every day, the nearer we get to the opening. Not all of them are going to understand what you're doing. Most of them hate Indians. There's bound to be trouble."

Abraham patiently watched while Alex delivered his explanation. "But," Abraham said, shaking his head, "what happened yesterday happened because that white boy make trouble. We the ones got hurt, just trying to protect ourselves. It don't make no sense."

It never will, Alex thought. And there doesn't seem to be anything I can do to explain it to you. Or change it. Because it doesn't have anything to do with right and wrong, which are the concepts that you intuitively understand and live by. Instead, it has to do with power and fear and prejudice, which are beyond you.

It's his eyes, Alex thought. There's no guile there, no wariness, nothing that says, *What's the catch? Don't bullshit me, I'm on to you.* He'd never seen eyes like that, not in his own time. Everyone then, back in New York, was too smart to behave that way, to *be* that way. The task was to find that nature in oneself, that simplicity. Failing that, the least he could do was not destroy it in one who had it.

"What will we do?" Abraham asked. "What will them Indians do?"

"I'll take care of them," Alex said. "You tell me what to do. You get their food ready; I'll take it to them." I'll take care of them, sure, until Custer sells them to Barnum for the circus, he thought. There's got to be an answer somewhere.

"You gonna look out for them? Just like it was me?"

"As near as I can."

Abraham nodded. He sat back in his chair. The door opened and Elias came in, glancing in their direction then looking closely at them, aware, by the attitudes of the two men, that some bond had been sealed, some bargain struck.

"You giving one of your lessons tonight, Alex?" Elias asked. "The chief of the police going to let you stay here with us niggers?"

Uncle followed Elias into the room. He put a bulky flour sack on his cooking bench. "We got sweet potatoes tonight. Some bacon." He went into the back room to take off his coat.

Elias pulled up one of the chairs and sat down. His mouth was still swollen where the rock had hit him. He tried to speak without moving his lips, giving him an even more impassive expression than normal. He resembled a goateed, thin-faced, irritable ventriloquist. "Something soft, Uncle," he said. "My mouth isn't up to anything difficult."

"Cook them potatoes till they soft as butter, just melt in that poor mouth." He opened the belly of the stove and poked the coals to life.

"What did the chief say this morning?" Elias asked. "Besides for you to stay away from us. I'm sure he told you that."

Alex nodded. "He said to keep Abraham away from the Indians."

"Of course," Elias said, his tone muted but still scornful, "keep away the one person that cares about them and let in all white boys looking for trouble. Yes, that makes sense."

"Don't make no sense at all," Abraham said.

"That's right, Abraham," Elias said, quietly. Uncle put the sweet potatoes on a grate inside the stove and came to sit at the table with them.

Alex looked around the table and saw that they all were looking at him. As if he were somehow responsible for Brannon's edict. Kill the messenger, he thought. Especially Elias. Tonight Elias seemed to burn with pain and bitterness.

"Let's not have any history lesson tonight," Elias said, coldly, his words as clipped and precise as he could make them. "Let's do something different. We've sat and listened as you've told us stories about our fine colored legislators, about school systems being established for colored people and poor whites, about all the good that's come out of the Reconstruction of the South." His voice trembled with controlled anger. "What I would like to know is when is it going to get good for *us*? When is there going to be some change? When can we stop having to put up with always being in the wrong? The answer to white society's problems, nine times out of ten, is *get rid of the nigger*. When the hell is that going to change?" He stopped, he was breathing heavily. The room was dead quiet; Abraham and Uncle were looking at Alex. "Forget the past. I know you're smart, we all know that. You've got information that we're never going to have," Elias went on. "So for our sake, give us something useful. Tell us what's going to happen. Tell us the future."

The sound of the potatoes beginning to split and hiss was loud in the silence. "I can't do that," Alex said. "I can't tell the future."

"Then, goddamn it, tell us what you think!" Elias's fist hit the table.

A sudden gust of wind blew the burlap curtains into the room. Rain began to fall outside, slowly at first and then heavily. Yes. He could tell them. He could tell them that before the year was over the Union troops would all be pulled out of the South, part of a deal to free the South in return for the presidency for Rutherford B. Hayes. That small wars would be fought between whites and blacks in South Carolina, Louisiana, and Florida, that lynchings and beatings would make it deadly for any black man or woman to attempt to achieve any measure of the freedoms promised them by law. That the Ku Klux Klan would soon achieve real power. That Reconstruction was over, and blacks would begin the long slide backward for the next hundred years until in his own time prejudice and stupidity would still rule in much of the country. That he could walk down any street in New York, or in fact any large city, and hear people using the word *nigger.* He could tell them that, and he would see any hope they had for the future die. Because they would believe him. They had seen too much of the past to doubt him. Let them live, he thought, let them at least have hope.

He shook his head. Elias snorted and stood up, his chair scraping loudly, his disgust evident. "Just what good are you, anyway?" he asked. "What the hell are you doing here? Why do you stay? You're like some vulture sitting on a limb, waiting. What for? What is it you want with us? What good can you do with your history, your little lessons. You know what we need, I know you do. Why don't you tell us something we can *use,* something valuable?" The black man walked to the window, pulled up the burlap, and looked out at the driving rain. He pulled the curtain closed and fastened it at the bottom.

Uncle stood up and went to the stove, opened the door and

peered in at the potatoes. He got a long fork and prodded one of them.

"Brother Rabbit," he said, straightening up and hanging the fork back on a nail. "One time Brother Rabbit was very hungry, had nothing to eat. His children and wife was crying. Rabbit going to have to leave that old hollow tree where they lived, get something for all of them, or they going to die." He took the cast-iron black frying pan from a hook on the wall and put it on the hot stove.

None of them broke the silence while Uncle worked. Uncle was telling a story.

"Brother Wolf was also hungry. He always hanging around that rabbit house just waiting for a chance to get in. Brother Rabbit knew of this, but still he had to go out, otherwise, like I said, they was to die. But before he left, Brother Rabbit told Mama Rabbit and the little ones not to let anyone in at the door, less they sing, 'You stay when I'm away. Stay and keep the home.'"

Uncle unwrapped a piece of bacon and sawed off thick slices. He threw them in the frying pan and rewrapped the chunk of meat. Abraham watched the old man with wide-open eyes. Elias stood by the window looking at the floor. Uncle lighted the kerosene lamp and the warm yellow flame seemed to dry out the damp air.

"But Brother Wolf was right out behind that ol' hollow tree and heard Brother Rabbit sing the song. When Rabbit left, that wolf sneak around the front and knock on that door. 'Who's there?' asked all the little rabbits. 'It's your daddy,' said ol' Wolf. 'Let me in.' Then he sing the song. 'You stay when I'm away. Stay and keep the home.' Well, those little baby rabbits and Mama Rabbit just roll on the floor laughing. 'You ain't our daddy,' one of them called out. 'You Mr. Wolf. Our daddy ain't got no cold, he sing sweeter than that. You just go away.'" Uncle got his long fork and pushed the thick slices of bacon around in the pan. The hot fat began to sizzle, and the smell of bacon mixed with the smell of roasting sweet potatoes.

"Now up in the top of that hollow tree was Mr. Turkey

Buzzard. He just sat there where he could see everything, down in the inside of that hollow sycamore where the rabbits lived, and also on the outside where Mr. Wolf was trying to get in. He don't say nothing, just sat up and watched.

"So that wolf go away, but he never give up. He goes out to the woods and practices and practices until he can sing just as sweet as Brother Rabbit ever could. Then he come back and hit on the door. 'Who's there?' cry the little ones. 'Who's at the door?' Then that ol' Wolf says in a voice sound just like Brother Rabbit, 'It's me, your daddy, and I come home with some *fine* food. Open the door!' Then he sing, 'You stay when I'm away. Stay and keep the home.' And he sings it just as sweet as Brother Rabbit. 'It's Daddy!' cried the little rabbits, 'and he brought something good to eat! Open the door! Open the door!' " Uncle turned over the slices of bacon. Abraham was leaning forward in his chair.

"But before they open it, that ol' Turkey Buzzard seen what's going on. He decide to take a hand. Buzzard ain't no friend of the wolf as they both fight over the same food. So ol' Buzzard stuck his head down the hollow of that tree and say in a big booming voice, 'Don't you open the door! Don't you open the door! It ain't your daddy. It's the wolf, and he fixin' to eat you all up.' Then that Buzzard just fly away. He off and flappin'. So the rabbits keep that door shut tight, and shout for Wolf to just go away 'cause they ain't going to open up. Brother Wolf, about this time he get sick and tired of this and want to get shed of it. He give the door one last kick and head on off into the woods where there's other animals to eat. And no butt-in buzzards to spoil things."

Uncle pushed the frying pan onto the back of the stove, opened up the belly, looked at the sweet potatoes and tested one with his fork. He pulled out a beat-up tin plate and forked the potatoes onto it. "Set the table," he said to Abraham. Abraham rose and took the pile of heavy china plates and handed them to Alex.

"Pretty soon Brother Rabbit comes home with a load of nice sparrow grass for everyone to eat. He hit on the door, sings his song, and waits to be let in. He waits and he waits, and after a good long wait finally they open the door and he hop inside. The whole family say, 'Hallelujah! Daddy is home! He's bring a load of sparrow grass.' And they commence to eat. When they full, they tell Brother Rabbit the story of how the wolf tried to trick them into opening up the door. 'I got all that part,' Brother Rabbit say when they had finished. 'What I want to know is how come I had to wait so long when I come home and hit on the door? And how come you decide to let me in anyway?'

" 'Well,' one of the little ones pipes up, 'Mama say it was the Lord God what told us it was Mr. Wolf. When *you* knock and sing, we just wait to see what the Lord say. When he didn't say nothing, we figured it must be Daddy and open the door. And there you was with the sparrow grass.' " Uncle put the frying pan with the bacon on the table. Alex could smell the hot pan burn the wooden table.

Everyone sat down and passed around the sweet potatoes and bacon. Alex waited for more of the story, but when Uncle stayed silent he decided that it must be over.

"I don't like buzzards," Abraham said. "They're a lonesome kind of bird. Baldheaded. Give me the creeps."

Alex cut open the black skin of the potato. Sweet fragrant steam billowed out. He wondered if it were against custom to ask what the point of the story was. He decided to keep his mouth shut and see what came of it.

"Buzzard's an ugly bird," Uncle said, "no question of it. God made all kinds of creatures." He looked hard at Elias, who was mashing up his potato. "Not up to us to judge which ones are useful and which ones aren't. Brother Rabbit might think that ol' buzzard was a beautiful thing."

"Brother Rabbit didn't know it was the buzzard that spoke," Elias said. He blew on a small spoonful of potato and put it carefully into his mouth. He chewed gently. "He thought it was the Lord."

"That's so," Uncle said, nodding his head, "that's so. Course some might say the Lord was speaking through ol' Mr. Buzzard. The Lord sometimes picks an unlikely vessel to carry his word. Might be the Lord, might just be ol' Buzzard. You never can tell, Elias, 'less you can see into the future. No man can do that. You just got to wait it out.''

They ate in silence. The sweet meat of the potato cut the salt of the bacon. They went well together, just like Uncle said.

Chapter 20

During the day John Raven dragged his sleeping bag farther into the woods. The trees were low and stunted on the slope of the hill, but they gave him cover. It was best to be careful. He crawled back into the bag and slept.

Later in the afternoon he rose and washed in the small nearby stream. He built a fire and cooked a cake of cornbread in his frying pan. The sounds of the woods were around him; birds, laying claim to territory, chattering squirrels, chipmunks, and occasionally the sounds of larger animals moving carefully. John Raven sat by his small fire and watched his cornbread cook, and he listened.

The men he had shot were trespassing. They had been told to stay off the reservation, but men such as these did not listen to what Indians told them. They knew they would eventually have their way, no matter what the Indians wanted. So John Raven had shot them. He did not kill them, there was time for that later, but he had hurt them. These men were the arms and legs of the companies they worked for. To kill them would have hindered the company, yes, but would have changed nothing. What he had wanted to do was to attract the attention of the company. Now the message would be clear.

What else could he do? Telling them to stay away did no good. If the tribe did nothing it was likely that the company would come in and search and find uranium. The tribe would receive little compensation and would be left with a ruined land and mountains of radioactive tailings. The people would sicken and die as they had done in other tribes who had let this company in. He could not let them do that to his people.

So now he had their attention. Now he must plan his next move, a move that would be both symbolic and very real. Men would have to die if he were to force a decision from those in decision-making positions. The only way for the Indian to progress in a white world was to react against it.

They had attempted to work within. Even in the beginning. In the old days, the Sioux transition to the white man's world had been relatively painless. They had maintained good herds of cattle, and their community spirit was strong. But eventually control of their land passed out of their hands and into the hands of the government. White farmers were allowed onto the land. The best lands were seized, and they were left with only the poorest, and little of that. They could not support themselves. Now the big mining companies would come in and take more of the land, cut roads, dump their wastes into the rivers, destroy what little was left. Without land, the people would die.

He pushed his hunting knife into the heart of the bread. He put the bread on a rock to cool and pulled it apart and covered the fire. The smell of the cornbread reminded him of his days in the white boarding schools, far away from the reservation. First they had cut his hair; long hair was bad, un-Christian. Then they showed him pictures of Jesus and his disciples, all of whom had long hair. Then they taught him that war was bad, that the life of the warrior was un-Christian. And then they would all sing "Onward Christian Soldiers." And so it went, until he escaped from their schools and made his way home.

And then his father had gone away and he had been left alone with his mother and her whiskey. And then he had been at Wounded Knee, and it was there that he learned his true calling, there he had had his first vision of his father. He had been set upon the path that led to this hillside. Soon he would come to the place where the soldiers would again die.

Chapter 21

Albert Riddle had them lined up in their morning formation. Albert was becoming more and more military as the opening day approached, conducting his morning inspection as if he were General Sherman, and the chair-pushers his crack cavalry troop. He wasn't, and as the line of ragged men showed, they weren't. But Albert played, as always, to some internal reviewing stand that saw only with Albert's eyes. To Albert the line of men and chairs stood at respectful rigid attention. The rolling chairs were transformed into fiery mounts, trembling with pent-up energy, tossing their fine heads, and stamping their hooves. Albert heard the distant sound of bugles and the whip and snap of flags in the cool, crisp air.

"All right, men," Albert said, pacing back and forth. "I've got a special assignment today. The commissioners have detailed us to help with the stock out at the yards." A small groan went up from the ranks.

"You there, Jenkins." Albert whirled on one of the groaners. "Who is Mrs. Mary G. Este and what is her contribution to our Centennial?" Albert's riddles were becoming more and more esoteric. The morning pop quizzes were beyond most of the men. Only Alex and a few others were able to supply answers with any regularity. Alex's mental storehouse was beginning to bulge, though, and he had cut back on his input, finding the key to the questions to be a concentration on the unusual. Albert was no longer interested in prosaic weights and measurements. He wanted stand-out personalities and awe-inspiring achievements.

Jenkins, one of the duller pushers and a general malcontent, silently scuffed at the ground and looked surly.

Albert's eagle eye scanned the ranks and fell, as usual, on Alex. "All right, Balfour. Tell Jenkins who Mrs. Este is. Jenkins, listen up and learn something."

Jenkins gave Alex a look of undisguised hatred. "Mrs. Mary G. Este," Alex said, drawing himself up to attention and ignoring Jenkins, "is a sculptress exhibited at the Women's Pavilion."

"What is the subject of her work?" Albert questioned.

"She has executed a bas relief of Iolanthe, daughter of the king."

"Exactly. Now can you tell us what material Mrs. Este employs?"

"Butter, sir. The piece is sculpted entirely of fresh creamery butter. Or at least it was fresh at one time."

Albert peered closely to see if Alex was twitting him, then nodded. "Precisely, Mr. Balfour. Take heed, Jenkins." He left-faced and resumed his pacing. "As I said before, we've been detailed to the stockyard to help with the unloading of the animals. I want you to leave your chairs here and board the wagons at Belmont Avenue. Report to the foreman at the yards. After you have completed the work there you may utilize the rest of the afternoon, if any remains, to resume your studies. One more word before you're dismissed." The muttering pushers fell silent. "I want you to stop congregating in the Main Building, and in particular I want you to stay out of the French Exhibit. I know that the women there are a primary attraction to you men, but I see little in the way of learning going on there and much jawboning." He stared at the line of men with a flinty expression, then nodded. "You men are dismissed."

The men pushed their rolling chairs back to the storage

room and headed for the wagon that would take them to the stockyards. For the last several months the stock had been moving into the stables. There were horses, hundreds of horses from tiny Shetland ponies to giant Clydesdales, oxen, sheep, hogs, goats, rabbits, chickens, geese, and turkeys. And, as Alex noticed as the men disembarked at the yard, a herd of buffalo still in transit. A small herd, fifteen adults and four calves, but still sizable enough to cause trouble.

They had been brought in special wagons, built solely for the transporting of oversize animals, one or two to the wagon, depending on size and temperament. The entire trip, from the prairie lands of the Midwest, had taken months and involved a complex arrangement of boats and wagons. Each leg of the journey was fraught with the sort of brute danger that only a buffalo or rhinoceros can provide.

By nature, the buffalo is an intractable animal. The bulls weigh in at one ton and the cows at a bit more than half of that and tend to go wherever they please, whenever they please. The only sure way to stop them is to kill them, which is not an easy task. Threats and force are meaningless, fences merely an annoyance. They have tiny eyes, and brains to match.

Alex stood by one of the oversize wagons as the gate was let down to free the first of the bulls. A heavy reinforced ramp, leading into the fenced enclosure that was to be the herd's home, had been pushed up to the wagon. The foreman, a big-boned, well-muscled Irishman, bossed a work gang that included regular stockhandlers, and today the push-chair crew. The men stood to the side of the wagon looking up at the giant bull, who gazed unblinkingly out of the gloom, over the heads of the crowd.

Alex had noticed that the greater part of his own crew had melted away as soon as they had arrived at the yards. Now, looking up at the buffalo, he understood why.

The bull turned his shaggy head and looked at Alex. Alex felt the vast weight of incredible stupidity behind the gaze, giving it a force that seemed both malevolent and curiously distant, as if the animal were gazing through him to another place or time. He had the feeling that the buffalo saw him not as a man or a living thing, but some species of movable plant or perhaps simply a shadow that flitted before him.

Suddenly, without any noticeable motivation, the bull lumbered forward and onto the ramp, which sagged beneath its bulk. As it passed Alex, massive and inexorable, he noticed its dry, dusty smell. From inside its gut came a sound that was like the grinding of two great rocks, a rumble that seemed to come not from the beast but from somewhere deep within the earth. The ground literally trembled as the bull stepped off the ramp and plodded off into the enclosure. An audible sigh of relief came from the small crowd.

"Now, that was simple, wasn't it?" the foreman asked. He motioned away the now empty wagon and moved the next in line up to the ramp. Alex found that his job as well as that of most of the others, consisted of maneuvering the wagon into place, lowering the ramp, and simply standing by as the great beasts lumbered down and into the grassy ring. That was until the last, a huge bull, stood at the top of the ramp and decided that he would stay where he was, unmoving, staring out at some other buffalo world that did not include men, or ramps, or a Centennial Exhibition.

"Why don't you just let the wagon stay here until he decides to come down," Alex said.

The Irishman looked scornfully at Alex. "Yes, and what if he never decides to come down? Do we leave him here forever? He's a beast, nothing more. If we want him to come down then he'll be coming down. I've a job to do and I'll do it."

Alex shrugged, aware that he had no standing here, no expertise or rank. To these men he was one of the sissies who pushed people around in chairs.

"Let's get a rope on him, boys," the foreman said. The stockmen looked at each other until one of them picked up a rope that was hanging on a nearby fencepost.

"Look, Pat," the man with the rope began, "maybe that chair yahoo has a pretty good idea. If that animal don't want to come down, there's damn little that we can do to force him.

Maybe we should ought to just let him stand there till he gets hungry enough to come down and graze."

The man with the rope got the same look from the foreman that Alex had received earlier. The man flushed and looked at the ground. *Who's the yahoo now,* Alex thought.

"Boys, we'll be bringing him down if I have to go up there and carry him down on my shoulders. Now get that rope around him. If you're afraid to do it then I'll do it myself."

The man with the rope looked at the foreman, spit on the ground, and turned to face the buffalo. With practiced movements he shook out a loop, twirled it once, and tossed it over the great shaggy head. The bull didn't move, or even notice as the man gently tightened the noose until it was snug. He swaggered over and handed the rope to the foreman.

The Irishman nodded and moved toward the bottom of the ramp. He was standing slightly to the right of the ramp in a direct line between the buffalo and a stout gatepost directly behind him. He pulled on the rope until it was taut. He wrapped the rope around his right wrist and had one of the men tie the remainder to the post behind him. The buffalo did not move.

The man, the rope, and the buffalo formed a curious, almost straight line, a geometrical equation. The line was pulled tight from post to man to beast. The Irishman planted his feet, drew in a deep breath, and flexed his back muscles. He assumed a tug-of-war stance and nodded to the other men.

"Sing to him, boys," the Irishman said. "Sing him a pretty song while I draw on this rope—we'll soon coax this great beast down."

And then the buffalo moved.

You would have hardly noticed, had he not been roped. He seemed to settle back on his haunches, as if testing the strength of the tether. The rope tightened, and the foreman grunted and threw himself back against the weight. The coils around his wrist cut off the blood and began to dig into the skin. "Turn loose," one of the stockmen yelled, but it was too late. The buffalo's head jerked, as if to flick away an annoying insect, a short pull to the left. The two coils around the Irishman's wrist popped straight and tore his hand off before anyone could move or even speak. The men stood stunned, watching as the Irishman lifted his arm and looked dumbly at the stump as it suddenly spurted blood. He sank to his knees and a low wordless moan bubbled from his throat.

"Somebody find a doctor," Alex shouted as he knelt by the man. "Hold it tight," he told the Irishman. "Give me your bandanna," he said to one of the men standing beside him. Alex knotted the kerchief around the man's forearm. The flow of blood slowed as Alex pulled the bandanna as tight as possible. He tried to stand and slipped on the blood-slick grass. "A doctor," he said, getting up. "For Christ's sake, isn't there a doctor around here?"

The Irishman still knelt, staring now at his hand lying on the ground. He was deadly pale, blue eyes wide with shock. "Lord, Jesus, I've lost my hand," he said, and began to cry.

Two men came running up, one with a black bag.

"I'm a vet," the man with the bag said as he knelt by the Irishman. "I'm the best you're going to get for the moment. Oh, Christ." He glanced up at the men standing around them. "Help me get him to the stables. We'll lay him down there, and I'll try to stop the bleeding."

Four men helped the Irishman to his feet and half carried him off toward the stable. Alex watched them for a moment, and then he turned and vomited. No one looked at him. Except the buffalo. Alex wiped his mouth and looked up at the bull as he looked down at him with small dumb eyes. He snorted, perhaps at the smell of blood, then looked away, back to his own world, far away, where there were no men.

• •

Alex handed the plate to High Cloud. High Cloud lifted the cloth cover, looked at the food and handed it to Little Spring. She nodded, and Alex sat down beside the small fire built into a rock-lined pit. The three sat in a triangle around the burning sticks. It was evening, not really dark yet, and the flames cast a warm glow. Little Spring pushed half of the food onto another plate and handed it to High Cloud. He took it and set it down beside him.

"Aren't you hungry?" Alex asked. "Hungry?" High Cloud said. "I have not been hungry for many months. Not since we were brought here. Have they stopped the big black man, the buffalo man, from coming?"

Alex nodded. "They said it would cause trouble. Abraham wanted me to bring the food. I will help you if I can, just as he would."

The Indian picked up a slice of bread. Usually the food was left over from the kitchen where Uncle worked. "It is the bread made from the white powder," the old Indian said. "Not real bread. There is no strength in this powder. If we eat this we will grow weak and sick." He pushed the bread around on the plate. "The black man, Abraham, has been our only friend here." He pronounced the name in three distinct syllables: *A-bra-ham*.

"I will be your friend now," Alex said. He thought he saw Little Spring glance at him, but when he looked at her she was chewing a piece of bread and looking into the fire.

The old man picked up a beef bone and took a bite of the meat. He chewed for a minute. "This meat is from a white-horn, the white man's buffalo. It is thin and stringy meat. I cannot understand why you prize it."

"It's what we are used to," Alex said.

The old man nodded. "That still does not explain it. All of your food is weak. Only the black drink with the sweet powder has any strength. I have grown to like that drink. I will miss it."

Alex knew he meant coffee, but he didn't understand what the Indian meant when he said he would miss it. "I can bring you coffee," he said.

"Soon we will be gone," the Indian said.

How could he know that they were planning to get rid of them? That the deal with Barnum was in the works. "I don't understand," he said.

High Cloud put the beef back on the plate and pushed it away.

"We have been here long enough. I cannot eat this food any longer. I must have real food, meat from the blackhorn, the buffalo. The buffalo is my brother. We have been away from him too long. I will lose my strength if I do not see my brother."

He sat up straighter and looked out over the fire. "I allowed myself to be brought here. I thought it would be more helpful to my people to come to this country and learn your secrets. I would have liked to die with the others, but there was little help for the people that way." He pulled a short pipe from a leather pouch. He packed it with tobacco and lighted it. "At one time they told me I could not smoke here. I do not pay attention to such people. What could they do to me? Make me a prisoner?" The old man seemed to smile as he puffed on the pipe.

"And so we came, High Cloud and Little Spring. I came to this place to learn the white man's secrets, and she came to care for me. I have seen this place, learned your speech, seen the machines and the wonders that you have here, and now it is time to go. I have learned all that can be learned."

Alex wondered what the Indian thought of the machines and the goods from all over the world. The marvels of this century were displayed before the old man as if stocked on the shelves of the greatest trading post in history. "What have you learned?" Alex asked. "About all of this," he said, gesturing into the dark around them.

The old man puffed on the pipe and stared into the space between Alex and Little Spring.

"I have learned," he said, "that beneath all of your marvels there is a great weakness. You are a clever people. You have built these things called machines to do many things for you. To lift water, dig in the ground, make false-hides, cook your food, carry great weights, many things. They make your life easier."

He knocked the ashes out of the pipe and placed it back in the leather pouch. He picked up a stick and stirred the fire, sending a shower of sparks into the night sky.

"The weakness?" Alex asked.

He nodded. "You have no spirit. Your lives are easy, you have many goods, but you have no purpose. There are many of you. You have a great energy to own things, but there is no happiness inside you. You possess much, but the spirit eludes you the way the rabbit eludes the bear. You are a poor people who desire nothing more than to have everything. You lie, you cheat, you take it all, until you can stand up in your councils and say, see, we have all the world's goods, we have all the land, now it is ours and we are truly great. But you do not understand. You cannot own the land. You cannot own people. You can only own yourselves, and that is the one thing you do not seem able to possess. You are not at peace." High Cloud stood. He glanced at Little Spring, and she went into the tepee.

"At first I thought the black men among you were different. They are buffalo men, and as such they are closer to me. It is true that they have more of a sense of themselves, but they carry a great shame. They allowed themselves to be your slaves and they must live with that. Abraham is different, but he is a simple man. His mind is not like the others'.

"So now we will go back to our people. We will tell them these things. We will tell them that you are more numerous than the grasshoppers, and you are powerful like the bear, and you possess great weapons. We will tell them that we will probably die, but we must fight. You will only allow us to live beneath you. That sort of life is not worth living."

The old man went into the tepee and pulled down the entrance flap. Alex sat watching the coals of the fire. He felt ashamed. The moon had risen in the sky. As he walked back through the night, the pale light outlined and silvered the pavilions and fountains and walkways, but he did not find it beautiful.

Chapter 22

He lay awake, trying to sort it all out. The days were moving too quickly. Events seemed to pile up against him like dead leaves blown before the wind. Images wheeled in his head, replacing one another with sudden kaleidoscopic shifts. He watched, helpless, unable to stop the movement, to find the meaning in it. And always the questions: What should I do? Is it time? Will it change? What is right?

He got up early and ran, hoping that the familiar exercise would help him put things into perspective. It didn't. The rest of the day was spent chair-pushing. He found several exhibits that diverted him and that he thought Twain would enjoy. He was anxious for Twain to return—the writer was the most modern person he had met in this time. Talking to him was a relief and a challenge. Their differences were less encumbered with cultural baggage than his relations with either the blacks or the Indians.

And so when he sat with the Indians that night, he was no closer to a plan or an answer than he had been the night before. He saved the food from their evening meal. A soft rain fell outside. Little Spring tended the small fire in the center of the dirt floor of the tepee. They sat on piles of buffalo robes. Alex suddenly realized that the tepee, by virtue of the small smokeless fire, and the soft pile of robes, was considerably more comfortable than the shack with the hard wooden floor and the thin cornhusk mattress where he usually slept. So much for the rigors of the savages.

High Cloud watched Alex over his cornbread and his squirrel stew. "Real food," he said, gesturing to his plate.

Alex waited while they ate. He watched Little Spring. She always had the same response to him: none. She could see him; he was sure of that. But she paid absolutely no attention to him. She never spoke. He knew it was physically possible for her to talk. He had heard her speak to High Cloud, and he had heard her on that long-ago night when they had made love.

She was a beautiful woman, and if his stares bothered her she gave no indication of it. Long black hair, classic high cheekbones, brown skin that appeared as soft as the doeskin dresses she wore. He remembered touching that skin, yes, quite as soft as it looked. And beneath the skin the lean sure muscles of the deer. He shook off the memory. During the day she did beadwork and sewing, using bone needles and wooden tools. He had brought her a package of sewing needles, but he never saw her use them. He spoke to her occasionally but she did not acknowledge him.

"You told me last night you were going to leave," Alex said. "They won't let you. You're a prisoner. How do you expect to get away? Where will you go?"

High Cloud put down the empty plate. "Many questions," he said, looking at Alex. As always, Alex felt the weight of the Indian's gaze. The old man never seemed to look at anything without actively considering it. People, trees, blankets, whatever he looked at he thought about as if all things had some sort of life. And perhaps, Alex thought, they did.

"Several days. Soon. First, we must pack what we can carry. There is food, our weapons, all of these things. Little Spring will do this. Then we will leave."

"Where will you go?"

"Home. To our people. They must be told what we have learned. They must be made ready to fight."

Alex felt a wave of exasperation, as if he were dealing with a small, recalcitrant child. "Do you know how far it is?" he asked. "How will you travel?"

High Cloud looked at Alex as if he were dealing with a similar child. "We will walk. We will steal ponies. Perhaps we will ride the iron horse. That is how they brought us here. It is far, but we are here. It must be possible to return. That is not a concern to us. It will be done."

Looking at the lean leathery face, Alex understood that High Cloud meant exactly what he said. There was no confusion here, no hesitancy. In his own time, such resolution would only be seen on the faces of the insane, those who walked the streets and muttered about nuclear radios in their heads, conspiracy theories, and the imminent end of the world. Or by the instructors at expensive, confidence-enhancing business seminars. Everyone else hedged his bets, left a little room to back-pedal if need be. It was the intelligent way to exist in an uncertain, unfair, modern world.

The old Indian had a face wrinkled by years in the sun, a body that was thin but looked to be whipcord tough. Arms that reminded Alex of the hard lean jerky he used to buy at liquor stores before he got old enough to know that beef jerky and a beer was not a balanced meal. But as Alex looked into those dark unwavering eyes he knew that the old man could do it. He actually could walk out of here and across the continental United States, no matter who was chasing him. Or he would die. That was the alternative, but it didn't seem to bother High Cloud.

"What weapons do you have?" Alex asked. He felt himself drawn into the possibility of the escape. Just a few minutes before he had scoffed at the idea, but now, in the face of High Cloud's confidence, he found himself willing to accept it. And believe. He looked around at the tepee and the two Indians, and he felt himself a part of this world. Who was he to say the old man was crazy, that he would never make it?

High Cloud went to a mound of blankets, pulled one back and lifted out an unstrung four-foot bow that looked as if it had been made from the antler of a deer or an elk. He laid the bow in front of Alex and put six arrows beside it. "They brought my bow along when we came. They let me keep it. They think that I am too far from my home, my people, to use it, that my medicine is weak. They trust too well in the might of their own world. I have this bow. I have a knife. Little Spring has her knife. We are people, and you are white men. It is enough. You judge everything by what you see, or what you think you see." He stared at Alex. Alex could feel himself being measured.

"I will tell you a story," High Cloud said. "My people live in the land of the Great Turtle. This is the land which the whites would like to steal from us. We know this, we have known your people, the Bluecoats, for many years. We have gone to the forts; I have done this myself.

"When we have need of new horses there are several ways to acquire them. One is to steal them from the Crows. But when it is too cold, we take them from the soldiers.

"Your soldiers do not like our land. They are restless there. They see nothing but emptiness. They want only to amuse themselves. Sometimes we go to the forts, and we offer the soldiers a wager. We take one of our horses, and we offer to race any of the American horses that you have. The soldiers look at our horse. He has no name, but he is the horse of Walks Tall. He is a small horse, small even for an Indian horse. And he has much hair. He looks very much like the animals you call sheep. And he looks very sad, although I don't know why this is." High Cloud placed a stick on the fire. In the flare of firelight Alex could see that the old man was staring into the flames.

"Walks Tall goes to the soldiers and challenges them to a race. The soldiers always accept. They are proud of their horses, and they think our pony is a poor beast. They are quick to take any advantage, that is the way of the whites. Walks Tall mounts the pony. He is a tall heavy man, and his feet come near the ground. And he carries a very large club. Many goods are wagered.

"The horses go off, Walks Tall beats the pony with the club, the Indian pony wins by a neck. Another race is proposed, the whites accept, again Walks Tall beats the pony with the large club. This time he wins by a length. The soldiers cannot accept this. Everything is wagered; horses, blankets, rifles, food, many goods. The finest American horse is brought out.

"This time Walks Tall throws away the club, and the pony runs like the wind. He is twice as fast as the American horse. The last half of the race is run with Walks Tall riding backward, facing the pony's tail. He makes many faces and beckons the other horse to come on. The soldiers truly hate this. But it always happens this same way." He looked up at Alex. "You see, the soldiers think the club is to make the pony run faster, actually it is to keep him from running too fast before everything has been wagered. The pony does not look like the horses they know, so they think he is inferior. The soldiers also think this about our people. We do not look like him so we cannot be as strong or clever as he is." He stared at Alex, the flames reflected in his eyes. "One day your people will lose a big fight because of this mistake." High Cloud gestured to his bow. "My bow will kill as easily as any rifle here in your show. And it does so quietly."

Alex had an image of High Cloud and Little Spring lying outside the exhibition gates, shot to death, their quiet bows and arrows and knives scattered around them on the ground. This was no horse race. He couldn't let them do it. They would surely die.

"You said you needed to see the buffalo. Would you stay if I showed you a herd of them? Would that help? Later we could decide what to do, after the exhibition opens and the authorities have other things to worry about."

High Cloud laughed. "You have no buffalo here. Only those whitehorns. They are not worth seeing."

"No, it's true. Over at the stockyards. They brought them in yesterday." He thought of the big Irish foreman, kneeling in the grass holding his bleeding stump. He pushed the memory away.

For the first time since he had met him, High Cloud actually looked interested in what Alex was saying.

"I have been to the place where they keep the animals," High Cloud said. When we first came, they took us around this camp to try to frighten us with your cleverness. They let us walk about as long as a white was with us. They do not fear us here in their own country. Take me to the buffalo. I would see them. I have need of it."

Alex nodded. "Tomorrow's my day off. I'll check with the big police chief; I think he will let us do it. You will stay?"

"I will see the buffalo," High Cloud said. "Then we will decide what is to be done."

"Good," Alex said, standing up to go. "I will talk to him tomorrow."

High Cloud also stood. "No," he said. "I will go tonight."

"He won't be there tonight," Alex said, confused. "He won't be in his office until tomorrow."

"I care nothing for your chief. Tonight I will see the buffalo." He turned and knelt at the pile of blankets.

Alex watched with a cold dawning realization as High Cloud pulled a long knife from the pile and pushed it into the waistband of his pants. He was wearing elkskin pants and a dark wool shirt. He took off the shirt and tied on a chest ornament made of porcupine quills. He slipped on a pair of soft moccasins.

"Wait a minute," Alex said. "What do you think you're going to do?"

The Indian stood and turned to face him. "I am going to meet my brother. This does not concern you." He turned back to Little Spring and spoke to her in Sioux. She nodded to him. He picked up his bow and two of the arrows. He pushed back the flap of the tepee and stepped outside.

The air was heavy with mist. Alex stepped out behind High Cloud. They stood silently for a moment, listening. High Cloud turned to him and spoke in a bare whisper. "The guard is asleep. He is always asleep at night. Go away."

"No," Alex whispered back. "I'll come with you." He had to keep control. He had told Abraham that he would take care of them; now he could see the whole cloth of that promise beginning to unravel. Besides, he was the one who told him about the buffalo. He was responsible.

High Cloud stared at him. Alex could imagine the Indian

deciding whether or not to just kill this bothersome white man and be done with it. High Cloud nodded. "You will come."

Suddenly it was no longer an interesting form of historical study, or an idealistic notion, or the matter of promises to be kept or broken. It had escalated to a plane where death was a part of normal life, either dealing it out or accepting it. This Indian always lived there, lived with the immediacy of death, his own or others', and was willing to make decisions concerning these deaths. He did this with the ease that Alex might use in deciding what Molly might prefer for dinner. By electing to go along with High Cloud he had chosen to participate. High Cloud would expect him to behave accordingly.

High Cloud stood listening once more and moved off around the back of the Government Building. Alex took a deep breath and followed.

Alex had always been struck by the relative lack of security at the exposition. There was a fence, but not a particularly high one, and there were guards, but not very many of them. At night there was very little in the way of patrolling by the police. He tried to imagine what that sort of security would mean to an exhibition of this size in modern-day Philadelphia. Images of ransacked and vandalized buildings, gangs of teenagers carrying off the world's goods, smoke curling from burning structures; total chaos.

They stayed off the main roadways, running easily through the gardens, two figures ghosting through the night. There was a moon to guide them, although High Cloud seem to know where he was going without consulting Alex. Alex wondered vainly if High Cloud was impressed that he could keep up with him, then realized he was comparing his endurance to that of an old man. They passed between the hospital and the Gliddon Guano Building, a tropical forest recreated to show the miracle powers of bat guano as a fertilizer. Alex had laughed at the idea of a guano building until someone had explained to him that bat shit was a major fertilizer of the time, and a multimillion-dollar business.

In the near distance, dimly lighted from inside, seeming to float in the mist, Alex could see the outdoor exhibit known as

Bartholdi's Electric Light, which was the right arm and torch of the Statue of Liberty.

They came to the exposition fence, found an unlocked gate, and continued due north toward the stockyards. High Cloud seemed to gather energy as they ran, sucking it in with the damp night air and expending it as he lengthened his strides. His was the fluid grace of an animal, a deer or a wild horse. Alex began to fall behind. This was not jogging, this was running. High Cloud did not slow or look back.

Alex estimated that they had run at least two miles when he had to slow down. By the time he reached the stockyards he had no idea where High Cloud was.

The compound fence was made of metal pipes that ran through heavy metal posts. It surrounded several acres with crude bleachers rising along the far end. Beyond the bleachers, past a wide grassy roadway, were low wooden buildings where many of the horses were stabled. Alex could see the large humped unmoving shadows of the buffalo on the far side of the arena.

And then he heard High Cloud chanting. The buffalo shadows shifted. The beasts stirred and came to consciousness as if a spell had been lifted.

He knelt to crawl beneath the bottom rung of the fence, and as he moved on all fours he leaned on the severed hand in the tall grass beneath the fence. The fingers curled in response, encircling his wrist with a feathery grace that forced a choked cry from him. He started up and slammed his neck into the thick pipe above him.

He blacked out for a moment, opening his eyes to a thick tussock of grass that appeared in his confusion to be a stand of trees. Memory returned, and he scrabbled back away from the hand. He pulled himself up. Pinpoints of light swirled before his eyes.

He leaned against the fence and breathed deeply, clearing his aching head. High Cloud's chant drifted across the field. He walked unsteadily toward the humped shadows.

Halfway across the enclosure, he stopped. He could see clearly now, see the buffalo as they shifted their massive weight from side to side, see High Cloud as he moved among them, touching their dusty flanks, running his hands along their bodies as if feeling for a weakness, or a special strength, searching for something that could not be seen but only felt. The animals moved away from his touch, but only slightly, as if accepting it as necessary, but not desired, something to be borne for the moment.

High Cloud stopped and appeared to whisper to one of the great shaggy heads. Then he pulled his bow from his shoulder and fitted an arrow. Alex wanted to shout. He wanted to keep High Cloud from the act that would lead unfailingly to pain and trouble and worse. But he couldn't. Time and fate curled around this moment, but he could no more stop it than he could stop the arrow loosed from High Cloud's bow as the old man grunted with the effort, and the cow grunted in surprise. The arrow entered her and tore not merely into her vast body, but through it, the razor-sharp iron arrowhead emerging on the other side as a pointed excrescence. She went to her knees, rumbled deep within, a terrible and curious sound, and rolled to her side. And died in a long exhalation that went on and on until it seemed not merely breath, but the animal's soul that streamed from the flared black nostrils, wet with blood and departing life.

High Cloud knelt by the black form, working his knife beneath the skin. Alex walked closer, carefully skirting the other buffalo, now motionless, dreaming their buffalo dreams, until he could see and hear the knife as it slid along an invisible line, parting skin from flesh and fat, as sure and as fine as the line between past and present, life and death.

Chapter 23

Molly watched Special Agent in Charge Frank Owen look around his small, green-walled office with obvious distaste. She couldn't tell if he was more disgusted with the jailhouse color of the walls or with her persistent questions. He rubbed his face, stared at the ceiling, and, finding no comfort there, sighed and looked back at her. His swivel chair was tilted so far back she half expected him to fall over, then suddenly come up blasting, service revolver clutched in a classic double-handed grip, dealing death and destruction to both the office and the pain-in-the-ass reporter from the *New York Times*.

She had waited for three days, usually in the crummy outer waiting room, sometimes here in Owen's office, as the FBI, local police, sheriff's men, and Indian agents put together a posse to trail John Raven into the Badlands where no one wanted to go.

"The goddamn reservation itself is two-point-five-million goddamn acres of butt-busting rock," Owen said, holding his arms wide to indicate two-point-five-million goddamn acres. "And it looks like a picnic ground compared to where we're going."

He sighed again. "Listen to me. I'm starting to sound like that idiot Blanchard. I've been out here two weeks and I'm going native. J. Edgar never mentioned Indians when I signed up. Three years of law school, and now I've got to ride a horse down into the biggest ditch in the world."

"I think the Grand Canyon is bigger," Molly said mildly. Over the last few days she had, against her will, come to like this large, out-of-his-element FBI agent. He was so ill suited for this particular job his plight had assumed comic proportions. At least to her.

"Why did you join the bureau? After years of law school most bright young men join organizations that offer the prospects of legal fame and large amounts of money."

"Defending the rights of bloated corporations," Owen said. "Somehow it didn't appeal to me. I grew up with 'The Untouchables.' Do you know how many men joined the FBI because of that TV program?" She shook her head. "More than you might imagine. When I was a kid my dad took me on a tour of the FBI building. The one where the agent fires the machine gun at the end. That's what did it, that goddamn guy with the machine gun, blasting away, shredding a life-size paper target of a bad guy in a hail of bullets. Do you know how many times I've been allowed to shoot a machine gun since I signed on? Once—that's how many—in training school." He shook his head. "Now I've got to ride a horse. I've shot a machine gun more times than I've ridden a horse." The phone rang.

"You're asking me?" he shouted into the phone. "How do I know how many pack horses we're going to need? Don't we have Indians working on this? If they don't know, who does? All I know is we're starting tomorrow morning and I want the pack horses, the Indians, the trackers, and everybody else ready and in place first goddamn thing. Now take care of it and stop bothering me." He started to slam down the phone and then replaced it gently, remembering that Molly was watching.

"You don't suppose I could talk those two Indians who bushwhacked me out at Henry Sands's place into going along. Or that Will Two Horses?" he asked. "Somehow my Indians don't seem up to the caliber of your Indians."

"They're not exactly *my* Indians," Molly said. She had purposely stayed away from Will Two Horses for the last several days. "But after your midnight raid, I doubt they have much sympathy for your position."

He waved a hand. "That was a mistake, I admit it, off the record. I'd only been around a few days, and Blanchard talked me into it. He was a local; he was supposed to know what would work. It was goddamn embarrassing. Off the record, remember?"

She nodded. It had taken her two days of being meek and inoffensive to convince Owen that she wasn't out to hang him or the bureau. He still didn't trust her, but he would never trust any reporter. He was always very careful with his "off the records."

Owen stood up and walked to the one window in his office. It looked out on a nearly empty parking lot, a beat-up aluminum diner, and a long row of used-car dealerships, each with a small herd of dented oversize cars and crudely repainted pickup trucks. In his several days of staring out the window he'd never seen any of the cars actually move, but the pickups were traded and replaced with surprising regularity. "I suppose you're going to want to go with us tomorrow," he said.

"No thanks," she answered, standing. "It's too cold at night, and I've been on a horse enough to know what a pain it's going to be." Besides, she thought, I don't think John Raven is down in that ditch. "If you catch him, I want to talk to him, but I'll leave the camping out to you boys." She attempted to keep most of the sarcasm out of her voice when she said the word "boys." It never hurt to reinforce people's stereotypes. That way when you broke those same stereotypes you had the element of surprise on your side. As well as righteous anger. He nodded glumly, still staring out the window. "Let me know what happens," she said, pausing by the door.

"Aren't you going to wish us luck?" he said. "Off the record."

"No," she said. "Try not to hurt anyone, though."

He shrugged and sat back down at the desk. "No one gets

hurt," he said. "Not if I can help it. The job is to catch a man who tried to kill two other men. All this cowboy-and-Indian shit is just incidental."

• •

Molly drove her rental car to her motel on the outskirts of town. The motel was part of an area known as The Strip, which featured package liquor stores, fast-food joints, and cowboy bars that advertised dusk-to-dawn topless dancing. She drove carefully, mindful of the cars that pulled out without warning from the line of businesses. Back in her room she tossed the car keys on the bed, sat down at the Formica desk, and stared at the blank screen of her portable computer. She ought to write a story, file something, but there wasn't anything new. Raven was still missing. The law-enforcement people had still not gotten their search effort together, and it looked like a long dry haul until something broke.

She thought about going back to New York. Her nightly call to Alex had turned up nothing. He was still away, wherever "away" was. At least out here she would worry less than if she were sitting around the house waiting for him to return. And then there was Will Two Horses.

She stood up and took off her jacket. She threw it on the back of her chair and cursed softly as it fell on the floor. She lay down on the bed, jammed her hands into her jeans pockets, and stared at the ceiling. *Will Two Horses.* She thought of how he had looked at her, back there at Wounded Knee. There was too much in that look—too much worry, too much care, too much something else that she was afraid to identify. She was afraid to identify it because she felt it too, unwanted, unasked for, but there it was just the same. She frowned and shook her head. What the hell was going on? She wasn't some fourteen-year-old kid. She had a man at home, a man she was in love with. He might be a little flaky, a little too prone to self-examination and disappearing into thin air, but she loved him and had for quite a few years. Why this sudden surge of feeling for an Indian lawyer that she hardly knew? How could these two emotions, love for Alex and, what? romantic interest in Will Two Horses? exist at the same time? One would think that they would be mutually antagonistic. But it was not so. *Mysteries of the heart,* she thought, she'd never been any good at them. She was better at the normal mysteries, the ones that the newspaper paid her to unravel. Or at least report.

She got up off the bed and found her address book in her pack. She would call Will. He was the key to John Raven. She had put off calling him for two days, but it was time to either get to work or go back to New York. Business, this was business, she thought as she dialed. He answered on the first ring. His office was an old Airstream trailer on the reservation. He also lived there.

"You tired of sitting around with the FBI?" he asked. "They had any luck finding John?"

"Not yet they haven't. They go down into the Badlands tomorrow. Is he down there, Will?"

There was a long silence from the other end. "I don't know," Will said.

"You don't know or the line is tapped?"

"Probably both," he answered. "You want to come out here, or should I pick you up?"

She thought about it. She didn't want to visit his trailer, even if it was his office. It was important to keep everything on neutral territory. "Pick me up," she said.

"I'll be there in half an hour."

She hung up the phone and tried to forget everything that wasn't connected with John Raven. If she could get to him before the FBI did, she would have a real story. Too complicated, all of it, she thought. Stick to basics, pay attention to your job, establish your priorities, and find John Raven.

Chapter 24

"The way I heard it," Alex said glumly, "it took all of twenty minutes for them to figure out who had killed the buffalo. The arrow was buried under it, and the damn thing was too heavy for High Cloud to move. They found it when they turned the animal over." Alex was slumped in a green plush easy chair in Twain's hotel room. Twain was on the bed. It was afternoon, but Twain was dressed in a purple dressing gown and alligator-skin slippers. For the moment he was not smoking. He was drinking a glass of whiskey.

"This is a sad tale," Twain said. "And of course they charged you with it. Naturally they would have, after assigning you keeper of the savages. I'll warrant Chief Brannon was none too pleased. Can't say as I blame him. Wouldn't do to have redskins running around slaughtering the livestock. Bad for morale. So what's he say he's going to do?"

"Well, I haven't been charged with anything yet. But he said at our last meeting that the commission will allow Custer to sell the Indians to P. T. Barnum. They're Custer's, evidently, by right of battle. He's allowed to do whatever he wants with them. I doubt that this latest incident will change those plans. It'll speed them up, if anything."

Twain nodded. "I'm sure old P. T. will jump at the chance. Indians were a big draw at his museum, but he's run out of his supply. He tried out-of-work Irishmen, but people noticed they were a bit pale. Rumor has it that he's buying up every oddity from here to Calcutta for a new circus. Yes, P. T. will take them if he can." They were both silent for a moment. Alex tried to imagine High Cloud and Little Spring as participants in a circus. The image wouldn't come.

"Were you ever to P. T.'s museum?" Twain asked.

"No," Alex answered.

"Odd," Twain said, looking up at the ceiling. "Everybody who ever lived in New York has seen P. T. Barnum's American Museum. You could hardly escape it. A dead person would have trouble missing it." He glanced over at Alex.

Alex had decided that the only course of action in situations such as this was to keep quiet. The more he tried to explain the inconsistencies of his past, the worse it sounded. Particularly around Twain, who was maddeningly adept at pointing out the flaws in his stories.

"Marvelous place," Twain went on. "He had a band up on the roof, worst band you ever heard. There was no more tune in them than in a horse. P. T. wanted them that way, said that the noise of that band drew people to him, then their awfulness drove them inside.

"No one ever complained, though. At least about the museum—plenty complained about the band. Once inside, you completely forgot that P. T. had talked you out of a quarter to see the place. It was filled to the rafters with curiosities. You couldn't swing a cat without knocking over at least ten oddities from faraway exotic locales. Mummified mermaids, petrified eyeballs, Siamese twins, cannibals—you name it, and he had it. Oh, yes, he'll want your Indians, and he'll get 'em."

"Doesn't anyone understand that one should not buy and sell people?"

"Haven't I heard this song from you before?" Twain asked, sarcastically. "Yes, these are people, but that's just a technicality. These are Indians, savages, and most of them are involved in a fight to the death with the United States Army. In my travels throughout the West, I've seen a lot of them, and on the whole I found them lazy and unclean. And those are their good points." He put his empty whiskey glass on the bedtable. "By instinct, inclination, and profession they are nothing so much as a nation of beggars. If P. T. takes them into the circus they'll lead a life far superior to any they'll find on the plains with their own tribe. I see the circus as a kindness, not the hell you're making it out to be." He looked at Alex with raised eyebrows.

"This is America, the land of the free. You don't buy people and put them in cages."

"Alex, I don't know whether to swear at you or cry over you. We put criminals in cages, don't we? If these particular Indians were brought in by George Custer then they most assuredly qualify as criminals." Twain got out of bed and stood in front of Alex. His rust-colored hair was mussed from lying in bed, giving him a slightly mad look. "I'll grant you their appearance is not one of particular savagery here at this show, but if you met them on the open plains I'd not go a single cent on the likelihood of you retaining your hair. But I see by the set of your jaw that I'm not going to change your mind."

"I don't think you will," Alex said. The problem was, he wasn't so sure about that. Most of what Twain said, the parts about Indians being dirty and beggars, was wrong, but Twain had a point with the rest of it. He remembered how quick Little Spring had been with her knife on the man who tried to get into their tepee, and High Cloud's arrow as it pierced the buffalo. Had the knife and the bow been used on other men, guiltless white settlers perhaps? And just who *was* guiltless? Custer and the army with its "only good Indian is a dead Indian" philosophy? Settlers who rushed to stake out huge chunks of Indian land? Prospectors who panned for gold on their sacred grounds? The Indians who fought to keep their land?

He watched Twain hang up his dressing gown and put on a shirt. He asked himself the same question he'd been asking for the last several days. What was he going to do about the Indians? Brannon had made it clear that their days here were numbered. High Cloud had made it clear that he was going to make a run for it soon. Should he just stand back and let matters take their course with the inevitable clash? Could he stand back and watch when death, probably the Indians', was the likely outcome? It always came back to the same question: if it were possible to influence events, should he? Where did his responsibility lie in a moral landscape littered with dangerous contradictions and deadly inconsistencies?

He stood and watched as Twain fired up one of his cigars. There was only one option, he decided. Maybe there was only one option in any such situation. Quite simply, he would do what seemed correct to him *personally.* He would forget history, reject cultural differences, ignore the larger issues. He would make it personal and goddamn the inconsistencies and ambiguities. He would be his own man. Part of the gloom seemed to lift from his soul.

"I talked to your boss this morning," Twain said. "Mr. Albert Riddle. I have a lurking suspicion that the man's brain is cracked. But at any rate, he's turned you over to me for a day or so as a personal guide. He said you'd push me around in a chair if I liked, but I declined. Somehow it doesn't seem very democratic."

"Thanks," Alex said as they went out the door. "You'll find walking the grounds to be excellent exercise."

"I hadn't thought of that," Twain said, stopping to inspect the ash end of his cigar. "I'm not much for exercise. My biceps have all the muscle tone of an oyster wrapped in an old rag. And my legs won't go much better. Maybe we'd better get that chair after all." They walked down the hall toward the stairs.

"I'll take it easy. I've got two exhibits for you to see. In light of your interest in invention."

Twain stopped in the lobby of the hotel and asked for any messages at the desk and then steered Alex toward the door. He gave a mock bow and a wave of the hand. "Guide on," he said.

• •

As they walked to the Main Building Twain explained the purpose of his two-day trip to New York. "Since I was planning to stop here anyway, I decided to see if there might be some profit in it. I couldn't steal Howells's thunder, as his article was already lined up for *Harper's*. So I settled on a piece for *The Atlantic*. We don't need another wonders-of-the-exposition article. Howells and a thousand others will fit that to perfection, so I've been hired to work up a piece on the people who actually do the work here. A behind-the-scenes look, as it were. I'll write about chair-pushers like yourself, cooks and shoeshine boys like the Negroes you live with. Something amusing and informative. With your permission, and that of your friends, it should work out rather well. What do you think?"

Alex tried to picture Mark Twain in the little shack with Elias and Uncle and Abraham. He saw only disaster. But on second thought, maybe a disaster like that would be good for Twain. He tried to imagine Twain suggesting to Elias that all Negroes were either shoeshine boys or cooks. What the hell, they were adults. Why not throw them together and let them sort it out for themselves?

"All right," Alex said, unable to suppress a grin. Twain looked at the smile and frowned. "We'll try it," Alex said. "If nothing else, it will be interesting."

Twain's frown lifted, and he nodded. "Good. I'm still to be working in secret though. I'm not even allowed to tell Howells I'm here. *The Atlantic* wants to spring it on its readers. So don't mention my name to anyone. I'll remain Mr. Langhorne as far as the public is concerned."

• •

The section allotted to Chile was right inside the main door. The main part of the exhibit was the usual profusion of maps, books, drawings, and furniture. There was a mummy, dark and shriveled. Mummies were very popular, many of the countries had at least one on display. Alex led the way through the Chilean exhibit. "Did you know," he said to Twain, "that the Egyptian railroad fueled all of their trains for ten years with mummies? They stacked them up like cordwood in the tenders and slid them into the firebox as needed."

Twain stopped to look at a map made of human hair. Pictures made of human hair were almost as popular as mummies. "I didn't even know that Egypt had a railroad," he said. "Much less that they'd had one for ten years."

Alex stopped to consider. Had he screwed up again? He had so many small facts stored in his head he was never sure which ones were from what time. Usually it didn't matter; around Twain it did. "Here it is," he said, changing the subject. He pointed at a model in a glass case. It was a long tube with the side cut away to show a round ball inside. At the far end there was a fan—powered by a steam engine.

"What the hell is that?" Twain asked, coming up beside him.

"It's a device designed to supercede railroads. A long, airtight tube with a ball inside for freight. The ball is seven feet in diameter and is blown along at velocities of up to one hundred miles an hour. At least that's what it says. What do you think?" He watched as Twain bent close to examine the model. The thing had attracted Alex simply because it was an idea that seemed almost contemporary to his own time. As a kid he'd seen drawings for just such pneumatic railroads in *Popular Mechanics*. Usually along with articles and schematics of cars with wings, boats with wheels, and self-cleaning houses.

"Hmmm," Twain said. "Might work. You'd have to have a series of fans along the way to keep up the velocity." He nodded to himself and bent closer to look at the printed explanation. He took out a notebook and wrote something down.

Alex had a moment's pause as Twain began writing; he'd meant this as a mild joke, not something Twain would really want to invest in. He forced himself to relax. He'd never heard of the Mark Twain Pneumatic Railroad, so he was probably safe.

"Clever," Twain said, straightening up. "I'll look into it. What else have you got?"

Alex smiled. "I saved the best one for last. We had to do a tour of all of the state buildings and I found something inter-

:sting in Massachusetts. We'll take the exposition train so you won't have to expend any energy."

Twain nodded. "It's true, I've got to conserve myself. Just his morning I was lying in my bed and I suddenly realized hat in 1977 I'll be one hundred and forty-two years old. If I'm :o be any use at all in those days I've got to save myself now. Too much walking, especially outdoors, and it's good-bye, :anary."

Alex tried to remember how Twain would eventually die. He couldn't remember exactly, but he was fairly sure it wasn't ung cancer. Not that the man wasn't asking for it with the :onstant cigar. For a moment, he felt a chill as he realized he was contemplating the eventual death of the man he was standing next to.

The small train that ran the circumference of the exposition :ook them at a leisurely pace while Alex pointed out the sights. They circled around the huge Agriculture Building. 'Please," Twain said, "no exotic seeds, no prize yams." Finally, the train slowed and stopped at the small station at the :nd of Belmont Drive. A short walk past a row of state buildings brought them to Massachusetts. Inside, after strolling past glass cases filled with rock samples and models of various manufacturing processes, Alex steered Twain to an exhibit hat had been shoehorned in beneath the stairway to the second floor.

"I found this the other day and thought you ought to take a ook at it." He pointed to a table with a piece of electrical apparatus bolted to the top. There was a conical tube on top of a square base with several large batteries attached to the side. A wire ran from the base of the machine, off the table, and under the stairs. There was no accompanying explanation, but Alex had recognized it for what it was, and he thought he :ould explain it to Twain. He did not expect to be believed. In :act he thought it might be dangerous if he *were* believed. But ne'd take the chance. In a few years, Twain would look back on the moment and remember it vividly.

"May I help you gentlemen?" a voice behind them asked. They both turned and found a young man with black springy hair, broad mustache, and matching muttonchops. The man was coatless and had a large posterboard underneath his arm. He had a Scottish accent. "This is my exhibit," he said, almost shyly. "I'll explain it to you if you like."

"Well . . . yes, I guess so," Alex said. "We don't want to take up too much of your time." He hadn't thought that Bell would be around until closer to opening day. What he didn't need was Twain investing in the telephone, which would genuinely make him a millionaire in just a few short years. He knew that Twain wrote for pleasure, but it was the pressure of keeping up a lavish life-style that kept him to his enormous output. Without that economic impetus he might choose to spend his creative energies tossing off curmudgeonly broadsides aimed at all his pet peeves. Not exactly *Huckleberry Finn.*

"My name is Alec Bell," the man said, leaning the posterboard against the wall. He shook hands with both of them. Twain introduced himself as Samuel J. Langhorne.

"The purpose of my invention is the transportation of the human voice by means of electricity. When I say the human voice, I mean exactly that. The person at one end of my device will hear the actual words and the actual voice of the person speaking on the other end. I call this invention the telephone." Alex glanced at Twain, who was looking politely attentive. "If you gentlemen will remain here and allow me a few moments to go to the other end of my apparatus, I will give you a demonstration."

"Certainly," Twain said, raising his eyebrows at Alex, who nodded in agreement. "We'd like nothing better."

Bell gave them a short bow. "Please remain here. In a few moments, if you will listen to this device," he tapped the edge of the black conical tube, "you will hear my actual voice speaking to you from the other side of this very building." He gave them another small bow and excused himself.

Twain moved in behind the table and bent over the apparatus. He wiggled the wires on the side of the box and peered into the tube. "Empty as a beer closet where painters are working," he said. He looked up at Alex. "Seems like a nice young man. A bit on the milk-and-toast side, but nice enough

His proposition needs to be taken with a ton of salt, but I'm always open to a new idea."

A faint clicking sound came from the device. Both of them leaned close. A faraway voice, tinny and scratchy, but identifiable as Bell's issued from the tube. "Ahoy, ahoy," the voice said. "To be or not to be, that is the question." Twain looked at Alex with raised eyebrows. There was a moment of silence and then the sound of a throat being cleared. Faintly at first, but then louder as his confidence grew, Bell began singing a Scottish ballad that seemed to feature an outlaw and a wee bonnie lass. They listened to several verses. Twain straightened up and stepped back. Even standing away from the telephone they could still hear Bell's tinny voice working away at the song.

"The question is not how it works," Twain said, "but how to stop it." They stared at the telephone until Bell ended the song. In a few minutes he was back at the table with them.

"Very impressive," Twain said, Alex nodding agreement. "But I have several questions. First of all, is it possible to speak into this end and be heard where you were, and secondly, is it possible for both parties, one at either end, to speak at the same time? Or must each wait until the other is finished before speaking?"

Bell looked down at the table. "As yet we are able to speak in only one direction along the line, but we feel sure that we will have solved that problem in the near future. At this point one person listens to the other, and then responds by telegraph. And it will not be possible to speak both at once because the speech would perforce be unintelligible."

Twain nodded. "Have you heard of the multiple telegraph?" he asked.

"Yes, of course. In fact I have done extensive work on a device of that nature. While it would indeed be advantageous to send multiple messages along one line, I feel that, in the long run, the ability to actually hear the voice of the other person outweighs almost all other considerations."

"Yes, well, it certainly has its appeal," Twain said. "And carried to its logical conclusion, it brings you to my prospective invention, the Mental Telegraph. Does away with all the wires and attending apparatus." They all stood without speaking for a moment. Alex could almost see Bell trying to decide if Twain were serious, joking, or insane.

"Well, we wish you all the luck with your machine," Twain said, smiling. "What did you call it?" Bell supplied the word. "Telephone," Twain repeated. "Yes, of course." After a round of handshaking, Twain led the way back through the building and outside.

He looked around the yard in front of the building and drew a cigar from the inside pocket of his coat. "I don't give a damn," he said, "I'm going to smoke. They can shoot me if they want to." He lighted the cigar.

"You were being a little hard on him, weren't you," Alex asked. They both turned toward the train stop and began walking.

"Well, I hate to encourage every cub who comes along, especially if I don't agree with his notions. That's a very pretty invention he's got. Think of a man being able to hear his mother's voice from far away—but as far as business applications go, I don't see the worth of it. It's the Multiple Telegraph that will take the prize, mark my words. Besides, will it transmit profanity? We don't know, but I suspect not, and if not it would be of no use to me. And if you had one in your home every oyster-brain with his own machine could use it to sing imbecilic ballads at you until you went to the asylum. No, I'd not go a cent on it." They walked in silence for a moment as Alex told himself several times to just keep his comments to himself. Eventually Twain would not only own a telephone, but would, he recalled, invent the telephone booth. Early users protected their privacy while on the telephone by putting blankets over their heads, and Alex could not picture Twain with a blanket over his head.

"Now, that air train we saw at the Main Building, that's a different horse," Twain went on. "That's a ten-strike invention and the place for a man to lay his money. Take my advice on this one, and you'll never be sorry."

Chapter 25

The air in the room was thick with the by-products of Twain's cigars, the kerosene lamp, the coal stove, and Uncle's fried chicken. The burlap curtain had been tacked up, but the still outside air remained outside, as if unable to displace the heavier air within. Twain was at the head of the table; Abraham, Alex, and Uncle arranged at the sides, and Elias sat, tilted back in his chair, at the end.

The meal was awkward, mostly silent, Twain uncharacteristically so. Alex could feel the tension. It seemed to lie in the room like a volatile invisible gas, pooling and curling around their legs, waiting for some stray spark of ignition. After eating they cleared the table and Twain smoked while each waited expectantly for something to happen. Abraham and Uncle were patient; Elias, half-smilingly cynical, almost enjoying the strain; Twain wary; and Alex embarrassed and uncomfortable. The door opened quietly and Cato, a dark yellow shadow, slipped in and sat on a box against the wall.

"You are a cook, a professional," Twain said to Uncle. "It shows in the chicken." Uncle nodded his thanks. "I have been blessed with Negro cooks for much of my adult life." He looked around the table at the men who were watching him. He put both hands flat on the table, as if testing the strength of it. He seemed to understand that it was up to him to make the first move.

"In the summer we, my family and I, live with my sister-in-law and her family in the country. A number of years ago their cook told me a remarkable story. I wrote it up, just as she told it, and published it in *The Atlantic*. First piece I ever sold them." Twain paused, as if waiting for someone to ask him to continue. No one did. Alex had decided before the evening began that Twain was on his own, that he would not help him over the rough spots.

You could almost see the story settle over him. His eyes became distant, looking into the past rather than seeing the present. "Her name was Aunt Rachel, and she was a large woman. Sixty years old with undimmed eye and unabated strength. She was a cheerful, hearty soul, and it was no more trouble for her to laugh as it is for a bird to sing." He took the cigar from his mouth. It always surprised Alex that Twain's drawl was intelligible even when he had a cigar clenched between his teeth. Twain looked around, then placed it on the table so the burning end projected over the edge.

"It was our custom to sit on the porch of an evening and chaff her and watch her laugh. As I watched her one evening a thought occurred to me. 'Aunt Rachel,' I said. 'How is it that you've lived sixty years and never had any trouble?'" He waited for a moment, then added, "Understand I had never heard her sigh nor seen her when there wasn't a laugh somewhere in her. But the look that she gave me that evening sobered me considerably." He looked up from the table. Elias slowly lowered his tilted-back chair upright and crossed his arms over his chest. The two men looked steadily at each other for a moment.

" 'Has I had any trouble, Mr. Clemens?' Aunt Rachel asked. 'I was born amongst the slaves, and I know about slavery, for I was one. As was my husband. We had seven fine children, and I loved them just the same as you love yours. The Lord don't make any child so black that the mama don't love them. She wouldn't give them up for nothin' in the world. I was raised in Virginia,' she went on, 'but my mother she was raised in Maryland.' " Twain's voice was changed. He had, in his telling of the story, taken the role of Aunt Rachel. " 'Mama was terrible when she got started—my land, she could make the fur fly. When she'd get into them tantrums she had a word that she used, she always had this one way of speakin', she'd say,' " Twain straightened up in his chair and said in a high, forceful, commanding voice, " 'I want you to understand that I weren't born in the mash to be fooled by the trash! I is one of the ol' Blue Hen's Chickens, I is!'

"Evidently people from Maryland call themselves the Blue Hen's Chickens," Twain said dryly. "Or at least Aunt Rachel said they did. Aunt Rachel said she remembered that phrase so well because her mother used it with great emphasis and often. And so she used it herself. She had one memory of her mama in particular. They were in the kitchen when Rachel's little boy Henry came running in. Henry had hurt himself badly, cut his wrist and busted his head right up on the top of his forehead. 'They was niggers flying roun' the kitchen,' Rachel said, 'but they wasn't flying fast enough for Mama. She was a hollerin' at them to get this and that and then they talked back to her. Well, she just reared back and said it, said, *"Look-a-heah, I want you niggers to understand that I wasn't born in the mash to be fooled by trash. I'se one of the ol' Blue Hen's Chickens, I is!'* " She cleared out that kitchen and bandaged up that child herself."

Twain fell silent for a moment and Alex glanced around the table to see how the story was being received. The expressions on the faces of the others had not changed appreciably. So far, it seemed that he was the only one mortified by Twain's use of the word *nigger* and the dialect.

"Anyway," Twain went on, "one day the slaves got word that the woman who ran the plantation had gone broke and they were all to be sold at the auction in Richmond. They were all taken there and Rachel had to watch as first her husband was sold and taken away, and then each of her children until they were down to Henry, the littlest, and her pride. She told them she'd kill them if they tried to take him. But they did, of course. Before they tore that little boy from her he clung to her and said how he'd run away and then work and find her and buy her freedom. She fought them as best she could, and she was a great strong woman. But they beat her."

Alex could see Uncle nodding his head. Twain was staring at the rough wood tabletop. "Years went by. Rachel worked for the man who bought her, a man who became a Confederate colonel. Eventually the Union took the town and came to her house to set up their headquarters. The man who owned her, and his family, had run away. She stayed on, quite happily, to be the cook for the Union staff, eager to be of some help. They were good to her, these soldiers, told her if anyone meddled with her she should just tell them to walk chalk, for her to remember that she was among friends. So one day she went to them and told her story. She asked them if any of them had seen her little Henry, they'd know him by the scars on his wrist and on his head. But they hadn't seen him, and they told her that Henry probably wouldn't be so little anymore, as thirteen years had gone by since she had last seen him.

"So one evening there was a soldier ball in her kitchen. Evidently it was a very big kitchen. Aunt Rachel said she hated those balls, that it rasped her to have common soldiers dancing around her kitchen busting things up and making a mess. She'd put up with it for a while. Then she'd just chase them all out. On this night the soldiers were from a colored regiment sent to guard the officers at their headquarters. One boy stood out, a tall handsome fellow, the best dancer among them, with a fine-looking yellow woman as his partner. And this fellow and his partner danced right in front of Rachel and made fun of her red turban. 'Git along with you, rubbage!' she said to them. The man stopped his dancing for about a second, but then he went back to smiling and laughing and making fun, and pretty soon everyone else was laughing, so Rachel just lit into them. She was hot, she was blazing." Twain looked around the table at the others, who were unconsciously leaning toward him. Even Elias, with his slight, sardonic smile, was watching closely.

"That Rachel straigthened herself up and planted her fists

on her hips and said, 'Look-a-heah! I want you niggers to understand that I wasn't born in no mash to be fool by trash. I is one of the ol' Blue Hen's Chickens, I is!' Then she marched on those boys and drove them right out of that house. At the door, the tall, good-looking boy stopped for a minute, but she stared him down until he shook his head, and then he turned and left her alone.''

There was a small creaking sound as Cato shifted on his box. For a moment a breeze from the window stirred the air. In the morning she was back in the kitchen. She was baking biscuits. She was leaning over with one hand on the door of the hot stove and the pan of fresh hot biscuits in her other hand when a black face came up under hers with the eyes looking up and for a minute she just looked and then she knew. Her hand began to tremble and then the biscuits were on the floor. She grabbed that boy's hand and pushed back the shirt off his wrist, and then she went for his forehead and pushed back the hair, and then she cried out 'Lord God, Heaven be praised, Heaven be praised, I got my own again!' ''

No one moved. Alex thought he could hear each man breathing, could almost hear the beating of their hearts.

"Back on that porch, the evening had stretched into night. Aunt Rachel stood there, black against the stars, and I couldn't see her face, but I could hear her. I hear her right now. 'Oh no, Mr. Clemens,' she said to me. '*I* ain't had no trouble. And *so joy!*' ''

Twain sat with his head back and his eyes closed. He roused himself, shook the cloth of the story from him, and picked up his cigar. He looked at it, almost sadly. Then he put it in his mouth and looked around the table.

"How much did you pay that woman for her story?" Elias asked.

"What?" Twain asked.

"I asked how much you paid her for her story. You got paid, didn't you?"

"Yes, I did. It's customary."

"It was the woman's story, you said. You put it down just as she told it. I just wondered how much you paid her for it.''

"I paid her nothing. I was paid since it was I who wrote it Since she could neither read nor write, she was incapable o writing it for herself." His voice was level but carried a tone that Alex had never heard from him before. "I assume the point that you are making is that I owed her something fo supplying it. That, my friend, is not customary."

Elias shrugged his shoulders. "What is custom is not neces sarily what is right. Whatever happened to her husband and the other six children?"

Twain studied Elias for a long moment. "I don't know. She didn't say."

"I guess she just got back the one son," Uncle said, shaking his head. "It's true there's some joy in that. But most the family still gone, most dead I imagine. At least scattered so' they can't get together again. It's sure that woman had a mess of trouble in her life. Most of us colored can tell you stories just like that, Mr. Twain. How big is that 'lantic book o yours?"

"Ain't that big," Cato said from his position against the wall. "Ain't no book big enough for all the stories I heard tell."

Twain looked at Cato for the first time. He turned back to the table and sighed. "I seem to have missed fire here. The point of the story was that in the midst of all her trouble, there came to this woman great happiness. That she found her los son. I meant nothing more by it."

"Always something more to stories," Uncle said. "That the power of them. Sometimes even the one that's telling them don't know all that's there. Sometimes it pays a man to look again at a thing he thinks he knows, just to see if he can learn from himself. That's the most important kind of learning. And the hardest."

"Perhaps," Twain said.

"You tell one, Uncle," Abraham said.

"Yes," Elias said. "I'm sure Mr. Twain would like to hea one of your stories. Uncle is our storyteller," he said to Twain "The people in this small community, especially the children rely on Uncle for his stories. They are our philosophy, our history."

"I would appreciate it," Twain said.

Uncle looked around the table and then down at his hands, thinking. His skin was thick and wrinkled, the knuckles large with work and age. He rubbed the palm of one hand against the top of the other and there was a rasping of dry callused flesh. He nodded to himself.

"Rabbit met ol' Frog on the road. Each was looking for something to eat for his dinner. Rabbit thought he might like some greens out of Miss Sally's garden, or maybe some roastin' ears or some cabbages or some sparrow grass. Frog, he wouldn't hold with such truck. He was looking for flies or other sorts of bugs. On this day, it would have been better for ol' Frog if he'd just nodded and spoke polite and passed on his way, but that was not the way Frog was built. See, Frog was a wagering animal, and the thing he liked most was to wager on himself."

Alex looked at Twain, who was smiling. Uncle did not notice either of them.

"So ol' Frog was sittin' in the road watching Rabbit just comin' on, and he got to thinking. Between all of the animals of the forest the ones that hops the most and the best was Frog and Rabbit. There was Cousin Toad, but he was an ugly thing and of no account. And while he could see that Rabbit was a prodigious hopper, he was sure that when it came to that particular means of travel, he, ol' Frog, was second to none.

" 'Hold on there, Mr. Rabbit,' said Frog. 'Good day to you.'

" 'Good day to you,' said Rabbit, stopping and scratching at himself with his hind leg.

" 'I wonder if I might to bother you for a minute of your time.'

"Rabbit didn't care much for Frog, but he'd been brought up polite. 'All right, but I'm in a big hurry,' he said. 'If I don't get to that garden soon it'll be too late for me to get my dinner.'

" 'Quick is what I been wanting to speak with you about. I seen you coming down this road lippity-clippity, and I said to myself, Frog, that Rabbit is one fine hopper, but he cain't hold no candle to one such as yourself, and I'd be willing to wager on it.'

"Rabbit knew Frog, and how he was always so high on himself. That kind of talk just grated on him till he was ready to do something about it. And that's the kind of animal that Rabbit was. If he didn't think something was right, he'd just do something about it, 'specially if he might see some amusement in it. So he said, 'What is it you got in mind, Frog?'

"'What I was wondering, Rabbit, was if you'd be wanting to run you a hopping race with me. Just to see who is the best at it in this country.'

"Mostly it was the tone of it that scratched him. Anyway, Rabbit said he'd be glad to take him up on it, but he couldn't at the moment as he had to get his dinner for his family. So Frog say tomorrow would do, so Rabbit say all right, they just meet right there at that same place and they have that contest. Then each said good-bye and went on about his own business."

All of them were watching Uncle as he told the story. The old man sat quiet for a moment then stood up and went to the shelf and got down his gray stoneware jug of dandelion wine. Abraham put the crystal glasses on the table. Twain picked up one of the glasses and held it toward the light.

"Now, Rabbit," Uncle said, pulling the cork from the jug, "thought he could have won such a race, no matter what. But there didn't seem to be no fun in it that way." He poured the wine into the glasses and handed them around the table. He held one out and Cato took it.

"Down in Miss Sally's garden was an old shed that her daddy used to keep his tools and such. Rabbit had been forced to hide in that shed on more than one occasion, so he knew it. Leaned up in one corner was an old shotgun and a box of shells. Now Rabbit, after he eat several cabbages, went in the shed and fetched out those old shells and carried them home.

"That night he emptied the shot from the shells and his wife sewed up a little cloth bag with a drawstring. Then he write out a note on a scrap of paper and put it all away. The

next day he set out for just that spot where he to meet
Frog later on. There, at the side of the road, he leave that bag
and that note. Then he hid himself in some bushes where he
could see.

"Pretty soon along came Frog. He stopped right at the bag.
He kind of pushed at it with his foot, and then he saw the
note. Frog picked it up and read it. 'Fast Pills,' the note said.
'Eat just one.'

"Well, Frog peeked into that bag and saw all those little
shot pills and got to thinking. Then he up and ate one of them
fast pills."

Alex looked around the table and found all of them smiling.
Even Elias looked amused.

"I'd bet he'd go and eat more than one," Abraham said.
They all laughed.

"That's right," Uncle said. "That Frog got to thinking even
more on it, and you know what he figured. Pretty soon he'd
eaten every pill in that bag. About then Rabbit went down the
field a ways and got on the road and came hopping down just
like he was coming from home.

" 'What's in the bag, Frog?' he asked.

" 'Nothin',' said Frog, kicking the bag off the road. 'Don't
mind no bag, just get yourself ready to be whipped in a hopping race.'

"Brother Rabbit just nod and line up alongside Frog. 'All
right, Frog, you just say "Go" and we'll commence to see who
is the best hopper.'

"So they hunkered down and Frog hollered 'Go' and Rabbit
sat back and watched as Frog pushed down with his hind legs
and grunted and went nowhere. Old Frog tried again, but he
just sat there, solid as a gob of mud.

" 'What's the problem there, Brother Frog? Your hop looks
like it's done git.'

"Frog looked at Rabbit and gave another heave, but it
wasn't any use. His belly was sagged down to the ground, and
he might as well been nailed to that spot.

" 'Who the fastest now?' Rabbit ask.

"Ol' Frog was quiet for a minute while he tried to riddle it out. The only thing he could figure was that those pills not only didn't work, but had somehow robbed him of all his hopping power. But just as quick he saw that it didn't matter anyway.

" 'It won't be no use to tell anyone about this,' he said. 'We didn't wager nothing, and no one will believe you anyway. It might take a while, but I'll get my hop back and no one will know no different.' Then he smiled that big wicked frog-smile that was just full of spite.

" 'Maybe so,' Rabbit said, grinnin' back at him. 'But I saw Mr. Fox coming down the road just over that hill, and he's looking mighty hungry. You just explain it all to him.'

"And with that, Brother Rabbit hopped on down the road."

• •

For a few moments Twain was quiet as they walked along the stretch of fence that bordered the exposition. It was not late, but the park was closed and few people were out walking. They hurried toward Twain's hotel. The night had grown cool. A small wind curled around them, stirring up the dust.

"I understand I didn't use my best hold with that Aunt Rachel story," Twain said, turning up the collar of his coat. "It's not the first time I've misjudged an audience. But I felt about as small as a homeopathic pill when that old man used my own 'Celebrated Jumping Frog' story on me. To say nothing of his moral. That was a shot that hit and hurt."

"Oh, I don't know. I doubt he's ever heard your story. Besides, I don't think he was referring to you with the moral. I think he was speaking in general."

"Bah, a cow could have seen what he was getting at. 'Some animals are full of shot,' he says, 'and some animals are full of shit. Usually it's the same animal.' An oyster-brain could have understood he was talking about me. And the thing that really gravels me," he stopped and turned toward Alex, his voice rising as he wagged his finger in Alex's face, "the thing that makes me feel like an imbecile, is that, by God, his ending for that jumping-frog story was better than mine!"

Chapter 26

The pounding woke them. Elias opened the door as the rest of them pulled on their clothes. A policeman handed him a note that had Alex's name written on the outside. "Come to my office," Alex read. And scrawled at the bottom by an impatient hand, the word, "Immediately." It was unsigned but there was no doubt who had sent it: Brannon.

• •

The first thing he noticed when he walked into the office was the arrow. It was lying on a pile of papers on Brannon's desk. The shaft was stained a rusty brown, the feathers bedraggled.

"You failed me, Balfour." Brannon was in his chair behind the desk. His arms were crossed over his uniformed chest. His face was stern, his voice tinged with a mocking sadness.

"What do you mean," Alex said, clearing his throat. He was on the defensive before they'd even begun. He was nervous. He was guilty. He found it very difficult not to look at the arrow.

"I gave you a job, a responsibility, and you failed me."

"You told me to keep Abraham away from the Indians. He hasn't been near them." He wanted to stop justifying himself, but he couldn't. Even before he walked into the room he knew what the meeting would be about. Everyone at the exposition had heard about the buffalo. Everyone knew it had to be the Indians. He knew Brannon would blame him.

Brannon shook his head. "Let us not evade the issue. I also told you there was to be no more trouble." He leaned forward and touched the feathered shaft.

"What are you getting at, Brannon?" Alex asked. He felt like a child standing in front of his father, waiting for punishment. He had stood so, many times. It did not matter whether or not he had been guilty, or innocent. He had been afraid. "If you've got something to say, get it over with."

Brannon stood and picked up the arrow. He walked around the desk. "How was the hunt? Did it amuse you? Did your friend enjoy it? Perhaps this evening the two of you can run off and attack a wagon train." He stopped in front of Alex.

Either Brannon knew he'd been with High Cloud, Alex thought, or he was pretending he did. If he knew for sure, he was playing with him; if he didn't, he was fishing. Either way it wouldn't help to lie. "I didn't want him to do it," Alex said. "I couldn't stop him. I suppose it was my fault, but there was nothing I could do. Not that it makes much difference."

"No." Brannon shook his head. "It doesn't make any difference at all. The point is," he held the arrow up and smiled, it was a very cold smile, "you failed me." Alex stood silently. Just as a child he had stood before his father and heard the same words, *you've failed me,* applied to any number of situations. Only after he had become an adult had he realized that failure had never been the issue; the lectures and punishments were institutions of power. His father had the need of power, even over his own child. The issue was control; then, and with this man, now.

"The arrow went all the way through," Brannon went on, conversationally. "My men pulled it out unbroken. Amazing. You have to admire the Indian's strength and skill. Sharp as a razor." He walked away a few steps. "The Indians don't use flint anymore. They take the iron from the wheels of the wagon trains they capture." He turned back to Alex. "Custer will be here day after tomorrow. Barnum as well."

And so it was upon them. No more ifs and whens to confuse the issue, Alex thought. Two days. "And you're still going through with it? Selling them to Barnum?" he asked, though he knew the answer. He was trying to give himself time to think, to plan.

Brannon laughed. "Oh, yes, they'll be gone in two days. You should be happy; it relieves you of your responsibility. And mine. There'll be trouble enough when we open, without those two. No more fights, no more midnight hunts, no more savages to coddle. We've treated them well here, and they didn't appreciate it. Had they tried to be more cooperative it might not have ended this way."

"Cooperative?" Alex shook his head, anger beginning to edge away his fear. "Bullshit. Custer attacks their village and kills their friends and relatives. He takes them captive and eventually drags them all the way across country to dump them here. They're expected to live in a tepee staked out in the middle of the fairgrounds, ogled and taunted by every fool who walks by. Now you're going to turn them into circus clowns, and you expect them to be cooperative? To be grateful?"

Brannon stepped close to Alex. They were the same height, but Brannon was heavier, his uniform tight over his upper body. His face was flushed. He pressed the arrowhead against Alex's chest. " 'Shit,' is it? 'Ogle'? 'Taunt'? Oh, those are fine words, my boy." Alex felt the point of the arrow begin to cut into his skin. "Let me tell you something." Brannon went on, emphasizing his words with little jabs of the arrow. "There was a time when those two were treated very well, very well indeed. I tried to help them, but they rejected my kindness. The woman chose the company of a colored man over mine; so now they'll both pay the price." Alex thought he could feel blood running down his stomach. He wanted to step back, but he wouldn't. "And something else." Brannon was almost whispering. "If you try anything to help them, or if the nigger interferes, it will go hard with you, I can promise you that. Very hard." He gave the arrow a sharp twist and stepped back.

"Now get out of here."

• •

He would not look until he got back to the house. He knew it was foolish; Brannon couldn't see him after he left the office. But he never cried when his father hit him. He would not stop to look now. In the back room he unbuttoned his shirt. His skin was torn and a trail of blood stained the waistband of his pants. He found a scrap of cloth and pressed it over the wound. Two days.

Chapter 27

Molly and Will Two Horses sat in the old pickup truck on the edge of a great ravine. The series of connected canyons, dug and torn from the earth by the wearing and upheaving action of time, climate, and geology, had achieved such purity of desolation that men were reduced to the simplest of words to name it—the Badlands. Will had turned off the motor and the sound died away. There was only the wind as it whipped up over the lip of the gorge.

Will Two Horses looked out over the land and was silent, not because he hadn't words, but because he didn't need them. She realized that much of his appeal, at least for her, lay in his elemental reaction to events. She hadn't seen this in him at first, maybe it was hidden beneath his antagonism, a defensive mechanism that was automatic when dealing with unknown whites. But he was different from the men she came in contact with. He didn't seem to always explain, to have reasons and excuses. Most of the people she knew, and she had to put herself in this company, seemed perpetually off balance. To have foundations of shifting sand. She had never really noticed it, but the contrast of Will's solidity made her aware of it. People were always waiting for the ethical ground beneath them to move and demand new compromises and positions. It wasn't as if she didn't think Will Two Horses prey to all the confusions and foolishness of modern life. She didn't see him as the Noble Red Man, a romantic figure, but there was always that quiet, fundamental base.

I'm too far from home, she thought, I need the canyons of Sixth Avenue to steady me. I need my own land. "Is he down there?" she asked.

"What do you think?"

She contemplated the impossible terrain and tried to imagine herself or anyone else voluntarily heading into it. "Well, there's a whole posse of FBI men, Indians, and various law-enforcement personnel going down there tomorrow morning. They think he is, though I can't imagine it."

Will nodded. "It's a hell of a place to hide out—there's no getting around that. If you've the supplies, the talent, and the will, you could stay gone forever. If he wanted to, John Raven could make it down there. None of the ones who are following could, and won't. They'll be back in three days. Four, if the FBI man, Owen, is any good." He sat wearing his cowboy hat, arms crossed over his chest, looking out over the massive gulch. He had on a red-and-black checked flannel shirt with snaps instead of buttons; blue jeans and boots. He looked at her. "No, he's not down there."

His answer surprised her. She hadn't expected him to be so definite. "Do you know, or are you just guessing?"

"Both. John stays in an old shack back in the hills, an abandoned sheep herder's shack. He doesn't exactly live there, not all the time, anyway, but he keeps his stuff there. I went up and checked it out right after I heard what he'd done. He couldn't have gotten there before I did. His camping gear was gone, which meant he'd taken it with him when he shot the two guys. He knew what he was going to do when he left his place. He had a plan. He didn't shoot them just because he ran across them while he was out riding the reservation. And then there was the horse." He paused but she didn't interrupt.

"He got the horse from old Aunt Flower. She's not really his aunt, not by blood anyway. She lives even farther out in the hills than John does. They were friends—he'd help her out when she needed it, pack in supplies to her, make sure she was all right in the winter. I talked to her. She gave him the horse he's riding. A good horse, she says."

"Does the FBI know any of this?"

He shook his head. "Nobody would tell them. I doubt if they could have found either John's place or Flower's, even if they knew the general direction to look."

She had to ask it, even though she was somehow afraid of the answer. "Why are you telling me?"

He looked out over the canyon. "Something happened back there, when you and I were at Wounded Knee. I could feel it. I don't understand it any more than you do, but it's there, in the air, just as sure as the wind or the clouds. You don't need to say anything; I understand your position, but I'm not going to pretend that you don't mean anything in all of this. I know you've got a job to do, and you're going to do it. All I'm asking is that you go along and try to see things honestly and clearly and try to get the real story. If you're willing to do that I'll help you. I've got a stake in it, too. John's my client, and he's my friend. He's going to need me in both capacities before this is over." He didn't look at her.

"I always try to see things honestly," she said. He nodded, still not looking at her. "Maybe if I hadn't seen what happened out at Henry Sands's the other night I wouldn't be leaning in the direction I am, but I'm more interested in John Raven and the problems that made him do what he did than I am in the FBI getting their hands on him. You can trust me."

His eyes searched her face for a long moment as though he could find any lie hidden there or in her heart. She could actually feel him looking at her. He nodded. "Can you ride a horse?"

"Yes, quite well."

"You'll need camping equipment, a sleeping bag, and trail clothes. Not much but tough quality. I'll take care of the cooking gear and the food. I don't want to go right away, say, four days from now. We'll wait until the FBI gets back from their trip—then you can tell them you're off the story until something definite turns up. All right? Then we'll take off and you'll drop out of sight until we find him."

"I'll need to go back to New York to clear things with my editor—he's not going to like it. He'll never approve it over the telephone. I'll be gone two days, maybe three. I'll get what I need and meet you back here after Owen gets back up out of there." She gestured to the canyon.

"It won't be easy," he said. "It isn't the Badlands where we're going, but it's bad enough. We can figure something else out if you're not up to it."

The smile she gave him was humorless. "I'm up to it. And about what happened back at Wounded Knee—whatever it was, or whatever you thought it was, let's both forget it. I can't do this job if you think there's anything between us. You agree to that?"

His eyes held hers for a second before he nodded. She looked out the window and wondered why she hadn't told him about Alex, that she lived with someone. They watched in silence as the sun lowered toward the horizon. He opened the door and stepped out. After a moment's hesitation she joined him on the rim of the canyon.

The wind had dropped and in her down vest she was warm enough. It wasn't the cold that made her shiver, it was the desolation.

"Is he crazy, Will? You'd have to be crazy to go down there."

"I guess that depends on your definition of crazy. According to most white values, he's crazy. Belief in a sun god and talking animals would just about certify anyone in your world."

"And the business about being descended from Crazy Horse?"

Will loosened a pebble from the dirt with the toe of his boot and kicked it over the edge. They both listened as it ricocheted off the rock walls. "There are legends, well, maybe not legends, but stories about Crazy Horse. You won't see them in books because most books are written by whites and whites tend to mistrust speculation. But according to these stories, Crazy Horse had a lot of trouble with his women." He smiled at her. "It seems to be inherent in our Indian nature. He had several wives, one of them he stole from another man.

Another wife was a Laramie Loafer. You know what that is?" She shook her head.

"Whites tend to think of the Indians as all living on the plains. But a lot of them lived around the army forts. They were called Laramie Loafers, or Hang-around-the-Forts. In fact, many of the tribes spent the winters around the forts. Then in the summer they'd fade back into the hills and go on the warpath again. The whites didn't like it, but there wasn't much they could really do about it. Crazy Horse never lived like that, of course, but he fell in love with a woman who was born and brought up around the forts. He met her while she was visiting one of the summer camps. He took her away from there, and she lived with him until Custer attacked the village where she was staying and captured her. Crazy Horse was away at the time, or the outcome might have been a little different. It's sometimes said that she had his child, though other's say it was Custer's. Crazy Horse had another woman who bore him a daughter, but she died of cholera. Any one of them could have other children that we know nothing about. In fact it'd be odd if they hadn't. No one really knows. So maybe John Raven isn't so crazy after all." They both turned and watched as the sun went down, flaring bright orange and coloring the sky. They walked back and got into the truck, and he drove her, mostly in silence, back to the motel.

She packed her bag and made plane reservations out for the next day. She sat on the bed and watched stupid shows on television until she fell asleep. The next day, in the airplane as it flew eastward over the Badlands, she found herself looking for Frank Owen and his men and found herself looking down at the brown wrinkled land and wondering where John Raven was in all of it. And where Alex was, and where she would be.

Chapter 28

Alex pulled up the collar of his jacket and put his hands in his pockets. The cool evening had emptied the dooryards and stoops of the long line of shanties. On warmer evenings the row was alive with men standing in small groups, sitting on boxes, talking and laughing or just watching; a few women and fewer children. But tonight there were only the blank faces of the rough-board shacks and, from time to time, the faint sounds of singing from within, the thin smothered sound of religion and, perhaps, joy.

He couldn't sleep and hadn't wanted to talk to Uncle or Elias. There was too much to work through. Now that Custer's arrival was imminent, he would have to put some sort of a plan in motion if he expected to help the Indians. And he expected to. He wasn't sure why. Maybe it was because he had been with Little Spring, or hunted buffalo with High Cloud, or that he was sick of seeing them pushed around. Or maybe Brannon reminded him so much of his father that he had to oppose him. Or maybe because it just wasn't right, handing them over to Barnum for the circus. Whatever the reason, he was going to try to get them out.

He passed the last of the shacks and crossed the empty field at the edge of the unofficial exposition. He could see and hear the burning torches and the snatches of calliope music and shouting men.

Twain was off somewhere at a dinner after a day on business in Philadelphia. Alex was glad he was gone. He didn't want to see him until he had decided what he was going to do. Twain was an ally, one he thought he could trust, but he needed to know what sort of help he required before he could ask for it. There was little time now for contemplation or agonizing over niceties. Two days.

He stepped into the flickering light of the torches. The crude midway had been strewn with straw to soak up the mud, giving the line of shacks and tents the air of a strange carnival, one that could exist only in the night, or in the night's imagination. He stopped and bought a thick meat sandwich from a man who had set up a grill. "Buffalo meat," the man said, as Alex paid him fifty cents. "Fresh off the prairie." Alex looked at the sandwich, half-expecting to see an arrow hole. He wondered how the man had acquired the buffalo so quickly.

The basic structure of the plan was fairly obvious. He had to get the Indians out, that was the most difficult part, and get them back where they came from. The only practical way would be to take a train to as far as the train went, then get on horses and ride the rest of the way. He would need money. He ate his sandwich as he walked the midway, hardly hearing or seeing the barkers and hucksters gesturing to him.

Money. The only asset he had was his knowledge. What did he have that someone else wanted. He touched the front of his jacket. The zipper. Twain wanted to invest. What would that change? Alex knew that Twain had invested in, and would continue to invest in, an automatic typesetting machine. Over the years this outlay would drain him financially until he would be forced to leave the country and lecture abroad to pay off his debts. Why not alleviate that pain with the zipper? He was still running the chance that it would change Twain in some way, keep him from writing, but he had to do something. He would chance it.

He stood looking at the torches that lighted the carnival, the canvas tents, the straw strewn about, and the rest of the plan fell into place. It was dangerous, but what wouldn't be? The time was over for worrying; he had to act. He had the broad structure, the details would come. And if they didn't he would improvise.

• •

"Balfour, what are you doing here?"

Alex looked around and saw he was standing at the end of the carnival and Albert Riddle was peering up at him. The little man was everywhere.

"The same thing everyone else is doing, I suppose," Alex said. "Fooling around, looking for somewhere to spend my money."

Riddle nodded. "Want to see Serena's tits? She sees all, she shows all." He motioned with his thumb to the tent where the fortuneteller held forth. Alex looked at the painting over the doorway of the tent. Serena, at least in the painting, was white, fat, and not very mysterious looking.

"And if you want something else, something a little more, well, you know, she'll oblige. For a price, of course."

"Christ, Albert, you're into everything around here, aren't you?"

Albert thought a minute while he tried to decide if he should be upset by Alex calling him Albert. He preferred Mr. Riddle, especially from his employees. He shrugged. "A man's got to make a buck," he said. "Seriously, Balfour, she's one hot woman. I can recommend her."

Alex shook his head. "No thanks. I'm not interested." He started to walk away, but Riddle caught his sleeve. "Just a second. One more thing. You're a friend of that big nigger that hangs around here." Alex nodded. "Tell him to stay away. It makes people nervous to see him shadowing Serena's tent. It ain't decent having a nigger hanging around." Albert stepped back. Alex decided that he no longer found the little man and his obsessions amusing.

"Albert," he said, "you're disgusting." As he walked away from the man he found himself possessed of a curious lightness, as if the solution to his problem, or at least having a

workable plan, combined with telling off one of the local big-
ots, had freed his spirit from the malaise of uncertainty. Two
days. Not much time, but time enough.

• •

There had been no problem with High Cloud. The Indian
had grasped the idea easily enough. He had been shipped
from the far west to the centennial by rail, and he understood
quite clearly that a free trip home on the same conveyance
would be immeasurably easier than single-handedly fighting
his way across the country. As always, Little Spring gave no
indication of her thoughts.

Twain, on the other hand, as they sat at the Catholic Abstinence fountain the next day, served up a complication that
dwarfed all that had come before. A Goliath of a problem that
suddenly stood up and waved hello before striding forward to
smash everything in its path. Alex's smug satisfaction in his
planning and cleverness was swept away in the breezy simplicity of Twain's words.

"Custer's due in today, want to meet him?"

Custer? That couldn't be right, Brannon had said they had
two days. *Two days.*

It was midmorning, and they were having a glass of water.
Twain found the whole idea of abstinence and the fountain
amusing. "Wait a minute," Alex said. "What's he coming
for?"

"The Indians, of course. Why is it that we have so many
conversations two times? Surely you've not forgotten?" He
leaned forward and pretended to peer into Alex's face. "No,
that steel blade of sentimental morality is still evident. Men
like you never forget. A memory for inequity comes with a
bleeding heart. Indians, Custer, P. T. Barnum and his inesti-
mable and cursed circus?"

"Shit. He can't be here today, it's too soon."

"Well, you can tell him that when you meet him. Custer
sets his own schedules; you never know what the general is
going to do. Or when he's going to do it. You do want to meet
him, don't you? I should think you'd leap at it, one of the
heroes of our time."

Alex looked at Twain closely. Sometimes he said things that were too near the truth to be simply coincidental.

"You know him?" Alex asked.

"Ah, yes, our boy general. We've sat side by side at more than a few celebratory dinners. By the way, when you meet him, address him as "General." It pleases him. It's a brevet rank conferred upon him for exemplary service during the war. In today's army he's a colonel, and not very happy about it. At the moment I believe he's nothing, actually. He's in disfavor, relieved of his command for the time being. Although you'll notice that he pays little attention to such niceties."

"Why isn't he out fighting Indians?" Alex asked.

"As I said, he's on enforced leave."

Alex thought it over. How fast would Custer move? The answer was obvious, even knowing what little he did of Custer's nature. Very fast.

Alex felt a quickening, as if suddenly his life were about to be jammed into a lower gear and his was the hand, moving by command of some unseen overseer, that was about to do the jamming. He heard himself ask his next question with a certain amount of fascination, knowing that there would be no slowing down or turning back once it was out. "Mark, what did you have planned for tonight. Anything special?"

Twain thought about it for a moment. "Nothing special. I ought to be working on my Little People article, but our visit with your friends took the tuck out of that one. Smoke a few cigars maybe. What did you have in mind?"

"I thought we might bust the Indians out of here and make a run for the Black Hills."

There was a silence while Twain turned slowly in his chair to look at Alex. "Oh," Twain said. "On second thought, perhaps I'm busy." There was another long silence. "I assume you're serious."

"Yes."

Twain nodded and turned back away to face the fountain. He raised his glass and took a long drink of his water. He put the glass down and drummed on the table with his fingers.

"You don't see any way around it, I suppose?" Alex shook his head. Twain nodded. "I thought not." Twain sighed. "I've been waiting for you to come up with some sort of scheme about all of this." He waved his hand in the direction of the exposition. "But I feel a bit like the new bride the morning after her wedding. 'I expected it,' she said, 'but I didn't suppose it would be so big.'" He sighed again and sipped at the water. He put the glass down and made a face. "This just won't do. Let's go back to the hotel, and you can tell me what you've got in mind. Then I'll decide. I need a drink, a real drink. Water just can't carry the weight of such notions. Only whiskey will answer."

• •

Twain sawed off a piece of beefsteak and began to chew. Alex followed suit. The hotel dining room was still in the shakedown stage, and they'd found over the last several days that the steak was the meal least likely to go wrong. The meat was tough by the standards of his day, but Alex found the flavor more than made up for work it took to eat it. A diet of fat-producing corn, and the consequent loss of quality had yet to be discovered. This was grass-fed beef, lean and flavorful.

"Your plan is to hook the Indians out of there tonight while the guard and everyone else is sleeping? Secrete them somewhere until the next day when you can get them on a train out of here? And you'll go with them?" Alex nodded, still chewing. "How do you plan to pay for all of this?"

Alex swallowed. If Twain didn't go for this part the whole plan would have to be scrapped. "How would you like to buy controlling interest in my zipper-manufacturing concern?"

Twain's eyes widened. He sat silent for a moment. "That," he said, quietly, "is a deal. Now let me get it straight. You want me to figure out the best passage, procure the railroad car, and help you herd them out tonight?"

Alex swallowed. "That's it. I'd consider it a great favor."

"Jesus, when you ask a favor you go right to the top. Fifty-one percent of the zipper concern?" Alex nodded. "All right. I can think of several problems right off that a cow could put his finger on. Hoof, rather. First of all, there's always *someone* about, especially after you get off the grounds. Someone would see us. Secondly, where are you going to hide them while you wait for the train? How are you going to get them to the train the next day? Surely the alarm will have been rung by then."

Alex put down his fork. "I thought we'd start a diversion, something that would attract anyone who was still wandering around. I was going to keep the Indians at Abraham's. I haven't asked them yet, but I'm sure they'll do it. We'll put regular clothes on them and just walk out the next day. Nobody will expect Indians in white men's clothes."

Twain closed his eyes and looked pained. "You're costing me my appetite," he said, laying down his own fork. "It's too risky. Why don't we do this? Your diversion idea is right enough, but the rest won't do. I think I can wrangle us an invalid car from the railroad. I have friends in high places. I'll have it brought out here to a siding. The tracks are all around this place, and we'll take the Indians to your friend's shack, change their clothes, and walk them to the car once your diversion is underway. In the morning, the regular train will pick up the invalid car and you're out of here. We'll put a quarantine sign on it and no one will bother you."

"You can just hire whole railroad cars?" Alex asked.

"Of course, as long as you've the money. I've done it a number of times. My wife, Olivia, is an invalid."

Alex nodded. It sounded fairly safe. "And you'll do it?"

Twain nodded. "My sluggish soul needs some up-stirring. When I was out West at the beginning of my career, there was always a fire or an earthquake or a murder to keep me jumping. Lately I've sunk into a morbid torpidity. Even my cat has commented on it. As long as no one shoots a hole in me, it ought to be fun. I'll do it. Maybe I'll get some material out of it. Besides, you're going to make me the zipper king."

"Good. I believe it's worthwhile."

Twain smiled crookedly. "Oh, I'm aware of that. You've made your stand quite clear. I disagree with you, or at least your theories, but trying to stop you romancers is impossible. It's not the Indians you care about, or at least not these particular Indians. It's the *idea* of Indians that gets you worked up.

You read too many Fenimore Cooper novels." He shrugged. "I guess as long as my wife doesn't find out what I'm up to I'll be all right.

"Now," he said, leaning forward. "I'll go see to the railroad. We've time to get the car out here if I do it right away. You talk with your colored friends, and don't forget to find some spare clothing. I'll meet you back at the Indian encampment around five o'clock to introduce you to Custer. You make sure that the redskins understand what's expected of them."

"It sounds fine," Alex said.

Twain leaned back in his chair again. "There's just one thing I haven't been able to work into the equation," he drawled.

"What's that?"

"George Armstrong Custer." Twain sighed and closed his eyes.

"Just what the hell do you think he's going to do when he finds out you've stolen his Indians?"

Chapter 29

Alex squatted behind Serena the Fortuneteller's tent, and he watched Cato stuff a handful of greasy rags beneath a pile of trash and garbage. He made sure that the pile of trash was far enough from the actual tent, then nodded at Cato, who smiled, nodded back, and crept off into the night. As usual, Cato's death's-head smile did nothing to reassure him. Alex wiped the palms of his hands on his jeans and tried to swallow, but his mouth was too dry. He drew in a deep breath and held it for a moment. Then he stood and walked away, into the dark toward the shack where he hoped Twain was waiting.

• •

Earlier in the day he had explained to Uncle, Abraham, and Elias what he wanted to do. Abraham had immediately assented. Uncle, who had no real part to play, had simply shrugged, and Elias had glowered and said maybe. But if *maybe* meant no, it was too late now for anyone to change his mind. Cato, who'd included himself in, as usual, was to set up a line of potential fires behind the shacks and tents on the midway. All Alex wanted was a series of small fires, and he'd emphasized the word *small* a number of times, to draw everybody's attention away from the railyard behind the shantytown. Fire would draw everyone, even the guards and workers

t the railroad. Fire was the great disaster of these times, and
very able-bodied individual turned out to fight it, no matter
what else he was doing.

Alex went to the Indian encampment in the late afternoon
and waited for Twain. Twain didn't show up—but Custer did.
Surrounded by a group of younger officers, Custer had strolled
in, dressed in a blue blouse and Turkish officer's pants. He
carried himself with an air of proprietary confidence, laced
with mild disdain. If the exposition excited his interest, it
didn't show. A small crowd of workmen gathered as Custer
stepped into the yard of High Cloud's camp. Alex, without
Twain to introduce him, stood with the workmen. Custer and
High Cloud conferred in low voices while the group of officers
waited to one side. Little Spring stayed in the tepee. Custer
kept glancing at the tepee, as if he expected her to make an
appearance. If so, she disappointed him.

Custer seemed to be reassuring High Cloud of something.
The old Indian, indicating nothing by his expression, simply
watched as Custer spoke. Custer finished his business, waited
for High Cloud to respond and, when he didn't, motioned for
his men. He looked around the small encampment as if
checking to see that all was in order, nodded again to the
Indian, and stepped back over the low fence.

"General Custer," one of the workmen called. A look of
annoyance flickered over Custer's face; then he smiled and
turned toward the small crowd.

"Going to whip those redskins, General?" the man called.

Custer walked toward the workmen and stopped in front of
them. "The Indian is already whipped," he said, in a high
tenor voice. "The war is essentially over. There'll be fighting
yet, but nothing the Seventh Cavalry can't handle." He wasn't
a tall man, although he seemed to be. He had a decidedly
commanding air.

"I'd like to shake your hand, General," one of the men said.
"And just tell you we appreciate what you and your boys are
doing out West."

Custer nodded and stepped up closer. The men formed a
semicircle and began shaking hands. When he got to Alex,

Custer looked him straight in the eye and shook with a grip that hurt. Up close, Custer was even more handsome and assured than he had been at a distance, radiating strength and competence from his long blond hair to the tips of his high black riding boots. Alex could smell the faint odor of cinnamon oil, and he half expected to see a saber lashed to the man's waist and a pair of pearl-handled pistols jammed into his belt. History books had given him the impression that Custer was somehow effete and stupid, as if his hair, being blond and longish, made him vain and thereby weak. In the flesh, Custer appeared just the opposite. His hair was no longer than that of many of his contemporaries, and the fact he kept it obviously cleaner than most might have indeed indicated vanity, but it certainly wasn't a sign of weakness. Or stupidity. There was an aura about Custer that affected Alex just as strongly as it seemed to affect the men around him. But there was a difference between him and the other men, and that was his knowledge of how Custer would die. Over the other impressions of Custer floated the chilling feeling that he was shaking hands with not only a man who would soon be dead, but a man who would die one of the most famous deaths in history.

"General," Alex said. Custer turned back toward him. "Mark Twain sends his regards."

Custer frowned. "Twain? Here?" Alex noticed a small stammer on the letter *T*.

"He was to meet me here. He asked me to offer his compliments if he was detained."

Now Custer smiled. "Remarkable man, Twain. Very amusing. Are you also a writer?"

"Yes, my field is history," he said after a moment's hesitation.

"As is mine," Custer said with a smile. "Of course none of us will ever match Twain. I scribble myself, you know." Alex nodded. He knew that Custer had written at least one book on his life and adventures on the high plains. He also wrote regularly for magazines. Custer's writing style, in contrast to hat of most of the other writers of the period, was straightforward and honest.

"I've been trying to get Twain to write about me for years," Custer went on. "I'd like him to go on expedition with me. We'll be moving out soon, going to take on the Sioux. This would be a good trip for Twain. Don't suppose there's any chance of it, do you?"

Alex pretended to consider it. Now there was a complication that sent a shudder through him: Mark Twain at the battle of the Little Bighorn.

"I believe he's working on some sort of boy's book just now."

Custer nodded. "Well, no matter." He got hung up for a moment on the *m*.

"Do you have an interest in Indians, Mr. . . . ?"

"Balfour," Alex supplied.

"Balfour. Yes. I've a need for a writer on our coming expedition. I would give serious consideration to your application. Any friend of Mark Twain's . . ."

Alex held up his hand. "No, thank you, General. I do, however, have an interest in Indians. These two for example, I noticed you talking to the old gentleman."

"High Cloud," Custer said, looking back at the tepee. "An interesting specimen. One of the spiritual leaders of his tribe, a great warrior when he was a young buck. They won't let them stay here, you know, and I can't just let them go back to the plains. I had to wipe out virtually a whole tribe to capture him. The woman, too." He shook his head. "Barnum wants them, so I guess that's where they'll go. Coming to pick them up tomorrow." He stared off into the distance over Alex's head. "Well, it's been a pleasure, Mr. Balfour." He held out his hand. "If you change your mind about that position with the Seventh Cavalry, contact my adjutant." He turned to leave, but his attention was caught by High Cloud. He looked at the Indian for a long moment and turned back to Alex. "You know, Mr. Balfour, that Indian is a superb example of his race. Were I not Custer, I would be High Cloud." He turned and strode away, his retinue falling in behind him.

• •

Alex waited for a moment inside the door. The lamp was lighted, but the wick was low. Uncle was at the table, closer to the lamp. Twain was near the window, as if listening for something outside. Twain stepped toward him into the light and Alex felt a shock. He'd shaved his mustache off and cropped his hair so close to the scalp that it was barely discernible. He did not look like Mark Twain.

Twain smiled. "If anyone recognizes me in the course of this little adventure, I might as well scalp myself and lie down and die. My wife will surely do it for me if I don't." He rubbed his hand over the stubble.

"I don't think you have much to worry about in the recognition department," Alex said. "You missed Custer."

"I was busy. It took a while to convince the Philadelphia railroad to put a car out here. They promise to hook it up tomorrow for the regular run to Chicago. Fortunately I hadn't cut my hair yet, so my words carried a certain amount of weight."

"But you got it?"

Twain nodded. "It's here. And paid for. I rode it out from the city. I waited until they had it situated so I'd know which one it was. There's a whole herd of cars in the yard, and ours is just one of many. Is the diversion progressing?"

The door opened and Abraham and Elias came in. "Yes," Alex said, "Cato's setting up the fires."

"I'll light the ones at this end," Abraham said. "We get them all lit at the same time, they won't notice anything going on 'cept them fires."

"I don't like it," Elias said. "Someone's going to get in trouble for this, and I know right now it'll be a black man. Why doesn't he do the dirty work?" He pointed at Twain.

"Because he has to lead us to the railroad car."

"Don't matter nohow," Abraham broke in. "I'm doing it and that's that. These Indians are my lookout more than any one else's. Colored man stood around worrying about nothing but his own skin for too long—I'm going to light that fire, nobody else. You tell me when to do it, and it'll get done."

Alex looked at Elias. Elias stared back with hard black eyes that showed nothing but hate. "We have a chance here in this city, and you're going to destroy it for two Indians? I've seen this trouble coming since the day you walked through that door, Balfour. This is white trouble, and you're bringing it down on our heads."

"Trouble ain't no color," Abraham said. "We sit around and think of nothing but ourselves we ain't going to get nowhere. We'd be just as bad as whites if we decide it on the color of their skin. You know that, Elias. If we do it right, ain't nobody gonna know we did it."

"If we're going to do anything we'd better be at it," Twain interjected. "In one hour your friend Cato's going to light his first fire, and we'd better be in place when he does."

"I'll go with Abraham," Elias said.

Alex looked at him in the dim light, trying to see if there were some trick behind it.

"If he's going to do it," Elias said, "I'm going to make sure it gets done right and he stays out of trouble. You might not be worth it, but he is."

"All right," Alex said, and he turned to Twain. "You'll wait here. I'll go get the Indians and bring them back. It'll take me forty-five minutes." He was amazed how assured he sounded. He felt far from it. "None of the people who live along here are going to give us any trouble. It's the men in the railroad yard and at the carnival who might be a problem. We'll have ten minutes to get the Indians dressed and ready to go. Fifty-five minutes from now I want that fire lighted. By the time we get down there, we should have every able-bodied man who might cause trouble working to put the fires out. Five minutes after you light the first one, Cato should come up the line lighting the others. They're small and shouldn't get out of hand, but only we know that. It'll keep them busy."

Twain stopped him at the door. "Don't waste any time. I'll be in a sweat, and a few extra minutes to scout around might be useful."

"Sound like the story man got the whim-whams," Uncle said from his place at the table. "Come on, sit with me, we'll tell stories. I got one about a blue jay I think you'll like. Calm you right down."

Alex stepped out into the cool night and felt it dry the sweat that he hadn't noticed soaking his shirt. Whim-whams, oh yes, he knew the feeling.

• •

He lay underneath the Conestoga wagon, behind the wooden-spoked wheel, and watched the guard lean his chair back against the guardhouse. The light from a lamp in the shack silhouetted him against the doorway. He had just come on duty, and it was early for him to be sleeping.

High Cloud had volunteered to capture and tie up the guard. This was to occur shortly after the man took over and settled in. *Come on now,* Alex said to himself. *For Christ's sake, High Cloud, it's time.*

A shadow slipped beside the guard and tipped the chair over into the hut. Alex saw a brief look of amazement on the man's face and heard a startled yelp. The light in the hut went out. Alex crawled out toward the encampment.

High Cloud was waiting, standing next to a small pack. "Little Spring?" Alex asked, looking around. High Cloud nodded to the woman as she stepped over the fence into the yard. The moon was high and the sky cloudless, though Alex wished it were otherwise. It was bright enough to see the woman's features as she stared back at him. "I thought you were going to take care of the guard," he said to High Cloud. "We agreed on it."

High Cloud smiled. "She wished to do it. It did not matter to me. We are ready." He bent and picked up the pack and his bow and arrows.

"Goddamn it, you can't carry that bow. You'll have to leave it here. You can't walk around carrying a bow."

High Cloud put the strung bow over his shoulder with the pack. He motioned toward the tepee and Little Spring went to the flap and picked up her own pack. "I will take the bow," he said.

Alex swore to himself. "All right. We've got to go." They stepped over the low fence and walked quickly away. As they passed the guardhouse, Alex stopped and glanced in. The guard was on the floor, on his back, still sitting in his chair. In the pale moonlight, Alex could see the stain that ran the length of his jacket. It glinted wet and black, edging the gaping wound that ran from throat to waist. Alex could smell the stink of blood and excrement. He turned away, sickened. He tried to put it out of his head but it wouldn't go. He knew that the image of that awful wound would stay with him forever.

He caught up with the two Indians. Cato had shown him a loose wrought-iron paling in the fence. They removed it and crawled through. It saved them at least fifteen minutes. As they walked along the row of shacks, he wondered if there were men inside, watching and wondering what a white man and two Indians were doing there in the middle of the night.

He knocked softly on the door and went in. Twain stood up but didn't say anything. The Indians moved into the shadows near the corners of the room.

"I'll get the clothes," Alex said, stepping into the room where they slept. Abraham had bought the clothes with money Alex had given him. They had decided against elaborate disguises. Simple work clothes would call the least amount of attention.

He motioned the two Indians into the room with him and handed them their clothes. He made sure they understood what was required, then went back into the living area.

"You made good time," Twain said.

Alex noticed that Twain seemed to have lost his usual joking attitude. Somehow, it made Alex feel better to know that Twain was probably as nervous as he was.

Twain looked at his pocket watch. "We've got ten minutes before they start the fires. We should leave here in five minutes." Alex nodded and turned just as the front door slammed open and Elias stood panting in the doorway.

"They've got Abraham," he said, between breaths. "That bastard Riddle caught him behind the tent."

"Shit!" Alex said. He felt it begin to go wrong, begin to

twist away, out of his grasp. "You stay here," he told Twain. "Give us five minutes. Then come on the way we planned. We'll get Abraham away from Riddle." He glanced around the room and picked up his jacket. He pulled it on as he started out the door. As he ran, he felt the thump of his tape player against his side, and for a moment he doubted that any of this was real. He longed to wake up in bed or in a hospital and look around, groggy with sleep, and say that classic line, *Where am I?* But it did not happen, would not happen. He was too afraid to be sleeping, too afraid to do anything but run.

Chapter 30

A half dozen men surrounded Abraham and Riddle. Riddle was holding Abraham's arms behind him as if he were hand-cuffed, and Abraham, looking confused and frightened, allowed it. The incongruity of the huge black being held by the skinny little white man would have been laughable under other circumstances. Alex made himself walk slowly toward the group of men.

"Caught this nigger back behind Serena's tent," Riddle was shouting. "Had some matches in his hand. I figure he was set to burn something up."

"Why in hell would he want to do that?" one of the men asked.

Alex realized very quickly that as bad as it was, it could have been worse. Riddle was known to most of the exhibition workers as a fool. People might listen to him, but that didn't mean they would believe him.

"I'll tell you why," Albert said. "He's been hanging around here for the last month. He wants to see a white woman, and you know what I mean by that." Now he was shouting again. "By God, boys, he wants to look at one of our women. He wants to look at one of our women *naked*."

Several more men strolled up. Alex could see now that Albert was using the incident to drum up business for Serena.

It was good advertising. If a black man got hurt because of it, that was too bad. This was business.

"*Naked,* boys, and that doesn't sit right with me."

"Wouldn't sit right with anyone," one of the men said, "but how the hell's he going to see her naked by setting fire to her tent?" Some of the men laughed. "Think he's fixin' to burn all her clothes off?"

Alex glanced around. Elias was directly behind him. The look on the man's face shocked him. The skin was stretched taunt over the skull, his eyes were wild with hate. Several more men joined the crowd. In a few more minutes it would get out of hand and it would be too late. Twain would be arriving any moment with the Indians.

"Hold it," Alex shouted, pushing into the center of the circle.

"Don't listen to him," Albert shouted. "This doesn't concern you, Balfour." He pointed at Alex. "This man's a nigger lover, and you all know it. He lives with this nigger. He'll try to get him off, but we won't let him." There were a few murmurs of assent.

Alex could feel the crowd begin to warm to its work, as if Albert's invective, and the simple fact of standing close together, had set off a slow chain reaction, probably fueled by alcohol, that would arouse them to the ignition point if allowed to continue.

"Look," Alex began, raising his voice, "this man hasn't done anything wrong . . ."

"He's a nigger, ain't he?" someone yelled, and the crowd laughed.

"Didn't do *nothin'* wrong," Abraham suddenly shouted, his strong bass voice louder than all the others. "Just wanted to know, that's all, just stood around here because I wanted to know."

"Wanted to know what a white woman looked like," Albert shouted. "I think there's something wrong with that, don't you?"

Albert smiled at the chorus of assent from the men. "We

got him," someone shouted. "What are we going to do with him?"

"Let's whip his ass," Albert shouted. "Whip his black ass!"

"No!"

They all turned. Elias had climbed up on the raised platform in front of Serena's tent. He was standing with both arms upraised. "No, you white bastards. You've got the wrong nigger! You think he's dangerous?" He laughed. His eyes caught the torchlight and seemed to flicker with madness. "You don't need to be afraid of him. He's nothing. I'm the one you've got to fear." He hit himself on the chest. "*I'm* the bad nigger. *I'm* the one who hates you. That one is but a lamb. I am the *tiger*. I'd tear your hearts out and gladly eat them. I'd pluck your eyes from your head and cast them to the ground. Look at me if you want to hurt. Hate me."

The crowd turned to look in amazement at Elias and moved obediently toward the platform as if drawn by his curses. The tall, thin black man with the crazed eyes held them transfixed, a new channel for their hate. Abraham and Alex and Riddle stood alone.

"Oh, you devils, you white animals! You are the slaves, chained by your own fear," Elias shouted. He seemed on the verge of tears. "With your stinking fear and your pushing and your stealing. Goddamn every one of you to the hell you deserve."

"Just shut the hell up, nigger!" someone yelled.

"No! Kill me, that's all you can do. But you can't shut me up. I'll come back ten million times over. I'll ride you and your brothers into the grave, whipping you and goading you with my color and my pride. My pride is immense, awesome, and before it you are nothing, puny and impotent."

Alex was paralyzed by Elias's tirade. And by the anticipation of what the crowd would do. He knew he had to break away, that Elias was providing the means for him to get Abraham out, but now there was a new sound, a squeaking, scrabbling sound, and then a bark. Wheeling into the midway was Brannon on his dogcycle with the black man and his stick and the two dogs barking. Behind it all, providing a madman's notion of musical accompaniment, the wheezy calliope ground out its happy tune. Brannon stood up on the footrests as he rode, stood up in his uniform with the shiny brass buttons and he towered over the crowd, an apparition from some strange circle of hell. He pulled his rifle from the scabbard hung on the steering stick.

"You listen to me!" Elias shouted, leaning over and pulling a torch loose from the ground. "You've pushed us far enough. You bought us and you killed us and, by God, we've had enough!" He whirled the torch once around his head and the crowd stepped back. Elias whirled the torch again and laughed, a triumphant laugh that rose and lifted over the sounds of the crowd, over the whipping flame of the torch as he swung it around his head, and the dogs barking, and behind it all, unceasing, the demented calliope.

Someone shouted *fire!* and several men pointed toward the other side of the carnival. "Fire?" Elias shouted. "You want fire? Ask me. *Ask me for it!* I'll give you bastards what you want." Another man pointed to where Cato was doing his work, and shouted *fire* again. Elias laughed. And the world seemed to explode. Elias threw his torch into the doorway of the tent. The straw flooring and the canvas walls burst into flame.

Alex saw Brannon raise his rifle, the barrel bright with reflected flames, saw him raise the rifle and fire. Elias threw up his arms and fell off the platform. Alex looked back at Brannon and saw an arrow thud into the policeman's neck. Brannon dropped the rifle and clawed at the arrow, lost his balance and fell, clutching at the seat of the cycle as he went down. The cycle tilted up on one wheel, pulled over by Brannon's weight, held for a moment, then crashed to its side in a confusion of scrambling, howling dogs and twisting metal wheels.

Alex turned Riddle around and punched him in the face, dropping him like a stone. Alex grabbed Abraham's arm and pulled him away and began to run, lost for a moment in the confusion of shouting men and the blazing tent.

"Here, goddamn it!" It was Twain, shouting at him, his face pale, his shaved head oddly luminescent in the flickering light.

He held High Cloud by the arm. High Cloud thrust his bow high in the air with a triumphant laugh. At that moment Alex heard a high quavering wail that cut through the uproar like a cold knife slashing through soft unprotected flesh, and Serena, *she knows all, she shows all,* burst with a shatter of sparks through the wall of fire that was the doorway of her tent, her hair and veils and diaphanous costume a sheet of trailing brilliance that curled and wreathed her in a gown of incandescence, a fleeing holocaust that held as its center a dreadful scream, one that rose with the terrible flames higher and higher into the clear night sky.

He pushed them before him, Abraham, Twain, and the Indians, away from the awful flames, into the dark.

Chapter 31

"End of the line," Will Two Horses said, slowing the truck and stopping. The single-lane dirt track they had been following had faded into the surrounding grassland and disappeared. As the engine died, the trailing dust cloud caught up and surrounded the truck and the horse trailer. They sat in silence as the dust settled around them. One of the horses in the trailer sneezed.

"God," Molly said, looking out the windshield at the barren expanse spread before them. Somehow she didn't feel quite prepared for all the emptiness. It gave the impression of flatness even though the land was actually a succession of low rolling hills. Twisting ravines disappeared into the earth. In the distance the Black Hills were dark with pines against the bright blue cloudless sky. She was always struck by this sky, the enormous inverted bowl of it.

She pulled on the down vest she had stuffed behind the seat. She was wearing jeans and boots, a western shirt, and a cowboy hat. Will had been inclined to make fun of the hat at first, but its used and battered condition attested to some lineage. Also, she had pointed out, he was wearing a cowboy hat, and he was an Indian, which had led to a discussion of proper headgear for an Indian lawyer, which had led to a few laughs, which pretty much laid to rest the whole discussion of hats.

She opened the door of the truck and stepped out onto the grass. A spray of grasshoppers spurted up around her boots.

The only sounds were those of the light wind and the cry of a red-tailed hawk, wheeling high in the afternoon sky above them. She walked a few steps from the truck, knelt, and touched the dry earth. The ground cover was a mixture of prairie grass, weeds, flowers, and low spiny cactus. She stood and turned as Will let down the trailer's tailgate.

"Give me a hand," Will said, walking up the gate and releasing the horses. He ran his hand along their sides and talked to them. She waited while he untied the halter of the first horse and began backing him out. Once down, he handed her the halter, and she moved the horse away as he brought down the second.

They were both pintos, white with splashes of brown. Indian ponies, smaller than what the Indians called "American horses," but able to endure days of running with little or no rest. The one she was holding looked at her with intelligent brown eyes. She blew lightly into the horse's nostrils, saying hello.

"You do know something about horses," Will said, watching her.

"My uncle had a ranch in Colorado," she said. "I spent the first sixteen summers of my life there. I learned to ride and rope about the same time I learned to walk."

He nodded and tied his horse to the railing along the side of the trailer. She did the same and helped him unload the saddles, blankets, spare clothing, and camping gear. He spread it on the ground around them, checked it carefully, and packed it into bundles that would be carried behind the saddles. They saddled the horses and tied on the gear. He closed up and locked both the truck and the trailer. He checked everything again and pulled the cinch straps tight on both horses. He took a map out of his saddlebag and motioned her beside him. He squatted and opened the map on his knee.

He pointed to a spot on the map. "We're in Wyoming, not far from the border. I wanted to get us into another state to make it a little harder on the FBI if they decide to look for us.

We can leave the truck here—no one will run across it and report it. We're going to follow an old cattle trail all the way up into Montana. I've marked it in pencil so you'll know where you are if something happens to me."

She looked at his face. "What's going to happen to you?"

"Nothing, I hope. I didn't say it would, I said *if.*" He looked at her, then back at the map. "There's a lot of country between here and where we're going. We've got rivers to cross. There are plenty of holes for the horses to break their legs in, and there's John Raven."

"I thought he was your friend."

"Well, now, he is. But he might get a little spooked if he sees someone, two someones, trailing him. Of course, I guess he might just as well shoot you as me, but if he does, I'll at least know where we are. You, on the other hand, will be lost." He smiled at her.

"I can read a map," she said, standing. "Just where is it we're going?"

He stood up, folded the map and put it back into the saddlebag. He looked up and squinted at the sky. "It's getting late. Let's try to get a few miles behind us before we camp for the night."

"That doesn't answer my question." She untied her horse.

"Let's just say we're following John Raven. At least for now." He put his foot into the stirrup and swung up into the saddle. She did the same. He smiled again, leaned forward, and the horse started off at a walk. She watched his back, wondering whether or not to press the issue, and decided to let it go for the moment. She clucked to her horse and followed.

• •

Her editor hadn't liked it. His general rule was when a story died on you, you walked away until it either was buried or came back to life. Her point was that the story wasn't dead. It'd just gone into hiding. What she wanted to do was to go and look for it.

"I don't know, kid, it all sounds too iffy. From what you say you'll be out of touch for a long time, you might not find this

uy, we may need you for something else. It just doesn't sound
ke it's going to be worth the trouble."

They were sitting in the editor's office. She could look out
ver the newsroom at the other reporters. She'd traveled two
housand miles so he'd have a harder time turning her down
han he would over the telephone. Her editor wore suspend-
rs, which he referred to as braces. And called her "kid," even
hough he was only a few years older than she. He, like many
f the other editors, patterned his general style after the char-
cters in the thirties classic *The Front Page*.

"Harry, you're supposed to say it's too dangerous, that I
hight get hurt," she said.

"Yeah, that too." He nodded.

"Look at it this way—if I do find John Raven, it's going to
hake a hell of a story. We can do it as a series of think pieces
nd tie it in with the hard-news angle. The Plight of the Mod-
rn Indian, you know what I mean." If Will Two Horses
ould hear her talking this way he'd never take her anywhere.
lere in the office she didn't care what she sounded like, just
s long as they let her stay on the story. Even though she knew
 wasn't professional. When the two white men had smashed
pen the door and spotlit her without her shirt on, it had
ecome personal.

Harry tapped a pencil on a pile of copy while he thought.
Don't give me any bullshit now, you really think this is that
ig?" he asked. "It doesn't look like it from here."

"Harry, we've had two potential murders and my contact
hinks there may be more. If I find the Indian, great, I'll get a
rsthand story. If I don't find him, I'll be right there on the
cene when someone else does or he shoots a few more peo-
le. I've got good contacts with all sides involved. It's a classic
onfrontation between the old ways and the new, cowboys
nd Indians, good guys and bad guys. Except this time it's
ard to tell who the good guys are. It's got all the makings of a
ulitzer, Harry. Please, you know I don't usually cause you
ny trouble—let me do this."

She surprised herself. Not that she cared so much about the

story, but that she'd be willing to talk the way she did just to be allowed to stay on it.

Harry tapped his pencil some more, then punched up a file on his computer screen. He stared at the screen, hummed a few bars of "Back in the Saddle Again," and swiveled back around to face her. He gave a melodramatic sigh and said, "All right, I'll go for it. I want you to report in at least once every four days. You've got a maximum of two weeks on this thing. If nothing breaks by then, I want you back here at your desk with your apologies and excuses all lined up and ready to go."

"Great," she said, standing. "You won't be sorry." She turned to leave, wondering just how she was going to report in every four days when she didn't even know where she'd be. Another thought crowded in. "Harry, if Alex gets in touch with you, tell him what's going on. He's out of town, and I'm not sure when he'll be back."

Harry nodded and picked up his pencil.

"You're supposed to tell me to be careful, Harry."

"Yeah," he said, "that too."

• •

She'd stored her riding boots and clothes in Alex's basement the year before, when she'd finally given up her own apartment and moved in with him. Now, as she sat at the bottom of the stairs trying to decide what to take, she looked around the damp concrete room at the junk, most of it Alex's, piled to the low ceiling, and wondered when she would see him again. Most of the stuff was furniture and various goods brought back from his family's travels when he was a child. His father had researched his historical novels by going to the actual locations and eventually buying props to bring home and live with while he was writing. Alex had moved all of it from his family home in Connecticut years ago, and here it had stayed, collecting mold and mildew. She'd once suggested they throw some of it out, and she'd received a pained look and a shake of the head. The problem was, or one of the problems, that all of these things reminded him of his father, whom he had grown up hating, and at the same time his

other, whom he had loved. All of it was evidence of his
parental schizophrenia, souvenir and memories of his troubled yet irreplaceable past.

She took her sleeping bag, her hat and boots, and her rope.
She had been a calf roper and a barrel racer on her Uncle's
ranch, but had given up the racing when she'd heard the term
"barrel racer's butt" applied to one of her fellow contestants.
But she stuck to the roping and had been good at it.

She had jeans and shirts, and her down vest and jacket for
warmth. Anything else Will would have to provide. She stood
up, looked around one last time, and turned out the light.

At the top of the steps, she stopped in the doorway of the
kitchen. Somehow she had been hoping that he would be
here. He wasn't. For a moment she felt a great longing to see
him, to talk to him about what was happening to her . . .
but he was somewhere else with, no doubt, his own set of
problems.

She changed her clothes and packed her pack and looked
back once as she stood out on the sidewalk in front of the
house. Still no Alex. She shouldered her pack, put the hat
firmly on her head, and walked down the street to hail a cab
for the airport.

• •

"When I was a kid," Will said—they were riding the
horses at a walk, side by side—"not really a kid, I was seventeen, in my last year of high school, I used to come here with
John Raven." She glanced over at him but his face was lost in
the shade cast by his hat. "You remember I told you that at
Wounded Knee there was another kid with me when we
picked up the parachute-drop supplies?"

"You said another boy and a girl."

"The boy was John Raven. That incident, all of our experiences at Wounded Knee, made us more than just friends. People talk about Vietnam, about how they forged bonds of
friendship there. Wounded Knee was our Vietnam. Those few
weeks politicized us." He glanced at her and she nodded to
how she was listening. "John came from what you'd call a
broken home, though among Indians it was pretty standard. A

mother who drank, a father who eventually deserted then Then along came the American Indian Movement, and Joh had found his real family. He was a member of the NIYC, th National Indian Youth Council, which was kind of the SNC for Indians." He was quiet for a moment, as if deciding ho much detail he would go into, how much he would tell. Sh didn't encourage him one way or the other, knowing that h came to his decisions on his own. She waved a fly fror her horse's head.

"We used to come down here and ride for days." He looke around them at the rolling prairie. "There were no more pec ple then than there are now. Most of this land belongs to th power companies. Once upon a time it was all Indian lanc until the 1868 treaty moved us over into South Dakota. Any way, we'd ride along this trail and argue. By then John was militant, and I was more of a movement conservative. He fel along with the rest of the NIYC, that spectacular short-ter projects were preferable to long-term solutions. They wer reactionists; they felt they understood white society and tha progress could be made only at the expense of it."

"Sounds like a good definition of terrorism," she said.

He nodded. "One man's terrorist is another man's freedor fighter. It all depends on where you're standing when yo look at it. Anyway, my solution was to study hard and go t law school and do something about protecting Indian rights. He smiled. "Much to the relief of my parents."

"I thought Indians didn't have any rights. And that wa what you were fighting for."

He shook his head. "No, Indians have very specific right they've just been denied them. In the beginning, the white considered Indians to be wild animals, the same way that the considered blacks to be draft animals. But when they under stood that Indians had land, then they gave him rights so the could legally take the land away. Blacks were systematicall kept away from the white establishment, but law after law wa passed to bring the Indian into the fold. The government goal was to turn him into a white farmer. A passive farmer

Unfortunately, our culture is too strong and too alien for that plan to have much success." They were moving up the side of a long, low hill. At the top they stopped and dismounted, letting the horses rest and crop at the grass. They had been taking it easy, walking and occasionally trotting for short distances to acclimate the horses to the conditions of a long ride.

"So you and John Raven took separate paths," she said, lowering her horse's reins so he could graze.

"The goal is the same." he said. "We're just two different people."

"What did you argue about on these long rides?"

He shrugged. "The same things boys of that age always argue about. Life, God, women. He was much more spiritual than I was. Or am. When he was little, before his dad left, they spent a lot of time together in the woods. His dad was an old-time Indian, by that I mean he lived a lot of the old ways. He taught John to talk to animals, to look for omens, how to read signs, how to see the future. John believed all of that. Still does."

"And you?" she asked.

He reached toward her and lifted a strand of hair from where it had gotten caught in the corner of her mouth. His fingers brushed her cheek. She stopped herself from jerking away from him. She felt herself flush. If she allowed this one touch, how would he see it? And what would she allow next?

"Me?" he said. "I'm of a more practical nature. If there's any God I believe in I'd guess it would be the Law. I'm hyphenated. I'm an Indian-Lawyer. I believe in a lot of Western legal systems, and at the same time I can't deny what I am." He looked out over the grassland. "John Raven and I love the same things. We have the same goals. We're just going about it in different ways." He looked back at her and his face had a grim, faraway look, as if he could see some inevitable future. "I'm not even sure that his way isn't right. It can't work, it's doomed, but morally it's correct. He's fighting for what he believes is best for the tribe."

She wouldn't accept that, or perhaps she was still too aware of his touch on her cheek. "The noble warrior," she said, sarcastically, "fighting his last doomed fight?" She heard the sarcasm in her voice and wondered where her reporter's objectivity had gone. She was becoming too involved on several levels.

He looked at her for a long moment then gently pulled his horse's head up. "Let's go. We'll camp in a ravine. I don't want to push the horses too far the first day." They mounted up and rode along the down side of the hill. The sun was lower now, the long rays reddening the landscape, casting the hollows between the hills into dark shadow.

• •

John Raven sat beside his dead horse, touching the star-shaped blaze on the wide forehead. The horse had been called Morning Star, and he had stepped in a hole and broken his leg with such unexpected swiftness that John Raven had found himself on the ground and rolling before the dry sound of the bone breaking had registered in his mind. He had shot the horse quickly, before the real pain had come.

Of course it had been the raven, the one that had come that morning and sat on the low tree next to his bedroll. The raven had warned him of the coming danger, but he hadn't paid enough attention, and this was the result. He had begun traveling during the day. There had been no indication anyone was looking for him. And so when the bird had perched by his head and spoken he had been too full of sleep to understand. And now his horse was dead. He stood up and looked around but there was only the land. He wondered if the raven would return.

He gathered up his supplies and his rifle and slung them over his shoulder. He would leave the saddle—a man with no horse does not need a saddle. If he found another horse, he would ride bareback, the way he had as a boy. The death of the horse would not change anything. He would walk; in the end, the result would be the same. He knew what must be done. He climbed a small outcropping and looked in all four directions. He saw no indication of man. It was quiet; even the wind did not blow. He was alone and his life seemed a dream, no less real for it, but as if it were taking place in the mind of a man who was sleeping. No matter. Sleeping or awake, it was all the same.

Chapter 32

He taught her to make a stew of dried corn in an old coffee can and a large biscuit in the bottom of the frying pan. That was dinner, and though she would never have thought it, it not only sufficed, it was fine, as perfect a fit in this landscape as the tiny blue flowers on the squaw grass or the sweet smell of burning sagebrush in the campfire.

"What if it rains?" she asked. "You've got us camped in the bottom of a ravine, won't we wash out and drown if it rains?"

He looked up from the coffee he was brewing. "Ah, you're displaying your knowledge of woodcraft. Or ravinecraft." He stared up at the sky. "It will not rain," he said in a mock-solemn voice. "We Indians have ways of knowing these things."

"Why are we down here?" she asked. "It's sort of spooky."

He stood up. "You only have to climb seven feet up a dirt slope to get out. It's not exactly like I've got us down in the Grand Canyon." He shrugged. "Maybe it's some sort of racial memory. War parties used to hide down in these ravines, waiting for passing wagon trains. You know, ride up out of here screaming and whooping, naked as jaybirds, feathers in our hair, scare the shit out of the white settlers. Good place to hide when you were being chased by the soldiers. I feel kind of protected down here."

"Protected from what? John Raven?" She knew this was a
ore spot, had noticed it before and now pushed on it for a
esponse. It was a technique that she had learned over the
ears. She wasn't particularly proud of it, but it usually
rought results.

They were both sitting on the dry sandy ground, on oppo-
ite sides of the fire. He put a small stick under the wire
andle of the pot he was brewing coffee in and poured some
nto two metal cups. He handed her one of them. "Yes, John
aven. See, John's different from most people. You're never
ure just how he's going to react to things. I'm pretty certain
hat he wouldn't want me riding after him, and I'm *real*
ertain that he wouldn't want me bringing you along. And I
ave. Though for the life of me I can't remember why I said
'd do it."

"Because I can save him if we get to him first, that's why. If
he FBI finds him before the *New York Times* does, they're
able to just shoot him and ask questions later."

He nodded. "Right, now I remember."

"And what you're trying to tell me is that John Raven is
razy."

He cleared his throat. "It's not that easy to put a name to.
He just doesn't think the way most people do. Indian or white.
He thinks more like Crazy Horse."

"Crazy Horse?"

"Yes, like Crazy Horse. And he's on the warpath. He's shot
wo whites and if he's headed where I think he's headed then
here'll be more trouble. All this land was once Crazy Horse's
ersonal hunting ground and battlefield. All of it from here on
p to the Yellowstone was contested ground. Once the white
old miners made it into the Black Hills there wasn't any
topping them, and the whole of white civilization was right
ehind. This was where the big battles were, and John Raven
nows it. Hell, he *feels* it. I know, I've been over this ground
ith him."

"So we're down in this ravine because we're hiding from
ohn Raven."

"Let's just say that we're down here because I'd rather find out where he is before he finds out where we are. It might be my law training, but I'm sort of cautious about some things and anyway he's better at this Indian stuff than I am. I like to get the lay of the land before I charge." He drank from his cup and did not look at her.

It was one of the few times she had ever seen him less than completely sure of himself. And out here that made her nervous. Generally she felt very safe with Will Two Horses. Now she found herself sitting quite still, listening to the night, trying to hear if someone was creeping up on them.

"Don't look so worried," he laughed. "I'm not even sure that he's within a hundred miles. He may be in the FBI jail by now. It's been three days since we left, time enough to catch him if he were where they thought he'd be."

"But you don't believe that, do you? Why would we be here if you did?"

He looked steadily at her. "I can think of a few reasons, but yes, I think he's out here. Somewhere."

• •

John Raven pulled his blanket around his naked shoulders. He would have no fire tonight. He had thrown away his clothing, keeping only his belt and two strips of leather from his jacket that he had made into a breechclout. It was better this way. He would not eat, nor would he sleep. He was troubled that Sun Chief had taken his horse. He needed a vision. He pushed the blanket away and relaxed, surrendering to the cool night air.

He stayed where he was throughout the next day. He put pebbles between his toes and beneath his tongue and he sat very still and waited. His father had taught him that there were animals who would speak to men. That Sun Chief would speak through these animals. The next evening the vision flew out of the night sky, spiraling into his mind. He slumped to the side and opened his arms to the raven that soared down to alight on the blanket beside him.

He heard the large black bird speak. "You must be cold lying here on top of your blanket."

John Raven sat up to study the bird. "I have been waiting for you. I am sorry that I did not heed your warning."

The bird nodded. "Now your horse is dead."

"I need your help. I must know what I am to do. Sometimes it seems clear to me, and then it fades. My eyes refuse to focus. I would help my people, but the way is not clear."

John Raven watched as the bird preened one of his long glossy wing feathers, stripping it through his beak before he spoke again. "It is not clear because you have not truly chosen the path. You must declare yourself, and then your vision will be strong."

"I wish to help my people."

"Yes, you wish, but that is not enough." The bird threw back his head and rasped a harsh call that seemed to echo in John Raven's head. "You must prove your intentions in the old way. You must sacrifice to Sun Chief."

John Raven thought this over. When a warrior asked for the help of the other world, he promised to sacrifice at one of the annual Sun Dances. If his sacrifice was successful, he was assured of help. He would do this.

"I will offer my prayers to the Sun. But I will need a Medicine Woman. It cannot be done alone. You know this."

The bird dipped his head in agreement and his words were clear in John Raven's mind. "Yes, look around you and you will find all that you need. The Sun is in the sky, and you are here on Earth. If you have honor, you will succeed. I will help you, Little Brother. Together we will find a way." The bird flew up to his shoulder and looked into his eye. For a moment, John Raven thought the bird would drive its heavy beak into his eye and tear it out. The bird smiled and he heard him whisper, "No, not yet, John Raven, not yet." And then there was that laugh and the bird flew away into the air and disappeared, and John Raven fell back into his body, stirred on the cold ground, and stared at the great mass of stars above him and knew that he had found his help, had found the way.

• •

Will made their horses work harder now, galloping long distances before allowing them to walk. The small Indian ponies did not seem to mind the pace. Molly found her muscles accepting the ride, complaining less at the end of each day when they unsaddled the horses and went about their various tasks. It reminded her of her life on her uncle's ranch and made her feel sixteen again.

During their sixth day on the trail they were discussing John Brown, the abolitionist. Will saw him as a great leader, a man, who, though probably mad, had the moral right to the means he utilized to achieve his ends.

John Raven leapt up out of a ravine before them, naked save for the breechclout and a single raven feather tied into his long, free black hair. He had daubed his face with red mud, tracing long streaks down each cheek. He pointed his rifle at Will Two Horses as they reined in the ponies and sat staring at the near-naked warrior, the only sound the blowing ponies and the only movement the dust that surrounded them. John Raven made a small motion with the rifle that told them to dismount.

They stood by the horses as John Raven looked from Will to Molly, a long look that seemed to assess their worth, to feel them for strength or weakness. To Molly, who felt the gaze with a cold chill of fear, the flat black eyes that measured her seemed to be looking from a great distance. "You have brought me the Medicine Woman," John Raven said, still staring at Molly. "I thank you."

"What?" Molly said, looking at Will.

"John," Will said gently, "we've come to help you. Put down the rifle."

John Raven turned to Will. The rifle was centered on Will's chest. "You have been following me. I have seen the sun reflecting from your metal. The sun has chosen you. Has chosen this woman."

"Look, John," Will said, dropping his reins and stepping toward John Raven. The rifle moved up an inch and Will stopped. "She's a reporter for the *New York Times.* She wants to help you. To help us."

John Raven nodded. "Your part in this is over, Will. She and I will go on. I will need your horse. You will be rewarded for the gift of these things. Our people will know of this in the lodges. It will be spoken of around many fires."

Will looked at Molly, and in his look she saw uncertainty and doubt. In that moment she knew that there was nothing that he could do, and that whatever happened she would have to depend on herself. That there was a point where intelligence and control ran smack up against madness and then rules no longer applied. Life turns on such moments, and she felt hers snag and turn and knew nothing would ever be the same. She might live, but she would never see through the same eyes, feel with the same heart.

Will looked at John Raven and saw not his friend as he had been, but his friend as he had become, driven by whatever demons had beset him, cursed by several hundred years of pain until the present had been torn and cast out, and the mind left behind to be filled with a purpose that was singular and pure, to the point of blindness. John Raven did not see what was before him. He saw what his hate told him he saw, and Will knew that there was little left to importune, that reason had been shredded by the strong wind of madness, that their only hope lay in becoming what John Raven wanted them to be.

And John Raven was pleased. His old friend Will Two Horses had brought him a Medicine Woman, and the ceremony could be performed and he would be cleansed and pure. That she was white did not matter. There was a certain justice in it. He would use the white woman to make him strong in the fight against her own people. The bird had told him that he would find all that he would need, and he had.

"I must leave you here," John Raven said. "We will leave you your supplies. You will find your way."

"John, don't do this. Take the horse, take both of the horses, but leave the woman. She's no use to you. Or we can leave her and I'll come. Together we'll fight the Wasichus."

"No, I must sacrifice to the Sun Chief. I will take the woman. You will stay."

"This isn't the way, John. You can't beat them this way.

They'll only kill you. Our people learned this lesson long ago."

John Raven looked at Will as if he were a child. "And what have we to show for it? What good has it done us? Our people would be better off dead. Surely you see that? They are all dying anyway. It will be good to fight, to die for a reason. A bullet is cleaner than a whiskey bottle. Have you no honor? Have the white men's schools driven even that from you? What have they given you that is of greater value?"

John Raven moved forward and picked up the reins of Will's horse. Working one-handed he cut the supplies loose from the saddle and then took the saddle off and threw it to the ground. He motioned for Molly to mount her horse.

Will tried. There were three steps between them, six feet of space; he was halfway there when John Raven turned and hit Will with the stock of the rifle. Will crumpled to the ground. Molly saw a thin trickle of blood spill from the corner of Will's eye and drip onto the ground. John Raven caught her arm as she knelt, and he pushed her to her horse. He waited while she mounted, and then he swung himself easily up onto the other horse.

She turned in the saddle and looked at Will, lying on the ground. As she was led away she felt her fear grow inside her until she was weak with it, until she felt if it were even a tiny bit greater, she would die of it.

Chapter 33

They alternated between a gallop and a trot, riding faster than she ever had with Will Two Horses. John Raven stopped only once, to fashion a lead to her horse's bridle. And so they rode, John Raven leading, she holding on to the pommel of the saddle, scanning the hills, searching for help that was nowhere to be found. Before, with Will, she had enjoyed the absolute solitude, but now she hated it, unable to understand how any country could be so empty and useless.

At times she simply rode and stared at John Raven's back and hated him for what he was doing. He was bigger than Will Two Horses, very muscular, and he rode easily on the bare back of his horse. His hair was black, but had an odd, vaguely kinky look. His skin tones were dark, but the planes of his face were softer, more like a white man's.

Far above them, an airplane traced a white trail of vapor across the blue sky. She looked at it as they rode and wished that she could be seen, and believed: a white woman reporter for the *New York Times* being kidnapped by an Indian who seemed to be acting out a fantasy that now included her, something she had thought of as a story, a job, that now had become dangerous. She thought of all the reporters that had been taken hostage in the Middle East, and about how easily one could suddenly become part of the story, or how the story could become your life.

They stopped once to drink from a small stream and rode on until twilight. As they unsaddled her horse and set up a rough camp, she catalogued her options. There was nowhere to run to if she could get away on foot, and even if she managed to get on one of the horses she knew he would ride her down and catch her. She was good on a horse, but he was better. Her only real chance was to kill him, or at least incapacitate him, while he slept, *if* he slept. And she hadn't the slightest idea how to go about that.

Could she get his knife and stab him? Probably not. Was he going to rape her? He wore only a breechclout. She could see his penis beneath it as he moved. How deep into this fantasy was he? Could he be dealt with in any rational manner? And so the list of options was reduced to none, or at least to the only viable one, which was simply hold on and talk to him and hope that someone would find them or Will wouldn't be dead and could get help or she could talk John Raven out of whatever it was he had planned for her.

He did not even allow them the comfort of a fire. He made her sit near him on the ground as he ate. He had gone through all of her gear and found the remains of the biscuit she had baked the night before. She waited for him to offer her part of it. When he didn't she sat stubbornly, refusing to ask. Finally, it was too much to sit and watch him eat, so she asked for some.

He shook his head. "You are the Medicine Woman. You cannot eat until the ceremony is finished."

She shook her head in disbelief. She had never been refused food in her whole life, and she was hungry. "What do you mean, I can't eat? For how long?"

He looked off into the night, as if he could see into the distance.

"Two more days, maybe three. It depends on the horses."

She was shocked at how casual he was. "I can't go without food for three days. Or even for two. I've hardly eaten anything today."

He nodded. "Yes, it will be difficult. But you must be strong. is a great honor to be a Medicine Woman."

She couldn't believe he meant it, couldn't imagine going ithout food for so long. "Besides not eating, what are my her duties." She said it as sarcastically as she could manage, ut he didn't seem to notice.

"Normally there would be many duties." He waved a hand round them. In the dark, she could see his broad gestures, ut not his face. It was as if she were conversing with a ghost. But here, with only the two of us, we will find a tree to use as ur center pole; you will assist me with my preparations; I will ach you the songs to sing. I would not have it this way, but ay adviser has said we must do the best we can. It is enough r you to be a virtuous woman."

Without a campfire the night around them seemed huge, mitless, without reference. She found that her constant fear ad settled into a dull ache. She was tired and hungry and her nger overcame the fear as she sat and watched John Raven at. She was to be a virtuous woman. That was good news—it led out any immediate rape. But, in truth, he really didn't eem the type. From everything Will had told her, and what ttle she had observed, John Raven seemed to be a man with mission, a man who was not bent on general mayhem, but ho had a purpose. That he was probably insane seemed lmost beside the point, as if in this land and this night, uestions of sanity did not apply. Whether or not he was crazy id not make much difference to her situation. She was in it nd would have to abide by the rules of the situation itself.

"Why must we wait so long to have this ceremony? Why an't we do it right now and get it over with?"

He could see her there in the dark beside him. He did not hink she would try to run away, but he would have to tie her o make sure. She didn't seem to know it, but they were very ear the big highway. Tomorrow they would cross a small ver and then the highway. Then they would be back in the vild areas and safe.

"We need a tree. Here, there is only prairie. We will be

back in the mountains and there we will find a tree that i
suitable. Two days if we ride hard."

She did not reply and he knew she was angry with him. H
could not blame her. He was sorry she was a white woman
wished that Will Two Horses had brought him an Indian, bu
wishing would make no difference. He could have brough
Will along for the ceremony, but Will was a peacemaker an
would have spent the time trying to convince him to not g
ahead with the plan, to give himself up, to trust the whit
man's courts. That was Will's way, not his, and it had no
seemed to have done Will Two Horses or any of their peopl
much good. He was sorry he had been forced to hit Will.

"I understand that you are angry," he said. "But you mus
do what I say. Why were you with Will Two Horses?"

"As Will said, I'm a reporter for the *New York Times.*
Somehow in the darkness and under the circumstances i
seemed a thin thing to be. It was difficult to remember tha
this had once been just a story, a job. Essentially she spent he
time telling one set of people what another set of people wer
doing. Right now it didn't make much sense.

"Look," she said, "I understand what you did, what you'r
doing." She stopped and gestured into the night. "You're try
ing to help your people. I can help you. Give this up, go t
court; you were defending your land. Take the company t
court and win there. Get a decision that will do some good in
the long run. Will Two Horses can help you. That's why w
were trying to find you."

"No. It is no good. That way has never worked for m
people." He spoke angrily. "Now it is time for action. N
more words. First we will have the Sun Dance. I will sacrific
and the Sun Chief will give me aid. Then we will ride agains
the white man. We have beaten him before. We will wi
again. We will return to the battlefield. We will show that th
Indian will not be pushed off his land, that our honor will no
allow it. Or we will die."

She watched silently as he went to his deerskin bag and go
a strip of rawhide. Watched and felt fear rise in her and fil

er. She fought him as he tied her legs together at the ankles, and then her wrists. He spread out her blanket and rolled her into it. He sat for a while, watching her; then he lay down on the ground. Finally, she slept.

Chapter 34

"Goddamn it, boys, I'd go behind the house and curse if wasn't stuck on this goddamn train." Twain looked out th window at the passing scenery as he rubbed his head. "W came damn near to joining the majority back there, and that' a condition I'm not quite ready for."

"Where are we?" Alex asked, leaning forward and lookin out the window. It had been two days since the train left th exposition, and Twain was still talking about it, picking i apart, working it over.

Twain glanced out the window again. "Near Cleveland, believe. It's ugly enough to be Cleveland."

Alex nodded and sat back in the seat. He and Twain wer facing each other, by the window. The Indians sat on the floo of the car in the back. Abraham was asleep on one of the cots long legs hanging over the edge.

They were all dealing with the facts in their own separat ways. Twain had his novelist's approach, examining it fron every conceivable angle; the Indians seemed merely to accep events as they came, no matter how horrific or mundane; Ale: continually ordered the facts and made lists in his mind, at tempting to set priorities and decide on possible courses o action. And Abraham, because he had lost Elias and so wa most hurt, had shrunk from the pain and spent his time sleep ing, praying, or simply sitting, not even bothering to look out the window.

The train had stopped in Pittsburgh, and Alex had bought food and all the newspapers he could find. All of them had at least mentioned the fire and the shooting, and a few of them were trumpeting it as either a major conflagration, insurrection, race war, multiple murder, or tragic accident, depending on their particular bent.

Elias, Brannon, Serena, and the Indian's guard were all dead. Numerous others were injured fighting the fire. Alex read each account and felt the sickness of guilt and the shame of responsibility. He had saved the Indians, but three men and a woman had died in the process. Had it been worth it? He tried to push the issue away and concentrate on staying out of further trouble.

"How much longer do you think we can keep anyone from paying us a visit?" Alex asked.

"If you mean a railroad official, at least until we get to Chicago. We're paid up to there; after that there's room for negotiation. And as long as we keep our quarantine sign up we should be spared any tourists. This is a private car; we shouldn't be bothered."

Alex nodded and settled farther back in the seat. The constant clatter of the rails made him sleepy. When he slept he didn't think about his guilt. He found it hard to plan anything. For the moment, Twain's carefully hand-lettered quarantine sign seemed adequate protection.

"I'm getting off at Chicago," Twain said. "There's a certain lurid fascination in your adventure, but it's too much for me."

"I seem to recollect your saying a few days ago that you'd relish a little adventure."

Twain laughed harshly. "That was before I witnessed the mayhem of the other evening. I'll carry the memory of that poor woman on fire to my grave. No, I'm a married man, and I have children that cry out in the night for their father. I don't want to disappoint them. I'm going home as soon as we get far enough away to allow me to slink back from another direction. I'll negotiate your carriage for you when we get to Chicago, but that's it. It's time for me to throw in the sponge and withdraw from the canvas."

Alex didn't blame him. So far he didn't think that anyone had recognized Twain as Twain, the haircut and absence of mustache had ensured that, but unless Twain were willing to keep on shaving his head and face, someone would eventually recognize him. Better that Twain was out of it. If he could get them passage from Chicago on, then he would have performed more than Alex had ever hoped. Alex sat and watched Twain as he dozed in his seat. They had become friends, but he had already asked too much. The motion of the train rocked him gently. What else was there? Give it up, let go, sleep.

• •

Chicago. Alex was standing in line at a ticket window when the man behind him nudged him. "That sawed-off squirt in the spectacles keeps hissing at you," the man said.

Alex looked over at a short man standing against the wall. He was wearing a homburg hat and green rimless sunglasses. It was Twain in a very strange disguise. He thanked the man and left his place in line.

"Where the hell have you been?" Twain whispered urgently.

They had arrived in the middle of the night. Their car had been shunted onto a siding and uncoupled. Twain was gone when Alex woke the next morning. He had made sure Abraham understood that he was to stay in the car with the Indians and then he had left to find Twain.

"Where the hell have *I* been?" Alex said. "I've been looking for you."

"Who's guarding the despondent Negro and the two savages? Leaving that lot alone is like taking a smoke on a powder keg. I don't need to be found, but they need to be watched."

Alex was inclined to agree. "Sorry," he said. "I think they'll be all right. So, where have you been? And what's with the disguise?"

"I've been gathering information. It seems the jig is up. My benefactor declined the further use of his railroad car. At any price. The company isn't saying so directly, but it's clear they smell some sort of a rat. We can't get a train out of here because they're looking for us. I came up here last night and bought coffee for one of the guards. Seems two white men and two Indians are wanted for murder and assorted other crimes back in Philadelphia. And there may be a Negro involved. One of the white men was described as a 'strange-appearing bald individual.' That's when I bought the hat and the spectacles. Now listen—I've hired a coach. I wired my bank and got some money. We'll drive west of here until we reach Davenport. There's a train depot there where I'm hoping we're not such popular figures. They probably only telegraphed our description to the main stations. We'll all get out there, and you and the others can continue on west with all of my heartfelt good wishes. I'll take a train back East where I belong."

Alex nodded. Twain took his arm and steered him to the back of the station toward the baggage section. They went through a large door and found themselves on a back platform piled high with trunks and crates. Twain nodded toward the end of the platform where there was a large horse-drawn coach with a driver on top. Twain pushed him inside. In twenty minutes, he was back with Abraham and the Indians.

• •

It was near dawn the next day. They were standing at the edge of another railroad yard. Their few belongings were piled at their feet. They had arrived at the Davenport depot an hour before, and Twain had bought coffee for the lonely stationmaster who had a story to tell. Alex had begun to think that anyone in the country could be bought for a cup of coffee. Evidently their whereabouts, at least in general, were known. All stations were to be on the lookout for the five of them. The coach driver would take them no farther west, so Twain paid him off and sent him away.

They stood in the cool dawn looking miserably out over the

wide misty expanse of the Mississippi River. Twain gave a small snort and Alex turned to him. The smaller man tilted his head back and smiled. "I'll be goddamned," Twain said, looking back at the river. "I've got another idea."

Chapter 35

The path Twain found had probably been blazed by generations of truant boys intent on stealing a day at river's edge. And had they met one of those boys, or anyone else for that matter, this strange group would surely have been reported to someone: the police, the government, or the local lunatic asylum.

Twain had taken off his green spectacles (he referred to them as goggles), but he still wore his plug hat. Abraham, withdrawn and silent, followed Twain. The Indians still wore their work clothes, but they wore them poorly, not understanding buttons and shirttails. And Alex, who should have been leading, was bringing up the rear, lost in a labyrinth of questions, guilt, and indecision, his confidence slowly disintegrating. It was the same curious feeling that he remembered from standing in the surf at the seashore as a child. The sea rushes in and washes the sand from underneath your feet, and at the same time piles it up around your ankles. You are, simultaneously, trapped and off balance.

The path wound down a steep hill covered with thick, spiny underbrush almost to the water's edge. Twain made Alex, Abraham, and the two Indians sit in a small grove of trees. "Keep them under cover," he said. "I'm going to go see if we can do some business here. Stay put. I've had about as much adventure as I want out of this, so you be here when I get back." He gave Alex a hard look and left to climb back up the path.

As the morning wore on it grew hotter, and the flats of the riverbank began to smell of drying mud and dead fish. Small biting flies and mosquitoes went to work on exposed flesh. Alex sat and worried about what Twain was doing. The Indians slept, and Abraham simply stared out over the water.

High Cloud was smiling at him. Through it all, the old Indian had accepted whatever they told him, seemingly content to be headed west. Little Spring had followed, silent and impassive.

"It is hot," High Cloud said to Alex. "The other one has left us. Will he come back?"

Alex nodded. "He'll be back."

"We must eat. I will go find food."

"No," Alex said, suddenly realizing they had eaten very little in the last few days. But they would not move from this spot. Twain's obvious disgust with his leadership abilities had made it abundantly clear that to allow High Cloud to wander off would put an end to the last shreds of faith the other man had in him. Besides jeopardizing the entire group. "We'll stay here until he comes back for us." High Cloud didn't answer. Alex stared at the Indian. High Cloud smiled.

The afternoon crept on. Alex had given up trying to keep the bugs away. They bit his face and neck and his wrists and hands. He was sitting on the ground leaning against a small tree when he fell asleep. High Cloud strung his bow and left the grove noiselessly.

A breeze off the water woke Alex. The leaves of the trees rustled dryly. Small waves lapped the river's edge. He opened his eyes on the empty spot where High Cloud should have been, knowing instantly he'd screwed up once again. He wiped his face and looked around: Little Spring and Abraham, but no High Cloud. He got to his feet and crept to the edge of the trees and looked out at the river, which was very wide and empty. It was late afternoon, five o'clock by his pocket watch. He thought about asking the others where High Cloud had gone, but he knew it was useless. He considered filling his pockets with stones and walking into the river, but Twain would probably show up and pull him out and call him an ass for screwing *that* up.

When High Cloud slipped back into the grove, Alex was looking in the other direction and didn't notice. The Indian touched him on the shoulder and Alex jumped.

"Food," High Cloud said, holding up a dead dog with an arrow in the midsection. Alex felt the simultaneous urge to laugh and cry. The dog seemed to be a mixed-breed retriever with a golden-red coat and wide-open dead eyes. High Cloud laid the dog on the ground and squatted by it, working the arrow on through the body.

Well, shit, Alex thought, why not? His mind carried on a conversation with itself. We have now reached the absolute nadir. Mark Twain, the famous American humorist, has left us, and who could blame him? I've gotten several people killed and there's certainly no humor in that. I'm stuck with two Indians, one who hates me and one who doesn't care much one way or the other, and I've caused the mental breakdown of the only purely honest man in the group. And here is a dead dog for dinner. High Cloud glanced up at him curiously, as if he could sense the dialogue Alex was having with himself. Alex shrugged his shoulders and shook his head.

It was early evening, just beyond twilight, when Twain hove into view at the helm of a long flatboat. He guided the boat to a stop slightly upstream of where Alex stood. Alex went to the water's edge and caught the rope Twain threw to him.

"You came back," Alex said, as Twain stepped onto shore. Twain looked at him sharply. "You thought I wouldn't?"

Alex looked away. "No, not really. I knew you'd come."

"What the hell has he got?" Twain asked.

He was looking at High Cloud. The Indian stood at the edge of the trees, holding the limp, now gutted dog by the hind legs. In the dim light he resembled a strange commuter with a hairy briefcase.

"Dinner," Alex said.

• •

The days swam by easily, and Alex found a semblance of peace, as if whoever or whatever controlled the speed and intensity of his life had called time-out and allowed him a respite. The river became their world.

The raft was fifteen feet long and broad enough to seat three abreast without crowding. Twain called it a "glorified sneak-box" and had paid a dollar a foot for her. The front half was covered over, making a low dry cabin, and there were broad plank seats along the sides and across the back. It was steered by a long oar worked from the stern. There was a dirt-lined box where they could build a fire and a rough wooden trunk in the cabin to store the provisions that Twain had bought along with the boat. Power was supplied by the current, which carried them along at a leisurely four miles an hour.

They traveled both day and night. Twain told them that before the war this would not have been possible. The river back then was thick with traffic; huge lumber rafts, hundreds of palatial steamboats, scores of local river freighters, and numberless drifters. Whole families floated from one place to another in search of a better, safer, or simply different life. But the war had made river travel too dangerous, and after the war the railroads had finished off any possibility of renewed river trade.

They had the upper Mississippi pretty much to themselves. The banks were solid with seemingly impenetrable forest, only seldom broken by small clearings with rough cabins. Other humans were rare. The solitude was complete, and the river seemed to heal them.

Alex and Twain set up watches, and the hour before dawn became a favorite time for Alex. From the almost absolute blackness of night would come the first signs of dawn, the riverbanks slowly seeming darker than the sky. The scattering of stars would fade and the sky would become a shade of gray that Twain likened to kid gloves and cats. As day broke, the river would trail thin veils of mist that would gradually lift and

anish with the rising of the sun. The sky and river would
become red and then gold, and then morning would be on
them with clean blue skies and a feeling of both peace and
pleasant expectation. Twain had rigged lines behind the raft,
so they always had fish for a hot breakfast, along with baker's
bread, and when that was eaten up, cornpone with molasses.

Alex felt the gradual return of control, at least of himself.
The problems were still there, but the mental contortions had
left him.

Twain began to actually enjoy himself. He stopped talking
about finding a railhead and going home, and he expounded
at great length on all the facets of the river, learned during his
years as cub and pilot on the steamboats.

And Little Spring began to talk.

She could, it seemed, speak English. Quite well. Although
the first few days she limited herself to requests for food, she
eventually began commenting on their life on the raft.

One evening, late, after the fire had faded to glowing coals
and Little Spring had gone to sleep, High Cloud told her story.

"She is Crazy Horse's woman," High Cloud said, nodding
toward the covered area where Little Spring slept. "You are
right to return her to him, for he is not a man who takes such
heft lightly. Even from the general with the golden hair, Iron
Butt. The general has taken her away, and Crazy Horse will
revenge himself."

Twain snorted. "I'm sure the general is trembling in his
riding boots. But tell me, how is it that she suddenly is able to
speak? She has an astonishing accomplishment of our language."

High Cloud packed a short clay pipe and lit it. Twain
pulled a cigar from an inner pocket and took the burning stick
from the Indian. Both of them sat and puffed for a moment.

"She is the daughter of White Feather and Little Deer.
White Feather left the tribe years ago to go to the fort. He has
been a Laramie Loafer for many years. Little Spring was born
at the fort, and grew up there in the company of the soldiers."

"I don't understand," Alex said, "why Crazy Horse would
choose a woman who lived among whites."

High Cloud nodded. "That is one reason why we will defeat you. It is true that many of the Hang-around-the-Forts Indians are lazy and useless. They have come to treasure the white man's goods more than their own freedom. But many of our warriors winter over at the forts. They trade for the white man's guns and ammunition. They rest in comfort during the hard cold months. In the spring when the ponies have fattened on the new grass, they leave the forts and return to us in the hills. And make war on the same whites who fed them throughout the winter. With the same guns and ammunition that they have traded for buffalo skins. It is a good joke."

Even in the dim light of the moon and the campfire Alex could see the look of disgust on Twain's face. "Very amusing," Twain said. "Unfortunately, he's correct on one count. Those contemptible, shriveled-up reptiles who run the trading concerns find nothing wrong with selling the hostiles better guns and ammunition than the U.S. Army issues our soldiers. Custer has been in Washington testifying to it. That's why he's been cashiered for the moment."

"And Little Spring?" Alex asked. "What does she get from the forts?"

"Information," High Cloud said. "She has been very useful. But then Yellow Hair came and attacked Black Kettle's camp and took us away. It is said she has become his woman, his second wife. He has a white sits-beside-him woman who is his first wife. It is said that Little Spring was sent with me to your exposition because Iron Butt's first wife was jealous."

I can believe it, Alex thought. At least the jealous part. Little Spring was very beautiful and very desirable. That night with her seemed so long ago and far away. Only, what? A month? Six weeks? He remembered the feel of her skin, the lean muscles of her back, her quickness. He did not blame Custer for desiring her.

"She is with child," High Cloud said. "Some say it is Crazy Horse's, some say Custer's. She will not say."

Ah, Christ, he thought, or mine. Or mine. No. Could it be possible? He felt the chill of possibility and the shame of it. What had he done? Jesus Christ, *what had he done?*

Chapter 36

The sight of the blacktop two-lane highway came as a shock. She fought back a swift surge of hope. After days of riding through the empty hills and prairies, the road seemed more a stage prop than real. She knew it must be Interstate 90, one of the few highways to cross these northwestern states. It ran from Rapid City through Wyoming to Billings, Montana, and beyond. From her brief look at Will's map, she realized that they must be in northeast Wyoming headed north toward Montana. She scanned the road for cars, but there were none. It was early morning, another painfully beautiful day. The horses' hooves made a clopping sound on the blacktop. A frightened meadowlark started up out of a sagebrush.

She still had not eaten. It was her second day without food, and the pain was acute. At times, waves of nausea and weakness would flow over her, causing her to grasp the saddle pommel and fight to stay upright. As they crossed the road, she struggled against the urge to jerk away and ride hell-bent down the road, praying for someone, anyone, to come along and save her. It was a vain and futile hope, worse than useless. It would be stupid to antagonize John Raven. He had not really tried to hurt her, not in any active way. It was better to go along and do what he wanted until she had a real chance to escape.

They crossed a small river, stopping only to water the horses and to allow her to drink. She tried to fill the emptiness inside her with the cool clear water, but it did little to satisfy her need for food. John Raven watched her silently and rode on when she indicated she was ready. The day grew hotter. The sun passed noon and slowly crossed the empty sky. The land was hillier now, with low forested mountains visible to the east. They rode until dark and camped, and again there was no food for her.

The next day was so like the preceding one that she began to hallucinate that they were trapped on a loop of film that repeated itself endlessly, and that they had been on it always, that there was no before, and would be no after. The hunger weakness came over her more often, and she caught him glancing back at her as she clung to the saddle. Her thighs were chafed raw, and her head ached. When they stopped at midday to rest in the shade of a tamarack pine, he tried to explain to her that the hunger was necessary, that if she was to be the Medicine Woman, she must be pure, that it would soon be over, that he, too, would be purified and ready for the next step. Sun Chief would look with favor on them, he said, and the people would be free. She heard the words but no longer listened.

By that evening, he could see that she could go no farther. She sat on her horse as he walked, leading both horses, scanning the hills. Finally he led them to a steep slope covered with low brush and scree. They left the horses at the bottom of the hill and climbed to a flat area of hard brown rocky earth with a grove of trees that looked out over a small valley. She sank to the ground and watched listlessly as John Raven hobbled the ponies and set up their minimal camp.

She lay on her sleeping bag and looked at the tiny fire he had built. "You have done well," he said. He was sitting cross-legged on the ground. "We have traveled many miles. You have much strength for a white woman."

She thought over a list of sarcastic replies but didn't bother to voice them. She was weak and sick and exhausted, and she no longer cared about much of anything. New York seemed

ke some past phantom-life. The *Times,* what was that? What
ad newspapers to do with hunger? She thought of their
ouse, and the kitchen, and the elaborate, absurd things they
sed to do with food. Food was sustenance, life, not artifice.
er freedom in that past life, so natural as to be unnoticed,
ie now saw as precious and singular, and she marveled that
ie had never thought of it before. Life was not easy. Behind
ie scrim of normality, she knew that it was as hard and stony
nd uncaring as the ground beneath her. To take it for granted
as to pour it away, to see it sift between her fingers and
:atter in the wind.

"Eat," he said, handing her a small leather pouch. She
)oked at him wonderingly and pushed herself up to a sitting
osition. She opened the bag and found a grainy mass inside.
he put a small amount in her mouth and chewed. The sharp
ιste of berries and meat flooded her senses.

"Slowly," he said. "It is real food, made by Aunt Flower in
ιe old way. It will give you strength for tomorrow." He
)oked around them in the dark. "This will be where we meet
un Chief. It is a good place." He picked up a sharp chip of
)ck. "If the ground could speak, it would tell of many Indi-
ns and what they have endured here."

She continued to chew. She couldn't have bolted the food if
he had wanted to. It needed work before she could swallow
. But it was good. She drank from her canteen. That night
he slept and there were no dreams, and in the morning she
vatched the sunrise while she waited for him to untie her, and
or the first time in three days she allowed herself to hope.

Chapter 37

Alex had studied the history of American art in graduate school. He remembered a description of the great panorama paintings of the 1870s, a description he thought exaggerated, since none of the paintings exist today except in fragments. But as he floated down the Mississippi, he began to believe.

The massive panoramas were invented by enterprising showmen to satisfy the curiosity of an American public fascinated by the Mississippi River. Although civilization had spread to the far western coast, most of the population had never, and would never, travel on, nor even see the great river.

The panoramas were painted by artists who journeyed down the river, sketching as they went. Back in the studio they transformed these sketches into huge paintings that depicted the sights and natural wonders of the river. These immense works, one of which was said to be three miles in length, were hauled around the country and exhibited in circuslike tents, for a price, to eager audiences. Both ends of the paintings were attached to huge rollers. The painting would be rolled from one end to another as the audience imagined themselves comfortably floating the length of the mighty river.

The sights of the entire river were crammed into one length of canvas. As the artists grew bored with reality, they began to include details that lived only in their imaginations; strange

imals and odd aboriginal tribes, birds that flew from the
ges of ancient myths. And the men who exhibited the paint-
gs, interested in money rather than scientific accuracy, en-
uraged the artists in these flights of fancy. But amidst all of
e humbuggery and sham there was a certain spirit, the spirit
the river, that somehow remained imbedded even in these
obdingnagian fantasies. It was often reported by local news-
pers that the audiences at these entertainments left the tents
er a showing with a newfound sense of calm, a contentment
at could not be easily explained. Healings were sometimes
ported to have taken place after several viewings. Other mir-
les of a minor nature were attributed, at least by the
owmen, to the paintings. Whatever the truth of the matter,
ere was no denying the popularity of the shows. For several
ars they were exhibited all over the country and seen by
ousands of satisfied customers. And then, quite suddenly,
e fad withered and died, and the showmen dumped the
intings, selling them to small local museums and carnivals,
oving on to newer, more exciting popular amusements.

Alex watched the passing riverbank unroll over the days,
d he understood the sense of calm and contentment some-
nes experienced by those who saw the paintings. And then
ended. Whatever measure of peace the river gave each of
em was taken away and transformed as quickly as thought
elf. One moment they were moored at the mouth of a small
eek, cooking fresh-caught fish, and waiting for Little Spring
return from foraging for berries, and the next they were
oking up at two roughly dressed men holding guns at Little
ring's head.

"Ain't this pretty?" one of the men said. "We're just in time
r breakfast."

There was never a time, not even from the first minute, that
ey could have stopped it. It had the inevitability of fate, as if
e pleasure and peace of the preceding days had borne a
rsh hidden cost, and payment had fallen due.

They were scattered, expecting nothing: Twain and Alex on
e boat; Twain smoking a cigar and Alex cleaning his teeth
th a beech twig. High Cloud was watching the fish on the

fire, and Abraham was washing himself in the shallows of the river. They had no weapons other than High Cloud's bow and a few knives. And so it ended, and began.

"I want all of you lined up on the bank there right in front of your little boat. Anybody tries anything funny and they gonna be dead."

Alex and Twain looked at each other and moved forward to the end of the boat. They jumped onto the riverbank and stood watching the two men with guns. Abraham waded out of the water and stood beside Alex. His pants were wet, clinging to his legs. Water beaded like quicksilver the edges of his thick black hair. High Cloud still crouched beside the fire.

"Move it, old man. Up there with the others," the larger and dirtier of the two men said. He was a big man wearing buckskins, woodsman's clothes. He had several weeks of whiskers, flushed red cheeks, and rotten teeth. The other man was small with a pinched weasel's face apparently creased into what seemed to be a permanent grin. He wore heavy dark blue pants and a brown wool shirt. He had a runny nose that he wiped on his sleeve.

High Cloud stood and watched the two men for a moment then began to sing. It was a low, monotonous song and all of them stared at him.

Both High Cloud and Little Spring had abandoned their white men's clothes. They wore elkskin that was tanned a light brown, the color of autumn oak leaves. It had been chewed and worked by one of the old women of the tribe until it was as smooth and supple as flannel. High Cloud's pants were fringed, and his vest was decorated with delicate bead work.

Without a word, the larger man shot High Cloud in the chest. The impact knocked High Cloud back, down the short riverbank, and into the water. His arms were stretched high as if at the moment of death he had reached for something in the sky, perhaps the sun. As they watched, in the sudden stillness, bubbles rose from High Cloud's open mouth, and the red stain that grew on his bare chest ran down to the hollow of his neck and into the water where the tendrils of blood curled, and were carried away, and became one with the river.

"Just like little Phil Sheridan said, that's one more good one," the short man cackled.

"I like to set the tone of things right off," the big man explained. A small wisp of smoke eased out of the barrel of the gun. "That way we can all understand one another. That was his death song he was starting in on, so it was best to get it over with quick. He wasn't going to be nothing but trouble anyway. Them old Indians always are. Now I'd just as soon shoot another of you, truth to tell. It'd give us more room on the boat of yours. Probably it'd be the big nigger. He looks like he takes up the most room." He pointed his pistol at Abraham.

"Don't," Alex said, speaking without thinking. The clear, pure brutality of the killing had left him shocked and breathless. The idea of death so quickly and casually executed was beyond immediate comprehension. He'd seen men die before but never so perfunctorily. The barrel of the pistol swung over to center on his own chest. Then it was as if a massive hand settled around his body and began to squeeze. His bowels were cold and loose. In his mind he could see down the barrel of the gun to the blunt cartridge, see the man's dirty finger begin to tighten, see the bullet grow and feel its blinding, final impact.

"Don't, huh?" The big man laughed. "What are you, the leader of the expedition?" He glanced at the small man who snorted in appreciation of the high-toned word. "What the hell's your name?"

"Balfour. Alex Balfour."

The man nodded. "My name's King, and this here's the Duke." He waved the pistol in the direction of his partner. "We're kind of like traveling royalty. You wouldn't mind giving us a ride on your boat, would you?"

"Do we have a choice?" Twain asked.

The man swiveled toward Twain. "Who are you, short shit?"

"Sam Clemens."

The name made no impression. "The only choice you got is to live or die. It don't make a shit to me one way or the other what you choose." He reached over and put his hand on the Duke's shoulder. "Duke here's going to look you over for any weapons you might be hiding. You just stand still for it."

The little man giggled and went to each of them in turn, running his hands over their clothes. He took the opportunity to squeeze Little Spring's breasts, but she seemed not to care, as if he were beneath notice, or this world were beneath notice. She was watching High Cloud, whose blood was now so thick in the water that it had formed its own eddy and had stained the mud at the edge of the river. Small, flealike water beetles were feeding on it.

"Now the boat, Duke. You can have your fill of the squaw later." King stood patiently while the other man searched through the boat. After he was finished, King got them all aboard, making them stand on the wooden deck. He and Duke pulled High Cloud out of the water and disemboweled him. They threw the intestines into the water and pushed the body back in. The old Indian slowly sank from sight. The whole procedure was performed with the relaxed skill of the veteran hunter.

"Fish'll eat the guts and the body will stay down. There's some folks looking for us. Wouldn't want them to find the Injun and figure we're on the river." He rinsed off his hands and his knife. "And now, ladies and gentlemen, we begin our journey."

• •

They strapped Twain to the steering oar. Alex sat beside him with his hands tied in front of him. Little Spring was bound, hands and ankles, and thrown down in the sleeping compartment. Abraham was at the front of the boat, arms tied behind his back. The Duke and King were on the deck of the covered area, looking down on them and smoking Twain's stash of cigars.

"Those goddamn oyster-brained curs are smoking up all of my cigars," Twain said softly. "I'm glad they were cheap ones." He kept the boat hugging the Missouri shore, as he'd been ordered to do. The current was slower there, but there was less chance of being seen than on the Illinois side. Evidently the pair were wanted in Illinois, but not in Missouri. At least not yet.

"Is there anything we can do?" Alex asked. His job was to fend the boat away from any obstacles with the long pole. He glanced at Twain but found it impossible to keep his eyes off the two toughs for more than a few seconds at a time. Trouble always draws the eye.

"It doesn't look like it." Twain said. "They're imbeciles, but they're imbeciles with guns. That makes them too many for us. After that grisly scene back on the riverbank I think we can safely say that these two will do anything they please. We'll just have to wait and see what happens."

"Where the hell did they come from?"

Twain shrugged. "Their kind are common enough. I've met plenty of them out West and on the river, but back then I had my own gun to even the odds. They look to be down on their luck, probably ready for anything." He glanced at Alex. "When you get this far west you're beyond the help of most of our civilization. We were foolish to run the river without protection. I thought my previous experience and piloting ability would be enough. I'm an ass; I had forgotten about slime like those two."

Alex found it difficult to think of the Mississippi as the last outpost of civilization. But here it was. They were beyond most law and could expect little help from any authorities. They would have to get out of this by themselves, or stand by and watch while each of them was killed. Alex didn't think that these men were going to let any of them go free. They would use them as long as they were needed and then dispose of them without the slightest compunction.

"What do you suppose they'll do next?" Alex asked.

Twain shrugged. "There's no way of knowing. If we had some whiskey they might get drunk and fall off the boat, but we don't have any whiskey. Maybe they'll smoke themselves to death, but I doubt it. I think we'll be all right until we get to their destination. Then we're in big trouble." They sat quietly and watched the two men. The larger man was giving a speech or telling a joke, gesturing extravagantly with his cigar. The little man was grinning and watching. Snatches of their conversation floated back to them.

"Take them for all they're worth and then some . . . Got to get on top of that man and stay there until you used him all up . . . get some of that squaw."

The last phrase hung in the air between them. "Well," said Twain, "I've been waiting for that one. With men of this kidney it had to come sooner or later."

"You two shut the hell up!" the big man said, turning and shouting back at them. "You just steer the goddamn boat and shut up your cake holes." He nudged the smaller man. "Speaking of which, me and the Duke here are getting hungry. Get us some chuck."

Alex stood up and went to the provision box just inside the sheltered area. He could see Little Spring lying on her side on the pile of blankets. Her elkskin dress was pulled high on her legs. He could see the round swelling of her stomach. Now that he knew she was pregnant, it was obvious. In the dim light he could see her staring at the side of the cabin. Her eyes focused on that same faraway place that High Cloud used to visit.

A wrenching blow fell on his back and knocked him to his knees. He twisted to his side and saw King leaning over the cabin roof, holding a short club and smirking at him. "You want something from the squaw, boy? You had your chance with it. Now it's our turn. But first I want my goddamn feed, so get your ragged ass up and fetch it."

Alex pushed himself up, trying to catch the breath that had been knocked out of him. He struggled with the lid of the box, clumsy with his hands tied. He picked up a slab of cornbread and a jug of molasses and two tin plates. He built a small fire in the earth-lined box, and he hung a pot of beans and water for coffee over the flames. He felt fear and anger twisting in him. It was the feeling, he supposed, of all hostages; shame and terror and anger, all entwined until it seemed that there was no hope, no future, only the present, which just might possibly be lived through. His back ached where he'd been clubbed.

Twain watched him cook. Alex was embarrassed at the sympathy in the other man's eyes. He carried the plates of food and cups of coffee to the two waiting men. It was twilight, the river reflected the day's dying light up from the water.

"Ah, dinner is served. Thank you, my good man. Don't go away," King said as Alex turned to go back to his seat. "I think we need some entertainment to go with our vittles." Alex stood waiting while the big man chewed thoughtfully.

"Get down there with the nigger," he said, pointing with his spoon to the small deck area where Abraham sat. Alex walked to the edge of the cabin roof and stepped down to the deck. Abraham looked up as Alex squatted beside him. Abraham had been tied with the heavy rope they used to moor the boat. It was thick and rough, dirty and rotten in places, wound around his upper chest and arms. It had dried and tightened until it cut into his body.

"Get him up," King commanded.

Alex put his hands under Abraham's arm and helped him to his feet.

"I like a good nigger show, don't you, Duke? Before the war there was some good ones. Not so many, these days. Now I want the white boy to sing and Jim the Nigger to do us a dance. Maybe a cake walk."

Alex looked at King, and Abraham stared at the deck. He had said nothing since they had been taken. Any progress he had made over his great sadness seemed to have been taken away with their freedom. He looked at King, and then away, out over the river.

King picked up his pistol and cocked it. He pointed it at Abraham. "So long, Jim."

"Hold it!" Alex said, holding up his hands. He stepped between Abraham and the gun. He turned away toward Abraham. He could almost feel the gun pressing into his back. "Abraham, do this for me," he whispered. "I know you don't care for yourself, but do it for me. These men are animals, but we'll get out of this. Elias wouldn't want you to give up. Do this, and we'll beat these bastards."

Abraham looked up at Alex. His eyes were red-rimmed and sad. He nodded.

"All right," Alex said, turning back to King. "What do you want me to sing?"

"Coon songs, what else?" the Duke said. He spit over the side and snickered at King.

"Yes, of course," King said, lowering the pistol.

Alex thought for a moment, and began to sing. "Camptown ladies sing this song, doo dah, doo dah, Camptown race track four miles long, oh doo dah day." He looked at Abraham who began to shuffle around in a small circle. He stopped for a moment then went on. He sang all of it, then he sang it again. Then he sang every Stephen Foster song he could remember. He had a brief moment of qualm when he wondered if Stephen Foster had written the songs yet, and then almost laughed at the stupidity of the thought. Who gave a shit? Screw the time-line, screw the sacred status quo, none of it made one bit of goddamn difference when a man had a gun on you. None of it probably made a goddamn bit of difference anyway.

They lighted a lantern, and in the dim light he sang, and King and the Duke clapped their hands and laughed, and Twain kept them on the river. Abraham threw back his head and danced, and Alex felt the black man's pain and his own humiliation and the fear that made him do it, and he vowed that he would not let any more of his small family die if he could stop it. There were no rules here; the niceties and conventions of modern life were not applicable; they were laughable, and he would abide by a more basic morality that recognized only right or wrong with no tricky shades of gray, no ambiguities. If it meant he must kill these two men then so be it, he would kill them, and gladly.

He watched Abraham dance and felt his own tears of rage for the man, for High Cloud, for Twain tied to the rudder, and Little Spring lying below.

And around them the empty river whispered in the dark.

and his own voice was flat and harsh in the night, but no one heard him, no one saw their light or the two men clapping and laughing, no one wondered who was having such a good time to sing and dance on the river. No one cared.

Chapter 38

She lay on the hard ground and listened to him chant. The sound of his voice had brought her out of a deep sleep. Her hands and legs were tied but she felt curiously well. As if the three-day fast had taught her things about herself that she had not known; that she was strong and could endure. She had been forced to reconsider life from the standpoint of one who was in danger of losing it. And she saw the thinness of much of her existence. In a way it was like those dry, papery seed pods that people used for dried flower arrangements: if you held them up to the light you could see through them, but inside was the seed, as hard and solid as rock.

The sun had just cleared a distant range of saw-toothed mountains. John Raven, dressed only in his breechclout, faced the sun with eyes closed and upraised arms as he chanted. He stood absolutely motionless. When he stopped and there was silence, it was as if some natural phenomenon had ended, a steady rain, or the wind. All the elements of this harsh land suddenly seemed separate and distinct: the brown rocky ground, the bright sun, the blue sky and the two humans. He went to her and untied her. She sat up, rubbing her wrists and ankles. "Today," he said, "we will celebrate Sun Chief." He sat down on the ground and handed her the bag of dried meat and berries and her canteen. She ate and drank as he talked.

"The Sun Dance is very old. It has been part of my people for many years. When the whites defeated us, they tried to take it away."

"What's the significance of it?" she asked. "Why are *we* doing it?"

"There are many reasons to dance." He scanned the valley that spread before them, but there was no movement anywhere. "If the ceremony was performed well, it was a sign that Sun Chief would help his people find the buffalo during the year. There would be little hunger in the camps. Individual warriors would have made vows to Sun Chief; the sacrifice at the annual ceremony was the payment for the vows. Other warriors danced simply to prove themselves."

"And you?" she asked, holding out the bag of food to him.

He shook his head. "I am not allowed to eat, it is forbidden." He reached toward her and picked up the canteen and drank. He screwed the top back on and set it gently beside her. "Why do I dance? I made a promise to Sun Chief that I would. It will help in the coming fight."

For just a moment, it seemed almost ordinary. As if they were two friends on an outing. "Look," she said, leaning forward, "we can stop all of this. I can help you. Will Two Horses can get you a fair trial. You don't have to keep fighting. There's no point in it." She tried to stop herself. She knew it wasn't the way to go about it, but it just came out. He stared at her, and she felt afraid. His expression was hard and flat. He looked up at the sun. "It is time," he said.

• •

She didn't know whether he was praying or singing or both. He had a small bone whistle that he blew to punctuate his chant song. He had chosen a tree for his center post, a tall lodgepole pine that was stripped of limbs on the bottom twenty feet of its straight trunk. He had her saddle rope and several feet of rawhide string. She was still not sure what he expected of her.

He cut the rawhide into two equal lengths and lashed them to the end of the rope. He threw the rope over the bottommost branch of the tree as if he were going to hang someone.

They stood for an hour as he chanted and blew the whistle. The sound of his voice and its monotonous rhythm and the heat of the sun lulled her nearly into a trancelike state and when he turned to her and stopped the chant it took her a moment to surface.

He bent and pulled a hunting knife from a sheath he had strapped to his ankle. He took the knife and held it out to her, handle first.

"Take it, Medicine Woman," he said.

She just looked at him. She had no idea what he wanted her to do.

"It is for you to make the cuts." He gestured to his chest. "You will make four cuts." He drew two parallel lines with his finger on each breast. The lines were around four inches long and two inches apart. She still didn't understand. He reached out with both of his hands and took her hand and put the knife into it. The bone handle was warm. He clasped her hand around the handle and moved the knife to his chest. He pressed the point into his flesh. A tiny drop of blood welled up and formed a red bead that hung from the blade.

She felt her breath quicken. *I could kill him.* He still held her hand, but a quick thrust and it would be over. *I would be free. He would be dead.* He squeezed her hand and pushed the knife into his breast and pulled it down. He gasped, and she cried out. She tried to drop the knife, but his grip held her fast. The blood coursed down his chest and stomach.

He positioned the knife two inches over and made the next cut. This time he did not gasp. His eyes were on her, staring deep into her, past her to somewhere else. She could feel his whole body through his clasped hands, held impossibly stiff, vibrating with tension. He looked down and moved the knife to his other breast.

"No," she said. She could smell the blood. She felt her knees grow weak. He pulled the knife down again, moved it over and made the fourth cut. She looked at the four parallel lines of blood that traced heavy streams down his stomach and into the leather thong of his breechclout. He loosened her hand and dropped to his knees.

She thought he had fainted. She would run down the steep hill and catch her horse and ride away, escape. He looked up at her, his eyes wide with pain. He held out the rawhide attached to the rope. "Put it through the cuts," he said hoarsely. "Tie me."

She took the rawhide. He stood up and faced her. She looked at the blood welling from his chest and thought she would vomit.

"Do it!" he shouted. He took her hand and placed it on his chest. He pried up the cut and stuffed the rawhide under the skin, using her finger to push it beneath the muscle. It was warm and wet and horrible. She began to cry.

He pulled the rawhide out the parallel slash. "Do it!" he shouted. "You must do it. You must help me!" Crying, she forced herself to thread the rawhide beneath the warm thick muscle on the other side. He grunted once and then sighed when she pulled it through.

His hands were wet with blood, but he quickly tied each piece of rawhide to itself where it attached to the rope. He held the rope out in front of him, pulling lightly. It held, the skin and muscle pulling slightly away from his chest.

"You will take the other end of the rope," he said. "I will dance. When Sun Chief sees us he will be glad. He will take me and I will see what must be done."

She wiped her bloody hands on her jeans and went to the tree and the other end of the rope where it hung over the bottom branch. She was dazed, only half conscious as she clasped the rope. "Tighten it," he commanded. She pulled on it and took up the slack. He began to chant again and dance in a shuffling manner, toward her and the tree. When he got to the base he began to back away, and she played out the rope. He blew on the whistle and the sound was high and thin, the cry of an eagle. She watched him dully as the rope slipped through her sticky hands.

The idea came to her, almost unbidden, as if from a watcher who stood outside her body, as if this spectator had leaned over and whispered it into her ear. As he shuffled forward she saw it clearly, saw what she must do. This was madness and she must be free of it.

As he reached the base of the tree, she continued to pull. He raised his hands and grasped the rope but she kept pulling. He went up on his tiptoes and she dropped to one knee and wrapped the rope around the base of the tree. She wrapped it three times around and tied it into a knot. She was beginning to hyperventilate, her breath coming in gasps. She jumped back from the tree and saw him hanging at the end of the rope. There was no way he could bend down and untie himself. His arms were still outstretched grasping the rope. She turned and began to run.

The scree on the slope slid out from under her. She caught herself and, sliding and scrambling, she skidded down the steep slope. She glanced back up and could see him still in the same position beneath the tree. She lost her balance, fell, and got back up running. She glanced back and saw him begin to lift himself slowly, as if he were going to climb the rope. The muscles of his arms and back stood out in sharp relief. Somehow he'd gotten the whistle in his mouth and was blowing it in a series of short bursts.

She could see the horses where they had left them, tied to low bushes. Their heads were raised, looking at her as she slid down the slope. She looked back at John Raven. He had pulled himself up until his head was even with his hands. She stumbled backward, watching as he let go of the rope and fell, jerking once when the rawhide tore through the flesh of his chest. He disappeared, cut off from view by the lip of the ledge. She screamed and turned and ran.

The brush was thick and thorny and the bridle rope was twisted and tangled into the short limbs. She worked at the knot, willing herself to slow down and be careful, trying to keep her shaking hands from snarling the reins even further.

She heard him hit the loose rock on the slope.

She undid the knot and pulled the reins free.

The scree slid down the hill with a scrabbling sound and she could hear his footsteps as he ran.

She got the horse turned around and she swung up on its
re back.

She pulled the horse's head up and dug in her heels when
blew a sharp piercing scream on the whistle. The horse
red and John Raven caught her leg and pulled her off down
o the dust. The horse danced around them. She could see
stamping, plunging hooves around her head as they wres-
d, and the horse tried to get out of the way. The air was
ck with dust, she could taste it. John Raven was on top of
r, and there was blood dripping down on her as he sat up,
addling her, blowing the whistle. Her arms were pinned to
ground by his knees. His weight crushed her chest.

He clutched her left hand by the wrist and lifted it to the
y. "You must do this!" he shouted. The twin flaps of flesh on
chest had torn loose and were spraying blood. He was
vered with a layer of dust that coated his body over the
eat and blood. He held the hunting knife in his right hand
d the blade flashed in the sun. Her heart was pounding as
e struggled beneath him, kicking him in the back with her
ees as she tried to squirm away. He held her left hand to the
ound and put the blade of the knife against the first joint of
r little finger. "Now you must do this. You are Medicine
oman. It is time for you to sacrifice. It is time, it is
e . . ." And he pushed down and cut the end of her finger
, and she screamed, and he raised both hands to the sky
d rose up on his knees and shouted. She saw him fall to-
rd her, growing larger as he fell, smothering her beneath
bloodslick chest.

Chapter 39

"Keep this scow in the center of the river," King said. He was standing next to the cabin, looking out over the muddy water. "Too goddamn many people." He was frowning, watching the few local traders in their flatboats along the edges of the river.

Since morning, they had been aware that not only was the river traffic increasing, but signs of civilization, small towns and individual houses, had begun appearing on the river banks. Twain had been up all night, keeping the boat away from hidden snags and sandbars. To Alex, who had sat up much of the night with him, the river was nothing more than a black swath against the slightly blacker riverbank against the night sky. Only the stars provided relief, a backdrop that accentuated the obscurity of the foreground. Twain had piloted them through without incident. But now even his mustache, which had begun to grow back in, seemed to be drooping, and his already hooded eyes were on the point of closing altogether.

"Look, King," Twain said. "I've got to sleep. Let somebody else steer this thing for a while."

King transferred his gaze and his frown to Twain. "You'll keep at it till I tell you to quit. Once we get past this town we'll put in and lie up for the day. You can sleep then. Tomo

w we'll find a place and stop for supplies. You people eat
 much. Too goddamn many people on this boat. Got to do
nething about that." He went back to watching the river.
oo goddamn many people," he repeated to himself. He
nbed back up on the roof of the cabin and kicked Duke,
o was sleeping with his hat pulled down over his eyes.
'atch them," King said, lying down. "It's my turn to sleep.
ou see a good place on the other side of this town, put in
d tie up until tonight." Duke sat up sleepily and grinned at
thing in particular.

Twain bit off a piece of cornbread. It had gone moldy so
ng said they could have it. Alex had broken it into pieces
d handed it out. Abraham's arms were still tied to his sides,
 Alex fed him his share. Each time he put a piece in the
n's mouth he had to endure the questioning look in his
·s. But Alex had no answers. He had finally realized that all
 analysis led nowhere, that a thing explained is not a thing
derstood. Here he was, the man who had the answers of the
ure, prisoner of two homicidal cretins who held him in
adly control. It was quite clear that his position as man-
m-the-future conferred no benefit when it came to mortal-
 he could die just as easily and quickly as High Cloud had.
t last night the last shreds of civilization had been burned
 of him.

He had given Little Spring her share of the cornbread. She
d eaten it, indifferently. He had no words for her, either of
pe or encouragement, and she did not look to him for them.
He and Twain brushed the mold off the bread and ate.

"We've got to make our move tonight," Alex said, quietly.
ain nodded. "They'll kill Abraham or Little Spring next,"
·x went on. "Or maybe me. They need you to pilot the
at, but they're not going to let the rest of us hang out here
ever."

Twain looked at him curiously, the half-closed eyes widen-
, with interest. " 'Hang out here forever'?" he asked. "Hang
·?"

"You turds shut the hell up," Duke yelled from his perch on
· cabin roof. "You ain't got nothing to talk about." He

picked up his pistol and pointed it at Alex. He made litt
shooting noises. "Blow your goddamn head off."

After a while Duke tired of watching them and transferr
his attention to the riverbank, where he pretended to sho
various buildings and boats.

"I'll be goddamned," Twain said softly. "I know where
are." He looked at Alex who leaned closer. "This town
Hannibal, Missouri. I grew up here. I thought things we
starting to look familiar. From Hannibal on down to Ne
Orleans I know every bend in the river."

"Shut the hell up!" Duke shouted, raising the pistol ar
sighting along the barrel. "Bang, you're dead."

• •

They tied up on an island several miles downriver fro
Hannibal. Twain slept. They were still tied. King let them
ashore one at a time to relieve themselves, but he made
other concessions. Either King or Duke was awake at
times, and a pistol was always close to hand. Around fi
o'clock, King decided it was safe to get back out on the riv
The late afternoon breeze had freshened, and the s
was beginning to cloud up. Twain predicted rain befo
morning.

Alex cooked the last of the beans and bacon and gave it
King and Duke. After eating, they sat on the cabin top ar
smoked Twain's cigars. They had put Abraham back wi
Alex and Twain where they could keep an eye on all of the

"Duke," King said, speaking loud enough so that the thr
in the back could hear, "I think it's time we enjoyed ourselv
Last night we had us a nigger dance. Tonight I think we
help ourselves to some of that Indian poon tang."

Twain looked at Alex. Alex felt the words cut into hir
He'd expected it from the beginning. When it didn't happ
the first night, he'd begun to hope that King and Duke h
spent so much time together they'd acquired sexual prefe
ences for each other.

"I believe I'll go first," King said to Duke, turning to wat
the three men, "and you can have what's left over. You st
out here and keep a close eye on those three bastards." I

stood up and stretched. "Look at 'em. Like three monkeys all in a row."

The clouds had thickened, and lightning flashed in the distance. "Gonna rain, King. I stay out here, I'm gonna get wet." Duke was looking up at the other man with his demented grin.

"That's too goddamn bad. Someone's got to look after those three, and I can't do it and get no lovin' at the same time." He jumped down from the cabin top and walked over to where Twain, Alex, and Abraham sat.

"You got any complaints?" he said to them.

"You oyster-brained, shriveled-up reptile, you small-souled . . ."

King kicked Twain. "You aren't fit," Twain went on in the same monotone, "for anything but to be stood up on a street corner and used for dogs to piss on."

King hit him in the face. Blood trickled from the corner of his mouth. Because he was still tied to the steering oar, he could do no more than turn his head away from the blow. "Steer the goddamn boat," King said. "You can listen to me give it to the Indian. I'll take care of you later." He turned back to the Duke. "You watch them, you hear me? Anybody makes a move you kill him. I don't give a good goddamn about any of them." He ducked down into the cabin.

"You'd best not get him mad," Duke said, swinging his legs over the edge of the cabin. "You get him mad and there's no telling what he'll do. He's mean when he gets mad." He picked up the gun and held it in two hands, pointing at them. "Ol'King going to put it to the Indian. Then I get me a taste." He giggled.

The wind picked up, blowing riffles on the water. The trees on the banks began to bend as the front came through. The sound of thunder was followed by the sound of fist on flesh. Alex heard the hollow thump of Little Spring's head on the wooden flooring.

"Ol' King likes to tender his meat up before he tastes it," giggled Duke. He was bent over the edge of the cabin trying to see in. Alex had a brief hope that he man would fall on his head.

Duke hopped down off the roof and stood to one side of the opening, peering in. He kept glancing back at the three tied men.

In their minds they could see the big, dirty man as he bent over Little Spring. The wind had picked up even more, and the thunder rolled closer, almost synchronized with the sounds from below.

King began to curse, and the boat began to rock gently. Beside him, Alex noticed Abraham breathing heavily. He looked at the black man and saw his chest heaving, his muscles beginning to bulge around the thick rope wound around his chest.

Duke was crouched down now staring into the cabin, the pistol hanging in his hand. A clap of thunder drowned out the beating. A slash of lightning lit the boat and the river a harsh electric blue.

Alex felt Twain inch himself upright. On his other side, Abraham grunted and inhaled and held his breath, straining at the ropes. Alex saw the muscles bulge and writhe beneath the skin as Abraham threw back his head and began to raise his arms.

Twain pulled the ten-foot-long steering oar out of the water, the thick handle firmly in his hands. The next bolt illuminated the wild look on Twain's face as he struggled upright, lifting the oar out of the water. With the next crash of thunder, a cry broke from Abraham as his ropes parted with a tearing snap. Duke heard the cry and looked up at them, just beginning to straighten as Twain swung the oar overhead. The lightning streaked across the sky and all of them looked at the oar as it arced high, drops of water spraying from the blade into the wind. The sky opened up and the rain poured down. The blade fell with a terrible weight onto Duke's head with a thick, heavy thud that shook the boat. Alex was on his feet as the man hit the deck. He could feel Abraham behind him as they leaped down into the cabin.

King, on his hands and knees, snapped his head toward the

doorway. The scene was frozen into a crude pornographic snapshot by the next series of lightning strokes: King's pants down around his ankles as he prepared to mount Little Spring again. She was sprawled under him on her stomach. Alex acted without thought, kicking King square on the testicles with every ounce of strength in him, putting all the misery and frustration of the last several days into the blow. He felt the soft sack smash beneath his shoe. King roared like an animal, fell to his side, and curled into a ball.

Little Spring rolled into the shadows. There was a brilliant orange flash and a deafening crash, this time from inside the cabin, and she was crouched on her knees pointing King's pistol at the doubled-over man. The gun blasted again and the cabin was bright with the muzzle fire and thick with the sudden stink of gunsmoke and filthy bodies and sex and blood. The lightning next revealed the naked King with half his head blown off and blood welling from his chest and groin. Alex turned and stumbled out of the cabin as the gun went off again, and then again.

The air was clean and the rain cool against his face. He leaned on the cabin roof and heaved air into his lungs. Abraham helped Twain get the steering oar back in the water. The boat raced along on the churning river; Twain tried to steer them into the slower water near the shore while dodging trunks of submerged trees that threatened to snag them. Little Spring stepped onto the deck beside him and dropped the pistol into the river. He could see spatters of black blood on her torn shirt and exposed skin. Her face was battered and beginning to swell, but her look was triumphant, almost ecstatic. She leaned her head back into the rain and smiled. The rain ran in rivulets down her face and throat and arms and dripped pink onto the deck, where it collected and pooled beneath Duke, who stared up at them, eyes wide, his foolish grin gone at last, forever.

Chapter 40

"I'm telling you I know where they're headed." Will Two Horses stood in front of Agent Frank Owen's desk. The right side of his face was bruised a deep purple. He was dirty and tired and his feet hurt. He had walked and hitchhiked in from the spot where John Raven had left him horseless and senseless in the middle of the prairie. It had taken two days, and he was in no mood for cop bullshit.

Owen sat at the desk looking at the dusty Indian lawyer and wondered what he had done that had resulted in his being sent out on this case. Was it irreversible? Or was he doomed to a career of impossible no-win cases where the agent in charge is forced to deal with Third World immigrants and various minorities who hate his guts on principal and who would no more give him straight answers than they would inform on their sainted criminal blood-brothers. This Indian had made a fool of him once before. What was he up to now?

"All right," Owen said. "Let me see if I have it straight. You and the *Times* reporter were out in the middle of nowhere tracking down John Raven when he appeared out of a gulch, stole your horse, smashed you in the head, and kidnapped the lady." Will nodded. "You had information as to the whereabouts of this fugitive and you chose not to inform any of the authorities?"

"Goddamn right," Will said. "You people are too quick to shoot when there's an Indian involved."

Owen sighed. He had spent four miserable days down in the Badlands and all he'd found was sand, sagebrush, and sunburn. And now it turns out he'd been looking several hundred miles in the wrong direction. To say nothing of the fact, if this one was telling the truth, that a reporter for the *Times* was now involved.

He looked out the window and watched a used-truck salesman pointing out the finer features of a Ford pickup to an Indian wearing a ten-gallon hat with an eagle feather in the brim. Don't they know that possession of eagle feathers is a federal offense, his mind asked no one in particular, punishable by not more than ten years in prison? I could run that man in.

He sighed. He'd misspent most of his time out here listening to various locals, both Indian and white, give him advice that in the end turned out to be not worth a pile of coyote shit. Maybe it was time to cast his lot with the enemy. He couldn't do any worse than he'd been doing.

"Why have you come to us now, Mr. Horses? If we were too dangerous for you before, why are you here?"

"It's Mr. Two Horses," Will said, pulling up a chair and sitting down. "For one thing, John has crossed several state lines and added kidnapping to his other federal crimes. I have a fair grasp of the legal implications. Molly Glenn said that she thought you might be a cut above the usual law-enforcement gorilla."

Owen nodded. "I accept the compliment."

"Also," Will sighed, "I'm afraid John Raven has gone completely over the edge. I could get some of the boys together and try to catch him, but, as I said, we're talking state lines here, and besides, I'm not sure we could do it without someone getting hurt. I'm not sure *you* can do it without someone getting hurt, but if you're as smart as Molly thinks you are, then maybe you'll listen to reason and plan it so we've got a chance of bringing John in without killing him or harming Molly."

Owen nodded again. "I'm listening."

Will studied the other man for a minute and nodded back. "May I have a cup of coffee?" For two hot dusty days and two cold nights he'd been dreaming about a cup of coffee. Owen went to the office door and asked the deputy outside to bring in two cups of coffee. He went back to his desk and watched the deputy cross the street in front of the office and go into the beat-up diner across the road. The deputy was back shortly with two Styrofoam cups.

Will thought about how he could best present his plan. It would go against the grain of any regular lawman, but he thought maybe this one really was different. After his initial screw-up at Henry Sands's place he hadn't done anything else that was too offensive. That in itself was an indication of more than usual cop intelligence.

They sipped their coffee until Owen cleared his throat and leaned forward. "All right, Will Two Horses. Where's Raven going? Where do you think we can catch him?"

Will glanced out the window at the far mountains. Somehow it felt like a betrayal. He knew it wasn't, knew that John Raven had lost his hold on the real world and had to be helped. Christ, had to be stopped. What John was doing was wrong. His reasons were correct, and the moral weight was behind him, but he was a hundred years too late.

"He's headed for the Little Bighorn," Will said. "John Raven thinks he's the legitimate son of Crazy Horse, and he's about to reenact Custer's Last Stand. The part of the Seventh Cavalry will be played by whatever Park Service employees and tourists are in the area. The anniversary of the Last Stand is coming up June the twenty-fifth. It can't be coincidence. That's what he's heading for. He believes he can make a statement this way, that the world will sit up and take notice if he does this."

Owen sat back in his chair. "Well, he's right about that. Especially if he gets a New York reporter killed in the process." He stood up and walked to the door. "I'll get the maps. You tell me what you think we should do."

Chapter 41

Little Spring wanted to gut them. But for Alex it was too much. He didn't mind that they were dead: in fact, seeing them stretched out on the deck gave him a grisly pleasure. In the few days they had ruled over them, he had come to hate them that much.

It was early morning, just after dawn. The first stirrings of freedom and escape had grown into something akin to euphoria, a flushed, pleasant feeling. "Dump them," Alex said, "let's get them off the boat. I don't care if they float, I just don't want to pull up to the dock and pick up supplies with two corpses on deck."

Little Spring nodded. She was sitting on the roof of the cabin. Her face was swollen and bruised where King had beaten her, but even so there was a look of life about her that he had not seen since they had begun their odyssey. It was as if she had needed something to fight against, a true and obvious danger that she could overcome before she would agree to join them.

Alex could understand it. When he had jumped down in the cabin and seen King on his hands and knees, he had felt a surge of hate and power that was electric. At that moment, fate had switched sides, and they had seized the opportunity and freed themselves. And now he felt washed clean, as if all the niggling little creatures of doubt had been rinsed away in the blood of righteousness. The problems were still there: Custer, getting Little Spring home, Abraham, but they no longer were dragging him under. He had helped kill two men. Questions of ethics are difficult to entertain when you're standing next to two dead bodies.

They pulled Duke up on the edge of the deck and balanced him in a sitting-up position. His head was misshapen but whole, the look of surprise still on his face.

Twain puffed on a cigar as he stood looking at the corpse. "His head was full of axle grease," Twain intoned. "He was a bad boy who had been led astray by his choice of companions. But we care not. He deserved his ignominious end. We consign him to this river with relief." He pushed the Duke over and the body spun off into the current. They had to get Abraham to help with King. They had put his pants back on, no easy task, and none of them wanted to touch him as he had a number of holes in him and he was covered with dried blood. That was until they found the money. One of his pockets contained five hundred dollars and a full body search turned up over a thousand. After they were sure they had gotten it all, they balanced him on the gunwale.

"This one was worse, far worse," Twain said. "He was a crawling insect, a contemptible black and infamous excuse for a human being. He was a man with not a mind, but a skull full of reason-debauching maggots. He was a wretched goddamned pig-headed tapeworm." He looked at the others assembled in a semi-circle on the deck. "Yes, I am mixing my metaphors, but this man has driven me to it. He demands it. He has made me ashamed to be a man. And it is only the thought that there is a hell that calms me. The bullet, or in this case, bullets, were a merciful instrument of death. Too merciful. It is a great pity that he died so quickly. Have a cigar." He pushed his half-smoked stogie into King's cold mouth, ash end first. He rolled the body over the side and stared at it for a moment as it floated alongside the boat.

"I ain't never seen a man as dead as that," Abraham said.

"Yes," Twain said, "he's dead all over." The two of them looked at each other and smiled.

Twain picked up the long pole and pushed the body away. It spun in an eddy and drifted off, toward the center of the river.

"I guess they never expected us to fight back," Abraham said.

"Well," Twain said, looking at the big man appraisingly, "no, they didn't. They mistook us for the sort of men they were used to, and that was a mistake. Reminds me of a true story." Twain sat down at the steering oar. "When I was a boy I was out fishing. I was with several companions and all of us had elected to not attend school on this particular day. We were walking along the riverbank, and we came across a man with a pole in his hands and his line in the water. We asked him if he were getting any bites, and he said this curious thing. He said that he wasn't getting any bites from the fish, but his worms sure were going after him. We thought no more about it until later that same day." Twain looked out over the water, remembering. Alex had sat down, but Abraham was still standing, watching Twain.

"It was getting onto evening, and we were on our way back, when we came across that same fellow. Only now he was stretched out on the riverbank, stark dead. We were a little nervous about it, but we got up close and took a look. The man's hands and arms were swollen up as tight as a tick and had little holes in them. Then one of us picked up his can of worms and saw the man's mistake. He had him a can of baby copperhead snakes for bait. They do look a lot like your common nightcrawler. He'd mistaken the snakes for worms, and he'd paid a heavy price as a result. Not unlike our two friends now consigned to the river."

Twain leaned back on the oar and looked up at Abraham. "Ever since we left the exposition you've been moping around like you lost your best friend. I understand that, you did lose your best friend. But death comes in many forms, and it comes to all of us. A man might get bit to death by a can of baby snakes, or a man might die in the service of his friends. Elias did a brave thing back at that fair, and he did it knowing the probable outcome."

Abraham nodded. "Uncle would have told a different story, but the meanin' probably would have been the same. You saying that what some people might see as a weak creature might turn out to be powerful? That we shouldn't be quick to judge."

"That's right," Twain said. "That, and there's a lot of different ways to die. Some foolish, and some worthwhile."

Abraham looked at Twain and nodded. He looked out over the river and nodded again.

"What now?" Alex asked.

"Well," Twain said, "I figured we'd just hang out here on the boat for a while. Maybe Abraham can catch some fish and we'll pick up supplies the first town we come to. We ought to strike St. Louis sometime late tomorrow. That's far enough away from whatever was chasing you. We can get transportation there, me back East and you in whatever direction you're headed in. Two days ought to give you enough time to come clean with me about all of this. I haven't wanted to stir the matter before, but now that we have some time I'd appreciate an explanation. In many ways I am a fool, I understand that, but I am God's fool and his works must be contemplated with respect." His eyes were serious. "No more bogus stories. I've never been one to hold a grudge against a good lie, but I'm tired of having my leg sawed off."

Alex looked at Twain and then out over the river. " 'Hang out,' huh?"

Twain nodded. "That's right. And don't forget the zippers."

What the hell. If there was anyone in this time that he owed, it was Twain. And if there was anyone in this time who would understand, or at least listen to his explanation with consideration and sympathy, it was Mark Twain. As far as breaking the rules of history, well, he'd lost interest in rules. The concepts involved were too abstract in a world that was overwhelmingly pragmatic.

Abraham was at the front of the boat, fishing. Little Spring was on top of the cabin, facing forward. The air was clear and clean, cool, the sun high in the sky, beginning to warm them. The river was brown and swift, whole trees would sometimes rear up, like huge spiny water monsters, then disappear. Branches and chunks of wood swirled around them.

He had imagined the moment as being a release, the pouring out of his great secret. The Future. But what could he tell? What would be right? How about the history of future wars? Should he skip the minor incursions and go straight to World War I, and then II, explain the complicated circumstances of Korea, and wind up with Vietnam? Expound on trench warfare, poison gas, psychological torture and the wonders of the atomic bomb? How do you explain the Nazis? The Bolsheviks? Do you illustrate with various atrocities? The Holocaust, the bombing of Dresden, My Lai, the destruction of Cambodia, Afghanistan, germ warfare, neutron bombs. Adolph Hitler, Joseph Stalin, Pol Pot, Big Daddy Idi Amin, Baby Doc, and Muammar Khadaffi.

And if history is not defined by wars and despots, then what? The advances in medicine that have cured the common diseases of Twain's time, tuberculosis, and syphilis? But what about the new environmental diseases we've given ourselves; lung cancer, heart disease, to say nothing of AIDS.

Let's see, he thought, how about machines? These people have great faith in machines. The automobile? Should he tell Twain about rush hour? How could he explain that people would sit in cars for hours every day waiting to go distances that could be covered on horseback in the same amount of time? Pollution? He could feel himself working his explanation into every available corner. How about social advances? The voracious robber barons of this time, although some of them were among Twain's greatest friends, had been eradicated. But we replaced them with greedy developers and businessmen who would sell anything down whatever river was available if there was profit in it. At least the robber barons left behind railroads and mines and buildings, something useful.

Where was the good stuff? Here was a man who gets his mail delivered in New York at least twice a day and he, Alex, sometimes had to wait five days for a letter to get across town. Where were the advances? Surely there was something to be proud of. There must be *something*. Velcro. I'd tell him about Velcro, but he probably wouldn't believe it. He already thinks the zipper is high tech. Digital watches? He wouldn't understand the point of them. What *was* the point of them, anyway?

Dumping caution in the river, he simply said it. "I'm from the future. From the twentieth century."

They both sat quietly as a great blue heron lifted from a nearby tree and slowly flapped his way toward the other side of the river. "Is that so," Twain said.

"Yep," Alex said.

They sat through another silence. "You know," Twain said, "once you start a stretcher like that, you should be able to follow up with some detail. It lends a bit of credibility to it." He shook his head. "Forget it. I guess just because a man uses unusual expressions and has an interesting method of fastening up his garments doesn't make him a man from another planet. I was hoping for an explanation that I could use in a story. I honestly thought you were going to tell me you were from Mars, or the moon. I'd have believed that."

They stopped in a small town and bought a ham and some bread and some eggs. All afternoon as they floated along Alex thought about it, trying to come up with something that would have answered, but it just got worse. Should he have told Abraham of all the future indignities and pain that his race would be faced with? Should he tell Little Spring that her people would be slaughtered and put on reservations and cheated until they constituted the most deprived, poverty-stricken, alcohol-ridden, and poorest people in the United States of America?

No, he couldn't tell any of them any of that. There must be some good, something to be proud of, but he couldn't think of it.

And then he remembered his tape player. He went to the storage box where he kept their provisions. He got out his jacket and felt in the pocket. He was at the side of the cabin and the others were paying him no attention. He opened up

e Walkman and looked at the tape. *Little Richard: Greatest
its.*

Play it for Twain? No. How the hell would you explain
ittle Richard to Mark Twain. Besides which, Twain would
ant to patent the tape player, batteries not included because
ey hadn't been invented yet. He leaned back against the
abin and slipped the player back into the jacket. Here it was,
is big moment, and it had turned out to be impossible. He
as not proud of his time. Revelations of its wonders would
e no kindness.

• •

That night and the next day slipped by as quickly and easily
s the river itself. It was a pause, a moment of respite, and
en it was over. "St. Louis," Twain said, nodding toward the
harves and docks ahead of them. "End of the line."

Chapter 42

They stood on the levee and looked out over nearly a mi of empty wharves. Their boat was tied a few hundred fe upstream. Alex could see Abraham sitting on the deck, fish ing. Little Spring was watching him. They were talking. Sh had refused to leave the boat, and Abraham had volunteere to stay with her. He had regained much of his old spirit, b Alex was afraid that part of him had been damaged beyor repair.

"In my day, twenty years ago," Twain said, interruptir Alex's thoughts, "there used to be a solid mile of wide-awal steamboats here." He was looking down at six beat-up-lool ing steamboats; two sternwheelers and four sidewheeler "Now we have half a dozen sound-asleep ones. This is woeful sight." He swept his hand over the empty wharve "This whole area was piled high with mountains of freigh armies of drays, people all over, rivermen everywhere. Now see a handful of ragged Negroes, most of whom seem e) tremely fatigued, probably with whiskey." He sighed ar shook his head.

"Where did they all go?" Alex asked.

"The rivermen?" Twain shrugged. "Hard to say. Into th common herd. I guess such things are inevitable. In the ear days, steamboating killed keelboating; now it's the stean

oat's turn. The railroads make the same trip in less than half
ne time, so there goes your passenger traffic. Towboats fin-
hed off the freight business. A towboat can drag six or seven
eamboat loads downriver all at once, and do it a hell of a lot
neaper. No, the steamboat is dead and more's the pity." He
urned away from the wharves.

" 'The old, old sea, as one in tears/ Comes murmuring,
ith foamy lips,/ And knocking at the vacant piers,/ Calls for
s long-lost multitude of ships.' " He smiled at Alex, head
lted back. "Let's go find a drink, poetry makes me thirsty. I
eed something more interesting than river water. I'm tired of
rinking mud. Besides, if we stay much longer I may begin to
eep."

They walked carefully over the broken sidewalk to the main
bad that ran along the levee. Twain hired a cab and they rode
nto St. Louis, rivermen of a sort, perhaps not as grand as
nose of earlier days, but having had more than their share of
dventure, and more than ready, after an unusually arduous
ip, for a drink.

•   •

The Southern Hotel was everything Alex could have asked
r in the way of authentic deep-South charm. Overstuffed
nairs in a lobby glittering with mirrors, gold and cut-glass
nandeliers, pretty blond waitresses rather than the usual
aiters, and drinks served in heavy decanters with sprigs of
int adorning the rims. Alex surveyed it all and wished he
ere here on vacation, wished he could enjoy it, wished Molly
ere with him. Molly, where was Molly? What was she doing?
id she miss him?

"Now that I've had the opportunity to mull over your brief
xplanation of the other day, the notion that you've arrived
ere among us from some distant future, I've come to like it.
ll admit that at first I thought it a little bogus, but on reflec-
on, it's quite a darling. In fact, if you don't mind, I might just
ook it for my own use." He pulled out the thick wad of
reenbacks they had taken from King and put it on the table
front of Alex. Alex glanced nervously around the room, but
o one was looking at them.

Twain laughed. "This room has seen a sight more mone than that sliding across the table. I want you to take it all. remember with a small amount of pain the accusation flung i my face by your friend Elias, that I had taken my story of th old darky woman and given her nothing in return. There wa just enough truth in that shot to hurt. So you can have m share." He put his hand up and rubbed his head. His hair ha begun to grow back but it would be months before he woul look like his old self again.

"It's an interesting problem, this idea of going back into th past. I believe I can get a book out of it. That's why you ca have my share, in payment for a good idea. I'll never be abl to use our river adventure; no one would ever believe it. Be sides, we'd probably go to jail if it ever got out. But maybe thi time-travel thing will come to something." He signed. "We'v had our fun, but it's time for me to get back into harness."

"Where would you go," Alex asked, "if you could go bac in time?"

Twain got out a cigar and put it in his mouth. "I've though about it some since you brought it up, and I believe I'd g back to old King Arthur's court. I'm interested in the Englisl and I'd like to know the truth of that time. It'd also be a goo place to put a few modern suggestions into the mill of histor Do our English cousins some good."

Alex sat forward. "If you could really go back in time, you' try to change things?"

Twain looked surprised. "Wouldn't you? If you had tha ability and you could change things for the better, wouldn you? I would think it would be one's duty to do so." It was now clear to Alex that Twain didn't believe him, never ha That he saw it as an interesting joke. He briefly considere going back to the boat and getting the tape player, putting tl earphones on Twain's head and cranking up Little Richa and *then* seeing if Twain believed him. But the only purpo would be to prove that he was telling the truth, to settle tl score. Not reason enough.

"Tell me something," Alex asked. "One day in Philadelph we had a discussion on the nature of man." Twain nodde

He struck a match on the underside of the table and lighted his cigar. "You said man was merely a machine. Have you changed your opinion in any way?"

Twain blew a puff of smoke toward the ceiling and watched as it floated upward. "I guess I have," he said gruffly. "Always remember that a humorist has a professional lock on opinion holding, which means I may change my opinions at will, much like a politician, and not be charged for it. Unlike you civilians. But yes, on contemplation, I'd have to say that while my argument was correct, it was limited. What I learned on our boat trip was, well, several things.

"I saw a man, High Cloud, die simply because it was evident that he was not going to knuckle under to another man's will. And back at the exposition, when the rest of us were standing around with our mouths open and our thumbs up our behinds, that same Indian shot Brannon, coolly and as accurately as death itself. Brannon was the danger and he reacted correctly, in his terms, to it. This was an heroic act, especially under the circumstances. Had he lived I'm quite sure he would have returned to his people, apprised them of our strengths and weaknesses, and made a great war on us.

"And then there are our friends Abraham and Elias. Abraham personifies simplicity, goodness you might say. As a man, he was completely undone by the death of his friend, who was also a hero. And by the continued harassment of those two malignancies, King and Duke. And they were evil, or at least King was, to the core. Men who had, by circumstance and sheer will, become savages.

"And so we have a red man who is heroic, two black men, one almost angelic and the other the soul of bravery, and a white man who is an infamous devil." He nodded to Alex. "If your point is that it is beyond the nature of machinery to be men of such extremes, then I'll grant you your argument. And retract my earlier one. I concede, you win by default." He puffed on the cigar and looked out over the room. While they had been talking, the other tables had filled up.

"I have one other question," Alex said. "If it is possible to save a man's life, or even men's lives, is one always obligated to do so? No matter what the circumstances?"

Twain looked at him evenly. He put the cigar onto the heavy, cut-glass ashtray in front of him. "Of course," he said. "Provided the men's lives are worth saving. I wouldn't budge an inch to save a man like King, or a troop of his ilk. But innocent men, moral men, yes, I don't think there's any question."

"I said only one more question, but I have another. Is Custer a good man?"

"I think so. He is a vain man, but then so am I. As are you. As are most men, particularly powerful men. Why do you ask?"

"No reason. I think I will leave here tomorrow, if possible. I'll take Little Spring."

"And Abraham?"

"Will you take him back with you? There's no need for him to go on; it's not his fight. Never was, really."

"All right." He finished his drink, picked up his cigar, and stood. "We've things to do. I must wire my bank once again, and we've train tickets to buy."

Outside the door they stood for a moment, looking down the narrow street and at the people walking by. It was still odd to see so many people.

"You know," Twain said, not looking at Alex, "knowing the future is a funny proposition. I don't think I'd want that burden, not a bit of it. Knowing the present is bad enough. It's sort of like death, which is, of course, awful, but the sentence of death is worse. Better that a man remain in the fog than stand in the pain of that clarity. I'll cast my lot with my present. The future might make a good book, but I wouldn't want to live it."

Chapter 43

In the end, it wasn't quite as easy as he thought it would be. But then none of it had been. Abraham decided that he was not going back; he would go with Alex and Little Spring.

"Come this far, I'm going to finish it."

"I appreciate it, Abraham, but I can get her home on my own. You've done enough—God knows you've done more than ever should have been asked of you."

"Wasn't your fight to begin with, Alex. You helped all you could and you got us this far, but I'm going along. These were my Indians, my responsibility first. I'm going to finish it. Colored men have just as much reason as white to finish what they start." The look on his face backed him up. He was going if he had to walk all the way.

"Three tickets to as far northwest as I can get," Alex told the man behind the ticket window. The man adjusted his green eyeshade and studied a map.

"Let's see, I can get you to Bismarck, which is pretty goddamn far north, and then I don't know how far west the line goes. Changes every goddamn day. I'm pretty sure we've made Fort Lincoln, got the Seventh Cavalry keeping that line open. Long as there isn't any goddamn snow." The man chuckled. He had several teeth missing.

"What's the date?" Alex asked. The sudden realization that he might be too late gave his bowels a cold squeeze.

"Date? June the goddamn first. Hell, there's still probably snow up there. Summer don't come till the Fourth of July. Autumn starts the fifth. What you want? A one-way to the end of the line? Wherever the hell that may be. First, second, or third class?"

"Three one-ways. Second class," Alex said, not paying much attention. June the goddamn first. A little more than three weeks until Custer rides down on the Sioux at the Little Bighorn. Maybe enough time, maybe not. The ticket agent asked for one hundred eighty dollars, and Alex peeled the bills off King's wad. He wondered for a moment who had been the original owner of the money. Probably a bank somewhere up the Mississippi. It was now going for the cause, whatever that was. Alex shook his head, amazed at how he had ever gotten involved in all of this, if the ability to move back in time extracted these moral quandaries as an entrance fee, a sort of bride price, a ride on an ethical roller coaster. *Step right up, the experience of a lifetime, have fun, see the past.* But you *will* pay the price. Or maybe he was just soft-headed, as Twain had pointed out on a number of occasions.

They stood on the platform, their pitiful pile of gear stacked at their feet. Of their group, it was he and Twain who stood out as unusual. The rest of the platform was crowded with black families, surrounded by mounds of household goods and boxes of clothing. "The Exodus of 1876 is what it's being called." Twain said. "They're going to Kansas. Things are getting a little warm for Negroes in the South, what with the Ku Klux Klan and other groups of oyster-brained asses. I'll tell you, Alex, some men's heads weren't meant to put ideas in, they were meant to throw potatoes at." He looked at the crowd of black men, women, and children. "These folks are headed for a harsh land. I know, I've been there."

In the distance they heard the whistle of an approaching train. "Thanks," Alex said awkwardly, holding out his hand. Now that the moment had come, he found that the customary entiments sounded faintly ridiculous. "You got us here; I ouldn't have done it without you."

Twain shook his hand. "I'm not sure I want to claim credit n this case." He looked away, as if thinking. "I think that perhaps we are only the microscopic trichina in some vast creature's veins, and that our adventures are the natural processes of that creature's life.

Alex groaned. "Not another theory of What Is Man."

Twain laughed. "These things bear thinking about; it's all that separates us from the rest of the animal kingdom. At any rate, I've had as much fun and interest as I want for a while. You've stirred all the torpidity out of my soul. I won't need to go to gypsying again for quite some time."

"Well, I've put you through a lot of grief. You stayed with us when you didn't have to."

Twain took a cigar out of his pocket and peered up the rack. The train was still out of sight. "Well, I guess that's true." He waited a moment, thinking. "It reminds me of a story." He took out a match and struck it on a nearby post.

"A group of people were sitting around at a wake. The deceased had died a rather unusual death. The man in question had run an impressive whiskey-making operation in his backyard, and it seems he slipped one day and fell into a rather large barrel of mash, whereupon he drowned." He puffed on his cigar for a moment. "The widow was carrying on something awful, crying and wringing her hands, lamenting. One of the other mourners, a man who was a partner in the whiskey business, decided to lighten the widow's load. 'I wouldn't take it so hard, ma'am,' the man said. 'I think he died happy. He got out three times before he drowned, twice to go to the bathroom, and once to smoke a cigar.'" Twain contemplated the ash of his own cigar for a moment.

"The point is, Alex, I could have gotten out of the barrel any number of times, but I didn't. Some men like it in the barrel—you and I are two of them. You've got an inflated moral sense that makes you do what you do; I have an incurable curiosity to see what will happen next." He studied Alex for a moment and then went on, "You still interest me; you have from the very beginning. I'd like to know what happen on your journey, but I believe that you've got to go the last par by yourself. As to why you're doing it, well, you can't help it it's the way you're built. If I were you, I'd just accept what yo have to do, and quit worrying about what's right and what' wrong. Otherwise, you'll just wear yourself out. You see, it' not what you do that's so important, it's that you do it at all It's the search, the attempt, that separates us from the animal: That and the formulation of absurd theories on the nature c man." He smiled and held out his hand as the locomotive spewing steam and ashes, puffed by them and screeched to stop.

Alex shook his hand again and turned to herd the other onto the nearest car. When he turned back, Twain had walke away to stand under the veranda. Alex got on, found a sea and opened the window. Twain was standing, arms over hi chest, head back, peering out of his deep-set eyes, as if h were looking at something very far away. Then he shook hi head and walked back to the edge of the platform. He looke up at Alex.

"Goddamn it, I can't help it, I've got to ask. Several day ago I told you that no man wants to know of his own end. lied; every man wants to know, as long as it's far enough i the future. Tell me, what's the verdict?"

Alex looked down and thought of one last piece of busi ness. "How about a trade? Forget the zipper?"

Twain looked pained. "I was counting on that to see m through my old age."

"Wouldn't you rather know if there was going to be any ol age?"

Twain looked down at the ground. "All right, goddamn it.

Alex was glad that he didn't have to lie. "Years. Lots them. More than enough. And books. Great ones. They wi say that you and your work changed the course of America literature."

Twain nodded and smiled. "Literature, huh? I don't believ that could sound any better, even if it were true."

"It's true, believe me."

Twain looked at him for a long moment and nodded again. "Thank you." He put his cigar back in his mouth, waved, and turned and walked into the station.

Alex felt him go. Felt the presence of the man leave him. He was surprised at the loneliness that flooded into the space that Twain had just left. He sat back in the seat and looked at Abraham and Little Spring and wondered what he would do without Mark Twain to help him.

• •

They were lucky. Most of the travelers back on the platform were traveling due west from St. Louis. The northern train remained uncrowded. Second class was the mode of travel for most ordinary folk; those using the train because they had to get from one place to another as opposed to those in first class, who were traveling for pleasure. Third class was reserved for immigrants, mostly the Irish who were headed to the Northwest to work on the railroads. Third class was unpleasant, two rows of wooden benches on either side of a converted freight car. Second class was bearable, rows of horsehair-stuffed seats facing one another. First class was luxurious.

Alex considered changing their tickets to first class but decided against it; Abraham and Little Spring would not fit into that upper-class white world.

The second-class car had an enclosed toilet at one end and a stove at the other. Everyone in the car used the stove to heat water for coffee and for shaving and washing. They bought their food from vendors at the numerous stops along the way. The conductor rented them boards to lay between the seats for beds, and straw-filled pillows for their heads. For four days and nights they rode due north and then began to ease west, picking up and dropping off scores of locals who rode the train from one small town to the next.

Alex tried not to plan anything, knowing by now that it was virtually useless, that chance had more to do with what happened than any plan that he might conceive. If they were indeed trichina, as Twain thought, inside some creature's veins, the creature was at least headed in the correct direction.

In Fargo they turned west and the train population became at least in second class, rougher and almost exclusively male. Fur traders, drummers, and soldiers shared the car with ever increasing numbers of railroad workers who were headed to rail's end to join the men already working there. Most of the men stared at Little Spring and ignored Abraham. There was some curiosity toward Alex, who was seen as the leader of the group, but he was able to deflect most of the questions and hostile glances without trouble.

The days and nights passed quickly. He tried to achieve a sort of Zen-like empty-mindedness, attempting to damp down his eternal moral niggling, which he now recognized as his own particular reflexive response to fear and uncertainty. The main question that occupied his mind was Little Spring.

As they rode, Abraham and Little Spring side by side on the opposite seat, he became increasingly aware of her "condition." Perhaps it was because he was thinking about it, but she seemed to become more and more visibly pregnant with each passing day.

He had been operating under the impression that the baby belonged to one of three people: Crazy Horse, the leading candidate; Custer, a close second; and, God forbid, himself. He hoped he was a distant and unlikely contender, but there was no way he could dismiss the possibility.

When the train sighed and slowed to a stop at Bismarck, he was no closer to a solution than he had been when they first climbed aboard. But he was certain of one thing. Well, fairly certain. In the future, if he had a future, he would resist sexual temptation no matter where and when it struck. At least as long as Molly wasn't involved. The idea of a future peopled with his own descendants, born before his own parents had even existed, was a knot too Gordian to unravel. He wondered what Mark Twain's opinion would be of that one.

End-of-track turned out to be only several miles outside of Bismarck. Alex studied a map that was posted in the train station. There was a lot of blank space to the west of them, all unexplored territory, and a few, pitifully few, rivers and trails that were clearly marked. He supposed they could buy them lves horses and camping gear. They still had plenty of money left; they could simply ride across the blank sections of the map until they got to where Custer would end up. But it was a long way, and he wasn't sure he could navigate them on journey like that without becoming hopelessly lost. Perhaps little Spring could lead them, but somehow he was reluctant to turn that task over to her. She still remained distant where he was concerned, and he had to admit that he did not trust her. He had seen her kill the guard at the exposition, or seen the evidence of the killing, and he had seen her shoot King as many times as she had bullets. The only person, besides High Cloud, he had ever seen her be pleasant to was Abraham. She was a mystery to him, an unknown, and he was not yet so lost or without resources that he would turn to her for help.

He got them two rooms at a rough hotel, making sure that the other two understood they were to stay in those rooms, and he began trying to find some way for them to get close enough to the Sioux to turn Little Spring loose. In the end, he found the solution in a saloon.

The saloon, as an institution, played a great role in the life of a western town. It was the civic center of the community, a place to catch up on the news and pass along important information as well as gossip. So for the price of a drink, usually whiskey or brandy, it was possible to answer virtually any questions about a particular place or person. Depending on how long you were willing to persevere, and how sober you could remain. Fortunately for Alex, his problem had a three-drink, one-afternoon solution.

But it was Twain that made the difference, once again. While they had been on the river, in those first idyllic days, Twain had reminisced at length on his days as a pilot on the Mississippi. One of the men he remembered fondly, and with great admiration, was a pilot named Grant Marsh. So when Alex thought he heard the name again from the mouth of a short, hard-looking man who was willing to talk as long as Alex bought, he seized on it.

"Did you say Grant Marsh?" Alex asked.

"Give us another round, bardog," the small man said, mo
tioning to their two glasses.

Momentarily diverted, Alex looked at the label on the bottl
as the bartender poured. It had a crude drawing of a winc
with the name Block and Tackle at the top. "Could I see th
bottle," Alex said. The bartender handed it to him. At th
bottom of the label it said "One drink and a man will walk
block and tackle anything."

"Pretty good whiskey," his drinking partner said, holdin
his glass up to the light.

"What was that name again?" Alex asked.

"Block and Tackle," the man said. "My name's Jacl
Crabb."

"No, the name you said before, not the whiskey."

The old man looked puzzled. "There's lots of names o
whiskeys. Red Dynamite, Brave Maker, Joy Juice, Dus
Cutter . . ."

"Not whiskey—you were talking about a boat."

"Red Disturbance, Apache Tears, Corpse Reviver," the mar
had closed his eyes and was chanting the names almost reli
giously, "Jig Juice, Miner's Friend, Nockum Stiff . . ."

"Wait a minute," Alex said, putting his hand on the man'
arm. "Nockum Stiff? You're kidding."

Crabb opened his eyes and looked at Alex's hand on hi
arm. "I never kid about whiskey."

"Grant Marsh," Alex said, now that he'd regained th
man's attention. "You said you were a teamster, you wer
going up the Missouri on a boat. That the captain's name wa
Grant Marsh."

Crabb nodded. "That's right. Grant Marsh, captain of th
Far West. Commissioned by the Seventh Cavalry to haul sup
plies as far up the Yellowstone as possible. Which they figur
is going to be farther than anyone else has even gotten. She'
built special with a low draft, don't draw hardly any water a
all. They say she can navigate on a heavy dew." The mar
knocked back his drink and stared at Alex's glass. Ale:
pushed it over to him.

"When do they leave?"

"Soon as they finish with the loading tomorrow morning. uster and them's already headed out. They're going to meet p down on the Yellowstone before they make their run on the dskins. Going to whip 'em once and for all, least that's what ey say. I tried to sign on as a scout, but they didn't need me. guess I'll skin some mules instead."

Alex thought about it. The man was drunk, but he seemed know what he was talking about. This Grant Marsh had to e the same one Twain had talked about; how many river ilots named Grant Marsh could there be? If he could get em on the boat it would solve a large part of their transpor- tion problem. It would put him in contact with part of the eventh Cavalry, but at least not Custer. He wondered if uster would remember him from their meeting at the exhibi- on. He motioned the bartender over and pointed at both asses now lined up in front of his drinking companion.

As Alex pushed through the batwing saloon doors, he could ill hear the little man, back in his whiskey world.

"White Mule, Taos Lightning, Forty Rods, Lamp Oil . . ."

• •

It wasn't hard to find the steamboat; she was being loaded y torchlight. He found the captain and Mark Twain's name ot them passage. Alex told Marsh, a tall man with gray mut- onchop whiskers and the air of a Kentucky colonel, that he as a reporter for the *New York Sun,* sent out to cover the big idian fight. He would be traveling with his Negro servant and h Indian woman who acted as his guide and interpreter. larsh didn't care. If he was a friend of Sam Clemens's, the nest riverboat pilot he'd ever trained, he could ride wherever ie *Far West* was going. Stay out of the way, Marsh said, find a oot on the deck to camp out, and he'd watch out for them. nd when he got back to New York, say hello to that son of a oyote Clemens. Alex allowed as how he would, the very first nance he got.

And so in the morning just as the sun began to warm the iist off the river, the steamer *Far West* cast off from the dock nd started up the Big Muddy to the headwaters where it ined the Yellowstone. On deck were Alex, Abraham, and ittle Spring. Mark Twain had saved them again.

Chapter 44

Molly rolled over and looked up at John Raven. He wa
standing over her, talking, gesticulating with his hands. H
had put a layer of moss over his chest wounds, and he ha
found a shirt in her saddlebag and tied the arms over the mos
to hold it in place. He had dug up a thick red clay and groun
it with water and painted his cheeks and arms with lightnin
streaks. He was going on again about his ancestors, his glori
ous past. She was sick of his babbling.

They were camped next to a creek in a grove of cotton
woods. They had been there for several days, living on frog
that John Raven cooked over the fire.

She rolled back on her side, ignoring him. "You will com
with me. It is still not finished. You have sacrificed, and that i
good, but we must finish our fight."

No More. I can't do it. She had hoped he would let her g
That it was over.

"You are the witness," he went on. "As Medicine Woma
you will witness the fight. It is your work. You will tell th
world what has happened."

"Go away," she said. After a minute he went away an
crouched down by the small campfire. She lay on her arm an
looked at her hand. He had dressed her wound with the sam
moss he used on himself. He had tied it up with cloth he ha

n from the same shirt he had used as a bandage. It was an
flannel shirt, one of her favorites.

The first day she had been in shock, unable to do anything
re than cling to the saddle as he led her horse at a slow
lk. They had camped that night and stayed by this little
am ever since. Her hand and arm ached with a dull pain
t made her sick to her stomach.

She understood that he was crazy, that he no longer had
control over his actions. She understood that, but it did
make her hate him any less. She lifted her hand, looked at
grotesque bandage. Alex had given her the shirt for Christ-
s, years ago; it was white-and-blue checked, as soft as a
en. She looked at the bandage and felt the anger begin. She
ed him, but this was different. This was sharper and de-
nded revenge. It began as a small flame. She would tend it,
l it would grow.

An Indian woman would consider the mutilation an honor.
n Raven explained it to her as if it would make a differ-
e. It was a ritual that Indian women were expected to take
t in, to ensure the efficacy of the Sun Dance. They would
off their fingers, sacrificing one joint at a time. She would
l quickly; Sun Chief was pleased with them. There was
re, but she no longer listened. She had her anger to nur-
.

He had cut off her little finger at the first joint. She remem-
ed the bright flaring moment when she lay beneath him
l his knife came down and she screamed. . . .

She would live through this. She looked away from her
d, at the small fire, and thought of Alex. How she missed
. She would not give up. And John Raven would pay.

Chapter 45

For some reason, and he was afraid to question it, thi
were going smoothly. The *Far West* steamed up the Misso
and into the Yellowstone with the workmanlike grace of a f
craftsman performing a familiar and pleasant task. The Y
lowstone itself was a trickier river, swift and deceptive,
Captain Marsh turned out to be as good as Twain had sa
and the strong engines, broad beam, and shallow draft s
them through. They camped out on the covered deck of
steamboat. The weather was good, and the trip had been e
and interesting. There were the usual questions about Ab
ham and Little Spring, but Alex was becoming adept at sp
ning his story of writer and retainers. By the time they dock
he had bought supplies from the sutler on board and e
three horses from the civilian stockman who was supply
the army with mounts for the Indian campaign.

They picked up the horses as soon as they landed.
army herd had been sent ahead from Fort Lincoln to meet
boat. Alex knew that Custer was due in the next few days,
he hurried his preparations and purchases as much as po
ble without calling undue attention to himself. He picked
two Indian ponies and an army horse. The army horse was
Abraham, as the Indian ponies were too small. The civi
purchase of a horse clearly marked with the initials u.s. on

shoulder was illegal, though common, and it was added
lucement to leave the area quickly. His story of being a
iter had filtered through most of the officers on the *Far West*
d had been accepted without question. Custer had a policy
always bringing along the press on his campaigns so his
ploits would be written up quickly, and to the general's
·cifications. One more writer, even one with an entourage,
s not unusual.

The big horse cost him one hundred fifty dollars, but the
dian ponies were a bargain. Their original purpose had
en as gifts for whatever scouts Custer deigned to reward.
e unrecorded sale of two of them would never be noticed.
bought saddlebags, saddles, and other gear from the quar-
master, all negotiations having proceeded nicely after a
ge bribe was offered and accepted. Alex was throwing
ney around as if it didn't belong to him, which it didn't.

His plan extended no further than getting Little Spring into
se proximity to her own people. After that he intended to
urn East with Abraham by whatever means possible, de-
nding on whatever opportunities presented themselves and
w much money they had remaining. The idea of being com-
·tely on their own, dependent on only their own resources,
pealed to him.

As he sat by their smoky campfire, he realized that he had
gun to settle in and enjoy the feeling of competence that
ne with successfully outfitting them. He could see now how
uch he had come to rely on Twain, deferring to him on all
ijor decisions, and most of the minor ones. He had slowly
t his self-confidence, sinking ever lower until he reached
 nadir the night King made him sing and play the fool
iile Abraham danced. Even the memory of it brought a flush
 his cheeks. The same memory convinced him to buy two
ns, a Spencer carbine with a ten-tube cartridge box, and a
·lt .45 pistol. He would carry the Spencer in a saddle scab-
rd, and Abraham could carry the Colt in his belt.

And so two days after they had disembarked from the *Far*
st, early in the morning in the dark cold hour before dawn,
, Abraham, and Little Spring loaded their gear onto their

horses, mounted up, and began their journey south. As th
rode quietly out of camp, it occurred to him that he w
headed directly into one of the most dangerous locations a
situations on earth. The realization filled him with a nervc
sort of energy, a light, fluttering feeling of fear and anticipati
that promised a kind of personal testing, a weighing of I
courage. If he passed the test, it would wipe clean his rece
past, his indecision and his shame. If he failed he would me
likely be dead, and all questions of honor and courage wo
be moot.

The landscape was flat, cut with long, shallow ravines th
had to be crossed and often necessitated long detours. T
only trees were lone stands of cottonwoods that lined the fe
creeks where they sometimes stopped to water their hors
Little Spring rode with no problem, obviously born to
Abraham turned out to be reasonably skilled, having spen
fair amount of time on various mules when he was young
and though Alex found himself chafed and muscle-sore afte
day in the saddle, he was generally none the worse for it. Th
had made reasonably good time after he began to get a ser
of the land and how to avoid lengthy detours. He estimat
they had made thirty-five miles by sundown.

Two days later, in the early evening, they camped in a
vine, the now dry bed of an old creek. The grass in the ravi
was yellowish-green with a seed stem that was white a
furry. He thought of it as foxtail, but Little Spring said t
Indians called it greasy grass, and the more he looked at it t
better the name fit. At any rate, it was soft to sit and sleep c
As they were in the ravine, they could have a small fire wit
out worrying about being seen, and the horses were down c
of sight. He realized the trip was taking longer than he thoug
it would, but they were closer now, and as the end neared
needed to take a stand, a position.

He sliced up and fried a chunk of side meat and brown
slices of rough bread in the pan grease. As he crouched by t
fire, soot-blackened cast-iron pan in hand, he almost laugh
at his recent culinary efforts. No room for the Cuisinart in I
saddlebags. Sorry, had to leave the crepe pan at home.

After eating, they drank coffee and sat on their blankets. Alex leaned against his saddle and watched Abraham stir the fire with a stick. Little Spring stared into the red-orange coals, watching the sparks flicker up into the night.

"There's going to be a big fight," Alex said. He hadn't planned on telling them what they were doing or what was going to happen, but the impulse to explain, perhaps to justify, came over him. They were alone on this great plain, three puny animals crouched by the side of a fire, and it didn't seem fair or right that he held not only their fate, but the fates of others. The responsibility was too great, the night was too big and dark, and he was unsure, and often wrong.

"Custer is going to fight the Indians. He will try to wipe them out, to finish for once and for all this battle between the white and the red man," he said.

Little Spring looked at him over the flames. "We know this," she said. "That is what the horses and Bluecoats are here for." Abraham nodded.

"But the Indians will win," Alex said.

"Yes," Little Spring said. "It is as High Cloud said it would be."

Alex shook his head. "But in the end you will lose. I need to explain this to you. If you understand, it may be possible to change things. Not much, but just a bit. We can save lives."

"What you mean they going to win, but they going to lose?" Abraham asked.

Alex sat up straight so he could see over the fire. "Here's what will happen. The Indians have a giant camp down on the Little Bighorn river. The army knows they're down there somewhere, but they don't know just how large the camp is. They're sending out three detachments to try to surround the camp, from the west, from the south, and from the northeast, where we are. Custer is coming from our direction." His ever present voice of historical purity was telling him to shut up, but he was tired of listening to that voice, tired of worrying about it. He wasn't out to make radical changes. The Indians were going to get screwed whatever he did; he just wanted to ease the blow.

"You'll have to take a lot of this on trust. But the way things are now, Custer's going to ride into that camp and the Indians are going to wipe him out to a man. Because of that, the government is going to swear revenge on every Indian in the United States, and they will have it. If the battle didn't happen, if the Indians would just avoid this fight, maybe there won't be this great cry for revenge."

He looked at Little Spring. "I'm afraid High Cloud was wrong. The Indians aren't going to win, no matter what. There are too many whites. They are too strong. You've seen their engines, you know what they can do." He shook his head. "The best that can be done is to salvage something from what little is left."

"How do you know this?" Little Spring asked. Her voice was hard with disdain.

Alex shrugged. "I just know it. You must believe what I say; it will save the lives of your people. Save them now and in the years to come."

"My people do not want to be saved. They want to keep what is theirs."

"I understand that, but it is the future you must consider. The revenge will be great. It will go on and on for many years, even after the whites have forgotten why it began. Your people will become very poor, very sick, whole tribes will die out. The children will have little chance to grow up to a normal life." At his mention of children she put a hand on her swelling abdomen. He saw how inexplicable this moment must seem to her. Why should she believe him? But he had to convince her; she was the key.

"You must warn your people—they must escape before Custer and his men come. They are adept at this. They can hide for many more years. To kill Custer will lead to disaster."

Both Abraham and Little Spring were silent.

"I will take you to your people," Alex went on. "You must warn them. If we can reach them soon they will be saved."

Little Spring nodded. "We can reach them if they are where you say they are. I can lead us there."

They rolled up in their blankets, facing the fire. Alex

watched the lowering flames and wondered if he was screwing up. There was no way to know. He believed what he had told Little Spring. It was undoubtedly true that the Indian would be punished for the next hundred years for what was about to happen. If he could stop that, or at least mitigate it, it would be worth it. He was saving lives that would be lost. There was a danger there, that men who did not die would produce children who would not have been born, would do things that would not have been done. But wasn't history large enough, resilient enough to absorb these possibilities, to even out over the long run?

He sure as hell hoped it was.

Chapter 46

Agent Frank Owen walked out onto the porch of the National Park Service visitors' building and stood waiting for Will Two Horses. They had been there for two days, riding the perimeter of the park and scouting possible hiding places and access routes. It was beginning to get on his nerves. He had been on stakeouts for longer than two days, but this was different. He was used to sitting in cars drinking coffee out of Styrofoam cups; here he rode a horse and drank lukewarm water out of a canteen. Today's FBI, he thought. John Dillinger would laugh his ass off if he could see this.

The Little Bighorn battlefield was situated on the Crow Reservation, two small islands of federal parkland in a million and a half acres of Indian reservation. There was a green cinderblock visitors' building with exhibits, a movie theater, bookstore, and a small, well-kept federal cemetery that looked to Owen like a miniature of Arlington National Cemetery. Every year thousands of visitors tramped the surrounding hills and stood before the stone obelisk marking the spot where Custer and his men made their last stand.

"Two days now. Why haven't we spotted him?" Owen asked.

Will shrugged. "He's good at hiding."

"Shit. He's got two horses and a hostage to hide. There's just not that much cover."

"Custer missed an Indian encampment of five thousand men, complete with tepees and a herd of two thousand horses. His Crow scouts saw it, but he couldn't make it out. Believe me, it's possible to lose a couple of people and a few horses around here. It looks flat, but the ravines cut it all up. You can hide a hell of a lot down in one of them."

"But he's got to be close. Tomorrow's the day."

Will nodded, looking up the long hill where the battle markers and obelisk sat on the dry hillside. It was early morning, but there were already tourists pulling into the parking lot. Tomorrow, the actual anniversary of the battle, the place would be jammed. John Raven would do it tomorrow. He might be off his head, but he would still keep that line of reasoning: make the most of the symbolism. He'd started out in this whole thing to make a point. Somewhere along the way his mind had lost its grip, but he would hold on to his purpose. Only the attack would not be symbolic, Will thought, it would be real.

"Let's ride it again," Owen said.

"All right," Will answered. They'd get the horses and ride the hills, but they wouldn't find John Raven. They wouldn't find him until he was ready to be found. Eventually they would, he did not doubt that. But not today. Tomorrow.

Chapter 47

He opened his eyes. He was looking at the point of Little Spring's knife as she crouched in front of him. No, he was not dreaming. Abraham held his hands together and wound a piece of rope around his wrists and tied it. Alex looked at him.

"Got to do it, Alex. You just sit quiet."

Little Spring smiled.

Abraham finished and stepped back: Alex sat up. He gave an experimental pull on the ropes, but there was no give. It was just past dawn. Little Spring stood up and walked around to the other side of the now-dead campfire. He didn't even know what to ask. Or maybe what he had to ask was so obvious that it didn't even need asking. Why had Abraham tied him up? What the hell was going on? He held his bound hands up. "Anyone want to explain this?"

Abraham was rolling up his and Little Spring's blankets. "You be able to slip out of that without too much bother," he said, not looking at Alex. "Use your teeth on it. You can pick that knot." He stood up holding both blanket rolls. "Little Spring and me going on by ourselves. We have to take you horse so you don't try to catch us."

"Where are you going?"

Abraham nodded toward Little Spring. "To find he people."

Alex shook his head. "Wait a minute. I thought that's what vas trying to do. What we all were doing. Why am I being t behind now? What's changed?"

Abraham and Little Spring looked at each other, and he ·dded again. "We go to find my people," she said. "To warn em," she added fiercely. "You told us last night that there ·uld be a great fight, that Yellow Hair would attack my peo- ·e on the Greasy Grass. We will warn them that Custer mes. They will be ready. He has fought us before. He de- ·oyed Black Kettle's camp on the Washita. He killed the ·en, and the women and children as well. He will not kill ·s time. We will kill him." Her dark skin was flushed. Alex ·d never heard her say so many words all at once.

He felt a small moment of relief. They hadn't understood ·at he'd been trying to tell them. He would explain it; they ·uld untie him, and they would resume their ride. It would just like it had been before. "There will be a fight only if ·ur people want it. If we ride today, we can find them and ·u can warn them. Yes, I want to warn them as much as you ·. If they leave their camp and move north, the soldiers ·n't find them. If there isn't any fight, there won't be any ·ling. If there isn't any killing, there will be no retribution, · revenge from either side. The Indians will have time to ·an how they will deal with the white man. You know they ·n't be beaten. We talked about this last night."

Little Spring shook her head. "*You* talked about it last night. ·u have forgotten what High Cloud told you when we first ·et. He told you that there is a great weakness in you, in your ·ople. That you have no spirit; you have only things, only ·jects, machines. Our people have a great spirit. High Cloud ·t it would be enough. We will kill you."

Alex shook his head angrily. "Some of those objects they ·ve are weapons, repeating rifles, Gatling guns. They will be ·ed against you. In the end, you can't win no matter how ·eat your spirit is." He put his hands on the ground and ·shed himself up. His muscles protested, sore from yes- ·rday's ride. He turned to Abraham. "Surely you understand ·s. I can see how she might not see it, but you have more

perspective, more knowledge about our world. If Custer ar
his men are killed it will be worse than if the Indians los
There can be no fight. You tell her. Tell her she must warn h
people to leave, to get out of here."

Abraham looked steadily at Alex. "No," he said. "I wor
tell her." His eyes seemed to narrow, as if he were remembe
ing. "You want them to run away. To let the whites take the
land without a fight. I ain't going to tell them to do that. That
what *my* people did." He looked hard at Alex and for the fir
time since he had met him he saw real anger in his eyes. "O
foreparents fought, in Africa, but after that we gave in, l
them keep us for slaves. You expect me to tell her to let h
people to do that? White man take them for slaves, take ever
thing that they have, you know that. What's to stop then
They ain't never stopped taking what they want before. No,
won't tell them that. I'll tell them to *fight*. I'll tell them to ki
every damn white man they run across, kill this Custer and a
of his men."

"Abraham," Alex thumped his chest with his tied hand
"I'm white. Should they kill me, too? We've been through a l
together. Doesn't that count?"

Abraham's expression didn't change. Alex realized that th
habitual expression of mild pleasantness, the look of gent
bemusement, were gone without a trace.

"That's why I tied you loose. You can get away. You unt
yourself and walk back to where we came off that boat. You l
all right." He waited for a moment and then went on. "Th
problem you ain't never got straight on, is you mix up yourse
with the rest of the whites. You expect me to like them ju
because I like you." He shook his head. "Elias told this to yc
back at the fair. Colored people don't like white folks, ar
that's the truth. Did any slave ever like his master? Only the
that are fools. You're not a bad man, and you can't help it
you're white. I don't hold that against you personal. But wl
help you whites against these Indians? It was a white ma
killed High Cloud. Tried to hurt Little Spring. It's white me
who are going to kill her people. No, I won't tell them to ru
Me and Little Spring going to find them and tell them to sta

nd fight. Stay and kill as many as they can. There ain't noth-
ng else to do. You run, Alex, you run the other way. Other-
vise you going die, too. And I can't help that."

Alex looked at Little Spring. She was still smiling, a triumphant look. He made a last effort. "And what about your
aby?" he said. "If you wipe out Custer, that baby will be
orn into a world where every white man will be against it.
very man's hand will be raised against that baby. He, or she,
von't have a chance."

Little Spring's smile disappeared. "And what chance will
ny baby have if we don't fight? Do you think the white man
vill let my baby be free if we don't fight?" Alex didn't answer.
he truth was, she was probably right. He had the sickening
eeling that what he'd tried to do was wrong. He'd misjudged
verything.

"I've seen you watching me," she went on. "Looking at the
aby. I know what you're thinking." She put both hands on
he sides of her abdomen. "You think this is *your* baby." He
elt himself flush. She laughed. "I've seen how you whites
ook at Indian women—I've seen it all my life. You want to
wn them the way you own your horses. You came to me in
he night, and I took you because I thought you were another
f the soldiers. That Long Hair was giving me to one of his
riends. All of our people had been wiped out on the Washita.
was a prisoner. It was expected. And I thought you were
omeone important. And after, when you disappeared from
he tepee, I thought you must be a spirit. But when you came
o the exposition, I saw that you were a man. An unimportant
vhite man. I have had a life of white men looking at me,
ouching me. Doing whatever they wanted." She shook her
ead. "No white man will ever touch me again."

Abraham turned and picked up both their saddles and
valked to where he'd tied up the horses. "All right," Alex
aid. He knew he'd been beaten, but he couldn't let it go.
What if it's Custer's baby. Are you going to help kill the
ather of your child?"

She looked at him with real disgust. "It is not Custer's baby.
le has not touched me for many months." She laughed. "You

believe anything. It is not Crazy Horse's baby either. High
Cloud made up that story; it amused him to do so. He said
would be useful in protecting me, that if the whites though
the baby was Crazy Horse's or Custer's, they would be les
likely to kill me. It was a trick. And you believed it." Sh
shook her head. "I wanted to kill you, but Abraham said
was not necessary. He is probably right. You will probably kil
yourself in some stupid manner." She turned away an
walked to the horses.

Alex watched them climb into the saddle and turn away
They were leading his horse. They moved off, the horses
hooves muffled in the soft grass. Neither of them bothered t
look back.

Chapter 48

Will Two Horses stood in the bookstore, looking back into the display room of the visitors' center at the Custer National Battlefield. It was beginning to fill with tourists. Small still-sleepy children, stout men and women bandoleered with cameras and binoculars, and uniformed Park Service employees. A few Crow Indian women worked the information desk and sold books. The walls of the room were covered with paintings and posters of Custer and his men being overrun by the Sioux. This was the big day of the year, June 25, the anniversary of the Battle of the Little Bighorn.

"I can't keep them in here for long," grumbled one of the rangers. "I'll give a little talk out by the flagpole, take them through the cemetery, but then they're going to want to go down the hill."

Frank Owen nodded. "Just give us time to get in position. We don't want any trouble."

The ranger nodded back, grimly. "Neither do we," he said, and he turned to the crowd. "Ladies and gentlemen," he began.

• •

They walked along the dry dusty path that twisted down the hill behind the visitors' center. Small white markers stood at intervals along the path, all inscribed with the words *Here lies an unknown soldier of the Seventh Cavalry.* Which wasn't true, all the bodies having been disinterred years ago and reburied up on the hill where the last stand took place. They stood on the edge of a deep ravine. A sawhorse blocked the path in front of them. Over the next hill and down to the right they could see the thick stand of cottonwoods that lined the banks of the Little Bighorn River.

"He's got to come out of there," Owen said, more to himself than to Will. They'd been over it and over it. There was only one really good place from which John Raven could approach the battlefield without being seen, and that was along the river, from behind the trees.

"It looks like it," Will said. He also thought the trees were the obvious place, but he wasn't as convinced as Owen. Just because it looked right didn't mean that John Raven was going to follow the script. He was too crazy and too clever to predict. Will said a silent prayer to whatever gods were listening, red or white, that Molly would come through this unhurt. She was always there, in the back of his mind. She'd been his responsibility, and he'd lost her. He realized now that if he'd been paying more attention to what was happening, and less to his romantic notions, she might not be in trouble. Foolishness. Falling for a white woman. They lived in two different worlds, as hackneyed and clichéd as that idea was—how could he ever expect anything from her?

There were no romantic notions now. The truth of the matter was this long stretch of grass and sage and cactus and these hills and the extreme probability that there would be trouble here in a very short time. He'd been that Indian-Lawyer for too long; he'd been on the edge, always splitting himself two ways, never sure of what he really was. Molly was the symbol, the representative, of another life. It was that other life he was reaching for, more than the woman. It was hard work being an Indian, and he was tired of it.

Owen had wanted to set up in the trees and wait; Will had wanted to stay back on the hill at the visitors' center. Down in the trees was too close; if they missed him he'd be by them and into the tourists before they could do anything about it. B

center was too far back; there would be tourists between
m and the river. They had made the obvious compromise.
ey would wait just beyond the big ravine where they could
down to the river. The Park Rangers had put up the saw-
rse to keep the tourists from going any farther along the
h.

"If we only had more men we could saturate the area. Se-
e it." That, too, had been a sore point, but not between the
o of them. The Park Service had rejected that idea. They
re extremely nervous about any untoward incidents that
ght occur on this special occasion. Some years back they
d staged a reenactment of the great battle; some of the boys,
h Indian and white, had gotten a little carried away, and
ple had been hurt. The whole fiasco had been effectively
ered up. But everyone concerned knew they'd been lucky,
d they weren't likely to get a second chance if something
nt wrong again. So they had been firm in their rejection of
outsiders, be they FBI or local law enforcement, coming in
protect their mass of unsuspecting tourists. They assigned
extra rangers to help out, but that was it. They would put
with Owen and Will Two Horses, but they were on their
n.

Owen stopped and held his rifle out to Will. "Hold this,"
said. The Park Service had allowed the rifle, an old but
viceable Springfield carbine, and as long as Owen pre-
ded it was a prop, a piece of history, and showed it to the
asional curious tourist, he was allowed to carry it.

Will took the rifle. Owen lifted his binoculars to his eyes.

"There's a mystery about this ravine," Will said. "During
battle a contingent of Custer's men known as the gray
rse troopers—they all rode the same color horses—piled in
re and tried to set up a defensive action. The Sioux sat up
t about where we are and picked them off one by one. The
ng is, they've never been able to find evidence of the bod-
. They've dug a number of test sites, but . . ."

"Shit," Owen said, softly.

Will looked where the glasses were pointed. The line of

trees. And then he could see it. A horse and rider. Comi
toward them.

"Oh, shit," Owen said again, and he looked at Will.

Will handed back the rifle and took the glasses. He adjust
them for his own eyes, and brought John Raven from a mc
ing blur into sharp-focus clarity.

"Christ," Will said. John Raven had kicked his horse into
canter. He was naked. His body was painted with a dull r
pigment that he had probably dug out of the riverbank. I
face was divided into two sections, one half completely re
the other decorated with a jagged streak that was meant
represent lightning. His torso was painted with more of t
lightning streaks and a series of red slash marks. Will conce
trated on the chest and saw that the red slashes were r
painted. They were real wounds. What had happened? I
moved back to the face. John Raven was laughing. In his h
was a single feather. He was carrying a rifle in his right har

Both Will and Owen looked around for some sort of cov
There was none. They were on the crest of the hill. Owen f
a chill begin deep in his bones. He had been in trouble
number of times, but it had never been like this. He had nev
fought a naked man who was painted with lightning strea
and riding a horse and laughing.

Will saw the look on Owen's face and felt a shaft of fear
his gut. Christ, he thought, if he's scared, what about me? I
had predicted this, he had known what John Raven would c
but now that he was in the middle of it, he wasn't even su
who's side he was on. He had wanted to be here to prote
John Raven and rescue Molly. But John Raven was beyor
protection, and where was Molly?

"Give me the glasses," Owen said, his voice tense.

"Just a second," Will said. There. Behind John Raven. T
movement had caught his eye. Oh shit, he thought, he
comes the New York Times.

A half mile down the hill, Molly rode up over the riverba
and kicked her horse into a gallop. Will focused the glass
She was hatless. Her long red hair was streaming out behi
her in the wind. Her face was blurred by distance and he

she looked grim and determined. She was riding with the
ns in her right hand and her left hand held curiously up
d away from her body.

"Give me the goddamn glasses!" Owen jerked them away
d thrust the rifle back into Will's hand.

"What are we going to do?" Will asked. His voice was
gh. He cleared his throat, trying to loosen the fear that was
ck there.

"Do you think he'll shoot?" Owen asked, ignoring Will's
estion. "What the hell's the girl think she's going to do?"
knelt down in the grass.

"How am I supposed to know?"

"You're the goddamn Indian." Owen watched through the
sses. "When they get close enough, give me the rifle. He
't hit anything at this distance." Will nodded.

• •

ohn Raven felt the muscles of his horse ripple and bunch
eath him. *It is a good day to die. To kill.* He could see the
little men up the long slope in front of him and knew that
y would be the first. He heard hoofbeats behind him. *My
thers. They have come to join me.* He laughed and began his
r cry, a high quavering wail. In his mind he heard the shout
ked up by other voices. He urged his horse into a gallop.

• •

Molly switched the reins into her bandaged left hand, al-
st dropping them. The crude bandage made her clumsy.
e horse sensed her indecision and slowed. With a cry of
er, she tore the moss and cloth covering from her injured
d with her teeth. She took the reins firmly in her hand and
the scab on the end of her finger tear open. She did not
se the pain. She felt only the wind, and inside, the great
ne of anger that had been building until it blotted out ev-
thing besides the hate and the need to stop John Raven. *He
pay.* Drops of blood flew from her hand into the wind.

• •

*My fathers ride with me. Crazy Horse. The Buffalo Man. Iron
le.* Iron Eagle who taught me to ride and shoot. They are
here beside me. Now will be the end of the whites who

have killed my people. The names of those battles and t
warriors who fought them are before me: *The Washita. Sitt*
Bull. Gall. The Rosebud. Wounded Knee. For a moment the la
around him wavered and he saw himself as a boy, back at t
takeover at Wounded Knee, as Frank Sun Boy Early River r
up on his bunk and his head disappeared in a spray of blo
and brains. A cry burst from John Raven as the land went r
and he aimed his pony at the two men before him, one star
ing, one crouched with large glassy eyes. The sun glinted fr
the eyes. He lifted the rifle and aimed.

• •

Molly pulled the coil of rope loose as she rode. Her bre
was coming in gasps; she was making little moaning soun
that she did not hear over the pounding of her horse's hoov
She lifted the rope from the saddle. Her body remembered t
old skills. Her balance was steady as she let out the loop. S
heeled her horse faster and watched John Raven as he rode
front of her. His horse slowed as he raised his rifle. She w
almost on him. She whirled the rope over her head. The lo
flew toward the galloping horse . . .

• •

And John Raven fired and saw the man, the kneeling m
with the glass eyes throw up his hands and fall ba
ward . . .

• •

And the rope flew toward John Raven but it had been ma
years and the loop missed the man and settled over the hors
head. Molly cried out in rage as she whipped the rope arou
the pommel of her saddle and pulled back on the reins. I
horse tried to stop, but the rope jerked tight, twisting Jo
Raven's horse to the side, and they collided and the world w
full of screaming, twisting horses, and slashing hooves a
dust.

• •

John Raven felt the horse hesitate, jerk, and begin to f
but it came so fast there was nothing he could do, and th
the horse was gone and it was he who was flying, and for o
second he thought he had become his friend the raven, but

round rose up to him and he slammed into it and he was
olling . . .

• •

The terrible fall swirled around her, but she saw him go
own, saw John Raven fall, and she was whole again.

• •

Will Two Horses watched in horror.

Frank Owen's face was a mask of blood. He had heard the
ullet hit and seen Owen flip onto his back. Owen's last
ords echoed stupidly in his head, "He can't hit anything at
is distance." He saw the horses collide and Molly go down,
ad the dust surrounded all of it until,

• •

John Raven rolled to his feet and ran. Toward him.

• •

Will watched as John Raven came out of the dust cloud as
born from it, springing full blown from the dust now layer-
g the red war paint and covering his sweating body. John
aven raised his rifle again to finish at last what he had begun
o long ago.

• •

Will Two Horses made his choice. He dropped to his knee
ad fired once and saw John Raven stop.

• •

John Raven looked up. And fell. The words of his death
ong spun thinly in his ears, drowned by the roaring of his
ood, and then there was only silence, and the great blue sky,
ad high above a single bird tumbling in flight, and John
aven's spirit lifted free and soared and joined his friend the
ven. Together they flew toward the sun.

Chapter 49

Alex ran.

The low hills were covered with high weeds, sagebrush, cactus, and dry prairie grass. Every step sent up an explosion of brown and green grasshoppers. Their constant whirring was the predominant sound of the prairie. The air was hot and dry, the land empty.

He ran with his provisions and belongings stuffed into a pocket torn between the lining and the outer back of his jacket. He tied the arms of the jacket around his waist. It had taken him twenty minutes to chew himself out of the rope. Little Spring and Abraham were far away by then, well beyond any hope of his catching them. He couldn't have changed their minds if he did. The white soldiers under Custer were about to descend on the Indian's summer camp and kill everyone. They must warn their friends and repel the attack.

He stumbled over a low cactus and fell to his hands and knees. He sat for a moment, cradling his left hand in his right. Several cactus spines and a few pebbles were jammed into the palm of his hand. Breathing heavily, he pulled out the spines and brushed off the pebbles. He got to his feet, looked around at the unvarying landscape, shook his head, and began to run again.

It gnawed at him, what he'd done and what he had to do, scratched at his brain and his conscience like some bug that had crawled into his ear and was working its way inward. He'd failed at getting the Indians out of harm's way, not only failed, but ensured that they would be solidly in place when the Seventh Cavalry rode down the hill into the valley of the Little Bighorn. The only option he saw now was to remove Custer and his men from the equation. If he didn't, Custer would ride down against a hostile force of several thousand well-armed warriors. Just as history said. But what history never said, because of course no one knew, was that the reason the Indians were in place and ready was because they'd been tipped off. Custer would not have his most lethal weapon, the element of surprise.

If he could convince Custer not to attack, he could achieve the same end as if he'd convinced the Indians to run away. The initial result would be a saving of approximately two hundred fifty whites and one hundred Indians. He was willing to take his chances that nothing would be seriously altered by his action. Or if it was altered, it would be for the better: the Indians would not be hunted down and slaughtered under the rationalization of honor and revenge.

And so he ran. By noon, the sun had already baked him raw and blistered the skin on his lips. He'd fallen several times; the skin on his hands was torn, and the knees of his pants were ripped open. He was exhausted. From the top of one of the rolling hills, the landscape appeared flat. When he was down in one of the little valleys, looking up at the next hill he would have to climb, or run, he felt the disheartened fear of a man lost at sea, looking up at one more towering twenty-foot wave that he would have to swim to the top of, or drown in. And as far as he could see, this plain was unending, waves of hills that seemed to roll on to the horizon.

A jumbled pile of boulders and a few scattered trees on a ridge drew him; he needed to rest and to make sure he was headed in the correct direction. He walked the last few feet, breathing heavily, anticipating the shade, bent down beneath a large overhang, and put his hand down on a rattlesnake.

The snake squirmed violently; it was like touching a fa garden hose that was cool, soft, and dangerously alive. H jerked his hand back and froze as the small area beneath th rock filled with the angry rattling of what seemed to be doz ens, thousands of rattlesnakes. He watched them, the mass c them lying together in the dim shade, some beginning to li sleepy heads, others slowly sliding into coils, as the cardina rule of Boy Scout rattlesnake lore locked into place: *don't move* Shit, what was it? They can't see? They can only sense move ment? They can't smell? Touch? Hear? What the hell was i But it was too much, screw the cardinal rule, he threw himse backward, away from the rocks. He hit the ground and rolle grasshoppers blasting away from his face as he tumbled ove cactus and rocks. He would have rolled over a field of razo blades to escape. He rolled until the dust choked him and h had to stop to breathe.

He got up on one knee and looked back at the rocks wher the snakes were a heaving, rolling mass of shadow. He stoo carefully, trying to slow his breathing and his pounding hear At least they didn't seem to be chasing him.

He looked around and walked toward the small stand c scruffy pines. There were four low trees in a square, providin a patch of partial shade. Their branches were thin, the needle sparse. He checked for snakes and sat down, aware now tha he was calmer, that his shirt was torn and his arms wer scratched and bleeding and there were cactus spines imbed ded in his right forearm.

He sat under the tree, pulling spines from his arm, consid ering his position. He was still east of where the battle woul take place. He was at least thirty miles away, probably more The problem was not so much distance, but climate and geog raphy. This was not like running a twenty-eight mile mara thon through the streets of New York or Boston, where th only dangers were potholes and muggers. This was runnin over a landscape littered with prairie-dog holes, sharp rock ravines, hills, rivers, and rattlesnakes. And the sun was bakin the moisture out of him, burning his skin and frying his brair He felt goofy with fatigue and heat.

He decided his best chance would be to head directly west until he hit the Little Bighorn River, and then run due south. He could probably run along the banks of the river or even down in the flat bottomland beside the water. The distance would be farther, but he would be sure of ending up in the correct spot, and the terrain should be less difficult.

The next decision he made was to stay right where he was for the next few hours. The sun would kill him if he didn't. He had a canteen of water, but he wasn't sure where he'd find more until he struck the river. He had some jerked beef and a slab of cornbread; he wouldn't starve in the next few days.

He sat on the hillside and looked out over the spectacular view. As he watched, the singular most overwhelming impressions were of his own aloneness, and the absolute emptiness of this world. There were no men, and there was no indication of man. He knew that somewhere out there were thousands of Indians, the Seventh Cavalry, and in the Black Hills probably hundreds of prospectors, but there was no sign of any of it. This was the ultimate in isolation—no cell door to bang on, no possibility of passing ship. It was a rare feeling that hardly anyone in his own time would ever have. No telephones, no radios, no televisions, no roads, no airplanes, no cars. Nothing. For hundreds of miles. And in the center of the desolate landscape, Alex Balfour, ex-history professor, future man, attempting to straighten out a glitch in history for which he himself was probably accountable. The thought, long lurking in the back of his mind, occurred as he sat: perhaps he was *meant* to be right where he was, perhaps all turning points in history are determined by men, and not just men contemporary with those events, but men from another time. He flexed his shoulder muscles. He was sore from falling, itchy from sweat and dust, scratched, torn, and beaten.

His head dipped and he slept.

He dreamt that Molly was beside him. A strand of her right hair was blowing across his face. It tickled his nose. Now it was on his hands. He opened his eyes. Ticks! His hands, his legs, were covered with ticks. Crawling upward, toward his head.

He scrambled out from under the trees. He stood and began jumping up and down, brushing frantically at his clothes. He had never seen so many ticks. He brushed them off his legs, and they stuck to his hands. They were everywhere. He started ripping off his shirt. They were on his face. He scrubbed his body with his shirt, still jumping up and down, as if afraid to leave his feet on the ground for more than a second at a time. He kicked off his shoes and pulled off his pants and found himself standing stark naked on the side of a hill, making strange sounds and acting like a madman.

He forced himself to stand still. Assess the situation, he told himself, they're only ticks, not rattlesnakes. They can't really hurt you, chucklehead. Sure, the voice of panic spoke up, *What about Rocky Mountain spotted fever? What about Lyme disease?* These little babies may not kill you as fast as a rattler, but they can make you very sick; these fuckers fasten on and *suck your blood.* Most of them were off him, and away from the trees there didn't seem to be any new ones. He methodically started at his feet and worked his way up to the top of his head. He didn't know if there were more hidden in his hair, and he wished he had a mirror to see his back, but after ten minutes of careful picking he thought he had them all.

He checked his clothes. He had ripped all the buttons off his shirt, and his pants legs dangled from threads at the knees. He tore them off, giving himself a pair of denim clam-diggers, the first Bermuda shorts ever seen on the western plains. He went back to the tree where he'd left his jacket, de-ticked it and belted it back on.

He looked at his pocket watch. Three twenty—he must have slept for at least three hours. He sipped from his canteen and began to jog down the far side of the hill.

He found the first Indian trail several hours later. It was so broad that he crossed more than a hundred yards of it before he understood what it was. The grass had been eaten by a massive pony herd, crushed by their hooves, and mashed by thousands of moccasins. The trail was churned into dust six inches deep, plowed into furrows by hundreds of travois wooden poles with slings loaded with tepees and household goods, pulled by horses too old or weak for war. He considered following the trail, for it would surely lead him to the big encampment, but after a few hundred yards he found it was too hard to run on the broken earth, like running on loose sand. He stuck to his original plan and crossed the trail. It was a half mile wide and the grass around it had been cropped close by horses for another half mile.

After walking for three more hours he arrived at the Little Bighorn River. The last hour he had been stumbling more than walking. He collapsed at the edge of the shallow river and dipped his dust-covered face into the cool water. It stung as it opened up the cracks and blisters on his lips. He stood up, felt a wave of dizziness, and immediately had to sit back down on a piece of driftwood. He put his head between his knees to keep from fainting. He looked at his Nike running shoes and thought what a great TV commercial this would make. Nike—takes a licking and keeps on ticking. No, something wrong there.

He put his head up and breathed the rapidly cooling evening air. His head slowly cleared. He untied the arms of his jacket and carried it to the low riverbank. He dragged over several chunks of driftwood and built a fire. The thought that he shouldn't have a fire stirred sluggishly in his brain, but he shrugged it off. If anyone saw it and joined him, he'd welcome the company.

He had nothing to boil water in, so he comforted himself with a chunk of the jerked beef and a piece of cornbread. Both were so dry he'd had to chew until his jaw ached and make several trips to the river for water. He finally got it all down and lay with his head on his folded-up jacket. It was too hard. He felt inside and found his tape player. He considered taking it out and playing it but decided against it.

His gaze and his thoughts wandered over the starry night sky. The moon was full and bright. Even though his body was exhausted, his mind continued to work. Back in New York, he lived for things of the intellect, for abstract beauty. That was all that was available. There he was dealing in the gray tones of symbolism. Here he was immersed in the stark blacks and whites, the contrasts of a difficult land. There he had run every morning for reasons of health and the way he wanted his body to look. Here he ran for life itself, perhaps his own, certainly that of others. It was a clarity of purpose that refined his senses and brought him alive to the world. He felt the light touch of the wind and breathed in air cooled by snow on the mountains, drank from the stream and felt the presence in the clear water of other men and animals who also drank from the same stream. The earth itself seemed to vibrate faintly with the movement of creatures in the night. An owl hooted in a nearby cottonwood. A wolf howled in the far distance. On the prairie a pack of coyotes yipped at the moon. He was not afraid. He slept.

• •

Molly sat on the ground, holding her hand, rocking back and forth. Will Two Horses bent to help her. She looked up at him and gasped and pulled away from his touch, and he knew that she was hurt deep inside, that anything that had been there before was now lost, cut away in pain, washed in blood. He knelt beside her and waited for others to come and help

Chapter 50

The dark night began to gray into first light at 3:30 A.M. He broke, cold and stiff from sleeping on the ground. He rolled over and peered at his watch until he could make out the hands, and then sat up, confused. Three thirty was the middle of the night. How could it be getting light? Then he remembered; he was in Montana, so far north that night fell late and day began early. He had slept for five hours, and his body felt as if it had been hammered flat. His legs and feet ached. He massaged his swollen ankles and wondered if he'd be able to lace his running shoes. He hobbled down to the creek and stood in the shallows, letting the icy water numb his pain.

Standing by the now-dead campfire, he gnawed on a piece of dried meat and realized that as bad as he felt, it could have been worse. The cold morning air swept his brain clean of any remaining dust balls of doubt. He finished off the bread, drank from the river, tied his jacket around his waist, and trotted off upstream.

He had run for at least an hour by the time the sun had risen over the horizon and cleared the distant mountains. By then he was wet with sweat and aware that he'd made a mistake. It was definitely easier to run between the banks that enclosed the river, down in the bottomland, but the twisting course of the Little Bighorn at least doubled the distance he would have had to travel if he'd been up on the bluffs above He wouldn't make it in time.

At first he'd tried to straighten his course by splashing across the shallow horseshoe bends, but his sneakers sponged up the water, causing the wet canvas to rub blisters on his feet He stopped, dried his feet, and carried his socks and shoes while he ran barefoot. The hot sun dried everything out in half an hour, but he was careful not to get wet again.

As he ran, he tried to order the sequence of events as they would now be occurring.

Custer would have spent last night on a night march, pushing his men without letting them sleep or even rest. By now they would be ten or fifteen miles from the big Indian village on the banks of the Little Bighorn, approaching from the southeast. If he was going to defuse the coming fight he would have to get south of the Indians, below the village, and stop Custer before he attacked.

Custer's first sighting of the village would come in the Wolf Mountains at a high observation spot known as the Crow's Nest. There, his six Crow Indians and his two civilian scouts would point out the distant pony herd and countless tepees. Custer would refuse to see it, or be unable to see it, saying there was no village and no pony herd. This would occur soon after the sun rose well above the horizon. Just about now.

He stumbled over a pile of loose river rock. He stopped to rest, panting, beneath the shade of a half-dead cottonwood. He leaned against the trunk and looked at his shoes, which were beginning to split along the seams. How far? He looked at his watch. How much time? He glanced at the climbing sun and tried to remember. Custer would soon divide his forces. Captain Benteen would be sent with two troops to scout the valley and seal off any Indian escape routes. He would then send Major Reno across the river with his men to charge the village. He himself would move ahead to the right and come along a ridge over the upper village and ride down to attack.

Alex ran. The steady impact of his feet on the hard ground jarred his muscles, still sore from the day before. The sun was just as hot as it had been, maybe hotter. His face and neck

ere painfully sunburned, and his arms were swollen from
ue cactus spines he'd been unable to dig out. His shirt was
ow in tatters, his pants in hardly better condition. As he ran
e found a tick in his hair swollen to the size of his thumb. At
ue outside curve of a bend in the river, in an ankle-deep bed
f shifting gravel, he glanced up at the far bank and slid to a
op. In the distance, shrouded in a shimmering haze of heat,
as a cluster of tepees. After standing stupidly for a moment,
e slipped into the line of trees. This had to be the upper end
f the village. Most estimates were that it stretched for at least
ve miles along the Little Bighorn. He would have to leave the
ver and go cross-country from here to the other side.

The village was on the opposite side of the river. If he could
each Custer before he split his command, he could convince
im that he had no chance, make him scout the village before
e attacked, make him *see what was there*. All he had to do was
et Custer to stop and look before he charged. Surely if Custer
uw that great mass of Indians even he would give it up. Alex
rouched in the grove of trees. Has Reno been sent in yet? Are
10se gunshots? Ah, Christ, there aren't any answers, there
ever have been. The only thing to do is to run.

He climbed up the crumbling bank, onto the low bluff that
verlooked the river. He stood for a moment, looking at the
nending roll of low hills, and he felt the sinking fear of
opelessness and began to run. He was back on the prairie,
ack in the long tangled grass and the sagebrush and the
actus, the earth exploding with grasshoppers at every step,
1e sun beating down drawing moisture and strength from his
uuscles, brutal, inexorable. He ran because there was no
ope, ran because pain was better than despair. He ran and
is skin was raw and burning from the sun and the scratches
nd cuts of a hundred falls, his legs were dull stumps that
1oved by memory rather than direction, his bones ached, a
ong agonizing throbbing ache that peaked with every pound-
1g step and echoed through his body building upon itself
ntil he was running not toward something, but simply run-
ing because to stop would be to die. Then he inhaled the
rasshopper.

It flew up, and he sucked it in and began coughing vio
lently, trying to dislodge it. It was stuck, a burning scrapin
lump that seemed to be still alive, clawing its way downward
Ah, Christ, is this how I'll die? Strangled to death on a fuckin
grasshopper. He couldn't breathe. He went to his knees. He
coughed one last time, and the insect came up with a wad of
phlegm and blood and legs and wings and plopped into th
dirt in front of him. Alex fell over and lay on the ground
trying to breathe through his nose, fighting lack of oxygen an
fear.

It was time. No question. This is what he had been savin
the goddamn batteries for. He sat up shakily and untied hi
jacket from around his waist. He got out the tape player, spill
ing everything from the pocket. He threw the jacket to the sid
and pawed through the last of his supplies. He put the ear
phones on, checked the tape, and pressed the play button an
the volume at the same time. When he ran in New Yor
passing through Washington Square, dodging dope dealer
and roller skaters, he always turned up the volume for that la
kick, that last effort when there was nothing left but pure wil
fueled by rock-and-roll. The music would short circuit th
pain, if it was loud enough, if the batteries had power, if th
machine still worked. He turned the volume up further.

Nothing. The empty hiss of tape.

And then it hit. Little Richard slammed into the piano, th
backup band cranked it up, and they were into "Lucille," an
Alex was running. The music pumped into him as Little Rich
ard tore into the first of twenty great hits. His feet had no pai
his body no weight. The adrenaline splashed into his blood
stream as fear and niggling doubts were banished to some fa
corner of the kingdom and he ran.

His shirt was almost nonexistent, not much left but colla
and cuffs. His legs were scraped and bleeding, his arms wer
pumping, and his breath bellowed in and out. He came ove
the lip of a hogback ridge, the volume cranked to the level o
eardrum destruction, singing along with his main man, Littl
Richard, the two of them hard in the grip of the music, ye
yes, "Good Golly Miss Molly." Alex was belting out th

rus when he saw the horses and men but couldn't stop,
dn't get the word out to his pain-deaf legs, and ran head-
into the galloping lead rider of Custer's column and went
n in a flurry of dust, lashing hooves, and shouting, cursing
. For a moment he was out cold, but Little Richard
ght him around.

Come on, baby, whole lot of shakin' goin' on,/ Shake,
, shake."

e opened his eyes. The blue sky above was empty, mir-
d by the heat and the sun. He stared up into it and re-
mbered. He climbed to his feet, took a deep breath, and
the earphones down around his neck. No more music,
made it, maybe there was time. He ran after the column.
w, a half mile away, fording the river, he saw the Indians.
y were screaming their war cries, snapping off shots, surg-
through the water and boiling out on the near side, a nest
nts stirred up by a little boy's stick, a hive of bees knocked
n and torn open. Alex ran, and now he felt true fear. All
had gone before was blown away with the gut-clenching
t of the warriors.

oo goddamn late. Reno had attacked. Custer was making a
for the far hill to make his stand. Too late and nothing left
to run because he had been running for so long that it is
soon for him to understand, too soon for his brain to halt
actions of his body. Then Custer spotted him.

uster. Buckskin pants with long fringe, blue-gray shirt
dusted a dull dirty yellow. Hair cut short, his ragged
skered face flushed, broad white hat pinned up on the
t side to allow him to sight his rifle while he rode. Custer
him, wheeled his horse around, and rode toward him. He
ed to a stop and pointed at his stirrup. Alex stuck a Nike
he stirrup and swung up behind the saddle. They rode
k the way Alex had come, over the ridge and down onto
far side where there were no Indians, no soldiers, no dust,
an odd, almost unworldly quiet. Custer pushed him off
the ground.

Get away!" Custer yelled. "Run! You've got a chance if you
" His horse danced around Alex.

"Call it off," Alex shouted. "It's not too late."

"You're the writer," Custer said, distracted for a mom[ent].
The horse would not be calmed. Its eyes were wild. Cu[ster]
wrestled with the reins until the animal was pointed bac[k at]
Alex. "From back at the exposition. Did you steal my I[ndi]ans?" Alex just stared at him. "No matter. Too late no[w."]
Custer stood up in the stirrups and looked back up the [hill.]
"Tell the world what we did here, writer. Tell them ab[out]
Custer and his brave men."

"You can get away," Alex shouted. "If you run you [can]
escape, at least some of you will get away. If you stay yo[u'll]
die. You'll all die."

Custer's horse reared and pawed at the sky, twisting a[s it]
came down. Custer laughed, his eyes seemed as blue an[d as]
bright as the sky. "Yes!" he shouted as he reined the h[orse]
around. "Yes!" He turned in the saddle and raised his han[d to]
Alex. "Glorious, isn't it?" He laughed again and raked [his]
horse with his spurs and galloped away, back up the hill [to]
his men. Alex watched him disappear, trying to decide i[f he]
should follow. And then he saw the Indian.

The Indian sat on his horse on the brow of the hill, wa[it]ing. Alex held his breath as the Indian made his decision [and]
kicked his horse into motion.

Alex ran. As he turned he thought he saw the Indian [pull]
his bow from where it was slung on his back, but he coul[dn't]
be sure, and there was no sane reason to stop and make s[ure.]
Abraham had taken all the guns. There was nothing he co[uld]
do but try to get away.

He heard the horse, heard the hooves on the dry earth, [and]
then the sound behind him stopped, and he thought the [In]dian had changed his mind. *Go after the other guy,* Alex's m[ind]
screamed, loyal to no one in the grip of panic. *That's Ge[orge]
Armstrong Custer. I'm nobody. I never hurt any of you. I trie[d to]
help!* Even now, even as he ran for his life, the irony [was]
obvious. Under other circumstances he might even h[ave]
smiled. Mr. Goodguy, helper of the poor, the oppressed, [the]
weak and the downtrodden, friend to red and black [and]
white.

He was knocked sideways. He looked down in horror at the
l arrowhead and four inches of wooden shaft sticking out
his left shoulder. And his horror was doubled when he
ized another foot or so of arrow must be sticking out his
k. There was no pain to speak of, just a sort of numbness,
f his muscles and nerves were still too surprised to actually
anything.

He turned around. The Indian had dismounted. He was
ring a breechclout and body paint. He stood watching,
ting for Alex to fall. When he didn't, the Indian dropped
reins and began walking toward him. The horse bent its
d and began to crop at the grass. The Indian reached for
knife.

Alex looked at the arrow sticking out of him and felt an
enaline rush of anger. He knew the Indian was coming to
sh him off. There was no mercy in an Indian; the notion
considered to be cowardly, shameful.

Alex reached in his pocket for his Swiss Army knife, then
pped. The idea of that was laughable—what was he going
o, use the tweezers to defend himself? He looked down at
hand. He was still holding the tape player. Through all of
he'd held on to it.

He pulled the headset from around his neck. He felt a flash
harp pain, but his left arm still worked, even though punc-
d. He let the set drop to the full length of the double cord.

Indian was twenty feet away and still coming. His face,
ch was painted black with red around the eyes and white
ts on each cheek, showed no emotion. He was moving
her quickly nor slowly, as if he had a little job to finish but
e was no particular hurry.

larger wave of anger washed over Alex. He had tried to
these people. Shit, he had almost been killed trying to
. He had been called an Indian lover, what the hell, he
an Indian lover. He swung the tape player around his
d. The Indian, for the first time, showed a little curiosity.
x swung the player around again. The Indian paused,
ght it over, and came on.

ow about a little music? a voice shouted in Alex's head. *A little rock-and-roll. Little Richard*? *"Good Golly Miss Molly"*? swung the tape player in a great circle. *"Tutti Frutti"*? *"L Tall Sally"*? A little switch flipped somewhere in his brain, he was over the edge. He laughed wildly. This time the Ind stopped.

"How about. 'A Whole Lot of Shakin' Goin' On'?" A shouted. The Indian, ten feet away, began to look perplex

"You shot me in the arm, you motherfucker." The t player was whizzing around as fast as he could crank it. tried to help all of you, and you shot me in the arm, and r you want to stab me with your goddamn knife. I've had it, ungrateful fucker!"

Alex jumped forward and smashed the tape player into Indian's forehead, right between the eyes. The Sony br apart, batteries flying one way, tape the other, and the Inc dropped straight to the ground and flopped over onto his b as if he'd been shot. Alex waited for the Indian to get laugh, brush off his breechclout, and stab him in the gut, he didn't. He lay still, in the grass.

There was a small dent in the man's forehead. Alex laug and it came out as a sob. He turned around and tried to r The palm of his left hand was slick with blood. He looked his arm and saw that it was covered. He could feel bl running down his armpit and pooling at his waist. He tro a few steps. He was so tired of running. If he could make i the line of trees, he could hide. Make it to the trees. He st bled along. Have to write a letter to Little Richard, he thou express my thanks.

• •

Will Two Horses watched as a uniformed Park Ran helped Molly up and led her toward the visitors' center. Ot rangers were lifting Frank Owen. Will turned away looked back down the hill to the line of trees. There wa man. No one had noticed him. Shuffling toward them. He wearing shorts, and he had an arrow sticking out of his up chest.

The wind was blowing from the man toward Will. Th on the silence of the prairie, born by the slight wind, he co hear it. The man was singing.

Home

Alex sat in his deep plush easy chair, his hand absently resting on the white gauze bandage beneath his shirt. He was reading. A small pain in his shoulder brought him out of his book. He looked up. He remembered the hospital in Billings.

They had put him in a room next to Molly. It was assumed that he was another victim of the beserk Indian attack, and neither he nor Molly had disabused the authorities of this notion. Owen, the FBI agent, was dead. As was the Indian, John Raven.

The doctors assured Alex that his wound was fairly straight-forward, nothing complicated or difficult. Remove the arrow, clean the wound, change the dressing. Muscle damage, missed the nerve, sore for a long time, no complications. Except that it became infected and he lay in bed for a month as they pumped him full of antibiotics. Finally his body won, and they let him come home.

Molly healed quickly. But there were nightmares. She would hear herself cry out in the night as the knife flashed again in the hot sun and the dust swirled around her as she fought. He would hold her until it left her.

Alex flipped open the book. He was working his way through the complete works of Mark Twain. He was reading *A Connecticut Yankee in King Arthur's Court,* Mark Twain's time-travel book set in sixth-century England. Alex remembered Twain at the restaurant in St. Louis, handing over payment for the book idea.

Alex touched the page and read it again. Chapter Fifteen. The main character, having been hit on the head and transported back to King Arthur's court, rides off on a quest with his squire, a young woman.

"And so I'm proprietor of some knights," I said as we rode off. "Who would ever have supposed that I should live to list up assets of that sort. I sh'an't know what to do with them; unless I raffle them off. How many are there of them, Sandy?"

"Seven, please you, sir, and their squires."

"It is a good haul. Who are they? Where do they hang out?"

"Where do they hang out?"

"Yes, where do they live?"

"Ah, I understand thee not. That will I tell eftsoons." Then she said musingly, and softly, turning the words daintily over her tongue: "Hang they out—Hang they out—where hang—where do they hang out; eh, right so; where do they hang out. Of a truth the phrase hath a fair and winsome grace, and is prettily worded withal. I will repeat it anon and anon in my idlesse, whereby I may peradventure learn it. Where do they hang out. Even so! already it falleth trippingly from my tongue, and forasmuch as—"

"Don't forget the cowboys, Sandy."

"Cowboys?"

Alex laughed, closed his book, and put it on the floor. He could almost see Twain, smiling, blowing a stream of cigar smoke in his direction, and telling him not to be such a chucklehead. His wound under the bandage itched. He stroked it lightly. He thought of Molly and Little Spring and Abraham. He remembered Abraham lifting a smiling Little Spring up onto her horse, tenderly, gently. Abraham had touched her hand, and at that moment Alex had known who the father of the baby was, and understood. Abraham was not the simple man he pretended to be. He never could have been, but all of them wanted it to be true, to believe in some essential goodness.

The telephone rang. He pushed himself up and went into the hall and answered it. Molly. She was back at work, writing a follow-up story, reliving her past.

"They killed Henry Sands," she said. He could hear her voice catch.

"Who did? When?"

"It just came over the wire service. Last night." She stopped for a moment. "They shot him down on his front porch."

"Who did it?"

"They don't know. Oh, Alex," her voice broke, "it could have been anybody. The police, the tribal police, the FBI. No one will ever know. That poor old man."

"I'm sorry," he said.

"Just a minute," she said and put the phone down. When she came back on her voice was calmer. "I don't know, does it ever end? Doesn't anyone ever learn?"

And how could he answer her? How could anyone answer her? "We learn," he said, "but it doesn't always help. Sometimes things are just too large, they've gone on too long, they can't be stopped. All we can do is try."

She sighed. "How do you do it?" she asked. "How can you stand it, going back, knowing what will happen and not knowing how to change it? Knowing that people will be hurt, will die?"

He pulled up a chair by the phone and sat down. For a moment he remembered the past, saw the faces of his friends, Twain, Uncle, High Cloud, and how they had explained the world. "Let me tell you a story," he said.

"Years ago I read an article on hurricanes and tornadoes in some science magazine. In the late fifties, down South, after a massive tornado they found a man, unharmed, sitting in a Cadillac up in a large tree. The man explained that he had been driving along a coastal highway, trying to outrun the tornado, when it overtook him. The Cadillac was lifted off the ground and into the sky. There was remarkably little turbulence as he flew along and the car remained upright and fairly stable. After his initial terror died down, he began noticing things being blown along around him: chickens, dogs and cats, even cows. Outhouses, sheds, roofs of houses, parts of trailers.

"And then he saw a mattress sailing along. On the mattress was a man, clinging to the edges, obviously still alive. They flew along beside each other, and then the guy on the mattress noticed the man in the Cadillac. He let loose of the mattress, raised his hand, and waved. The fellow in the Cadillac waved back. Rain obscured the car windows, and when it cleared again, the man and the mattress were gone. The Cadillac went down shortly thereafter and landed in the tree."

There was a long silence from the other end of the line. Twain would have told it better, Alex thought.

"What about the man on the mattress, did they ever find him?" Molly asked.

"Nope."

She thought about it. "So what's your point?" she asked.

"Well, several things. Sometimes you get in terrible trouble but there's nothing you can do but go along with it, ride it out. You just don't have any other choice. You do the best you can, but that's all that you can do. Secondly, I guess it's just that no matter how unbearable things are, no matter how slim the chances are for our escaping whatever dreadful fate we are faced with, most humans still have courage enough to wave, to make contact. You meet people along the way who are also struggling, trying to live and make things better. Somehow it makes it worthwhile. You met Henry Sands. You'll never lose that."

"And you had Twain."

"Yes, and others, for both of us. And here we have each other."

"Yes," she said. "We have each other."

• •

That night he held her and slept. And dreamed.

• •

He was running. Easily, effortlessly. The tall prairie grass was a bright green sea washing over small red, yellow, and blue flowers that grew tangled within the grass. He could feel the prairie, the grass and the flowers, and the wind that came cold and sharp down out of the surrounding hills, carrying the smell of old snow and tamarack pines.

He was in a valley, surrounded by black hills, beneath a brilliant blue cloudless sky.

It was as if he were all sensation, seeing and feeling with a clarity undimmed by thought. A faraway herd of buffalo moved at the end of the valley. Two antelope, white tails held high, leapt from a stand of high grass on his right, leapt and fled at his approach.

In the distance a troop of men on horseback rode up a grassy hill, away from him, and he ran after them and heard the faint call of a bugle, drawing the men away, drawing him toward them. There was a great freedom in all of it, and he was as much a part of it as the grass and the hills and the sky and the animals, and they were a part of him. The clear, clean wind poured in, filling him, and he was giddy with the joy of it.

This time it was a dream, he was sure of it. Dreams were flowers and deer and buffalo. The past was heat and dust and grasshoppers.

This time it was a dream.

This time.